THE DARK

EDITED BY ELLEN DATLOW

Blood Is Not Enough

A Whisper of Blood

*Vanishing Acts**

Alien Sex

Lethal Kisses

Little Deaths

EDITED BY ELLEN DATLOW AND TERRI WINDLING

The Year's Best Fantasy and Horror, Sixteen Annual Collections

Snow White, Blood Red

Black Thorn, White Rose

Ruby Slippers, Golden Tears

Black Swan, White Raven

Sirens and Other Daemon Lovers

Silver Birch, Blood Moon

Black Heart, Ivory Bones

A Wolf at the Door

The Green Man: Tales from the Mythic Forest

Swan Sister

*available from Tor Books

THE DARK

New Ghost Stories

EDITED BY
ELLEN DATLOW

A TOM DOHERTY ASSOCIATES BOOK
NEW YORK

This is a work of fiction. All of the characters and events portrayed in these stories are either fictitious or are used fictitiously.

THE DARK: NEW GHOST STORIES

This book is printed on acid-free paper.

A Tor Book
Published by Tom Doherty Associates, LLC
175 Fifth Avenue
New York, NY 10010

www.tor.com

Tor® is a registered trademark of Tom Doherty Associates, LLC.

Library of Congress Cataloging-in-Publication Data

The dark : new ghost stories / edited by Ellen Datlow.—1st ed.
p. cm.
"A Tom Doherty Associates book."
ISBN 0-765-30444-9 (acid-free paper)
1. Ghost stories, American. 2. Ghost stories, English. I. Datlow, Ellen.

PS648.G48D37 2003
813'.0873308—dc21
2003054336

First Edition: October 2003

Printed in the United States of America

0 9 8 7 6 5 4 3 2 1

COPYRIGHT ACKNOWLEDGMENTS

For Lori

ACKNOWLEDGMENTS

I would like to thank Kelli Bickman, Neil Gaiman,
Merrilee Heifetz, and Ginger Clark for their work,
and especially James Frenkel for his
faith in the anthology.

CONTENTS

THE DARK

INTRODUCTION

ARE YOU AFRAID of the dark? We tend to think that ghosts and hauntings are most active then. That's when you can be most frightened by unrecognizable sounds, smells, touches. But this is not always the case—occasionally a ghost comes out in the bright light of the day to exact revenge (justified or not), or to take care of unfinished business that was interrupted by violent death, or because he or she is prevented from resting by the living. But whether taking place in the night or in the bright light of day, ghost stories touch us powerfully precisely because they deal with that unknown province we are born to fear.

None of us—unless one believes the stories of those who have somehow been briefly dead because of a freakish circumstance that stops their heart, only to have it start again after a short interval—can really know what happens after we die. Many religious traditions claim we have souls, and who are we, the not-yet-dead, to argue? If we do, then perhaps we are virtually challenged to argue that there *are* ghosts, vestiges of ourselves. And how very compelling, how tempting, how delicious or painfully *conceivable* the possibility seems that the unfinished business of the living might be taken up by the newly, uncomfortably, or angry dead.

Ghost stories have been a popular and powerful tradition in fiction for centuries, beginning with Homer, the Augustan poets Virgil and Ovid, and Pliny. The ghost story, never restricted to the province of writers associated with the supernatural, has inspired writers of many literary traditions, including such luminaries as William Faulkner, Edith Wharton, Oscar Wilde, Kate Chopin, Muriel Spark, and John Masefield.

From the ghost of Hamlet's father, and Banquo's ghost's unexpected dinner appearance in *Macbeth*, through disturbing hauntings as in the classic novella *The Turn of the Screw* by Henry James, Faulkner's "A Rose for Emily," and short stories by M. R. James, up to eerie imaginings such as Graham Greene's terrifying "A Little Place Off the Edgware Road," Robert Aickman's disturbing short stories, and *The Haunting of Hill House* by Shirley Jackson, ghost stories have continued to maintain their hold on the literary imagination. Although ghost stories fell out of fashion during the 1980s (with exceptions such as Peter Straub's *Ghost Story*), with horror moving toward the psychological and more realistic terror tales of serial killers and dysfunctional families, there is no doubt that ghost stories have made a comeback. I think this is because when done well, they are frightening. They're about something we humans cannot avoid—death.

As readers, we are lucky that even though many writers turned away from the supernatural for a while, some of the best continued to create wondrous ghost stories: seasoned writers with plenty of new tricks such as Straub, Stephen King, Tanith Lee, Charles L. Grant, and Ramsey Campbell, and refreshing new voices such as Kelly Link, Glen Hirshberg, Christopher Harman, Steve Duffy, Terry Lamsley, Michael Marshall Smith, Paul McAuley, Terry Dowling, P. D. Cacek, Kathryn Ptacek, Peter Crowther, and others.

This book came about because over the last few years I realized that some of my favorite stories were extraordinarily moving, excellent ghost stories such as "Dust Motes" by P. D. Cacek, "Things I Didn't Know My Father Knew" by Peter Crowther, and "Each Night, Every Year" by Kathryn Ptacek, to name just a few. So in my contrary fashion, I decided I wanted to edit a new ghost story anthology that was filled exclusively with *scary* ghost stories. Nothing heartwarming. I hope I've succeeded and that these stories will raise the hackles on the back of your neck—make you want to put the book down and spend the rest of the night nervous of the slightest noise, the creak of a board, or the tapping of a twig against a window. Above all, they should make you think, as has been said of nuclear war, "about the unthinkable." For only by confronting the issues that bedevil us when we confront the finality of death can we start to understand the darkness in ourselves. And that darkness is, after all, whence come the fears you'll meet in the stories in this volume.

—Ellen Datlow
Manhattan, N.Y.
August, 2003

JEFFREY FORD was born and grew up in West Islip, New York, on Long Island. He learned early about ghosts from his grandmother, Maisie McGinn, who had seen banshees and fetches, and had, on the way home from school one day soon after the turn of the century, encountered the funeral procession for a man soon to die but still very much alive.

Ford attended college at S.U.N.Y., Binghamton, where he studied writing with the novelist John Gardner. He now teaches at Brookdale Community College in Monmouth County, New Jersey, and lives in Medford Lakes with his wife and two sons. The first ghost he ever encountered was in 1988, at Knight's Park in Collingswood, New Jersey, at 2:00 A.M. during a windstorm—a man playing the bagpipes, who played for ten full minutes and then suddenly disappeared.

Ford is the author of a trilogy of novels, *The Physiognomy*, *Memoranda*, *The Beyond*, and more recently of *The Portrait of Mrs. Charbuque*. His short stories have been collected in a volume, *The Fantasy Writer's Assistant and Other Stories*, from Golden Gryphon Press.

THE TRENTINO KID

JEFFREY FORD

WHEN I WAS SIX, my father took me to Fire Island and taught me how to swim. That day he put me on his back and swam out past the buoy. My fingers dug into his shoulders as he dove, and somehow I just knew when to hold my breath. I remember being immersed in the cold, murky darkness and that down there the sound of the ocean seemed to be inside of me, as if I were a shell the water had put to its ear. Later, beneath the striped umbrella, the breeze blowing, we ate peanut-butter-and-jelly sandwiches, grains of sand sparking off my teeth. Then he explained how to foil the undertow, how to slip like a porpoise beneath giant breakers, how to body surf. We practiced all afternoon. As the sun was going down, we stood in the backwash of the receding tide, and he held my hand in his big callused mitt, like a rock with fingers. Looking out at the horizon where the waves were being born, he summed up the day's lesson by saying, "There are really only two things you need to know about the water. The first is you always have to respect it. The second, you must never panic, but always try to be sure of yourself."

Years later, after my father left us, after I barely graduated high school, smoked and drank my way out of my first semester at college, and bought a boat and took to clamming for a living, I still remembered his two rules. Whatever degree of respect for the water I was still wanting, by the time I finished my first year working the Great South Bay, the brine had shrunk it, the sun had charred it, and the wind had blown it away, or so I thought. Granted, the bay was not the ocean, for it was usually more serene, its changes less obviously dramatic. There wasn't the constant crash of waves near the shore, nor the powerful undulation of swells farther out, but the bay did have its perils. Its serenity could lull you, rock you gently in your boat of a sunny day, like a baby in a cradle, and then, with the afternoon wind, a storm could build in minutes, a dark, lowering sky quietly gathering behind your back while you were busy working.

When the bay was angry enough, it could make waves to rival the ocean's and they wouldn't always come in a line toward shore but from as many directions as one could conceive. The smooth twenty-minute ride out from the docks to the flats could, in the midst of a storm, become an hour-long struggle back. When you worked alone, as I did, there was more of a danger of being swamped. With only one set of hands, you could not steer into the swells to keep from rolling over and pump the rising bilge at the same time. Even if you weren't shipping that much water and were able to cut into the choppy waves, an old wooden flat-bottom could literally be slapped apart by the repeated impact of the prow dropping off each peak and hitting the water with a thud.

At that point in my life, it was the second of my father's two rules that was giving me trouble. In general, and very often in a specific sense, I had no idea what I was doing. School had been a failure, and once I'd let it slip through my grasp, I realized how important it could have been to me moving forward in my life. Now I was stuck and could feel the tide of years subtly beginning to rise around me. The job of clamming was hard work, getting up early, pulling on a rake for eight to ten hours a day. There was thought involved but it didn't require imagination, and if anything, imagination was my strong suit. Being tied to the bay was a lonely life, save for the hour or so at the docks in the late afternoon when I would drink the free beer the buyers supplied and bullshit with the other clammers. It was a remarkable way to mark time, to be busy without accomplishing anything. The wind and sun, the salt water, the hard work, aged a body rapidly, and when I would look at the old men who clammed, I was too young to sense the wisdom their years on the water had bestowed upon them and saw only what I did not want to become.

This was back in the early seventies, when the bay still held a bounty of clams, a few years before the big companies came in and dredged it barren. There was money to be made. I remember certain weekends when a count bag, five hundred littleneck clams, went for two hundred dollars. I didn't know many people my age who were making two to three hundred dollars a day.

I had a little apartment on the second floor of an old stucco building that looked like a wing of the Alamo. There was a guy living above me, whom I never saw, and beneath me an ancient woman whose haggard face, half obscured by a lace curtain, peered from the window when I'd leave at daybreak. At night, she would intone the rosary, and the sound of her words would rise through the heating duct in my floor. Her prayers found their way into my monotonous dreams of culling seed clams and counting neck. I drove a three-door Buick Special with a light rust patina that I'd bought for fifty dollars. A big night out was getting plastered at The Copper Kettle, trying to pick up girls.

In my first summer working the bay, I did very well for a beginner, and even socked a little money away toward some hypothetical return to college. In my spare time, in the evenings and those days when the weather was bad, I read novels—science fiction and mysteries—and dreamed of one day writing them. Since I had no television, I would amuse myself by writing stories in those black-and-white-marbled notebooks I had despised the sight of back in high school. In the summer, when the apartment got too close, I'd wander the streets at night through the cricket heat, breathing the scents of honeysuckle and wisteria, and dream up plots for my rickety fictions.

That winter the bay froze over. I'd never seen anything like it. The ice was so thick you could drive a car on it. The old-timers said it was a sign that the following summer would be a windfall of a harvest but that such a thing, when it happened, which was rare, was always accompanied by deaths. I first heard the prediction in January, standing on the ice one day when some of us had trudged out a few hundred yards and cut holes with a chain saw through which to clam. Walking on the water that day in the frigid cold, a light snow sweeping along the smooth surface and rising in tiny twisters, was like a scene out of a fairy tale.

"Why deaths?" I asked wrinkle-faced John Hunter as he unscrewed a bottle of schnapps and tipped it into his mouth.

He wiped his stubbled chin with a gloved hand and smiled, three teeth missing. "Because it can't be any other way," he said and laughed.

I nodded, remembering the time when I was new and I had, without securing it, thrown my anchor over the side in the deep water beneath the bridge. The engine was still going and my boat was moving, but I dove over the side, reaching for the end of the line. I managed to grab it, but when I came up, there I was in forty feet of water, my boat gone, holding onto a twenty-pound anchor. The next thing I saw was old Hunter, leaning over me from the side of his boat, reaching out that wiry arm of his. His hand was like a clamp, his bicep like coiled cable. He hauled me in and took me back to my drifting boat, the engine of which had sputtered out by then.

"I should've let you drown," he said, looking pissed off. "You're wasting my time."

"Thanks," I told him as I climbed sheepishly back into my boat.

"I only saved you because I had to," he told me.

"Why'd you have to?" I asked.

"That's the rule of the bay. You have to help anyone in trouble, as long as you've got the wherewithal to."

Since then, he had shown me how to seed a bed, where some of the choice spots were, how to avoid the conservation guys, who were hot to give tickets for just about anything. I was skeptical about what connection a frozen bay had to do with death in the summer, but by then I had learned to just nod.

Spring came and my old boat, an eighteen-foot, flat-bottom wooden job I'd bought for a hundred and fifty bucks and fiberglassed myself, was in bad shape. After putting it back in the water, I found I had to bail the thing out with a garbage can every morning before I could leave the dock. Sheets of fiberglass from my less-than-expert job were sloughing off like peeling skin from a sunburn. I got Pat Ryan, another clammer, to go out with me one day, and we beached the leaky tub on a spit of sand off Gardner's Park. Once we landed, he helped me flip it, and I shoved some new occum, a cottony material that expands when wet, into the seams and recaulked it.

"That's a half-assed job for sure," Pat told me, his warning vaguely reminding me of my father.

"It'll last for a while," I said and waved off his concern.

Just like the old-timers predicted, the clams were plentiful that spring. There were days I would have to put in only four or five hours and I could head back to the dock with a count and a half. It was a season to make you wonder if clamming might not be a worthy life's work. Then, at the end of May, the other part of their prediction came to pass. This kid, Jimmy Trentino, who was five years younger than me (I remembered having shot baskets with him a few times at the courts in the park when I was still in high school), walked in off the shore with a scratch rake and an inner tube and a basket, dreaming of easy money. A storm came up, the bay got crazy very fast, and either weighted down by the rake or having gotten his foot stuck in a sinkhole, he drowned.

The day it happened, I had gotten to the dock late and seen the clouds moving in and the water getting choppy. John Hunter had told me that when the wind kicked up and the bay changed from green to the color of iron, I should get off it as quickly as I could. The only thing more dangerous was standing out there holding an eight-foot metal clam rake during a lightning storm. I got back in my car and drove to the Copper Kettle. Pat Ryan came in at dinnertime and told everyone about the Trentino kid. They dredged for a few days afterward, but the body was never found. That wasn't so unusual, given what an immense, fickle giant the bay was with its myriad currents, some near the surface, some way down deep. As Earl, the bartender, put it, "He could be halfway to France or he might wind up on the beach in Brightwaters tomorrow."

A week later I was sitting on an overturned basket, drinking a beer at the dock after having just sold my haul. A couple of guys were gathered around and Downsy, a good clammer but kind of a high-strung, childish blowhard, was telling about how this woman had shown up at his boat one morning and begged him to take her out so she could release her husband's ashes.

"She was packing the fucking urn like it was a loaf of bread," he said, "holding it under her arm. She was around thirty but she was hot."

As Downsy droned on toward the inevitable bullshit ending of all of his stories, how he eventually boffed some woman over on Grass Island or in his boat, I noticed an old Pontiac pull up at the dock. A slightly bent, little old bald man got out of it. As he shuffled past the buyers' trucks and in our direction, I realized who it was. The Trentino kid's father was the shoemaker in town and had a shop next to the train tracks for as long as I could remember. I don't think I ever rode my bike past it when I was a kid that I didn't see him in the window, leaning over his work, a couple of tacks sticking out of his mouth.

"Hey," I said, and when the guys looked at me, I nodded in the old man's direction.

"Jeez," somebody whispered. Pat Ryan put out his cigarette and Downsy shut his mouth. As Mr. Trentino drew close to us, we all got up. When he spoke, his English was cut with an Italian accent.

He stood before us with his head down, his glasses at the end of his nose. "Fellas," he said.

We each mumbled or whispered how sorry we were about his son.

"OK," he said, and I could see tears in his eyes. Then he looked up and spoke to us about the weather and the Mets and asked us how business was. We made small talk with him for a few minutes, asked him if he wanted a beer. He waved his hands in front of him and smiled, shaking his head.

"Fellas," he said, looking down again. "Please, remember my boy."

We knew what he was asking, and we all said, almost like a chorus, "We will." He turned around then, walked back to his car, got in and drove away.

We were a superstitious bunch. I think it had to do with the fact that we spent our days bobbing on the surface of a vast mystery. So much of what our livelihood depended on was hidden from view. It wasn't so great a leap of imagination to think that life also had its unseen, unfathomable depths. The bay was teeming with folklore and legend—man-eating sharks slipping through the inlet to roam the bay, a sea turtle known as Moola that was supposedly as big as a Cadillac, islands that vanished and then reappeared, sunken treasure, a rogue current that could take you by the foot and drag you through underground channels to leave your body bobbing in Lake Ronkonkoma on the North Shore of Long Island. I had, in fact, seen some very big sea turtles and walked on an island that had been born overnight. By mid-June, the Trentino kid's body had, through our psyches and the promise made to his old man, been swept into this realm of legend.

Almost daily, I heard reports from other guys who had seen it floating just below the surface only twenty yards or so from where they were clamming. They'd weigh anchor and start their engines, but by the time they maneuvered their boats to where they had seen it, it would be gone. Every time it was spotted, some mishap would follow—a lost rake head, a cracked transom, the twin-hole vampire bite from an eel. The kid was soon understood to be cursed. One night, after Pat Ryan got finished relating his own run-in with the errant corpse, Downsy, who was well drunk by then, swore that when he was passing the center of the bridge two days earlier, he'd seen the pale, decomposing figure of the kid swim under his boat.

"Get the fuck outa here," somebody said to him and we laughed.

He didn't laugh. "It was doing the god-damn breast stroke, I swear," he said. "It was swimming like you swim in good dreams, like flying underwater."

"Did you end up boffing it on Grass Island?" somebody asked.

Downsy was dead serious, though, and to prove it, took a swing at the joker, inciting a brawl that resulted in Earl banning him from the Kettle for a week.

I asked John Hunter the next day, as our boats bobbed side by side off the eastern edge of Grass Island, if it was possible the kid's body could still be around.

"Sure," he said, "anything's possible, except maybe you raking more neck than me in a day. My guess is that you wouldn't want to find it at this point—all bloated and half-eaten by eels and bottom feeders. Forget the eyes, the ears, the lips, the belly meat. The hair will still be there, though, and nothing's gonna eat the teeth."

"Could it be cursed?" I asked him.

He laughed. "You have to understand something," he said. "If I was talking to you on dry land, I'd think you were nuts, but this is the bay. The ocean, the bay, the waters of the world are God's imagination. I've known wilder things than that to be true out here."

The image of what was left of the kid when John Hunter finished his forensic menu haunted me. At night, while I was trying to read, it floated there in my thoughts, obscuring whatever story I was in the middle of. Then the words of the rosary threaded their way up from downstairs to weave an invisible web around it, fixing it fast, so that the current of forgetting couldn't whisk it away. One hot midnight at the end of June, I couldn't take thinking about it anymore, so I slipped on my sneakers and went out walking. I headed away from The Copper Kettle, to the quiet side of town. I'd been burnt badly by the sun that day and the breeze against my skin made me shiver. For an hour or more I wandered aimlessly until I finally took a seat on a park bench next to the basketball court.

I realized it was not chance that had brought me to that spot. They say that when you drown, your life passes before your eyes in quick cuts like a television commercial. I wondered if in that blur of events, the kid had noticed me passing him the ball, getting the older guys to let him play in a game, showing him how to shoot from the foul line. What before had been a vague memory now came back to me in vivid detail. I concentrated hard on my recollection of him in life, and this image slowly replaced the one of him drowned and ravaged by the bay.

He was a skinny kid, not too tall, not too short, with brown silky hair in a bowl cut. When I knew him, he was about ten or eleven, but he had long arms, good for stopping passes and stealing the ball. He was quick and unafraid of the older guys who were much bigger than him. What I saw most clearly were his eyes, big round ones, the color green of bottle glass tumbled smooth by the surf, that showed his disappointment at missing a shot or the thrill of playing in a game with high-school-aged guys. He was quiet and polite, not a show-off by any means, and I could tell he was really listening when I taught him how to put back-spin on the ball. Finding him in my thoughts was not so very hard. What was nearly impossible was conceiving of him lifeless—no more, a blank spot in the world. I thought about all the things he would miss out on, all the things I had done between his age and mine. Later that night, after I had made my way home and gone to sleep, I dreamt I was on the basketball court with him. He was shooting foul shots, and I stepped up close and leaned over. "Remember, you must never panic," I said.

Come July, the bottom fell out of the market, and prices paid for counts went way down due to the abundance of that summer's harvest. Not even John Hunter could predict the market, and so although we'd all made a killing in May and June, we were now going to have to pay for it for the rest of the season. We'd all gone a little crazy with our money at the bar, not thinking ahead to the winter and those days it would be impossible to work.

I started staying out on the water longer, only getting back to the dock when the sun was nothing more than a red smudge on the horizon. Some of the buyers would be gone by then, but a couple of them stayed around and waited for us all to get in. I also started playing it a little fast and loose with the weather, going out on days that were blustery and the water was choppy. In May and June I'd have written them off and gone back to bed or read a book, but I wanted to hold on to what I had saved through the flush, early part of the season.

One afternoon, in the last week in July, while over in the flats due south of Babylon, I had stumbled upon a vein of neck, a bed like you wouldn't believe. I was bringing up loaded rake heads every fifteen minutes or so. After two straight hours of scratching away, the clams were still abundant. Around three o'clock, in the midst of my labor, I felt the wind rise, but paid it no mind since it invariably came on in the late afternoon. Only when I had to stop to rest my arms and catch my breath an hour later did I notice that the boat was really rocking. By my best estimation, I'd taken enough for two count bags of little-neck and a bag of top-neck. While I rested, I decided to cull some of my take and get rid of the useless seed clams and the chowders. That's when I happened to look over my shoulder and notice that the sun was gone and the water had grown very choppy.

I stood up quickly and turned to look back across the bay only to see whitecaps forming on the swells and that the color of the water was darkening toward that iron gray. In the distance, I could see clam boats heading back in toward the docks.

"Shit," I said, not wanting to leave the treasure trove that still lay beneath me, but just then a wave came along and smacked the side of the boat, sending me onto my ass between the seat slats and into the bilge. That was all the warning I needed. I brought in my rake, telescoped the handle down, and stowed the head. When I looked up this time, things had gotten a lot worse. The swells had already doubled in size, and the wind had become audible in its ferocity. By the time I dragged in the anchor, the boat was lurching wildly. The jostling I took made it hard for me to maneuver. I had to be careful not to get knocked overboard.

"Come on, baby," I said after pumping the engine. I pulled on the cord only once and it fired up and started running. I swung the handle to turn the boat around in order to head back across the bay to the dock. Off to my left, I noticed a decked-over boat with a small, red cabin, and knew it was Downsy. He was heading in the wrong direction. I followed his path with my sight and for the first time laid eyes on a guy who was scratch-raking about a hundred yards to my left. He was in up to his chest and although he could stand, the walk back to the shallows by the bridge was a good four hundred yards. He'd never make it. Without thinking, I turned in that direction to see if I could help.

As I chugged up close, I saw Downsy move quickly back into his cabin from where he had been leaning over the clammer on the side of the boat. His engine roared, and he turned the boat around and left the guy standing there in the water. His boat almost hit the front of mine as he took off. I called to him, but he never looked back. I pulled my boat up alongside the guy in the water and was about to yell, "How about a lift," when I saw why Downsy had split.

Bobbing in that iron-gray water, trying to keep his head above the swells, was the Trentino kid. He wasn't the decomposed horror show that John Hunter had described, but his skin was mottled a very pale white and bruise green. Around the lower portion of his throat he had that drowned man's blue necklace. His hair was plastered to his head by the water, and those big green eyes peered up at me, his gaze literally digging into mine. That look said, "Help me," as clearly as if he had spoken the words. He was shivering like mad, and he held his arms up, hands open, like a baby wanting to be carried.

I sat there in the wildly rocking boat, staring in disbelief, my heart racing. What good it was going to do me against the dead, I didn't know, but I drew my knife, a ten-inch serrated blade and just held it out in front of me. My other hand was on the throttle of the engine, keeping it at an idle. I wanted to open the engine up all the way and escape as fast as possible, but I was paralyzed somewhere between pity and fear. Then a big wave came swamping the kid and slamming the side of my boat. The whole craft almost rolled over, and the peak of the curl slapped me in the face with ice-cold water.

The dead kid came up spluttering, silently coughing water out of his mouth and nose. His eyes were brimming with terror.

"What the hell are you?" I yelled.

His arms, his fingers, reached for me more urgently.

"Deaths," the old-timers had said, as in the *plural*, and this thought wriggled through my frantic mind like an eel, followed by my realization that what Downsy had been fleeing was the "curse." I took another wave in the side and the boat tipped perilously, the water drenching me. Clams scattered across the deck as the baskets slid, and my cull box flew over the side. I felt, in my confusion and fright, a brief stab of regret at losing it. I looked back to the kid and could see that he seemed anchored in place, his foot no doubt in a sinkhole. Another minute and he would be out of sight beneath the surface. I thought I'd be released from my paralysis once his eyes were covered by the gray water. I dropped my knife and almost thrust my hand out to grab his, but the thought of taking Death into my boat stopped me in mid-reach.

I had to leave or I'd be swamped and sunk just lolling there in the swells. "No way," I said aloud, with every intention of opening the throttle, but just then the kid made one wild lunge, and the tips of the green-tinged fingers of his left hand landed on the side of the boat. I remembered John Hunter telling me it was the rule of the bay to help when you could. The boat got slammed, and I saw the kid's hand begin to slip off the gunwale. I couldn't let him die again, so I reached out. It was like grabbing a handful of snow, freezing cold and soft, and a chill shot up through my arm to my head and formed a vision of the moment of his true death. I felt his panic, heard his underwater cry for his father, the words coming clear through a torrent of bubbles that also released his life. Then I came to and was on my feet, using my season-and-a-half of rake pulling muscle to drag that kid, dead or alive, up out of the bay. His body landed in my boat with a soggy thud, and as it did, I was thrown off balance and nearly took a dive over the side.

He was curled up like a fetus and unnaturally light when I lifted him into a sitting position on the plank bench at the center of the boat. A wave of revulsion passed through me as I touched his slick, spongy flesh. He'd come out of the water wearing nothing, and I had no clothes handy to protect him against the wind. He faced back at me where I sat near the throttle of the engine. There was a good four inches of water sloshing around in the bottom. I quickly lifted the baskets of clams and chucked them all over the side one at a time. I had to lighten the load and get the boat to ride higher through the storm. Then I sat down with those big green eyes staring into me, and opened the throttle all the way.

Lightning streaked through the sky, sizzling down and then exploding over our heads. The waves were massive, and now the storm scared me more than the living corpse. I headed toward the dock, aiming to overshoot it since I knew the wind would drive us eastward. If I was lucky, I could get to a cove I knew of on the southern tip of Gardner's Park. I had briefly thought of heading out toward Grass Island and beaching there, but in a storm like the one raging around us, there was no telling if the island would be there tomorrow.

I never tried harder at anything in my life than preventing myself from wondering how this dead kid was sitting in front of me, shivering cold. The only thought that squeaked through my defenses was, "Is this a miracle?" Then those defenses busted open, and I considered the fact that I might already be dead myself and we were sailing through hell, or to it. I steadied myself as best I could by concentrating on cutting into the swells. The boat was taking a brutal pounding, but we were making headway.

"We're going to make it," I said to Jimmy, and he didn't smile, but he looked less frightened. That subtle sign helped me stay my own confusion, and so I just started talking to him, saying anything that came to mind. By the time we reached the bridge and were passing under it, I realized I had been laying out my life story, and he was seeing it flash before his eyes. I did not want to die that afternoon with nothing to show but scenes of the bay and my hometown. What I wished I could have shared with him were my dreams for the future. Then I noticed a vague spark in his gaze, a subtle recognition of some possibility. That's when the full brunt of the storm hit—gale-force winds, lashing rain, hail the size of dice—and I heard above the shriek of the wind a distinct cracking sound when the prow slammed down off a huge roller. The boat was breaking up.

With every impact against the water came that cracking noise, and each time it sounded, I noticed the kid's skin begin to tear. A dark brown sludge seeped from these wounds. Tears formed in his big eyes, became his eyes, and then dripped in viscous streams down his face, leaving the sockets empty. The lightning cracked above and his chest split open down to his navel. He opened his mouth and a hermit crab scurried out across his blue lips and chin to his neck. I no longer could think to steer, no longer felt the cold, couldn't utter a sound. The sky was nearly dark as night. We fell off a wave into its trough like slamming into a moving truck, and then the wood came apart with a groan. I felt the water rising up around my ankles and calves. Then the transom split off the back of the boat as if it had been made of cardboard, and the engine dropped away out of my grasp, its noise silenced. One more streak of lightning walked the sky, and I saw before me the remains of the kid as John Hunter had described they would be. The next thing I knew, I was in the water, flailing to stay afloat amidst the storm.

I was a strong swimmer, but by this point I was completely exhausted. The waves came from everywhere, one after the other, and I had no idea where I was headed or how close I had managed to get to shore. I would be knocked under by a wave and then bob back up, and then down I'd go again. A huge wave, like a cold dark wing, swept over me, and I thought it might be death. It drove me below the surface, where I tumbled and spun so violently that when I again tried to struggle toward the sky, I instead found the sandy bottom. Then something moved beneath me, and I wasn't sure if I was dreaming, but I remembered my father riding me on his back through the ocean. I reached out and put my hands on a pair of shoulders. In my desperation, my fingers dug through the flesh and latched onto skeleton. We were flying, skimming along the surface, and I could breathe again. It was all so crazy, my mind broke down in the confusion and I must have passed out.

When next I was fully aware, I was stumbling through knee-deep water in the shallows off Gardner's Park. I made the beach and collapsed on the sand. An hour passed, maybe more, but when I awoke, the storm had abated and a steady rain was falling. I made my way, tired and weak, through the park to Sunrise Highway. There, I managed to hitch a ride back to the docks and my waiting car. It was late when I finally returned to the Alamo. I slipped off my wet clothes and got into bed. Curling up on my side, I quickly drifted off to sleep, the words of the old crone's rosary washing over me, submerging me.

The next day I called the police and reported the loss of my boat, so that those at the dock who found my slip empty wouldn't think I had drowned. Later on, when I was driving over to my mother's house, I heard on the radio that the storm had claimed a life. Downsy's boat was missing at the dock. Ironically enough, they found his body that morning washed up on the shore of Grass Island.

A few days later, it was also discovered that the storm had left some interesting debris on the beach at the south end of Gardner's Park, close to where I had come ashore. Two hikers came across pieces of my boat, identified by the plank that held its serial numbers, and a little farther up the beach, the remains of Jimmy Trentino.

I went to two funerals in one day—one for a kid who never got a chance to grow up, and one for a guy who didn't want to. Later that evening, sitting in a shadowed booth at the back of The Copper Kettle, John Hunter remarked about how a coffin is like a boat for the dead.

I wanted to tell him everything that happened the day of the storm, but in the end, felt he wouldn't approve. He had sternly warned me once against blabbing—even when drunk—about a bed I might be seeding for the coming season. "A good man knows when to keep a secret," he had said. Instead, I merely told him, "I'm not coming back to the bay."

He laughed. "Did you think you had to tell me?" he said. "I've seen you reading those books in your boat on your lunch break. I've seen you wandering around town late at night. You don't need a boat to get where it's deep."

I got up then and went to the bar to order another round. When I came back to the booth, he was gone.

I moved on with my life, went back to school, devoted more time to writing my stories, and through the changes that came, I tried to always be sure of myself. In those inevitable dark moments, though, when I thought I was about to panic, I'd remember John Hunter, his hand reaching down to pull me from the water. I always wished that I might see him again, but I never did, because it couldn't be any other way.

AFTERWORD

My favorite ghost story is "The Phantom Rickshaw" by Rudyard Kipling from his remarkable collection *Plain Tales from the Hills.* It is a story of a young woman who wastes away and dies after being jilted at the altar. The protagonist, the man who caused her demise, begins seeing her after she has died, passing him on the street in a rickshaw. There is a quiet beauty in the haunting, and an eerie resignation in the man's realization that her ghost has come from the grave to claim him. I read it when I was eight, and it is the only ghost story that ever really scared me.

TANITH LEE was born in 1947 in North London, England, didn't learn to read until she was eight, and started to write when she was nine. "Having," she says, "virtually wrecked, single-handed, the catering world with her waitressing, the library system with her library-assistance, and all types of shops with her mis-handling of everything," she was set free into the world of profes-sional writing in 1975 by DAW Books.

Tanith Lee lives with her husband John Kaine by the sea in Great Britain and is a prolific writer of fantasy, science fiction, and horror. Her most recent books include *A Bed of Earth*, *Venus Preserved*, and *Piratica*, a children's book. She is currently working on *Metallic Love*, a sequel to *The Silver Metal Lover*, and also a new fantasy trilogy. Her dark fairy tales have been collected in *Red As Blood, or Tales from the Sisters Grimmer*. Other stories have been collected in *Forests of the Night*, *Women as Demons*, *Dreams of Dark and Light*, and *Nightshades*, a novella and stories. Lee has won the World Fantasy Award for her short fiction and has had stories reprinted in several volumes of *The Year's Best Fantasy and Horror*.

THE GHOST OF THE CLOCK

TANITH LEE

I

I don't believe in ghosts. Assuming there is a soul, why should it hang around here if there is somewhere else it has to go? Oh, maybe there are recordings of past events that get left behind. Maybe even extreme emotions leave a kind of color, *like a stain. But that's it.*

So, this isn't a ghost story. Although it has a ghost.

MY NAME IS Laura. And there came a time when clever Laura found herself in bad financial straits—unable to pay the rent on her so-called "flat" in London (one room, and use of a bathroom down the hall) or for anything very much. My parents were long gone—my dad to that Somewhere Else I mentioned, my mother to Southern France with her "new bloke." She'd used him like camouflage and was virtually unfindable.

I ended up accepting the offer of a roof from my aunt.

Jennifer was my father's only sister. I'd seen her, once or twice, in childhood, but she had disliked my mother devotedly, so it hadn't been very often. I knew she had a house on the coast—I wont' say where, but it was a good address. I'd been a bit surprised to get her letter.

It was a long journey, and the train stopped outside some picturesque country station for about fifty minutes extra. My fellow passengers grumbled, but otherwise just carried on as usual, beetling over their ghastly twittering laptops, honking away into their bloody mobile phones. I went to the buffet and got a double gin-and-tonic. It was 11:30 A.M., but what the hell.

In the afternoon, when I had arrived and was waiting for a taxi, what struck me was the light.

I've heard the light is different—better—in Greece. Having never been there, I don't know if that is true. But certainly the English light that curtained the seaside town was sheer and crystal *clean*, as if the sea cast it up fresh-spun. When we drove out of the station and off up the bumping, winding, narrow roads to the hills, I looked at all the May-green woods and fields burning in this light, and the birds darting over like arrows with gold-tipped flights, and then the vast sweep of the sea itself, bluer than the sky.

This was a beautiful spot. The sort of non-resort the sensitive, England-oriented rich go for their holidays. Only I wasn't on holiday. And decidedly I was not rich.

Soon, we saw the house.

"Fair old place, that," said the driver, who until then had been unchatty.

I felt embarrassed. I didn't want to say my aunt lived here. I toyed with the idea of telling him I'd applied for the job of scullery maid, but that would be about a century out of date. Secretary, then, or personal assistant?

Lamely, I said, "Yes, isn't it."

And he and I left it at that.

We went up a winding drive, and the house, which had appeared so dramatically on a hilltop, now vanished behind broad stands of oak, pine, and hornbeam, and clouds of rhododendrons, blazing white and crimson.

Really, I suppose, it wasn't so big—not grounds or an estate, more a huge garden.

We passed under flowery terraces and roses, and then there was the house again, across a blank green oval of lawn.

It was a flat-fronted building, brown-skinned, with a large porch mounted on a little raised terrace, with a statue. I added up twelve windows along the top story before I stopped counting.

All right, it wasn't a stately home, but it was much more than just a *home*.

There was a garden all round, but to one side the land dropped in terraces, and over there, through the boughs of a cedar tree, the turquoise ocean appeared again, less than half a mile away.

The driver helped me with my bags, then left me. I watched the cab rattle off as I stood at the door. I'd expected by now a servant in uniform to come out to look down his nose at me. But no one had come, and when I finally jangled the old-fashioned bell, nothing happened either. Then I saw the electric bell hiding under the other one, and tried that.

Well, I did anticipate an employed door-opener of some sort at least.

But what eventually came was my Aunt Jennifer. She looked at me with all the contempt of any imagined butler, before the falsest of false smiles oozed up her wrinkled face.

"Laura! How lovely. Do come in."

THIS WAS MY aunt's big secret. She was mean. Wealthy people sometimes are, surprisingly so. It's how they stay wealthy, possibly. (I don't know how she was well-off when we hadn't been. I think it was from some kind of exclusive legacy.)

Really, if I'd thought, I'd have remembered enough from my childhood. I wasn't a stupid kid, less stupid probably than I've become since growing up. Twenty-five years back, when I was nine or so. . . . That weird thing over the individual ice cream, for example. "Just eat half, Laura, and save some for later. It will keep in the ice-box. . . ." But my aunt was mean not only in the monetary sense, but in her ways.

She had hated my mother. And I was, after all, half my mother, even if, as far as I was concerned, I'd really only ever had one parent, and he was dead.

I loved my father. He was kind and gentle, a dreamer who liked music, and silence. Death beglamored him for me even more—after the agony wore off. He had had a heart attack the night before I turned twenty.

Conceivably, I would have liked to get on with Jennifer, who had been his sister and so was, as I was, also partly *him*.

My bags got left in the wide walnut-brown hallway. We went into a sunny, rather dusty room, with long windows looking out over another lawn, the cedar, and the sea. The windows weren't very clean. All that—the dust, the windows—startled me. I mean, I'd lived regularly in a garbage tip, but I didn't expect that here—and definitely not amid this antique furniture and these Persian rugs.

The gardens had been very well kept, trees neatly trimmed to proper shapes and the lawns mowed to within an inch of their lives. So she *did* have a gardener.

My aunt told me I must sit down.

"You must sit down, Laura. You must be quite tired. But a cup of tea will put you right."

Then, another little shock. Jennifer crossed to an ornate eighteenth-century sideboard and switched on an electric kettle roosting there. Next to this was set a covered tray. Presently she brought everything to a coffee table between the two white-brocade sofas.

Unveiled, the tray held a plate of two dry chicken sandwiches, constructed perhaps in the early morning, two plain biscuits, and a banana past its first flush of youth. This feast was for me.

As she poured the boiled water on the tea (bags, of course) in the tarnished silver pot, I began to see the light. The garden she had kept up—for "appearances?" But she had no help in the house, or very little. No one to dust or clean or shine up the silver, let alone open the door. No one came in to cook meals either, or even make the poor old girl a cuppa.

She was sixty-seven by my reckoning. She looked older, having one of those faces that gets easily creased.

"I've given you a west-facing room, Laura. It gets the last of the sun."

Fine, I thought. Chilly first thing and too hot on a summer's evening.

"Lovely."

"Well, you must tell me all about yourself."

I glanced at her, and she sat there like a slightly overweight Venus flytrap.

Shouldn't I think of her like that? Should I be sorry for her, all on her own and not even able to afford, or too *afraid* to afford, despite her house, domestic help or even decent tea bags? Had she fallen on hard times? Was she lonely? Did she truly want to know me? She must have known my whereabouts at least, because her letter had come straight to me. But before that, I hadn't seen or heard from her since the funeral.

"There's not much to say, Aunt Jennifer."

"But you've made a bit of a mess of your life, haven't you?"

Yes, Venus flytrap.

"Not really. Companies are folding all the time in London. Everywhere. It's the economic climate."

"I blame these computers," she said darkly. "This Internet thing."

"Works of the Devil," I heard myself mutter.

"Always wanting something for nothing," she concluded, as if I either hadn't said anything or had simply endorsed her own suspicions. "And this man—*Even*, was he called?"

"Eden."

I sensed she thought I'd had an affair with my boss.

"He let you down," she said.

"No, actually—"

"American," she appended scathingly. "Oh, they did plenty of that, letting girls down, I can tell you, in the last war."

I wondered what she'd got up to during the blitz—to sound so pissed off. She would have been a bit young, wouldn't she?

"Eden was great, and when the sh—when the trouble started, he did everything he could to put things right for all of us. It wasn't his fault. But if you mean did I sleep with him, no. He was very happily married."

"Oh, yes," she said. She managed to look disgusted at my directness and wisely aware I was lying, both at once. "However, you lost your flat and your job. And I gather you have no savings."

This was like an interview—perhaps by the police.

"I didn't have very much anyway. Living in London is very expensive."

"I'm sure it is. Well, never mind. You're here now. I'll take care of you."

I felt in that moment like a child—small, thirty-four-year-old orphan. I wanted to say, *Stuff it.* Get up and stalk out, perhaps throwing the half-dead banana at the dirty windows first. But I didn't. I had less than five hundred pounds in the bank and less than forty in my wallet. My three bags contained every scrap I owned that I hadn't sold for next to nothing. Because of my almost freelance status with the company, my tax situation was in a muddle. I wasn't highly skilled, had no tremendous talents, and for every job I was likely to seek, there would be at least fifteen other eager or desperate applicants. It used to be people over fifty who had difficulty getting work. Then it was forty. I'd begun to believe the age had recently fallen even lower. I'd been stacking shelves in the supermarket when Jennifer wrote to me.

If I wanted a breathing space, I would have to put up with her.

After all, it wasn't so bad, was it? The house was uncared-for but lush, the gardens glorious, and the beach and swim-in-able sea just down the hill.

I thought, I'm stupid now.

"Well, Laura, if you've finished your meal, perhaps you'd better take your bags up and settle into your room."

Dismissed.

"Okay. Thanks, I will." I rose and said, feeling I still had to, "It's very kind of you—"

The horrible creeping smile squeezed over her face again. She was all overpowdered and rosy like a girl gone quite wrong, and her hair was thick and old and coarse and too brown, so I knew it was from dye, and not a very good one either. Naturally.

Oh, God, she made me sick. I was *allergic* to her.

She said, "That's all right, Laura. I know you had an unfortunate time with your mother, that can't have helped you. Anyway, pop upstairs now." She gave me directions to the room, with no intention of stirring herself to show me. Then: "I usually eat about seven. You'll find all the things ready for you in the kitchen. It's easy to find, the back stair is just along from your room, on the left."

I checked.

"You mean the way to the kitchen?"

"Yes," she said.

Hold on, I thought. Am I hearing what I think? She plans for me to go down and fix dinner. Scullery maid, did I say? But no, it isn't that. She just means there's some sort of cold stuff ready, and I'm to bring it upstairs to save her aged legs—

"I'm afraid," she added, arch and acid, "I don't have a microwave. You'll have to manage the cooking without. I've never accepted those things are safe."

I FOUND MY room without problems. It wasn't a maid's room—those, if there were any, were up in the attics, I expect. But it could have won a prize for Smallest Guest Bedroom in Britain.

After I'd propped my bags against the single bed, I edged past a huge, bearlike wardrobe and stared out the window.

The view was good—inland, to fields and beech woods honey-spread by a westering sun. It was already almost five. I knew that from my watch, not from any clock. The house *had* clocks—I'd passed one in the narrow side corridor that led to this very room. But none in my bedroom. She had presumably anticipated I'd bring my own.

There was a bathroom to the right of the room, down an awkward step. It had bath and lavatory and so on, even a hand-held shower attachment. There was some soap (not new) and a couple of towels, and toilet paper, bright green and rather cheap. The bathroom also had a tear in the lino floor covering and some loose wall tiles. But the flush worked, and the water ran hot. Why complain, I'd lived with worse.

But after I'd showered and re-dressed, I sat on my lumpy bed, smoldering in my anger.

She wanted a skivvy. I knew it. Had I known before I came? No. There had been nothing in the letter to indicate any of this. Or . . . could I be wrong?

All right then. Give it till tomorrow. And then if necessary, take off. Because it would be better to do almost anything than become maid-of-all-work for my Aunt Jennifer. Oh, I could bloody murder her—

It was then that the clock clanged in the corridor.

So we come to the clock.

I'd barely looked at it on my way to the bedroom, but when I came out again to locate the kitchen stair, I first walked back the short distance down the corridor and stared at the thing.

It was the ugliest clock, perhaps the most ugly piece of furniture I have ever seen.

It was about ten feet tall, made of some black old-looking wood that had a strong odor of must or rot to it, uncarved or decorated, except for a painting on its high-up face. A type of grandfather clock, I deduced, but the oddest thing was that where in such a clock there's usually a glass panel to look through, and so observe the swinging pendulum—even a door that can be unlocked in order to adjust the mechanism—in this model there was not, only the closure of unrelieved wood. Nor did the clock make any working sound. None of that deep *tugk-tockk* you hear so much of in a good atmospheric-period radio play. It had only made one noise, the single monstrous clang.

As I said, the face of the clock did have a decoration. First there were, in black, the Roman numerals. The hands were both firmly clamped to the VI, which was six all right—the actual time—but surely, if they had reached six and the clock had struck five minutes ago, the hands should now have moved on? I watched them a while, and nothing happened. VI was all it was going to be.

To return to the decoration, though. To the left side of the numerals was a woman's face, done like a mask. The style was old-fashioned—it looked eighteenth century to me. It was also nasty in some way I couldn't quite determine, save that, since it *was* a mask—though it had smiling red lips—the eyes were gaps of black, and in the black of each gap was a tiny silver point, so little that from that far below, I couldn't see what they were—but they looked like *pins*.

On the other side of the clock face was the image of something even less appealing. I took it for a monkey's head, this one wizened and evil looking.

Having inspected the clock, I turned round and found the backstair, a twisting, treacherous corkscrew lit by a couple of the narrowest windows. The kitchen was along a passage at the bottom.

Any doubts were canceled. Everything was shoved on the big wooden table, ready for preparation: vegetables, potatoes, a (shop-made) fruit pie. Placed in the middle was a postcard with a view of the town, on the back of which were instructions about the stove, the cutlery and plates, and where the fridge-freezer was with the sausages.

Apparently my aunt had faith I could cook. But she also perhaps knew how ineptly, or why hadn't she wanted something more elaborate?

II

"THIS IS ALL a little cold, Laura. Did you heat everything thoroughly?"

I said nothing, refusing now to play her game.

Before she started her critique of the food (including its late arrival), she'd commented on the *size* of my meal—"*Two* sausages, Laura? And all those peas, surely a young woman needs to watch her figure . . . and I thought I had left a cabbage out. The frozen peas were for Sunday."

Everything was fifth rate anyway. The sausages tasteless, the potatoes floury. Even the pie was flavored mostly with chemicals and had about three apple slices in it.

We ate in the dining room. This was another wide chamber, its windows giving on the lawn and the view of the sea. As daylight sank away, pink clouds and swallows came on, and then a high, blue-green dusk. By then I'd been back down for the appleless pie, and down again to make instant coffee. She didn't ask me to do this, she told me. And I obeyed.

And I kept thinking, I can't arrange a thing tonight. I'll sort all this out in the morning.

Was I spineless? Less that than rather tired.

The instant coffee, too, was not the kind that makes people alert, sexy and wise in the adverts. It was the kind you use to scare out the drains.

After dinner she opened the French doors, however, and said we should have an after-dinner stroll on the lawn.

Was she showing me what I would be missing if I rebelled and ran away?

The sea lay far out, adrift in the sky, dark now, and darker than the luminous dusk, just as it had been more blue than the sky before. The air was fresh and pure and smelled of roses, clematis, and salt.

"Tomorrow," said Aunt Jennifer, "perhaps you should make an early start. I'm afraid everything has got very dirty. Perhaps you should begin downstairs. You won't forget to clean the windows, will you?"

I drew a breath of the beautiful air.

"Where in your letter to me," I said, "exactly did you specify that if I came to stay in your house, I would automatically become your cook and cleaner?"

"Housekeeper, Laura."

"I see. Did you mention a fee then, the wages I'd get for being your . . . er . . . housekeeper? I seem to have missed all that."

"Oh, I can't afford to pay you. I can't afford that sort of luxury. But you're getting your keep, aren't you?"

I was, despite everything, dumbfounded by her relaxed demeanour. I thought, wildly, she's been dreaming this up, perhaps for years. Why? To get at my *mother*? At me? What had *I* ever done to her?

We'd been walking along the lawn all this time, as if engrossed in the most ordinary, friendly dialogue.

Now, around the bushes, the drop opened before us, a sailing away of the hill in air and darkness, quite dramatic. And I thought, Shall I just push the old cow over? But naturally, I would never do that.

And then she said, "Did you see the clock in the corridor near your door?"

"What has—"

"Didn't you think it rather peculiar?"

I said nothing, less from stern resolve than an inability to keep up with this.

"It has a story. That clock."

She was, my aunt, a very dumpy, unattractive figure in her sensible jumper, skirt, and shoes. Yet in the last of the twilight, she was melting to a shadow of her former self, a dumpy, *solid* shadow, lit now and then by a smeary flash of eyes.

"This house was built about nineteen hundred, only about a hundred years ago. Some playwright owned it. Some homosexual creature. He used to collect eccentric bits of furniture. I'm sure I have no interest in him or in them, and none of them remain . . . apart from the clock. The clock was one of his *finds*, and it's always been in the house. Quite a curiosity. One can't move it, you see."

Despite myself, I reacted. "Why not?"

"Because it was nailed to the floor of the upper story, and in such a way it would mean all the floor boards and the joists would have to come up, to pry it loose. I was warned about this. It's an eyesore, of course," she announced. "I don't imagine even you, Laura, with your extreme notions, would like it. At one time the previous tenants had it boarded up—but all that gave way and . . . well, I couldn't afford to have it done again."

"And besides," I added, "it's only in the corridor that leads to the back-stairs."

"Yes, quite."

Dark now. Night had come. The swallows were finished and instead, the odd bat was flitting over. I could just hear the sea, its slow sighing, so intimate, so eternally indifferent.

Jennifer said, "Did you see the two images painted on the face?"

"Yes."

"Youth and Age, they're called."

An explanation disconcertingly formed in my mind. The *mask* was youth—rather a quaint idea, I supposed—a hollow false face that didn't last and eventually had to come off to reveal what was truly there inside. Which was the evil-looking *monkey*? Yes, old age, the mischievous joker, it could make you ugly. *Animal.*

Was that precisely what was happening to Jennifer—mask ripped away, the mad beast beginning to show . . . ?

But she said, "All a lot of nonsense, of course. The interesting part is about the main body of the clock, the area inside the wooden frame."

The day had been warm. It was getting chilly now. A stiff light wind, blowing in over cooling sea, iced down my arms and through my T-shirt, and between my sandaled toes crept the breaking dew.

"So?" I said. Why was I indulging her in this? What the hell was the matter with me? Tell her to fly off the hill, the old witch. Or I should. God, there must be a pub around here somewhere—light, warmth, sanity, and booze.

Jennifer said, "It's haunted. The clock."

She said it with enormous relish. As if she were counting it, like her money.

"Oh, I see."

"It's only a story, evidently," she glibly said, facile in her absolute certainty that she was getting to me. Was she? I didn't believe in—"I found the history in an old book once, a library book, or I could show you. An unpleasant little tale. Most unpleasant."

"How do you know the clock in the book is the same clock?"

"Oh, the estate agent told me years ago, when I was buying the place. In case I found out, I imagine, and got ratty. Then when I read the story in the book, I recognized it was *my* clock, or rather the *house* clock. And the book gave a lot more details."

"You're obviously dying to tell me."

I tried to sound patronizing, but really just wished I'd keep quiet.

She would tell me anyway.

But then Jennifer said, "Well, I don't know, Laura. At this late hour. I remember what a nervous child you were—I don't want to alarm you. It's not a nice story. It might keep you awake. And you'll need your sleep if you're to get an early start on the house in the morning."

And then—*then*—the foul old bag turned on her clumpy heel and marched away from me, up the lawn, toward her economically faint-lit house. Leaving me with only the cold night and the indifferent sea, and the uneasy suspicion that if I didn't hurry after her, she might lock me out all night.

HAD I BEEN nervous as a child? Not especially. And yet there was a kind of something in me, always had been, a sort of feral awareness of . . . God knew what. Maybe that's why, in part, I don't believe in the supernatural. It's less that I don't than that I *won't*.

My father had been sensitive. Not afraid or cowardly, I don't mean that. But the rubbish of the world could get to him, truly upset him; reported cruelties in other countries, or my wretched mother. . . . It was why he'd died, I think. Worry, and trying not to worry, or rather never passing the worry on—to her, because he couldn't; to me, because he wouldn't.

I *hated* thinking of him like this, now sitting up in the awful bed, wondering—I couldn't help it—if Jennifer, his elder by three years, had tried to frighten him when he was a little boy. They'd both been kids when the war started and they were evacuated together to some farm. In my mind I had this picture of them in the unknown dark, he only about four or five, and *she* telling him horror stories.

All the time I sat there, I too was in the dark. There was no side-lamp, just the overhead bulb with the switch by the door. Another form of economy? Since, unless you wanted to sleep with the light full in your eyes, you had to turn it off before getting into bed.

Then the clock went off again. And I nearly jumped out of the house, let alone my skin.

This time, it clanged twice. But it was only just past midnight, according to my luminous alarm clock.

I thought (irrationally?), That's the other reason she's put me in here. So her damn clock can keep me awake.

Then, I heard the rustling sound.

Okay, I admit my hair stood on end. There I was in the spooky dark, alone, and here was this crepuscular little noise suddenly coming to join me, over there, by the door.

It's mice, I decided.

So I switched on the torch I'd had the sense to bring, conjuring country lanes by night, and shone it full at the doorway, expecting to pick up two or more little bright mouse eyes.

It wasn't mice.

There, pushed in under the door, were some sheets of paper.

I gaped at them. Then I got out of bed, crossed the intervening three feet of room, and picked the papers up. Then I switched on the overhead light.

The papers were handwritten, and I knew the writing, overornamented and tightly cramped, as if nothing must slip between the words or letters. It was hers. I'd seen it on her letter to me.

Disbelieving, despite the rest (and the obvious fact she must have crept soundless to my door in order to slot this under it), I read:

> *Laura, I remembered I had copied this from the library book I told you about. I thought you might be intrigued. I've pushed it under your door in order not to disturb you. Read it in the morning. No doubt, to your sophisticated mind, it will seem a very silly tale.*

How was that for contradictory malice? Also, she *knew* I'd be "disturbed," unless I was stone *deaf* and hadn't heard the clangs of the clock.

I sat down on one of the bed's rocky humps and read the remainder of the handwritten pages, which detailed carefully the story of the clock. They did read as if these passages had come from a book.

The clock, the text informed me, dated back to 1768, and had been made in France. In those days, it had had the normal glass window through which the pendulum might be seen, and the whole front of the lower clock might be opened in order to reach the workings. The face, then and now, was decorated with a macabre motif then current in decadent Paris, and entitled "Youth and Age," represented in each respective case by a mask and a distorted, monkeylike human head.

During the French Revolution, the clock reached England, brought over, for some inane reason, by fleeing aristocrats. And in 1820, it passed into the possession of an English family named Trente. They placed it in their country house, somewhere in the vicinity of Lathamfold.

Due to various reverses, there came in time to be only two females left to represent the Trente family: a young woman, Sabia Trente, and her elderly aunt, Eugenia. Both had experienced rather irksome lives, the old aunt unmarried and impoverished, dependent on her young niece who, apparently no longer rich, and quite plain, was herself without hope of catching a suitable man.

The book, or Jennifer, omitted to say much about the existence they led together in their failing country mansion, rubbing each other up the wrong way all the while, since they didn't like each other at all due to some quarrel in the family. Somewhat in the manner of an antique Cinderella, the aged aunt (she was sixty-odd, which must have been more like eighty in those days) was soon consigned to the servants' quarters and required to carry out quite menial work uncomplimentary to her years and status. Sabia Trente, meanwhile, lost no opportunity to "heap contumily" on the old girl's head, and in the end, they were deadly enemies.

By the year Sabia was thirty, youth's bloom gone and her last illusory chance of marriage with it, they occupied the mansion with only one actual servant. The grounds had run to seed and weed. Local farmers grazed their pigs and sheep on the meadows, and paid the Trentes a pittance to do it. The house was in bad repair, some of its roof down, and all its treasures sold.

All, that is, but for the French clock.

It would seem there was some sentimental or superstitious reason why Sabia Trente had *not* sold the clock, which might have brought a fair price as a curiosity, having become, of its kind, quite rare.

However, rather than having been sold, something else happened with the clock.

One night, aunt and niece had a real falling-out. For years, they'd been arguing, but on this particular night it came to blows. Sabia struck first, slapping the old woman across the face and head so hard she fell down. It was then that Auntie Eugenia reached for a fire iron. She in turn struck her niece a blow "harsh enough it clove the brain-case in twain."

Skull fracture accomplished, Auntie, in the rational panic of the amateur turned professional, dragged her niece to the tall clock, standing handy, undid the door, and with the super strength of fear and rage, stuffed Sabia inside. Then, Eugenia hauled the younger woman upright, propped her (presumably smashed head lolling and bleeding) against the pendulum—which naturally at once stopped moving—slammed shut the door and locked it. She then flung the key in the fire, where the heat soon deformed and disguised it. Last of all, the inventive homicide pulled down one of the frowsty curtains and slung it right over the clock, draping it from top to toe, and thus hiding its new grisly contents from view.

Jennifer's library book calmly commented that the old servant woman, if she at all noticed the clock had been shrouded, paid no attention, being used to the "eccentricities of her mistresses." And when the dead body began to stink? The clock apparently held most of that safely inside. The occasional whiff was put down to dead rats in the wall, an occurence of charming frequency.

Not even the disappearance of one of the Trentes was much noted. Both Sabia and Eugenia had long since ceased to frequent the village, or even the church. If the visiting pigs or farmers failed to see Sabia, trailing through the long grass of her estate in her ruined yellow gown, they doubtless only thought she had given up trailing, too, with her other renunciations.

As for the servant, "She asked no questions."

Incredibly, if all this were a fact, Eugenia then lived on in the Trente house for five more years before she "died of an apoplexy." The servant promptly left, stealing a few squalid items to assist her passage. Others came after the funeral, to clear and tidy the house. And that was when, of course, they found what was in the clock: a partly mummified, partly skeletal cadaver, held rigidly upright in its black-stained, pale yellow rags—which, once the curtain was fully off, was displayed as clearly as a mannequin in a shop window.

Some sort of investigation took place. It revealed, perhaps not amazingly, an account of what had actually happened, penned (boastfully?) by Aunt Eugenia in her journal and hidden in a concealed bureau drawer.

The clock meanwhile was broken open and the corpse removed and buried. A type of exorcism was reportedly performed. Exactly why was not specified. After that, the clock was sold at last, and went to unknown buyers.

Thereafter nothing was heard of it until early in 1909, when it reappeared at an auction, boarded all around with plain wood, and said very definitely to be haunted. This was when the gay playwright, who had formerly inhabited Jennifer's house, saw the clock and collected it.

His name was Shelley Terrence, and he had enjoyed some stage successes during the Art Nouveau era, enough to set him up financially and leave him bored. At first he was "*fascinated*" by the clock, inviting his friends of all sexes down for weekends to see it. But then they, and he, changed their minds.

> "Terrence alleged" said Jennifer's book, "that several of his guests had been woken at night in terror, on more than one occasion, by ghastly moans and cries issuing from the sealed-up stem of the clock. One of the guests, a certain Lady Devere Payne, claimed to have witnessed a pallid figure, in a yellow gown of the early Victorian years, lurching through the bedroom, from wall to wall—through both of which walls she passed unhindered—and wearing besides a scarlet, fringed turban, which the lady subsequently realized was really a mass of wetly matted hair and blood."

The guests fled, but worse was to follow.

Coming in late one evening, Terrence was standing talking with his manservant in the downstairs hall when both men heard a "creaking and groaning as of a ship at sea in high wind." Looking up, each man saw the same thing—the clock, which seemed to be moving quite rapidly across the top of the main staircase. It disappeared before reaching the stairs' opposite side, but not before they had also noticed shreds of yellowish material "billowing" from the spot where its door might have opened, had it still had one.

When they had gathered enough courage, Shelley and his man went to the room where the clock had originally been set down, and found it in a much altered position.

No surprise. Another exorcism followed. After which, it seemed, Terrence was advised against ousting the clock, and instead, recommended to have it ported to a back corridor and there nailed down with long iron farriers' nails, right through the floorboards and a joist.

This did seem to end the clock's personal activity. But by then, a name had been given the ghost: the Woman in Yellow. And she herself did not leave Shelley Terrence entirely alone.

She would manifest at random awful moments, such as when he stood shaving and abruptly saw her behind him in his mirror—a sight that so jolted him, he said, that he nearly cut off his ear. At last his nerves broke down, and he quit the house for America.

Thereafter another family, the pragmatic Jordans, lived there for a number of decades. It was they who had boarded up the clock entirely, but also they swore they did not credit ghosts and experienced nothing unusual during their tenure.

And after the Jordans, though the book didn't mention her, came my aunt.

PERCHED ON THE hillock in the bed, I put the pages down, all this information meticulously copied (or *invented*?—it didn't seem likely) by my own aunt.

That she was trying to frighten me, however, was pretty obvious. It was evidently all of a piece with her design for me here. To humiliate me and make me her unpaid servant—a curious reversal of Sabia and Eugenia Trente—wasn't sufficient. No, she wanted to give me nightmares, too.

Why did she have it in for me? I thought back, cautious. All I could recall was a dim, much younger version of Jennifer, making snide remarks about my mother's behavior, Jennifer's nagging voice gnawing away at my father, and more sharply at child-me: "Don't do that, Laura. That grass will get your skirt dirty, and heaven knows, your mother won't have anything ready for you to change into." Oh, and Dad's funeral. When she stood there, dabbing her bright, dry, hard eyes, and I hadn't made time to talk to her, all wrapped up in my own misery, and not wanting anyone else to see. As if to grieve was a humiliation.

Was that enough to make her want to get at me so much? Maybe. She was slightly crazy.

More to the point, was her scheme working? I mean, was I scared?

I switched on the torch, then switched off the overhead light. I left the torch burning by my bed. I lay down, listening, and heard only the vague sounds of wood and plaster settling toward the cool of earliest morning.

Yes, I was, if not nervous, unnerved.

I didn't think I could sleep. Then I did. I dreamed, of course. Not about the Woman in Yellow. I was meeting Eden at Heathrow to fly to the United States with him, and I was very happy about this, and then I found my passport had vanished, but there was my father, gray and old, saying, "I've got it here, Laura. It's all right." But we looked through the window of the caravan that was suddenly there and in which (in the dream) he'd been living, and it was full of *things*—*live* things—not really mice, more like ghastly little gingerbread figures—and they were eating the furniture—

And I woke up with my heart in my mouth, and it was light, 6:00 A.M., and the clock was striking ten.

III

I LEFT THE next morning.

Let me rephrase that. I tried to leave.

Having got up and dressed and herded my bags together, I bundled everything down the main stair to the hall.

It was by then only 6:20, and there was no sign of Jennifer. Though I suspected she was an early riser, it seemed not *this* early.

My plan was to use the phone I'd noted yesterday in the drawing room, and call the remembered number of the cab firm that had brought me here.

When I walked into the room, the sunlight was cutting through it from the east-facing windows, and I could see the ocean glittering away below, never now to be reached. But when I lifted the old-fashioned receiver of the telephone, there was no dial tone. I tried various things, nothing worked. I thought perhaps Jennifer unplugged the phone at night, and traced the wire around to its socket in the wall. But it was attached, and although I took it out and reconnected it, still the phone was dead.

Probably the machine itself had gone wrong and she frugally hadn't bothered to get it mended. Where then in the house would I find another phone that worked?

I searched the downstairs rooms, cursing myself now that I, abnormality among millions, had never invested in one of those mobiles I'd previously cursed on the train. Of course the one I'd used from the company had been recalled.

The rooms were all spacious, gracious, full of grand furniture and silk curtains, and all soiled and dusty and lit by sun. And phoneless.

I went to the kitchen then and made myself some of the foul coffee, double strength. Suddenly I thought I knew where the one operational phone would be. It would be in Jennifer's bedroom.

As I stood there in that dampish, still, shadowy, stone-floored vault, my body finally was prickling all over with a kind of fear. I *knew* I couldn't say to her, "I am leaving now. Let me use the phone to call a cab."

She would somehow (*how*?) prevent it.

She wanted me here, she really did. To play with, to get back at for imagined trespasses. And did she hope for me something worse than humiliation and housework?

Jennifer and Eugenia—just how much, by now, did the two of them have in common?

Then I visualized lugging my bags through the winding, twisty lanes, getting lost among fields and hedges, always glimpsing the sea and the way I should go, and not able to figure out physically how to get there. I thought of surly countryfolk who would detest me and refuse me use of *their* phones, of snarling dogs, bulls—the perfect layman's picture of the English Wild. Whatever else, it would be a long walk. It had taken the cab nearly an hour. . . .

So I thought of a cunning plot. I'm sort of a survivalist. Up to a point, I'll do what I have to, to escape, evade, get by.

SHE CAME DOWN at eight. By then I was cleaning the French windows of the drawing room. The rest of the room was dusted and hoovered, though not polished. You don't, even if on an economy drive, polish wood like that with *Busy Bee*, which was all she had.

I heard her stop in the doorway. Was she thrilled? Triumphant? Or at all startled that I'd actually given in?

"Hi," I said airily, only half turning. "Beautiful morning."

"Yes, it is," she said grudgingly.

"I've almost done in here. I thought you'd like this room sorted out first."

"Yes." Then she said, "So you decided you'd do it."

"Oh, why not?" I said. "For a while, anyway. It's a great house, it's good to tidy it up." Then I turned round properly. There she was, in a rather grubby white wrap, with her dyed hair in curlers and a scarf. I said, "Just one thing, I'm really sorry. When I was hoovering, I knocked into that table and the phone fell off. When I picked it up, I couldn't get the tone. I must have broken it. Of course I'll pay for the repair."

She blinked. That was all. Then her dire little smile came out like a hiding slug. "That's all right, Laura. It doesn't work anyway. I don't use the telephone much."

I gawped, *astonished*, and anxiously said, "But miles up here, and you live alone—do you keep another phone, for emergencies at least?"

"Oh, yes."

That was all. I turned back as if completely satisfied. Whistling, I went on sparkling up the windows with newspaper. I *was* satisfied. She did have another phone. Just a matter of finding it.

Then, as I gave the last burnish to the panes, I saw in the glass that Jennifer was now advancing through the room toward me, and . . . well, this frightened me. Was she violent? For a second, I pretended to go on obliviously rubbing the newspaper about, but keeping my eyes on her reflection. The image was virtually divided between outside and in, and she seemed to be passing through the cedar tree in sections, her stupid red scarf, wound over curlers, very vivid in the glass and in contrast, her wrapper looking rather like a long dress, and more yellow than white—

And then I knew what I was seeing.

It wasn't my Aunt Jennifer.

I whirled round, burning cold, in a terror the like of which I'd never ever felt—a sort of vertigo of fear. As if a hole had opened in the world and I was about to plunge through.

Nothing was in the room.

Not Jennifer. Nothing . . . else.

I made a noise, a silly noise.

After quite some time, I looked back at the window, and there was only the vague reflection of furniture held there among the branches of the cedar.

WHAT DO YOU do after something like that? If you're me, and you don't believe in ghosts, fairly quickly you put it down to hallucination caused by stress. And then you feel slightly better.

However, I was all the more keen to get out of the house.

She wanted breakfast, of course. Toast, cornflakes, marmalade—and tea, *not* coffee. I prepared that and she had it in the drawing room, taking the opportunity as she did so to write down on a notepad anything she thought I'd missed in my cleaning.

After all that, I explained I was just popping up to the loo. I guessed I'd get some comment about weak bladders or irregular bowels, but no.

Upstairs I went, but obviously not to the bathroom. I walked along the main upper hallway and looked into the rooms until I found hers.

Her room was disgusting.

I have lived, I've said, in tips, but she really had no excuse. The bed was tightly made. Otherwise, there was mess and junk everywhere—old newspapers in stacks, magazines, boxes of sticky old orange powder and makeup dried in tubes. And worse than this, half-eaten packets of biscuits, sweets that *seemed* half-eaten, then taken out and *wrapped up again in their paper for future use.* Another defunct banana lay rotting in a turpentine reek on the windowsill, to the glee of several flies. The room stank of that, of many saccharine things going off. Of her.

I opened windows, and then I looked for the phone. And it wasn't there. Which was insane, for it was nowhere else and I truly didn't believe even crazy Jennifer wouldn't have one. She must have concealed it cleverly. Where?

Perhaps I was chicken, I didn't want to start rummaging around yet. I'd have to tell her I would do her room this afternoon, make it nice for her, some crap like that.

Then I went down to get on with the drudgery, and unlike me, *she* had found something—my bags, thrust in the hall cupboard.

"Whatever are these doing here? I said take them up."

"Oh, I will, when I sort them out later. They take up too much space in my room like this."

I can sometimes think on my feet.

But perhaps I wasn't fooling her. Had she been looking?

A CURIOUS DAY. I labored like her slave. My arms began to ache, and my back hurt from bending and stretching. With the mirrors and the windows, I whistled and sang Mozart and XTC extra loud, and saw nothing beyond what usually reflects in glass.

I made lunch, (canned meatballs) and ate some with her. The meatballs seemed to give her a high. She started rambling on at me. I scarcely listened to her reminiscences. Everything had been much better then—maybe for her, it had been. And diatribes against men in general, lesbians in particular, the French, the Germans, the Americans, the Scottish, and those she chose to call "Negroes" (!). Also workmen, all of them, and the money-grabbing, work-shy, ne'er-do-wells who had ruined the British economy, and perhaps included, unspoken, me.

I wanted to kill her. It's a fact. I felt I, too, was going mental. Didn't care what I might come to do.

Acting Oscar-earning well, I smarmily told her I'd decided to clean her bedroom.

"No, Laura, that can wait. There's still plenty to see to on this floor."

"Okay," I said.

Sod her. She wasn't going to stop me now.

The old witch routinely had a rest after lunch, so she had told me—not in her bedroom but in one of the downstairs rooms. To this stroke of luck, I replied I'd clean up in the kitchen while she slept, so as not to disturb her.

"Oh, I don't sleep, Laura. I never sleep well."

"Just in case," Laura cheerily declared.

As I cleared the lunch things and went out, she was smiling to herself, a crafty slug smile. But this had gone far enough, and I meant to be out of this appalling house before nightfall. Even if I did have to walk all the way with my bags gripped in my teeth, and sleep on the beach when I got there.

Accordingly, all that afternoon I searched, mainly on the upper floor. I even got up into the attics by another narrow backstair—but they were such a shambles and draped so thickly with cobwebs, I thought perhaps she herself hadn't gone up there in a decade. I didn't find a phone. I began to feel she had lied when she said she had another, just to get me running in circles. (Somehow, during all this circle-running, I'd managed to avoid going anywhere near the clock. I'd even used the other bathroom.)

The hot afternoon light was abruptly slanting. It was nearly five.

There she was, standing in the lower hall, glaring up at me.

"Why ever are you up there? I expected tea an hour ago."

"Sorry, I'll get it now," I heard myself say, still with vague self-amazement.

"I told you not to clean upstairs yet."

"I haven't. Sorry," I said again. "I took a nap." Firmly I added, "I didn't have a great night."

She shrugged—placated? "Very well. We'll let it go. See to the tea now."

So I saw to the tea.

Inside me at last was a mindless—almost bestial—rising panic. I couldn't seem to pull myself around. I couldn't seem to confront her anymore, or make up my mind what it was best for me to do. And in about three hours, the sun was going down, down into the land, leaving behind a darkness that would smother even that coal-blue sea, which looked as if it belonged in Africa, but had somehow washed up here. As had I, who might also. . . . be smothered?

IN THE END, what I did was drag all my bags down to the kitchen, (having found another way onto the backstair from the ground floor; I wouldn't return to my "room"—or wouldn't go by the clock.) In the kitchen, I sorted through the bags in the mode of lifeboat intendees in movies. I was going to have to leave a lot behind; it would be too heavy to carry all that way.

At the finish, I had it all down to one single very heavy bag. This I then picked up and walked upstairs again, as I hadn't been able to open the kitchen door to the outside; it was stuck—or locked.

In the lower hall once more, I met her. She'd known, she must have done, all of it, even to my breaking point.

But, "What are you doing, Laura?" she asked. She had put on lipstick, as if for a celebration.

I moved across and paused, facing her at the foot of the main stair. She was between me and the front door. I put down my bag. I felt reckless.

"Sorry," I said again. "I just remembered I left the kettle on in London."

"You're leaving after all," she brilliantly fathomed.

"Sure am. I don't suppose you'll allow me to use the secret telephone to call a cab?"

"Certainly not at this time of night." (It was about seven). "They wouldn't come out. Not all the way up here. If you really insist on going, then you must do it in the morning."

"No. I'm not spending another night here. Not with you, or your specialty ghosts."

She smiled. What a giveaway.

"Don't tell me a grown-up woman, even you, is frightened by a ghost story."

"I don't give a toss about ghost stories. I just don't like *you*, Aunt Jennifer, or your behavior."

"It's mutual then," she said. We stood there in the cup of the brown hall, dusted by me, and the tiled floor wiped to a gleam as sunlight speared by in its death throes. "Oh, don't think I ever could forget the way you used to behave to me. You, a child. I used to think she put you up to it, that slut of a mother of yours. But I don't think she would have bothered. She'd got *him* where she wanted him. And she was busy making a fool of him. She killed him with her goings-on."

"Shut up," I said, but almost listlessly, because I half agreed at least on that. She didn't take any notice anyway.

"But you were a dreadful little girl. I always saw you sneering at me behind my back, laughing at me. Always trying to get me to buy you things—"

"For God's sake, I was a child—"

"She'd told you I was well-off, I suppose. And so it was 'Can I have an ice cream, can I go to the pictures, can I have that book on tigers—"

"Well, I didn't get them off you, did I? Oh, excuse me, I did get half an ice cream once."

She shamed me. Had I been a whining, gift-grabbing kid? We hadn't had much, and Jennifer, then, used to flash her money. And she used to promise me things, too, presents, and at first I'd believed her, but I never got them. Inside me now, the panic was boiling into rage. The hall was stifling and turning red with it. Like her furious self-righteous face.

"Then the funeral," she announced. "My own brother, and your father, and there you were, and you couldn't say a word to me, just 'Hallo, Aunt.' And later I think you said good-bye. Both of us standing there over his grave, and you wouldn't say a word. You couldn't even spare me a drop of kindness."

"My father was dead," I said bitterly.

"My *brother* was dead," she cried. Her eyes flamed like slices of razor, and then they went up over my head, up to the top of the stairs, and she let out—not a scream—a sort of yelp.

At once the blood-red light in the hall seemed to darken. Something out there had got hold of the sun. Instantly, the nature of my turmoil changed. My back, my neck, my scalp, were covered by freezing ants.

I stared at her. "What is it?"

She didn't speak. She simply went on gazing up the stairway, and still gazing, she began to back away, back through the door of the drawing room, and now her lipsticked mouth was hanging open.

I've no notion how, but I understood this was not part of the game.

As for me, for a moment I didn't think I *could* move. Then I knew I had to, because otherwise, if I just stayed there at the foot of the stairs, whatever—whatever was on them, coming down them, whatever that was—would soon be right where *I* was—and I didn't—no, I *didn't*—want that. . . .

So I somehow moved forward, to run after Jennifer through the drawing-room door, and at the same time, like Lot's misguided wife, I looked behind me . . .

And was turned, as she was, to an immovable pillar of volcanic salt.

Because what was standing still at the head of the stairs was the wooden clock, and what was coming *down* the stairs was Sabia Trente, not still at all, the skirts of her gown blowing round her, and her arms held up from the elbows, and her hands pointing with their grown-long fingernails.

You see such things on a screen, a book jacket, on the bloody Internet for God's sake, such images of Gothic horror, these evocations of dynamic terror. It doesn't prepare you for the actual thing.

There she was. And she was worse than anything anyone could ever physically mock up, or imagine.

Her face was white, blue-white, and marked by the fringe of blood that was still unraveling down her right cheek, and yet never reaching her already bloodstained gown or the stairs. Her forehead was red and also bruised black, and quills of bone stood out of her hair (like a Spanish comb), which was otherwise clotted scarlet with blood. Her face had features, all sunken in and withered. It was a fallen monkey's face, yet, too, like a mask—and in the place where her eyes had once been were only two bruised black sockets of nothing, each secured in her head by a shining silver pin.

All I wanted was to run. It was the sum of my ambitions. And I couldn't do it. Could not move.

And so Sabia Trente came down the stair and right up to me, and I smelled her stink worse than dead rats or rotting bananas, and then she passed directly through me, like a dank, dust-laden wind.

Perhaps I died for a split second when that happened. Perhaps my heart stopped. I don't know, can't remember.

It was just that suddenly she was past me, and I was still rooted there, watching her glide, as if she moved on ice skates over a rink, through the drawing-room door.

Darkness had come, premature night. Once before I'd seen this creature move across the room, seen her in the window. Now I saw her from the back. Saw her so clearly, *solidly*, even the creases of her dress and the bones of her corset under it.

And I saw my Aunt Jennifer, too, sprawled on a brocade sofa, screaming now, shrieking, and trying to bury her head in the cushions.

On which cue, Sabia Trente was raising up high a kind of stick, an iron thing like a wand with a strange, glowing tip—she hadn't had it a moment ago—and I knew it was the poker from a fire that had been out for more than a century.

She was going to return the compliment of the cloven brain-case, not on her murderous, no longer available Aunt Eugenia, but on the skull of Jennifer.

I told you from the start, I don't believe in ghosts. I don't. I flatly refuse to. If I did, I think I would lose my mind for sure and for real and for good. And so, in those moments that lingered between Jennifer and me and the gates of Hell, I saw it all, what had truly happened, and *why* this thing was here, and what it was, and what to do about it.

I was numb, had no feeling in my body, didn't really seem to be *in* it, except perhaps sitting tiny and high up behind my own eyes, like a lone passenger left on a train hurtling driverless to destruction.

For the train—me, driverless—was all at once rushing forward. It crashed headlong into the back of the stationary Sabia—I *felt* her—and I tore her apart with my hands, screaming myself now, over and over, "Go away! Get lost! Piss off—you don't exist!"

And she didn't exist. She was only air, and then she and her poker were gone. And at the head of the stairs, the clock became a black cloud and then was gone, too, back to its place in reality along the corridor.

I stood over Jennifer and I bawled at her now, "You made it up, didn't you, you fucking old bitch—*didn't* you?"

She whimpered. I struck her across the head. Not so hard. It was much better than a poker would have been. Then I pulled her to a sitting position and shouted abuse at her until she spoke. "I didn't . . . it was true . . . or at least in the book. Only not . . . not—"

"Not what, you cow?"

"Not that clock. Not *that* one."

SHE HAD WANTED to pay me out for all my seven-, nine-, and twenty-year-old transgressions against her. So she never quite lost track of me, and when the company folded, she was ready.

Yes, I was to have been her skivvy. For I must be punished. And muddled as Jennifer had become, she had invested in the invented memory of me as a sensitive, nervy girl, ready to be dominated and scared witless by a contrived ghost story.

Although, as she'd said, the story was true—at least in a bona fide book that carried the tale of the Trente murder and the haunted French clock. Even the piece about Shelley Terrence, though he had never lived in Jennifer's house—all these events had gone on somewhere else. For that reason, she had had to copy out all the passages. To photocopy the printed text would have revealed too much and given the game away.

She had read the story one idle afternoon and become obsessed enough to weave it into her retribution for me. And so mad, mad Aunt Jennifer, who wouldn't even pay to have her downstairs telephone repaired, forked out quite a sum to gain a rather poor reproduction of the Trente clock. This copy was then placed—*unnailed*—in the corridor by my elected bedroom. She had even arranged for its random striking.

Well, she was off her head. And her loathing insanity and my allergic anger seem to have been enough. For, yes, I take part of the blame. Without my side of it, I don't think it would have happened, she couldn't have done it on her own.

And what did happen?

Neither Jennifer nor I had ever had a child—in my case, from choice, in hers, I don't know. But we made a type of child between us, an *offspring* in that word's purest and most dreadful sense. For we fashioned the ghost of Sabia Trente between us, brought it to its unlife, and made it *run*. If simply that, our projected hating energy would have been sufficient to make the vengeful poker and its blow fatal—I've got no idea. Maybe. After all, I stopped it. I must have thought so then.

But, too, perhaps Jennifer and I merely hallucinated—visions of similar aspect experienced by more than one person at once aren't uncommon in the annals of the supernatural or science.

Whatever, as I said, this wasn't a ghost story, although it has a ghost.

And what happened *afterward?* Soon told. She did a lot of cringing and crying her dry, hard tears. But now I managed to make it clear I wouldn't stay another hour in her house.

I waited outside for the taxi, which took me away fast, so I just caught the 9:35 train to London. The phone? I hardly believe it myself—she, the arch-reviler of modernity, had a weeny little mobile tucked in her handbag.

As I was going out of her door, she came scurrying at me from the now thick-lit shadows of the house and pushed a paper bag into my hand. I thought it probably contained some stale sandwiches to give me indigestion, or some already half-eaten sweets. I wanted to slap it to the ground, but something made me take it. Otherwise, we parted without a touch, or another word. I didn't look at the paper bag until the train was drawing into London and I was going to throw it away. Inside was a hundred pounds in tens and a check for three thousand pounds. This was so obscene I felt nauseous. Or maybe that was only hunger, and the shock from everything else. I didn't throw up. I did cash and spend the money. And what does that make me?

I'M WONDERING, THOUGH, if you wonder . . . if, despite the clock's being only a copy, yet somehow it did draw back the vengeance-seeking Sabia's dead remnant, and only my vaunted stupidity drove her off. No. However, it's your choice. Somebody said it isn't the dead you need to fear, but the living. Too damn right.

Since that night, I've heard nothing more from Jennifer. Years have elapsed. Now and then I ask myself what she does, alone, when it gets dark in that house.

AFTERWORD

One of my most favorite and therefore most feared ghost stories is by the wonderful M. R. James. I first saw "The Ash Tree" on TV, and it scared me stupid, as most of his tales do—there is an aching and remorseless chill to his stories I've found nowhere else, a sense of the sheer ease in falling into the trap, and the implacability of the Inescapable. I subsequently read the story many times. It still horrifies me. The ash tree itself, filled by Something Unspeakable, and all too able to destroy, broods on the tale. Its shadow falls across the pages, and the reader's inner eye.

TERRY DOWLING was born in 1947 in Sydney, Australia, and always expected that his creative efforts would be directed into music and songwriting. After time as a soldier and primary-school teacher, he completed two degrees and spent eight years performing his songs on *Mr Squiggle & Friends*, one of the world's longest-running children's television shows. He made his first professional sale in 1982 and continues to be one of Australia's most respected and internationally acclaimed writers of science fiction, dark fantasy, and horror. In addition to editing *Mortal Fire: Best Australian SF* and *The Essential Ellison*, Dowling is the author of the linked collections *Rynosseros, Blue Tyson, Twilight Beach*, and *Wormwood*, and his short fiction is collected in *The Man Who Lost Red, An Intimate Knowledge of the Night, Antique Futures: The Best of Terry Dowling*, and *Blackwater Days*. His work has appeared in numerous "Best of" compilations and he has won many awards for his storytelling, the most recent being the Grand Prix at Utopiales in France for his computer game adventure, *Schizm: Mysterious Journey*.

ONE THING ABOUT THE NIGHT

TERRY DOWLING

LIKE THE GOOD friend he was, Paul Vickrey had kept to our first rule. He'd told me nothing about the Janss place, hadn't dared mention that name in his e-mail, but what precious few words there were brought me halfway around the world nineteen hours after it reached me.

Access to hexagonal prime natural.
Owner missing. Come soonest.

Suitably vague, appropriately cautious in these spying, prying, hacker-cracker times, "prime natural" would have been enough to do it. But hexagonal! Paul had *seen* this six-sided mirror room firsthand, had verified as far as anyone reasonably could that it was probably someone's personal, private, secret creation, and not the work of fakers, frauds, or proven charlatans muddying the waters, salting the lode, exploiting both would-be experts and the gullible.

The complete professional, Paul had even arranged for an independent observer for us. Connie Peake stood with Paul Vickrey and me in the windy afternoon before 67 Ferry Street, the red-brick, suburban home overlooking the lawns and Moreton Bay Figs of Putney Park, which in turn looked out over the Parramatta River. She promised to be a natural in that other sense: someone with a healthy curiosity, an open and scientific mind, and a respected position in a local IT business, recommended to Paul by a mutual friend as someone unfamiliar with the whole notion of psychomantiums and willing to help.

And now Paul was briefing her, giving her much of what he'd given me on our way from the airport. The Janss place would have been an ordinary enough, single-storied house except that its missing owner had bricked up his windows a year ago. At least a year, Paul was telling her, because it was all behind window frames and venetian blinds before then. Finally one of those venetians had fallen, revealing an inner wall of gray brickwork beyond, making 67 Ferry Street an eyesore and its reclusive owner an increasingly mysterious and unpopular neighbor.

"Seems Janss was a nice enough guy at one time," Paul was saying. "Friendly, always obliging. When he lost his wife and kids in the car accident, he went funny. He bricked up the windows, never answered the door. He abandoned the shed he was building in the yard, though he moved his bed out there and prepared meals and slept in the finished half. The neighbors still saw him around the place until two months ago."

"Surely local authorities did something," Connie Peake said. "Contravening building ordinances like this." We hadn't known her long, but Connie definitely seemed the sort of person who used words like "contravening."

"They never knew," Paul told her. "Not till the blinds in the living-room window there fell—in what used to be the living room anyway. Finally, neighbors did phone it in. The council investigated, and my contact arranged for me to be there soon afterward, as Janss's solicitor."

Which he wasn't, of course, but Paul was hardly going to tell Connie that. Who was to know that Janss hadn't had one since the inquest three years ago? Bringing me from the airport, Paul had explained that there was a sister in Perth who had come over for the funeral but seemed to have moved since then.

"A neighbor convinced them that they should break in, in case Janss had had a stroke or something and was lying there. He wasn't. The place was abandoned. So they fitted a new lock and stuck an inspection notice on the back door. My contact told me about the room."

"And now you have a key." His sangfroid had, quite frankly, astonished me.

"I do. If anyone challenges me on it, I'll say Janss and I had a verbal agreement. No paperwork yet."

"Provided he doesn't turn up."

"Provided that, though I'd just say someone phoned claiming to be him. Very thin, I know, but it's worth it. We have a window of opportunity here, Andy."

I could only agree. Hearing him talk to Connie now, I marveled yet again at how my only contact in this part of the world, a middle-aged former lawyer normally busy running his antique business, just happened to learn of this particular house halfway across the city, not through his usual antique-market channels but through an acquaintance who knew something about his interest in mirrored rooms.

"I'd like to see it," Connie Peake said, as if tracking my thoughts. "It's cool out here."

It was. A chill autumn wind was blowing across the river from the southwest. The big trees in the park across Ferry Street took most of the force, heaving and churning under a rapidly growing overcast, but screened off much of the lowering sun as well.

"Of course," Paul said. "We have to go around back. There's no front door anymore."

Connie frowned. "But—oh, it's bricked up, too."

The comment brought a thrill. More than Paul's e-mail, more than seeing the dull-gray Besser bricks behind the window glass in the red-brick wall where the living room used to be. There was a prime hexagonal in there, in all likelihood a genuine psychomantium and more.

Eric Janss had let the trees and bushes in his driveway and backyard grow tall. No curious neighbors could peer over their fences at us. Anyone seeing us arrive would be left with impressions of three well-dressed, professional-looking people talking out front, obviously there in some official capacity and driven inside because of the deteriorating weather.

Paul unlocked the sturdy back door and we stepped into an ordinary enough combination laundry-bathroom. There was a washing machine, sink, drier, and water heater to one side, a toilet and a shower stall to the other. What looked like a closed sliding door at the end led deeper into the house.

"It gets stranger from here," Paul said for Connie's benefit, closing and locking the back door behind us. "I'll have to go first."

At one time, the sliding door would have led into a kitchen. Now, as Paul drew it aside, it revealed a short, dim passage of the same drab Besser brick we'd seen behind the front windows. At the end of its barely two-meter length was another door, made of wood, painted matte black. Paul switched on his torch, waited till we were all in the passage, and slid the first door shut behind us.

"So most of the house is dead space or solid?" I asked, again for Connie's benefit.

"We can't know without demolition or soundings, Andy. Janss probably brought in the mirrors through the French windows facing the yard, then bricked them up behind the frames. None of this is the original house plan. He pulled down interior load-bearing walls, pulled up flooring, and anchored the new construction in concrete."

"And the neighbors never knew?" I said. "Never saw him bringing in bricks or heard him doing renovations?"

"Apparently not. He was just the reclusive, recently bereaved neighbor. Maybe he brought in stuff late at night or waited till people went on holidays. Who would have known? You saw how overgrown the driveway and backyard are."

"Can we get on with this please, Mr. Vickrey . . . Paul?" Connie said. 'I'm supposed to be back at the office by five. You wanted me to see the room!'

She didn't mean it peevishly. She just had things to do; things no doubt set out very meticulously in a busily filled diary. In another life she might have been a relaxed, even pretty, woman. But not here, not now, not this Connie.

"Of course," Paul said, and moved past us to push on the inner door. It opened with a spring-loaded snick.

Other torches shone back at us immediately, dozens, hundreds of them, in a sudden rush of stars. It was like walking onto a television set, that kind of dramatic, overlit intensity.

It was the single eye of Paul's torch, of course, thrown back at us a thousandfold from the mirror walls of Eric Janss's secret room.

"Oh my!" Connie said. "It's all mirrors!"

Paul, bless him, had been right. This *was* a prime and, with any luck, a true prime natural.

We stood inside a hexagonal room at least five meters in diameter but seeming larger because of the floor-to-ceiling mirror walls on all six sides. Even the wall behind us was mirrored, the door set flush in it as a hairline rectangle and barely visible, spring-latched to open at the slightest touch from either side. The floor was dark, varnished timber, but with little resilience to it; probably laid over concrete. The two-and-a-half-meter ceiling was matte black with a recessed light-fitting at its center. The only other features were an old-style bentwood chair and the reed-thin shaft of a candle stand next to it, a waist-high, wrought-iron affair and empty now. Whatever candle it had last held had burned right down. The chair and stand were at the room's midpoint.

Paul crossed to where two mirror walls came together and pressed a tiny switch concealed in the join. Soft yellow light from the ceiling fixture confirmed the reality, sent images of us curving away on all sides. What had already been a moderately large room now went on forever, every wall the wall of another room just like it, then another and another and another, on and on. It was as if you stood in, yes, a maze, or on a plain, or at the junction of promenades like those on the space station in Kubrick's *2001*, arching and curving off. *Very large array* came to mind. It was startling, riveting, overwhelming, all those linked, hexagonal chambers, all those countless Pauls, Connies, and Andys sweeping away in an infinite regress. You *knew* the room ended right there, hard and cold at silvered glass, yet that was nonsense now, impossible. We were at the center of a universe.

"You see why I e-mailed you, Andy," Paul said.

Connie Peake had her notepad out, checking the word Paul had given her earlier. "And this is a . . . psychomantium?"

"Probably is," Paul answered. "There are other theories."

"Psychomantium covers it," I said, trying to cue Paul to hold back, but it only made Connie more curious.

"No. Please, Mr. Galt—Andy—you wanted me here as observer for this first entry. What is a psychomantium? What are these other theories?"

"It'll bias you, Connie. You're meant to report only on what you see today, what is actually here in case the site ever becomes—"

"I know. But you and Mr. Vickrey both know I'm going to do a Net search the minute I get back to the office. You might as well tell me."

"All right. But help us here, please. Just observe. You can go verify whatever you want and bring questions later. Paul, best guess, how long have we got?"

Paul shook his head. "Can't say. It's not being treated as a crime scene. Janss has disappeared, but there's no suggestion of foul play. He may have just gone off."

"But you don't think so," Connie said. "Look, I'm trying to be of use. Say I've done a Net search already. What's a psychomantium?"

Another time I might have resented the presence of this officious young woman, but not now. It was good to be challenged on the fundamentals, especially on the fundamentals. Instead of pleading jet lag and letting Paul deal with her questions, I kept my attention on the earnest face, not wanting her to see Paul and me exchange glances, and didn't hesitate.

"Okay. Psychomancy was originally telling fortunes by gazing into people's souls. Catoptromancy was scrying using mirrors. The Victorians were especially fond of combining the two: building mirrored rooms so they could contact spirits of the dead. Mirrors are traditionally meant to trap the souls of the departed and act as doorways to the other side; that's why they used to be covered or removed when someone died. A psychomantium is a mirrored room built for that purpose."

"You believe this?"

Again I didn't look at Paul. This was the way to go and I hoped he'd see that it was.

"That they existed and still exist today, yes. That they permit communication with the dead, no. But others believe it, and I've been collecting psychomantia, mainly the modern ones."

"What, as oddments? Curiosities?"

"As something humans habitually do, yes. As a constant; part of a fascinating social phenomenon."

"So not just as functioning psychomantiums," Connie Peake said. "You want the range of possibility behind them."

Now Paul and I did exchange looks. *Where did you find this woman*? mine said. *I had no idea*! said Paul's.

Again, I barely hesitated. Connie was surprising me, changing the preconceptions I had of her. "Exactly. It's the infinite regress that's the common factor, and Janss has created it here using a hexagon, what I consider the classic form. The reflections in the angling of two facing mirrors have to be as old as reflective surfaces: the first virtual reality. It must have always been profound, something people just naturally hooked things onto. The French have the perfect term for it—*mise-en-abîme*: plunged into the abyss."

We gazed into that abyss now, the endless rush of corridors taking the three of us off to infinity, doing it in long curves, sending us to the left in one mirror wall, to the right in the next, back to the left, and so on. The ceiling light had seemed kind at first, pleasantly free of glare. Now my eyes had adjusted, and it lent a hard, almost clinical quality to the unending rooms and hallways, making me think of the oppressive cubicles in George Tooker's *The Waiting Room*. I couldn't prevent it.

"Have you seen many?" Connie asked, almost in a whisper. The faux cathedral space seemed to demand it.

"Not dedicated ones like this. Mostly you get full-length mirrors set opposite each other in drawing rooms and parlors that give the regression effect, or batwing dressing tables with adjustable side mirrors set a certain way. Sometimes it's hard proving they were intended as psychomantiums at all. There are a lot of hoaxes; descendants staging the effect for tourism purposes, claiming all sorts of things. Paul and I are looking for prime naturals, dedicated setups like this, with no trumped-up back-story to work through."

"And you've been lucky?"

"We've seen most of the famous ones," Paul said. "But it's the newer kind, the local ones, we're after. I've found four naturals, none as fine as this. Andy's located five, including a dodecagonal room—twelve mirror walls marked out according to the hours of the clock—a splendid octagonal, and two rather poor hexagonals."

"Using candlelight?" Connie indicated the candle stand.

"Almost always," Paul said. "It gives the most powerful—and traditional—effects."

"The most suggestive, I imagine. The most scary."

"No, powerful," I said, interrupting. "Look for yourself. This present lighting is effective. Janss knew to use a low-wattage, yellowish bulb, but it's like you get on mirror-wall escalators in malls and old department stores. It's not optimal, hence the candle stand. He wanted a controlled effect. So far as we can tell, all the naturals originally involved candles."

"Janss let his burn down," Connie said.

"And that's what we'll do," I said, letting Paul know that it was all right for Connie to know more. He'd accept the decision. "We'll sit here and let ours burn down."

"Turn about," Paul said.

"Turn about," I confirmed.

"You'll do it alone?" Connie actually gave a shudder. "It reminds me of that old skipping song we sang at school."

"I'm sorry. The what?" Paul asked.

"A skipping song." She gave an odd smile, part self-consciousness, part excitement, and recited it in the singsong rhythm of the schoolyard.

One thing about the night,
One thing about the day,
You turn around and meet yourself
And go the other way.

She gave another little smile. "The rope would be going really fast, and everyone kept singing it over and over till you had the nerve to turn around. If the rope was long enough, you'd either move back to where you started and duck out, or you'd keep changing directions on the word 'way' until you were out. The one who turned the most times won." She gazed off into the regress. "I guess Janss did his sittings mostly at night."

Now she had me. "Why do you say that? The room is completely sealed. It shouldn't make a difference."

"I think it completes the effect. He's got infinite night in here, but the sense of corridors leading off would be completed at night."

"It's less virtual."

"That's it." Connie checked her watch, but instead of reminding us she had to go, she surprised me again. "Can I stay part of this? I won't intrude. I'd just like to . . . well, know more."

"We'll consider it, Connie," I said, the best refusal I could manage after a long flight and having been awake for twenty hours.

"You hope to find Janss."

"We're doing this irrespective of Janss," I said too quickly, too harshly. "Excuse me."

"Can you explain that?" she asked. "Before I go?" Connie Peake was proving to be a master at this, and her enthusiasm was infectious.

Paul came to my aid. "Janss left no journals, no papers, doesn't seem to have had a computer. We probably won't ever know what he was really doing. We'll have to go by what he made here."

"It's like archaeology," Connie said and turned to me again. "That other word you said about using mirrors. Catop—catop—something."

"Catoptromancy. Catoptrics is the branch of optics concerned with reflection, with forming images using mirrors. Catoptromancy is scrying by mirrors. A catoptromantium is an arrangement, sometimes a room, for doing this."

I hoped my tone would warn her off, remind her that I wanted to examine the room with Paul. She did begin to move to the door.

"So you can't know for certain if a room was meant as a psychomantium or not?"

"No, the distinction has been lost." My tone was even cooler. *Please go, Connie, go.* "It's more dramatic to talk of contacting the dead. It gets the media attention." Why was I encouraging her?

"I bet. And I guess you have lots of models at home. Miniature rooms made of mirror tiles."

She'd done it again. I had to laugh. "Yes, I do. It's a hobby."

"It's more than that," she said. "You're trying to know something. Look, Andy, can I see you? Can we go for a coffee or a meal?" She was so direct it stunned me. It was as if Paul wasn't even standing there.

"Connie, ask me another time. I've just arrived. I'm jet-lagged and there's a lot to do."

"Of course. But another time. Please."

"Another time," I said, and we saw her out, to discover that the weather had turned. Rain squalls blew in across the river and the park, keeping farewells to a minimum. We watched Connie drive off, then hurried inside. Paul locked the back door behind us.

"Sorry, Andy. She was more high-maintenance than I expected."

"But valuable, Paul. We don't have a pedigree for this one, and the chances of demolition are considerable. It's all we can do."

Another time, we'd have postponed our first session, allowing for my jet lag, or Paul would have done a solo sitting. But we really didn't know how long we'd have, and we'd been at so few sites together that we wanted to make a start, to log the room's properties and just enjoy being there. Tomorrow we'd alternate solo sittings, overlapping a half hour or so to share information, then try another joint sitting later in the week, if we had that long.

Paul brought in a chair from Janss's makeshift bedroom out back and we sat with our camcorders and Pentaxes, taking footage and snapping dozens of shots, first by the overhead light, then using the new candle fitted in the stand.

It didn't matter that it was windy and rainy outside. In Janss's mirror room, it was lit as if for night. There were no windows for the rain to beat against, just blind brick. In a real sense, time had ceased to matter. We could have been anywhere, and in day or night for all the difference it made.

Though Connie had been right. It did make a difference. Of course it did. Doing this at night would complete something when the candle burned away. When darkness was restored.

We measured the room's dimensions next—smiling as we always did at the play on words—dividing the space into a clock face for easy reference. The door in its mirror wall was at six o'clock; that wall's juncture with the next, going clockwise, was seven; the center of that face eight; the next juncture nine, and so on. Twelve o'clock was directly opposite the door; the concealed light switch was at eleven, a tiny, cunningly hidden press button, virtually invisible unless you knew where to look.

We didn't move the bentwood chair, of course. Its position to the left of the candle was as Janss had last had it, his back not to six o'clock but facing the full mirror wall at two, with the eight-o'clock mirror wall behind. It had to be significant.

Paul and I were enjoying ourselves. His long-suffering wife, Cindy, had sent along a "care package," as she called it: chicken sandwiches, blueberry muffins, and a thermos of coffee, complete with a note: *Don't stay up too late.*

When we were finally settled in our chairs, we shared a modest candlelit meal with our myriad selves out along the ever-dwindling boulevards, remarking on whatever details of construction or effect caught our attention, even beginning to work out a timetable for the next day. Paul would do a four-hour morning watch before going in to the office. I'd do the late afternoon and evening, and he'd pick me up around nine.

Connie was right. I wanted to be there at night. Night did make a difference.

Inevitably we fell silent, looking off into the regress. As in other dedicated mirror rooms we'd logged, all the familiar things were there: the certainty of valid distance and genuine form, the sense of being watched, the uncanny stillness in which the smallest actions—gestures, sudden turns of head or body—sent immediate and startling motion across the lines, set crowds of ourselves gesturing, mimicking, almost urging stillness again by their manic imitation.

Paul and I knew the routine; nothing had to be said. We became utterly still, gazing into the deep, horizontal domains as Janss must have. In our sweaters and slacks, we made a dark knot at the heart of each chamber; faces and hands glowing in the candlelight like countless studies for Rembrandt's "Nightwatch." The corridors and mirror rooms took that calm as far as the eye could see, into the impossibility of dimensions that couldn't exist, yet did: space wrested from illusion, imposed on perception, demanding to be real.

We managed nearly two hours before jet-lag torpor made me call it quits. We hadn't let the candle burn away yet, but my journey across the world was already worth it. If Janss turned up right now, even if the police arrived and evicted us, we'd been in the Janss room at 67 Ferry Street. We were smiling as we went out into the rainy night and drove home.

I SLEPT LATE, lulled by rain on the roof and wind around the eaves, and never saw Paul leave for his early sitting. An old friend of Cindy's dropped by and I didn't get to Ferry Street until after five. The rain had continued. The harsh autumn wind gusted in the trees, and the park and the river were reduced to so many inkwash veils in the chill afternoon.

I was glad to lock the back door behind me, to place my bag in the laundry and enter the mirror room again. Paul had left the ceiling light on, with a precisely measured candle in the stand so I could do a burn-down. It would take two hours. My mobile was off. My checklist and clipboard were on my lap, my tai-chi chime ball in my pocket. There was a penlight in case it was needed; my main torch, camcorder, and camera were on the floor at my feet. Everything was ready.

At 6:00 sharp, I lit the candle, switched off the overhead light and returned to the chair, sitting with my eyes closed for maybe a minute so they could adjust. Finally, I opened them on the miracle of the mirror world.

I sat at the hub of an amazing wheel. Stretching away on all sides were corridors that existed only as reflection, arching off into replicated chambers of stars where other solitary watchers sat, eternally together, eternally alone. Each separate wall of the hexagon led into another hexagonal mirror room in which I was turned away, which then led into another where I was angled back, on and on, this way, that way, off to infinity, but with curves and archings according to counter-reflection and the imperfections and anomalies of the mirrors themselves.

In the ten-o'clock wall, lines of Andy Galt made an infinite corridor to the right. In the nine-o'clock wall, he arced to the left, then right, then left again in those puzzling alternations no one could satisfactorily explain. If I looked near where two mirrors joined, there was a boulevard, the sense of a shadowed avenue between infinite lines of Andy.

Mesmerizing didn't cover it. It was compelling, arresting, powerfully entrancing. I'd focus on a corridor, find myself staring at it, down it, across it, along all those curving lines of myself made into a string of honey-colored moons, party lanterns strung out forever along drained midnight canals and antique avenues. Yes, I was at the center of a universe. No other term came close. Janss had made himself a universe here, an orrery of realms in an arrangement few ever got to see, had brought endlessness into a red (and gray)-brick suburban home, put eternity into grains of sand and silvered glass.

I logged the usual tricks when they came, the catoptric anomalies triggered in brains not intended to face things like infinite regress: the twelfth or seventeenth figure out behaving differently, the conviction of a light source not my own, the sense of rippling or of movements delayed or prefigured somewhere among the myriad forms, the constant game of "Simon Says" you played until you were sure one doppelganger was truly, even purposely, out of sync.

Complex mirror reflections like this had no precedent in nature, hadn't existed for the eye and brain to adapt to in the evolution equation. Perhaps mirrors were the most profound, the most dangerous, the very worst human invention. They suborned the integrity of the mind, couldn't do otherwise. We were never meant to have mirrors more elaborate than calm pools, clear ice walls, lightning-fused sandglass, and sandstorm-scoured sheets of metal or mica, dishes of water, blocks of obsidian, screens of iron pyrites, or oddities like Dr. Dee's lump of polished coal.

In the second hour, torpor took its toll, had me nodding off until—using the old Thomas Edison trick—I dropped the chime ball I was holding in my left hand and woke myself.

That was the cycle until 7:52, when the candle was barely a finger's width above the cup. The rooms were dimming on every side, readying themselves for night. It seemed as bright as ever, but that was an illusion. My eyes had adjusted to what light there was, had made an Indian-summer noon out of a generous twilight. It was like the heat death of the universe out there, all that warmth and life being drawn away in subtle shifts, like some pattern of entropy replicated in an insect's eye. Janss had seen this, had been in *this* chair, seeing *these* gradations of night come.

Absurdly, I recalled the title of a Giacometti sculpture: "The Palace at 4 A.M." It felt like that dead hour now.

Connie's song was there, too, surprising me, the old schoolyard refrain about meeting yourself. That's what I'd been doing. Cued by the words, I turned, swung round in my chair. There I was on every side: flickering, faltering selves out in what was left of the vast, fading starwheel.

They trapped my eye, drew me image by image out into the regress. They were holding me there, fading, darkening. *Be easy now, easy. Be with us. Let it come.*

I felt a rush of dread, sudden and utter panic. The chime ball clanged against the floor; my clipboard clattered as I rushed for the switch, fumbled with it, brought up warm yellow light, saved us all.

Not tonight. No darkness tonight. I couldn't bear it. It was the jet lag, whatever. I'd do a burn-down at some other sitting. *We* would.

When Paul arrived at 8:53, he found me under the porch outside the bricked-up front door, sheltering from the rain.

NEITHER OF US had managed a burn-down, it turned out. Perhaps it had to do with the room itself, the circumstances of Janss's disappearance, the unseasonal weather, even Connie's song. We agreed that it might be something best done together.

I did a nine-till-noon sitting the next day, taking dozens of photos and more video footage, this time using a tripod and automatic timer for PR shots, and adding a sporadic commentary, anything to keep me from pondering why I hadn't let the candle burn away. It had been a crazy thing last night; it was irrational now, but I couldn't help it.

When Paul arrived for his five-hour afternoon session, he brought a lunch invitation from Connie. There was a twinkle in his eye as he handed me the car keys and gave me directions. He knew how on-again, off-again my relationship with Pamela was back home. This would get me out of the loop, he said. It was good for me.

I felt trapped but pleased. I didn't try to consider motives. I'd keep it easy, light and professional, and with luck, get more of Connie's enthusiasm.

We met at a café in a rainy village court in Putney. Connie had her hair out and wore a shiny black raincoat too blatant to be calculated.

"I looked up the mancy words," she said as I sat across from her. Her smile utterly transformed her face.

"The what? Oh, the mancy words. Right."

"I never realized people took it so seriously. Lithomancy: scrying by the reflection of candlelight off precious stones. Macharomancy, for heaven's sake: reading swords, daggers, and knives. Imagine specializing in that. Clouds: nephelomancy. Things accidentally heard: transataumancy." She pronounced the word so carefully, as if relishing it. "It's like people made them up for the fun of it. Came up with wacky names like those collective nouns you get: a murder of crows, a parliament of owls."

"A loony of researchers!" I said. I wanted to see her laugh.

We ordered the lasagne with salad and coffee, then sat watching cars go by in the rain. I let Connie bring us back to it.

"Andy, if it's a natural like you say, Janss had probably never heard of catoptromancy. Never knew the word, never knew any variants."

"So the room is a psychomantium, and all he was trying to do was reach his family. Maybe voices told him to do it; maybe he went quietly nuts."

"Surrounded by ordinary households and normal lives," she said. "Sat there while candles burned down. Did it again and again. Then probably sat in darkness, for who knows how long, without the reflections."

I couldn't help myself; I'd had a bad scare the night before. "Without reflections, but with the sense of all those rooms *still* there, those avenues filled with night. You can't help it."

Connie gave a shudder. "That's a chilling thought."

"It's part of the effect. Both Paul and I have let candles burn away." Not this time, I didn't add, and wondered why I didn't, why it mattered. "You feel the . . . pressure . . . of the rooms still out there, going on and on. You know there's nothing there, that reflections need light—"

"But the brain registers images for so long it can't give them up," she said, going to the heart of it. "A retinal afterimage thing. Like a ghost arm effect."

"And you can restore it all so easily. The little switch is right there, and your torch and your Bic lighter and matches. But the feeling is that they're still there."

"That's creepy, Andy. You're the master of all those rooms. They exist because of you."

"And the mirrors."

"No, you. It's *your* perception. *Your* conviction that they're still there. *You're* the activating factor."

The food arrived, but we let it sit a moment. "It gets stranger, Connie. Paul and I have confirmed it. When the candle finally does go out and you're in total darkness, it's as if your reflections, all the mirror versions you've been watching for hours, are pressing up against the glass. You even think you hear them moving in."

"That has to be hyperaesthesia. Anomalous perception. That's—"

"A mind thing, I know. It's exactly what it is. But it *feels* real."

We began eating, looking through the big window, again watching the cars in the rain.

"What if it's sciamancy?" she said between mouthfuls.

"It's what?"

"Sciamancy. What if it's a sciamantium: a place for making shadows, for reading shadows?"

I must have grinned in wonder, for she smiled back. "Andy, what?"

"You've been busy."

"I mean it. What if Janss made a shadow place? Not to contact spirits or read reflections—"

"To scry the darkness." It was so close to my own catoptromancy fixations that I felt alarm, genuine delight, true fascination. It was so good to share this. "Connie, maybe it is a . . . sciamantium."

"Night has to be psychoactive for us, doesn't it? You reach a point where a perception, even a misperception, triggers something in the psyche. You haunt yourselves. Janss, Paul, all of us. Everyone who tries it."

"I hope so. I hope that's what it is." All it is, I didn't add, didn't need to.

We finished eating. The plates were cleared, second coffees brought.

"It does have to do with light, doesn't it?" she said.

"Darkness."

"You know what I mean."

"It's an important distinction. Light running out, darkness being restored, what you were saying. We've always feared night, responded to it dynamically. We made use of that fear, and did pretty well, considering, but the primal response was to endure it, wait it out, worship and appease it."

"But mostly separate ourselves from it in sleep."

"Right. When we developed enough tribally, socially, to sleep safely. Then we modified the relationship over centuries, generations. Gas and electric light changed it, let night become romantic, a time for leisure and shift-work."

"The brain does learn."

"It has to. But only to a point. It's a dual thing: the adjustment *and* the remembering. My relationship with darkness was probably determined by how it was presented to me as a kid. Maybe Janss sussed it out, was taking the appropriate next step of embracing the night for *all* it is, revisiting it as a conditioned mind liberated from fearing it."

"The throwback fear thing hardwired in, but the framing culture telling us it's okay. Maybe the energy behind that fear *can* be directed differently. We don't do an ordinary lunch do we, Andy?"

"We didn't want one."

Connie smiled. "So Janss is a creature of his time, one more solitary watcher responding to what night has become for us. What *else* it has become. Something to inhabit and colonize, something to avoid. Have you ever tried infrared cameras?"

There she was, blindsiding me again. "What, and night-vision goggles?"

"Why not? It might give something."

"We've never been set up that way. We're more your boutique operation." Then it came out. "Connie, we haven't let candles burn down in the Janss room yet. Neither of us has."

There was kindness, instant understanding in her eyes. "So it might be sciamancy. The room could be a place for reading the form and nature of shadows, for creating intricate shadows, and both you and Paul sensed it."

It occurred to me then that if Connie was a natural, too, I should let her be one. "Make an argument."

"What?"

"Make an argument. It's a sciamantium. Convince me."

"All right. It's what we said. Janss was calling up the night. Humans have that ancient . . . an atavistic connection with darkness, *and* with the subtleties."

Subtleties. One word glossed it all. "He was creating an *effect* of night," I said, daring to believe it again.

"An *effect* of shadows and night that only the mirrors bring."

"Trying to reach his wife and son."

"You don't believe that any more than I do. It was accentuation. No, intensification. It mightn't even be related to the deaths."

"Go on."

I expected her to say that she should accompany me.

"That's all. I just know that you have to be alone in there, Andy, like Janss was. It won't work with the two of you. It can't work. If it's psychoactive, it has to be just the individual enabling what happens with the mirrors, *your* mind reacting to the shadows. And keep Paul out of there. You should keep him out. He has a family."

"I'll do a burn-down tonight."

Despite what she'd said about being alone, I truly expected her to ask if she could be there. Part of me hoped.

"Just be careful," was all she said, and we returned to watching cars in the rain.

I NAPPED FROM three till five. After enduring Cindy's jibes about going on a date with Connie, I relieved Paul just after five. We sat in the warm calm of the Janss room for a half hour or so, discussing everything but what Connie had suggested about sciamancy. One of us had to stay unbiased, and he didn't need to be burdened with additional labels and characteristics yet. That's what I told myself.

He finally left me to my evening shift, hurried out to the car and drove off through the bleak, wet evening. This time we'd agreed to leave our mobiles on. We didn't need to say why.

I filmed, I photographed, I did more commentary into the pocket recorder. I reached 7:00 P.M. without dropping my chime ball once. Everything was the same. Everything was different. Just the names: sciamantium and sciamancy took it from a familiar candlelight vigil to something new and unsettling: a night watch for shadowforms out in the marshes, the shadowlands, a warding off of unproven enemies in the backwaters of forever.

By 8:10 P.M. I was exhausted, ready to call it quits. It was all too still, too constant, too laden with immanence. No, not constant, I kept reminding myself. Now and then the hot blade of the candle did stir, perhaps from something as simple and immediate as my breathing or a microzephyr sneaking around the cracks and doorsills, finding a way in, and the lines of flames trembled, wavered, shook their points of light as if to catch my attention, as if to test me. *Did you notice? Did you notice?*

But mostly it was still, *we* were still, all of us in our articulated, nautilus chambers, our adjoining rooms.

The notion of a sciamantium kept me there, kept me resolved as the candle burned away, knowing that Janss had done this again and again, sat beside solitary flames made legion, watching himself parceled off into mirror chambers that gradually sank into night. He hadn't just been alone in a bricked-up suburban house, not merely in a fabulous mirror world, but at the focus of rooms destined for darkness. He'd made waiting rooms, filled them with light, then watched them empty out.

Waiting rooms, yes, where you waited for darkness to come, infinite, replicated darkness, growing, settling across all these real, unreal spaces. There could be no reflection, no possibility of rooms and boulevards when the flame died and the nautilus rooms emptied and slowly ceased to exist. Yet what if the opposite *was* true—if only in the mind? It was the old question of whether a tree falling in a forest made a sound if there was no one to hear it.

I kept wondering about defaults in the brain. How was mine dealing with the idea of all those darkening rooms out there, the prospect of what might use those boulevards when the light was snatched away? What was it devising even now to protect Andy Galt from inconceivable, unprecedented threat?

Minutes felt like hours. I'd look at my watch to find the hands had barely moved. It was like being on detention at school, time cruelly stretched and distended. The thought sent Connie's schoolyard rhyme running through my mind. But I'd already turned, faced where I'd been, met as much of myself as I could, my selves, going this way, that way, mocking me, taunting shadowforms in the infinite regress. The song's words were an incantation, a maddening litany. What had Janss been doing?

Then something caught my attention.

Did I imagine it, or was there a shadowing off in the distance—the false distance at two o'clock, where the images blurred into uncertainty? I blinked, took off my glasses and rubbed my eyes. There did seem to be something, a dimming, a shadowing out there.

I quickly looked about me. Behind and to the sides, the infinite rooms were as bright as ever, star chambers arcing off like settings for outdoor recitals. Carols by Candlelight. Madrigals by Mirrorlight. A Cappella, in the Waiting Rooms. Nothing had changed. It was only ahead, in the mirror wall at two, that there seemed to be a darkening, like a storm at the edge of the world, spilling a little to the sides, but only a little, and way out in those real, unreal, never-real distances.

It was impossible, of course. Physically impossible. Any shadowing had to be replicated, shared, made part of all the reflection corridors and boulevards on every side. It was basic catoptrics.

Or selective self-delusion. Something served up by fatigue and an overstimulated mind.

My adrenaline rush was real. I went into automatic observer routines, questioning everything. If the candle flame had been down at the rim, close to guttering, I'd have accepted it more easily, but two centimeters of candle stood well clear of the cup.

It was me. It had to be. Some optical trickery, some effect of jet lag. I'd been sitting and staring too long. My bored brain was entertaining itself. Finding things. Making things.

Or it was the room!

I reminded myself that the imperfections of an average wall mirror enlarged to the size of the Gulf of Mexico became waves twenty meters high. Could it be the mirrors? Part of Janss's intended effect?

He had to have seen this, had to have been in this exact situation. That was why the chair was angled so. Checking the anomaly at two o'clock.

And he hadn't survived it.

Or he had simply gone away, seen something that drove him off.

Again I removed my glasses, rubbed my eyes. Again I checked the image field. It was there, definitely there, something was, something like swelling, burgeoning night, or perceptual trickery in the glass or in the vision centers of the brain. Defaults, yes, that was the word. What were the defaults set there?

Enough. I'd give it up for tonight.

As a way of withdrawing, anchoring myself in the reality of 67 Ferry Street once more, I located the tiniest black dot of the light switch where it sat in the join at eleven o'clock, looked over my right shoulder to confirm the barest hairline of the door in the mirror wall at six.

One more glimpse, one more try, I decided, as Janss must have.

The shadowing was there—the spreading "darklands," whatever they were. I smiled at the fancy, a hopeless victim of autosuggestion now. It was crazy. Too much peering off into distances, making eyes track vistas rarely, if ever, seen in nature, never meant for eyes with a such a highly developed, reactive brain behind them. I simply wasn't sure what I was seeing.

I had my mobile. Now was the time to call Paul, to have him join me and verify what was happening.

Connie's words stopped me. I had to be alone with this, had to allow that the eye-brain link was overwhelmed, set to doing the only thing it could: imposing order, treating this as something real, even as crisis, but rigorously dealing with it. Of course there were shadows, optical tricks. Of course there was fear, feelings of disquiet and alarm. What we'd said about the night related to eyes and mirrors, too. Just as we were completing our connection with night, so too we were changing what eyes, what brains, needed to do.

The darklands seemed to be growing, pushing from the two-o'clock focus into the mirror rooms at one and three. Behind, everything remained as bright and steady as ever. It was in that two-o'clock spread that it was happening.

"Let it come!" I spoke the words to hear myself say them, aware of what an ominous line they would make on the audio track. I took more video footage, more photographs. I filled the time with deeds, filled with the dying of the light.

The flame sank closer to the rim.

My mobile rang. Thank God! Paul offering a reprieve!

But it was Connie.

"Andy, do you know what sciamachy is?"

Not now, not now, I wanted to tell her, but the word held me.

"Say again, Connie. What what is?"

"Scia*machy*. Not mancy, machy!"

"Not offhand. Something to do with shadows."

"Fighting shadows, Andy. The act of fighting shadows. Imagined enemies."

"Okay. Look, I'm nearly done—"

"Andy, what if it's a sciamachium?"

"Hey, look, thanks." I wanted her to go. I didn't want her to go. "Connie?"

"Yes?"

"Thanks. I mean it. I'm doing it. Alone. I'm doing it."

"I know. I know, Andy. But a sciamachium. Just call me when you're done, okay?"

"Promise."

She had known, I realized as I put the phone away. She was a natural and she had known.

The shadowing beckoned, teased at two, flexed dark fingers. *Look at me, look at me!* Everywhere else the rooms were bright and constant, seemed to be. I sat watching the darklands, wondering how they could exist, finally convinced myself that they spread only when I glanced away. It was using my mind, my eyes, to build itself.

I held the darkness with my eyes, daring it to slip into new rooms, consume new Andys. With all the bright rooms at my back, I held it at bay with my eyes and Connie's words, Connie's skipping song running through my mind.

Urging me. Connie the natural urging me to turn around.

I did so, looked over my shoulder at the eight-o'clock wall.

And there was dead-black night filling the glass, night the hunter pressed to it like a face at a window. The shadowing at two had been the bait.

I tipped forward in shock, slammed hard against the floor, reached for the first thing I could find—the candle stand—meaning to angle it up, to fling it at the dead-black wall of glass.

But stopped in time. Barely managed. Do that and I'd be in darkness when it shattered. Night would be everywhere, flowing out.

I scrambled to the eleven-o'clock corner, reached for the tiny button.

Yellow light filled the rooms. Most of the rooms. The black wall held at eight like onyx, obsidian, a membrane about to burst. The darklands shadowed off at two, but just the lure, just the distraction.

Now I flung the candle stand. Now it struck the glass, grazed and shattered the wall. The pieces clashed down, left dead-gray Besser brick beyond. At two o'clock, the darklands were no more.

WHEN PAUL ARRIVED fifteen minutes later, Connie was with him. They found me standing by the front gate in the wind and rain, cold and shivering.

"Janss didn't know he had to turn around," I told them as I climbed into the back seat. "He never turned around."

AFTERWORD

Because of how and when it happened for a fifteen-year-old living in Sydney in 1962, my favorite horror story has to be Fritz Leiber's "A Bit of the Dark World" from the June issue of *Fantastic* from that year. I have read it a dozen, maybe two dozen, times since, unable to keep away from Rim House and that unnamable presence amid those canyons. This Leiber connection continued with his 1978 novel *Our Lady of Darkness*, my all-time favorite horror novel. I took a copy with me when I explored Corona Heights in 1988 and then visited Fritz's home on Geary so he could sign it for me, a truly special occasion. If anyone was midwife to my own sweetly darkened life, it's Fritz. This story is for him.

Mike O'Driscoll has always believed his spiritual home to be the American West, despite having been born in London and brought up in the southwest of Ireland. Raised on cowboy films and science fiction, he grew up wanting to be the next John Wayne, but Clint Eastwood beat him to it. Undeterred, he ventured out to discover the world, cramming ten years into two so he could take the rest of the time off to fall in love, get married, raise a child, and teach a new dog old tricks.

He finally settled in Swansea, where he ran a video rental business for five years, and began writing short stories to fill the hours that might otherwise have been occupied with customers. His stories have been published in *The Third Alternative*, *Interzone*, and a number of anthologies in the U.S. and the U.K. O'Driscoll has also written film articles, and has a regular comment column on the TTA Web site, www.ttapress.com, and a horror column at the Alien Online (www.thealienonline.net).

THE SILENCE OF THE FALLING STARS

MIKE O'DRISCOLL

NOTHING IS INFINITE. In a lifetime, a man's heart will notch up somewhere in the region of 2,500 million beats, a woman's, maybe 500 million more. These are big numbers, but not infinite. There is an end in sight, no matter how far off it seems. People don't think about that. They talk instead about the sublime beauty of nature, about the insignificance of human life compared to the time it's taken to shape these rocks and mountains. Funny how time can weigh heavier on the soul than all these billions of tons of dolomite and dirt. A few years back, a ranger found something squatting against the base of a mesquite tree at the mouth of Hanaupah Canyon. It was something dead, he saw, and the shape of it suggested a man. Curious, the ranger crouched down and touched it. The body, or whatever it was, had been so desiccated by heat and wind that it started to crumble and when the desert breeze caught it, the whole thing fell away to dust.

No way to tell what it had really been, or if it was heat alone or time that caused its naturalization.

Fifty-year highs for July average 116 degrees. Anyone caught out here in that kind of heat without water has a couple of options. You can try to find shade, which, if you get lucky, will cut your rate of dehydration by about fifteen percent. Or, you can just rest instead of walking, which will save you something like forty percent. But the ground temperature out here is half again higher than the air temperature. Ideally, what you want is a shaded spot elevated above the ground. If you're lucky enough to find such a place, and if you're smart enough to keep your clothes on, which will cut your dehydration by another twenty percent, then you might last two days at 120 degrees max without water. If you're out of luck, then just keeping still, you'll sweat two pints in an hour. If you don't take in the equivalent amount of water, you'll begin to dehydrate. At five percent loss of body weight, you'll start to feel nauseous. Round about ten percent, your arms and legs will begin tingling and you'll find it hard to breathe. The water loss will thicken your blood, and your heart will struggle to pump it out to your extremities. Somewhere between fifteen and twenty percent dehydration, you'll die.

Which goes to show there is, after all, one thing that is infinite: the length of time you stay dead. There is no real correlation between what I'm thinking and the SUV that heads slowly south along the dirt road. Even when it pulls over and stops beside the dry lake running along the valley floor, I can't say for sure what will happen. I'm unwilling to speculate. Even when nothing happens, I don't feel any kind of surprise.

I scan the oval playa with my binoculars. Indians are supposed to have raced horses across it, which is why it's called the Racetrack. There's an outcrop of rock at the north end that they call the Grandstand, but I don't see any spectators up there. Never have. Below the ridge from where I watch, there are clumps of creosote bush and the odd Joshua tree. Farther north, there are stands of beavertail and above them, on the high slopes of the Last Chance Range, are forests of juniper and piñon pine. A glint of sunlight catches my eye and I glance toward the vehicle. But nothing has moved down there. I shift my gaze back out on to the playa, trying to pretend I don't feel the cold chill that settles on my bones. I look away at the last moment and wipe the sweat from my face. Thirst cracks my lips and dust coats the inside of my mouth. There's plenty water in my Expedition, parked half a mile further south along the road, but I make no move to return to the vehicle. Whatever is happening here, I have no choice but to see how it plays out.

A shadow moves on the playa. When I search for it, all I can see are the rocks scattered across the honeycombed surface of the dry lake. I scan them closely, looking for a lizard or rodent, even though nothing lives out there. The air is still and quiet, no breeze at all to rustle through the mesquites. Then something catches my eye, and the hairs on the back of my neck stand up. A movement so painfully slow I doubt it happened at all. Until it rolls forward another inch. From this distance, I estimate its weight at eighty to a hundred pounds. I glance at the rocks nearest to it, but none of them have moved. Only this one, its shadow seeming to melt in the harsh sunlight as it heaves forward again. There's no wind, nothing to explain its motion. All the stories I've heard about the rocks have some rational explanation, but there's no reason at all to what I'm seeing here.

Except maybe that SUV and whatever's inside it. I look back to where it was, but it's not there. I scan the dirt road to north and south and still don't see it. I search the playa in case the vehicle drove out on the mud, but there are only scattered rocks. The sun is at its highest now, yet I'm not overheating. I don't feel nauseous, and my heart isn't struggling. Maybe it's because I'm barely breathing. I stare along the dirt road for an age, looking for something I might have missed. But there's no trail of dust or anything else to signal anyone was ever here.

THE GUY WORE jeans and a loose-fit shirt; the woman had on shorts, T-shirt and a baseball cap. He was leaning over beneath the open hood of the Japanese SUV. A rusting stove lay on its back beside the road, and beyond it, two lines of rubble were all that marked a building that had long since gone.

The woman's face creased in a smile as I pulled up in front of the Toyota Rav4. I got out of my vehicle. "You need a hand here?"

"I think we've overheated," she said. I didn't recognize her accent.

The guy stood up and wiped his face on his shirt. "Bloody air-conditioning" he said. "I guess I was running it too hard. We're not used to this kind of heat."

I nodded. "How long you been stuck here?"

Before the woman could answer, a young girl stuck her head out the back window. "Henry Woods," she said, reading my name tag. "Are you a policeman?"

"No, I'm a park ranger."

The woman leaned over and tousled the girl's hair. "Ranger Woods, meet Cath. I'm Sophie Delauney. This is my husband, Paul."

I shook hands with both of them and asked Delauney if there was anything they needed. He frowned, then laughed and said he doubted it. "I suppose you'll tell me I should have hired an American car."

"No. You just had bad luck, is all." I leaned in over the engine, saw there was nothing I could do. "Could happen to anyone."

"Yeah, well, it happened to us."

I got some bottles of water from the cooler in the Expedition and handed them around. Delauney went back to fiddling with the plugs and points, unwilling, I figured, to accept that all he could do was wait for the engine to cool.

"How'd you find us?" Sophie Delauney said.

"We have a plane patrols the valley. Must have seen you here and called it in. I was up at Zabriskie Point, twenty miles north of here."

"I didn't see it," she said, shielding her eyes as she looked up at the cloudless sky.

"I saw it," the girl said.

"Did you, baby? You never said."

"I did. You weren't listening."

"Where you folks from?" I asked.

"England," she said. "We live outside London."

The girl frowned and shook her head. "No we don't—we live in Elstree."

"I know, dear, but Mr. Woods might not have heard of Elstree."

"I always wanted to see England," I said. "Just never seem to find the time."

"You should."

Delauney finally saw that merely willing it wasn't going to get the engine to cool any faster and came to join us. "Where you headed?" I asked him.

"Not far, by the look of things. Can you recommend anywhere close by?"

"About an hour's drive will get you to the resort village at Stovepipe Wells." I don't know why I didn't mention the inn at Furnace Creek, which was closer.

The girl piped up. "Do they have a swimming pool?"

I nodded. "Sure do."

Sophie drank some water. She wiped her hand across her mouth and said, "Do you ever get used to this heat?"

"Breathe lightly," I said. "It won't hurt so much."

After a quarter of an hour, I told Delauney to try it again. The engine turned over and cut out. He tried again, and this time it caught. "There you go," I said. "You should be okay now—just keep an eye on the temp gauge."

"Thanks for your help, Officer Woods," Sophie said. "It's much appreciated."

"It's what I'm here for."

They got in the vehicle. "Thanks again," Sophie said. I watched as they drove off, the girl hanging out the window, her mother, too, staring back at me. Alone in the ruins of Greenwater, I tried to imagine what she saw, wondering if she had seen something in my eyes I didn't know was there.

I PAID RENT to the government for the bungalow I occupied near Stovepipe Wells. It was small but even after six years, I didn't seem to have accumulated enough belongings to fill the available space. Rae Hannafin said it looked unlived in, said if I hated it that much, I should ask to be rehoused. She thought I was stuck in a rut, that I had been in the valley too long and that I should apply for a transfer. But I didn't hate Death Valley, or even the bungalow. Though I used to imagine that one day I would move on, over the years I've come to realize that I had reached the place I'd always been heading toward. It's not just the solitariness—it's the valley itself, which gets under your skin.

I sat in Arcan's Bar drinking Mexican beer. It was quiet; a dozen or so people, mostly couples, a few regulars shooting pool, half a dozen familiar faces perched on stools at the counter. Kenny Rogers, someone like that, on the jukebox. The young Hispanic behind the counter made small talk with a couple of girls. I caught his eye, he fetched another beer, set it down in front of me, gave me a scowl, and went back to work his charm on the señoritas. Jaime had been working there nearly two years and still complained about the customers treating him like shit. Just because he was Mexican, he told me one time. No, I said, it's because you're an outsider.

"That s'posed to make me feel better, man?" he asked.

"Yes," I said. "Because we're all outsiders here."

That was about the most I'd ever talked to him at one time. I'm not good at small talk. As a rule, I only talk when I have something to say. This is probably a failing on my part. Hannafin says that talk is a social lubricant, that it's part of what makes us human, even when it doesn't mean anything. I'm not convinced. Everything we say means something, even if it's not what we intended. But I had to admit that it worked for her. She seemed to be able to get through to people, make them understand her meaning without spelling it out. Maybe that was what made her such a good ranger, why she would maybe one day make assistant chief.

I took a pull on my beer and stared in the mirror behind the counter, looking for something to take me out of myself. It was getting to be a habit. I'd watch other people and imagine their conversations or what they were feeling, see if that made me feel any more human. Sometimes I'd see other men just like me, that same soft hunger in their eyes as they searched for someone or something to help them discover meaning in their lives.

"Hey, Ranger."

I came out of my reverie and stared at the guy who'd spoken.

"I was right." It was the guy whose SUV had overheated. "I said to Sophie it was you."

I saw her sitting at a table by the window, with her daughter. The kid waved. "You're staying in the motel?"

"You recommended it," Delauney said. "Look, ah, let me buy you a drink."

I was about to decline when I looked at Sophie Delauney again and saw her smile. "Sure," I said. "I'll have another beer."

While he ordered drinks, I walked over to the table. "Ranger Woods, what a surprise," Sophie said, and asked me to take a seat. "You live in the resort?"

" 'Bout a mile away."

"Where's your hat?" the girl said.

"That's for keeping the sun off my head, not the stars."

"You look different, but I knew it was you. Daddy thought you were someone else."

"You must have what we call the eagle eye."

"What is that?"

"It means you see too much," Sophie said as she stroked the girl's hair. I wondered what she meant, what were the things the kid saw that she shouldn't have seen. "Since you're off duty, is it okay if we call you Henry?"

I told her it was fine. Delauney came over with two bottles of Dos Equis, a glass of red wine, and a juice for the kid. I still felt a little awkward, but something about Sophie made it easy to be in her company. She steered the conversation so that I didn't have to say too much, mostly listen as they talked about their own lives back in England. She taught history in high school; Delauney was an architect. They'd made their first trip to America nine years ago, when they got married and spent a week in New York. Now, with their daughter, they'd come to see the West. They'd flown to LA, spent four days down there, doing the "Disneyland thing" and the "Hollywood thing," which was the way Delauney put it, rolling his eyes. They'd driven up to Las Vegas, had two nights there, before rolling into the valley this afternoon along Highway 178. The Greenwater detour seemed like a good idea at the time. Sophie's charm made me feel something like a normal human being. Sometimes I lost sight of that, and I was grateful to her for reminding me who I was.

I got another round of drinks and when I returned, Delauney asked me about the valley.

"What are the best places to see?"

"How much time you got?"

"A day."

"Don't try to squeeze in too much."

"He won't listen," Sophie said. "Paul has to turn everything into a major expedition."

He laughed. "Okay, tell me what I can't afford to miss."

I thought about it a while. "When you start to look closely," I said, "you'll notice all the things that aren't there." I wondered if Sophie understood, if she was capable of seeing what was missing.

She started to say something, but Delauney talked across her. "I'll stick with what is here. Like Badwater, and maybe a ghost town."

I nodded. "Chloride City's an old silver-mining town about a half hour northeast of here. Not a whole lot left up there, but there's a cliff above the town will give you some great views of the valley."

The girl said, "Ask about the rocks."

"The rocks."

"Daddy said they move."

Delauney seemed a little embarrassed. "Guide book said that rocks get blown by high winds across the surface of a dry lake." He sounded skeptical but willing to be persuaded. "Said they leave trails across the surface."

I took a sip of my beer. "I've heard that, too."

"Have you seen them move?" the girl asked.

"Never have."

"I still want to see them anyway," she said.

"Maybe," Delauney said. "But tomorrow it's the ghost town, okay?"

"You won't be disappointed," I said.

Sophie was looking at me. She seemed unconscious of the intensity of her gaze or that I might be aware of it. I wondered what she saw in my face, whether there was something there that revealed more than I wanted her to see. There was a spray of freckles splashed beneath her eyes and across the bridge of her nose. She was beautiful. I wanted desperately to know what was inside her head at that moment, but Delauney leaned close and whispered something to her. Something I didn't catch. She laughed and her face flushed red, and I didn't know what that meant. It was Cath's bedtime, she said. I smiled to let her know it was okay, but I could see she was troubled. She told Delauney to stay a while if he wanted. But I felt edgy suddenly, angry that she was going. I wished he'd kept his mouth shut.

"I gotta go, too," I said, standing up. "Early start in the morning."

"No problem, Henry," Delauney said. "Thanks for all your help."

I turned to Sophie. "It was good to meet you," I said, shaking her hand, using formality just to feel the touch of her skin. There was no harm in it. "Enjoy your stay. You too, Cath. Keep that eagle eye on your folks."

Sophie frowned, as if puzzled at something I'd said. I left the bar and set off out into the quiet darkness. It was less than a mile back to the empty bungalow, but it seemed like the longest walk I ever took.

BEFORE I CAME to the valley, I lived out on the coast. I was a deputy in San Luis Obispo's sheriff's department. I was good at the job and had ambitions to make sheriff one day. There was a woman I'd been seeing and I'd begun to think maybe she was the one. But things didn't turn out the way I planned. Something happened I hadn't counted on, one of those situations nobody could foresee. There was no time to think and what I did, I did instinctively. IAD ruled that it had been self-defense, but I knew as well as anyone the kid never had a gun. After the investigation, things began to fall apart at work and my girlfriend began to cool on me. A week after she left, I quit the department and spent eighteen months drifting round the Midwest, feeling sorry for myself and listening to songs about regret. Living in Death Valley cured me of that. Like Robert Frost said, whatever road you're on is the one you chose and the one you didn't take is no longer an option. I came here, worked as a volunteer, then after six months, got a ranger's post and in time, I saw there was no going back.

Some people find that hard to accept. This morning I got a call to check out a vehicle parked up at Quackenbush Mine. There was a dog in the back seat of the truck, a German shepherd. Her tongue lolled out her open mouth and she managed a feeble wag of her tail against the seat when she saw me. The window was cracked open a half inch but even so, it must have been over 130 degrees inside. It took me twenty minutes to find the driver, coming down from Goldbelt Spring. He was a heavyset guy, in shorts and vest, a 49ers cap hiding his close-cropped skull. Had a woman and two kids with him, boy and a girl about ten or eleven.

"Is that your truck down there at the mine, sir?" I asked him.

"The Cherokee, yeah."

"Your dog is dying in there."

"Aw shit," he groaned, lurching down the slope. "I knew this would fucking happen."

They always say they knew what would happen. Which, instead of justifying what they did, only compounds the situation. He bleated on about how he didn't want to keep the dog on a leash and how his wife kept on about how you had to because that was the rule and so, in truth, it wasn't his fault, he was just thinking about the dog. I led him back down to his vehicle, got him to open it up and lift the dog out onto the ground. Her eyes were glazed, her body still.

"She's still alive," the guy said. "I can feel her heart."

"Step back out of the way," I told him. I unholstered my gun, stuck the barrel against the dog's chest and squeezed the trigger.

The woman screamed.

"Jesus Christ," the guy said. "Jesus fucking Christ—you killed her!"

"No," I said. "You did that." I stood up and checked the vehicle over to see if there was anything else I could cite the son of a bitch for apart from animal cruelty. I gave him the ticket and drove off, leaving him to bury the dog in the dirt.

Heading south on the Saline Valley Road, I heard Rydell's voice crackling over the Motorola, requesting assistance at an incident in Hidden Valley. I responded and told him where I was.

"It's a vehicle come off the road, two people injured," he said. "Quick as you can, Henry. Hannafin's already on her way down from Grapevine."

I spun the Expedition around, throwing up a cloud of dust as I accelerated north along the dirt road. My heart was racing like it knew what I was going to find but the truth was, I had no real idea what to expect up there.

When I saw the truck turned on its side ten yards off the road, the feeling of anticipation disappeared, leaving me vaguely disappointed. Five kids were seated in a semicircle a few yards away from the vehicle. One of them, a fair-haired kid about eighteen, got up and came over to me. "I think Shelley broke a leg," he said, nodding toward the others. "And Karl's maybe busted an arm."

"You the driver?"

He hesitated before nodding.

"You been drinking? Smoking some weed?"

"No way, man, nothing like that. Just took the bend too fast, I guess."

All of them were cut and bruised, but only the two he'd named were badly injured. Shelley looked like she was in a lot of pain. I was splinting her leg when Hannafin arrived and went to work on the others. After we had them patched up, we put Karl and Shelley in Hannafin's vehicle and two others in mine. The driver made to get in front beside me, but I shook my head. "Take this," I said, handing him a two-liter bottle of water.

"What for?" He looked bewildered. "Oh man, you saying I have to wait here?"

"There's a wrecker on its way from Furnace Creek. Should be here in three hours."

The journey to Grapevine took the best part of an hour. The two in the back remained silent for most of that time, either too dazed to talk or wary of saying something that would incriminate their buddy. Or maybe they sensed my own unease, a feeling of disquiet that had been bothering me all day. I'd been expecting some kind of revelation, but all I had was the feeling that I'd been asking myself the wrong questions.

There was an ambulance waiting at Grapevine Station to take the two injured kids to the emergency room in Amargosa Valley. The other two said they'd wait at Grapevine for the tow truck to show up with their vehicle and driver. In the station office, Hannafin made fresh coffee while I stared out the window toward the mountains bordering Ubehebe Crater. She said something I didn't catch and I didn't ask her what it was.

"Is it any different today," she said, "from how it was last week?"

"They're the same," I said, though I knew she wasn't talking about the mountains.

She handed me a mug of steaming coffee. "You been keeping to yourself lately."

I felt weary and disinclined to have the conversation she wanted.

"What's bothering you, Henry?"

I sipped the coffee, trying to put my thoughts in some kind of order.

"It's good to see you've lost none of your charm and conversational skills."

I forced a smile. "I'm sorry, Rae," I said. "Got things on my mind, is all."

"Anything I can help with?"

I liked Rae, liked her a lot, but that's all it was. I wasn't looking for any kind of relationship. I was never much good at explaining such things, feelings, or their absence. "Just some stuff I have to deal with," I said. "Nothing that matters too much."

"A problem shared is a problem halved."

"There is no problem."

"I forgot," she said. "You don't have problems, ever." She bit her lower lip, I guess to stop from saying anything else. I didn't know what she might have wanted to say and I didn't care. I felt empty inside, empty and lifeless as the salt flats.

I drained my coffee and set the mug down. "None I lose sleep over."

"I think you should talk to someone."

"I talk to people all the time."

"No you don't, Henry. If you did, you wouldn't be losing touch."

"I'll be seeing you, Rae," I said, leaving the office. Hannafin was my friend, but that didn't mean she knew all there was to know about me. It was never that simple.

AT FIRST I saw nothing on the road. I drove past the Grandstand on my left and headed south another mile before pulling over, somewhat confused. I picked up the radio, intending to give HQ a piece of my mind. But before anyone could respond, I'd got out of the vehicle and was watching the small dust cloud that had appeared away to the south. I grabbed the binoculars from the dash. Between my position and the cloud, a vehicle was stopped in the middle of the dirt road. The dust cloud seemed to be moving farther south, as if marking the trail of some other vehicle, one I hadn't seen. Dry heat rippled across the exposed skin of my arms, sucked all the moisture from my mouth. As I stared at the dust cloud, it was pulled apart by a wind I didn't feel.

Nothing moved around the SUV. I scrambled up the slope to my right, moving southwest toward a patch of creosote bush. From there I looked down at the road, first at my own vehicle, then at the other, half a mile, maybe less, from where I stood. I squatted down in the scrub, removed the Sig Sauer 9mm from my holster and laid it on the ground. The sun was falling slowly toward the mountain behind me, but its heat seemed to have intensified. A sudden movement caught my eye. I watched through the binoculars as a man got out of the SUV and walked to the edge of the dirt road. He just stood there gazing out at the playa like it was a picture of beauty rather than heat and desolation. Two other people joined him, standing on either side. I tried to see what they were looking at, but nothing moved out there, not even the goddamn rocks. The mountain's shadow bruised the edge of the Racetrack.

A fourth person had arrived. I watched his lips moving as he pointed across the dry lake. Sound travels a fair distance in this stillness, but I didn't hear a word. There was something unsettling about the way he held himself, thumb looped into the belt at his waist, that made me feel numb and disconnected. After a few moments the first three set out walking, heading east across the playa. The last guy stood there a while, till they were two or three hundred yards out, then he followed them, taking his time, keeping his distance. A redtail circled above him and when he stopped to glance at it, the bird flew off to the north. A line of thin, ragged clouds chased each other away across the valley, as if anxious not to intrude. Beads of sweat dribbled from beneath the straw hat and down my face as I worked to fill the silence with the imagined sound of their footsteps crunching across the Racetrack.

Nothing made sense.

Long, thin shadows followed them, clawing the dry mud like the fingers of a man dying of thirst. The figures grew smaller as they receded into the distance. I clambered down the slope to the Expedition and drove south until I reached their vehicle. I thought about calling Rydell but wasn't sure what to tell him. All I'd seen was some folks set out across the Racetrack on foot, same as countless visitors had done before them. But if there was no mystery, then why was my heart racing so fast? Why couldn't I shake off the feeling that this was all wrong?

I stood by the side of the road, no longer able to see any of them, accepting that I had no choice but to follow. Strange, disorienting sensations flowed through my body, setting flares off behind my eyes and thrumming in my ears. I began to walk. The ground was hard and bone-dry, but even so, I found a trail of footprints. They were quite distinct, but what disturbed me was that there was only one pair, not four. I tried to ignore this and figure how long it would take me to catch up with the group. After thirty minutes, I should have been able to see them, but nothing moved out there. I quickened my pace. The mountains to the north and west punctured the sky, opening wounds that bled over the horizon and down onto the playa. Ten minutes later, I stopped and listened. Nothing, no birds, no wind, no voices. I unholstered the 9mm again, held it up and fired two shots. And was appalled when I heard nothing. My hand shook as I stared at the pistol. I'd felt the recoil, and the smell of cordite on the breezeless air contradicted the silence. I checked the magazine, saw that two rounds had been discharged. It was just the sound that had been lost, a realization that made my isolation more complete. If sound couldn't exist here, then what could? When I stared at the mountains enclosing both sides of the valley, I knew that even memories were not real in this place. I felt more alone than anyone had ever been, without even the company of the dead. With the light fading, I took a bearing on a western peak and set off toward Racetrack Road.

It took me the best part of an hour to find my vehicle, and by then, night had settled on the valley. I stared up, overwhelmed by the immense darkness. There was no moon, and the night seemed blacker than usual, as if half the stars were missing from the sky. It seemed the only way to account for the intensity of the night. I sat in the cab, radio in hand. I wanted to speak to someone, hear some familiar voice, but I was stopped by a doubt I couldn't explain. The feeling of wrongness persisted, had grown stronger in my head. It didn't make sense at first, not until I'd grabbed a bottle of water from the cooler, turned the key in the ignition, and flicked on my headlights. The road in front of me was empty and I was alone with the fallen stars.

I SAT IN the Expedition in the parking lot, feeling a deep weariness in my bones, the sort that can hold you for hours on end. My hand was on the door but I couldn't move. I watched cars come and go, people walking by like this was normal, like nothing at all had changed. I even saw Sophie Delauney walking across the parking lot, hand in hand with her daughter. She stopped halfway across the lot, turned, smiled, and waved at me. She seemed unaware of the people around her, and I felt my mind melting, my sense of being fading away in her presence. I thought maybe there were things she wanted to say, words she'd left unspoken. I felt the wrongness of letting her go without talking to her again, at least one more time.

But before I could go to her, Delauney himself walked past, though he appeared not to see me. He carried two large suitcases, which he stowed in the back of the Rav4. A vein began to throb in my temple. Drops of sweat stood out on my brow though the sun was low in the sky and the air con was blowing. He got in the driver's seat and started the Toyota. Sophie stood by the passenger door and glanced my way again. She looked right at me, but I knew she wasn't seeing me at all. Whatever look she had on her face, it didn't mean anything. By the time I got out of the Expedition, she'd climbed in beside Delauney and they were pulling out of the lot.

Later, I sat in Arcan's nursing a beer. Troubled by what I'd seen, I tried to cloak the strangeness in reason but I couldn't make it fit. The feeling that I was thinking about someone else had taken root in my brain. That I had no control of my own life nor any clear idea where I was heading. Maybe I'd spent too long in the valley. Maybe it was time to leave. Only, I wasn't sure I could.

Old Arcan himself came in the bar and made one of his regular attempts at playing the host. He claimed to be a direct descendant of one of the first men to cross Death Valley, but nobody believed it. His ex-wife told someone he'd been born plain Bill Judd. I watched him move from one guest to another, carefully selecting those on whom he wished to bestow his hospitality. Thankfully, I wasn't among them.

I found myself thinking about Sophie Delauney. They were the kind of thought I had no business thinking, that caused pleasure and pain in equal measure, but I thought them anyway. Some lives were full of certainties but mine seemed to be made up only of "what ifs" and "maybes." It should have been no surprise that it had become less real to me.

I ordered another drink and stared into the mirror behind the counter. The people in there seemed to have purpose in their lives, to know what they were doing, where they were going. If I watched long enough, paid attention to the details, maybe I'd discover how to make my life more real. Arcan was holding forth to the group of Japs sitting round a table across the bar. Jaime was working his routine on a blonde girl at the end of the counter. She looked bored, and I guessed the only reason she was tolerating his bullshit was the lack of any other diversion. I wondered if the real Jaime was having any better luck than the one in the mirror. And here was Sophie Delauney, standing just a few feet behind me and watching my reflection watch her, or maybe it was her reflection watching us. Do mirrors take in sound the way they do light? I don't think so. I couldn't hear anything, no music, no talk, not even the clink of glasses. It was a long time before I remembered myself and thought to say hello. But a second before I did, she beat me to it. She climbed up onto the bar stool beside me and caught Jaime's eye.

He was there in a shot. She pointed to my half-empty bottle of Dos Equis, told him to bring one of those and a glass of Merlot. I said I hadn't expected to see her again. She shrugged and told me they'd had a long day. Drove down to Badwater, where Delauney had decided to hike out on the salt flats. Went half a mile before the heat got to him and he returned to the car. Later, they went to Chloride City. She wasn't looking at me as she talked, but at the guy in the mirror, the fellow who looked just like me but whose thoughts were not the same as mine. The ache in her voice seemed to hint at some inner turmoil. I wanted to offer words of comfort and reassurance, tell her everything would be okay. But thinking the words was easier than saying them.

I asked if she'd seen any ghosts up there. She shook her head and smiled. No ghosts, just dust, heat, and silence. I understood about the silence but with all those ghosts up there, she'd expected something more. Why hadn't the inhabitants from Chloride City's second boom period learned anything from the first? I told her there were more fools in the world than she might have imagined. Gold wasn't the only illusion that drew people to the valley.

Did I mean that literally? I wasn't sure. I wondered if Delauney had seen anything out on the salt flats beyond Badwater, if his mind had been troubled by visions he couldn't explain. But I saw no sign of his existence in the mirror and didn't think to ask. Sophie wanted to know about my life and I told her some things that seemed important, others that kept a smile on her face. She told me Paul wanted her to have another child. She wasn't sure what to do. The dreams and ambitions she'd once had were largely unfulfilled, there were things she hadn't yet grasped. I understood her to mean that this was something she'd never told Delauney.

And then he was there, clapping me on the back and giving Sophie a proprietary kiss on the cheek. She fell quiet then, seemed to retreat into herself. I tried to maintain the connection to her but his voice kept intruding on my thoughts. There was nothing to distinguish his words from the other noises in the bar, a wavering chorus of sounds whose real purpose was little more than to fill the silence. A feeling of despair grew inside me as I watched Sophie close herself off. Her smile was gone and the lines around her eyes signaled the dreams she could no longer give voice to.

Delauney was asking me if it was possible to go to the Racetrack and join Route 190 heading west without coming back on himself. I told him it would add sixty or seventy miles to his journey, most of it on poor dirt roads. He nodded and said they might make the detour on their way out of the valley tomorrow. I asked him what he hoped to see up there. Same as anyone, he said; he wanted to see the moving rocks for himself, or at the very least, the trails they left in their wake.

I told him he wouldn't, no one ever did. He believed me, he said, but seeing beat believing any day of the week.

I WATCH THE shadows compose themselves. The way they move across mountains or desert dunes reveals how fluid identity really is. What we think of as solid has no more real substance than a whisper or a lie. It's just light and shadow that make the unknown recognizable, that sculpt unfamiliar surfaces into configurations we think we know. We stare a while at these faces or shapes, glad they mean something to us even if we can't name them, and then we blink and when we look again, the face has changed to something we can't recognize. We try to retrieve the familiar face, needing to see it one more time to confirm that it was who we thought it was, but the new image persists, erasing the old. It's like trying to see the two front faces of a line drawing of a transparent cube at the same time—it can't be done. One face is always behind the other. We close our eyes again and when we look one more time, there isn't even a face to see, just a shadow moving over rock, sliding into all its dark places. It was the kind of illusion that made me feel less certain about my place in the world.

I WOKE UP this morning no longer sure I am who I thought I was. I showered, dressed, and ate breakfast, feeling like an intruder in my own home. I sat in the Expedition, spoke to Rydell on the radio, and drove up toward Hunter Mountain, feeling I was watching another man try out my life. I had hoped to find some certainties up there, something to which I could anchor myself, but all I found was that everything flows. I didn't need to see it to know it was happening. Even the forests of piñon pine and juniper were farther down the mountain slopes than they were the day before.

In the spring, after heavy winter rainfalls, wildflowers turn certain parts of the valley into a blaze of purple, red, and orange. It wasn't possible to reconcile such beauty with that scorched and barren hell. If such a vastness could be transformed in what, in geological terms, was less than the blink of an eye, how could any of us hope to ever stay the same?

All those voices I heard on the radio—how could I be sure that they were speaking to me? If I couldn't be certain who I was, then how could they know I was the one they wanted to talk to? So when Rydell's voice came out of the radio, I had no way of knowing if it was really him. Short of driving down to Furnace Creek and standing right in front of him. And even then, there was no guarantee.

I heard Hannafin—or someone who sounded like her—asking where I was. I wanted to answer her but when I tried to talk, I realized I had nothing to say. I already knew where I was and where I was going. There was nothing Hannafin, or the voice that might have been hers, could do for me that I couldn't do for myself.

This person I had become had no more illusions. He was capable of seeing things as they really were. As he drove past the talc mines, across Ulida Flat and north into Hidden Valley, he was aware that the land was watching him. He heard the creak of Joshua trees, the distant groans of the mountain ranges, and the listless sigh of an unfelt breeze. And in those sounds he heard himself also, speaking in his usual voice, his tone neutral, the words precise, as he told them all they needed to know, the way he always did. Only it wasn't him talking.

THE SUV IS pulled off the dirt road onto the edge of the playa. The front passenger's door stands open. I glance up toward Ubehebe Peak, see no movement among the stands of mesquite. Approaching the vehicle, I move round the back and peer through the windshield. There are two large suitcases behind the rear seat. I continue on round the Toyota till I come back to the open door. I reach inside and grab the carryall on the rear seat. Inside is a money belt with close to four hundred dollars in cash, plus a book of traveler's checks. There's also a Nike fanny pack in there with three passports, a driver's license, and car-hire documentation. I look at the photographs, just for a moment, then put everything back in the carryall. On the floor by the front passenger's seat, there's a video camera. It's a Sony Hi 8 and the tape is about three-quarters of the way through. I sit on the running board, my feet resting on the ground, trying to decide what to do. The last thing I want to do right now is play the tape but I know that if I don't, I'll never find the answers I need. Flipping open the viewfinder, I touch the play button and get nothing but blue. I press and hold the rewind, listening to the machine whirr as the world runs back to where it has already been. I watch shadows grow westward from the Cottonwood Range and a strip of broken cloud that pulls itself together as it scrolls back across the sky. After a minute, I release the button and the tape rolls forward.

Sophie Delauney and her daughter walk out of their apartment at Stovepipe Wells, holding hands. They stop halfway across the parking lot, and Sophie turns, smiles and waves toward the camera before continuing on to the Rav4. The scene changes to a view of Ubehebe Crater from the north rim, stretching a half mile across and five hundred feet deep. The girl skips into the shot from the right, Delauney from the left. Something blurs the picture for a second or two, but I can't tell what it is—a hand or part of a face in extreme close-up. Delauney talks about how the crater was formed, sounding vaguely authoritative. The kid complains about the heat. Next, I see Sophie and the girl standing in front of the sign at Teakettle Junction. Delauney enters the frame from the left. The girl has a stick and she starts tapping out a rhythm on the kettles and pots hanging from the arms of the wooden cross. Sophie and Delauney start dancing round her, whooping like a couple of movie Indians. They look foolish but the girl laughs. No one seems to notice the single shadow that slips down the mountain behind them.

The scene changes abruptly, showing the three of them sitting in their vehicle, smiling and waving. After a second or two, I realize there's no soundtrack. They get out of the Toyota and start walking directly toward the camera, their faces growing in the frame. The jump cut I'm expecting doesn't happen. Instead, as Delauney draws close, the scene shifts slightly to the left and catches his face in profile as he walks past the spot where the camera had been. It catches the other two as they walk by, then turns and tracks them to the side of the road. Their smiles have disappeared, and they avoid looking at the camera until something prompts Sophie to glance up and say a single word, which might have been "Please." Moments later, she takes the girl by the hand and walks out onto the playa. After a second or two, Delauney wipes his face and follows them. The camera pans left and zooms in on the Grandstand to the north, holding the outcrop in the frame for what seems like an eternity. Nothing moves onscreen, even when I hold down the fast-forward button. When I release it, the camera moves upward to capture a clear and cloudless sky. The tape has played almost to the end.

The final shot is of Sophie, Delauney, and the kid, three hundred yards out on the playa, growing smaller as they walk on without looking back. And then the screen turns blue.

My head has started aching and the heat is almost intolerable. I put the camera on the seat, understanding what I have to do. At my vehicle, I grab the radio, press the call button and speak my name. Instead of voices, all that comes out is feedback and white noise. I try once more but whatever I hear, it isn't human. I lack the will to do this, but there's no one else. I load half a dozen bottles of water into a backpack, grab my binoculars, and head out onto the playa.

There are no tracks in the honeycombed surface. I walk five hundred yards due east, a little farther than I had seen them go before the tape had stopped. I figure they must have been looking for the rocks, or at least for one of their trails. I look north to where the slanting sunlight blurs the edges of the Grandstand. Shielding my eyes, I turn my gaze southward and pick out a few rocks of varying sizes scattered across the dry mud. There's little else to see out here, no signs of life. I head south and try not to think about the tape and the expressions on their faces as they had trudged past the camera. Almost twenty minutes pass before I am walking among the silent, unmoving rocks. Though I don't want to admit it, their watchful stillness bothers me. I don't want to think about what they've seen. Instinctively, I lay a hand on the Sig Sauer at my hip, drawing some comfort from the touch of the gun. There's a picture forming in my head. It's the haunted look in Sophie's eyes as she stared at the camera for the last time, just before she took the child's hand in her own and started walking. I'd like to think she looked back one last time, but I really can't be sure.

I search among the lifeless rocks for an hour. The ground is flat and the rocks are neither plentiful nor large enough to provide cover for anything much bigger than a gecko. Finally, as the sun falls toward Ubehebe Peak, I sit down on a rock, feeling dizzy and nauseous. I drink about half a liter of tepid water and pour the rest over my head. I raise the binoculars and see the vehicles where I left them, two dusty sentinels watching over the playa. As I shift my gaze northward, I'm startled by a flash of light from the mountains above Racetrack Road. I turn back to the cars, then search the slopes above them, looking for something up there in the creosote. I lower the binoculars and feel a tightness across my chest. I breath slowly, head hanging between my knees, and that's when I see it for the first time, the faint trail cut like a groove in the dried mud. It ends at the rock between my feet. It wasn't there when I sat down, I think, but I'm not certain. I'm spooked a little by it, even more when I notice more trails terminating at the other rocks lying nearby. I try to picture a rain-softened surface and a hundred-mile-an-hour wind pushing them along, but it's all in vain.

The flesh crawls on my back and for some reason, the air feels cooler. The silence is weird, and when I hear the two shots ring out, I need no further prompting to leave the rocks behind. I pick up the backpack, unholster my pistol, and set off at a slow trot north toward the sound of the gunfire. I don't think about what has happened, about the mess Delauney has got them into. Instead, I concentrate on getting there, on locating their position even though there are no further sounds to guide me toward them.

I pass the vehicles on the road, a half mile or so to my left, without having seen anything I don't recognize. But I keep on, another mile, until I realize I'm heading right toward the Grandstand. I don't turn back. There's no point, even though I won't find anything there. Nothing alive. Yet I have to see.

THERE'S NOBODY AT the Grandstand. I drink another bottle of water to quiet my despair. Shadows stretch out across the playa toward the outcrop, painting the surface the color of blood. For a while, I stare at the rocks, losing track of time. There are a dozen or so, scattered in a wide circle round the outcrop. Had these shapes seen Sophie? I grind the dust and dirt from my faithless eyes and when I open them again, I see that the rocks have drawn closer. The last rays of sunlight pick out their newly laid trails. My heart is racing, and the band across my chest tightens even more. At first I think I'm having a heart attack, that I'm really dying, but after two minutes, I realize that isn't possible. I focus on the nearest rock. It's eighteen inches high, a little more than that from back to front, weighing, I guess, about three hundred pounds. The ground is bone-dry, not even a whisper of wind. Even though I haven't seen it, I accept that the rock has moved. It's too late to matter a damn. I don't feel anything as I set off toward the road.

The sky is almost dark by the time I reach the two vehicles. The Rav4 stands empty like a ruin. I sit in my own vehicle and try to call HQ to report the missing people. But once again I get no proper signal, no voices other than my own to trouble the darkness. I keep trying, but nobody responds. After a while, I return to the Toyota. The camera is still on the seat where I left it, the tape stopped in exactly the same place. I press play and watch the blue screen, trying to see beyond it to what's on the other side. I let it run for a minute but it's a waste of time. Just as I'm about to stop it, the blue turns to white, which slowly reconfigures into a honeycombed pattern that moves back and forth across the frame. In quick succession, three shots ring out on the tape, the first sounds since Teakettle Junction. I am calm, I don't feel any fear, not until another minute has passed and a fourth blast sounds out and the screen fades to black.

Outside, I peer into the dark and see the more intense darkness of the

Grandstand looming up out of the Racetrack. It's no closer than it was before, I tell myself, though I no longer feel any inclination to trust my perceptions. An hour has passed when I climb back into the Expedition. Nobody has come. This time when I call HQ, I do finally get something, a voice reporting an abandoned SUV out at the Racetrack. I shut the power off quickly, drink more water and try not to imagine the rocks gathering out on the playa. I think about the voice I heard and what it was saying. Speaking only to myself, I respond, "You won't find anything out there."

And after a minute's silence, I add, "They're gone."

Hearing something, I get out of the car. I walk to the side of the road, feeling the weight of the night as it falls on the valley. I can't see anything but I look anyway, knowing the rocks are edging their way up from the south. I tell myself someone must have heard them, that someone will come. These are the certainties that sustain me. I can't stop myself from listening, so when they stop, it comes as a shock. Then, before I can register it, they start moving again, heading west, toward the road. I have no strength left. I sit down in the dirt to wait for someone to arrive, even though I already know that nobody is coming here, that no one else belongs. The truth is, I have as much right to be here as the dark. It's reason that's out of place here, that doesn't belong. Reason can't explain the rocks that roll, the moans of night, or the flakes of sky that drift quietly down to Earth, which, given time, I probably could.

AFTERWORD

My favorite ghost story is Lucius Shepard's "How the Wind Spoke at Madaket," though the nature of its ghost is difficult to pin down. It's not a ghost story in the traditional sense, though like the best of them, it relies on implication and suggestion rather than explication to achieve its visceral effect. We're never sure what triggers the elemental force at the heart of the story; its wonder lies in its ambiguity. There's an unsettling contrast between the evocation of peace and solitude and the moments of brutal, vividly described elemental violence. But what comes across most strongly is the interaction between character and place, the notion that landscape informs our consciousness at a deep level, that the forces that shape the physical world—wind, rain, heat, and so on—are analogous to the emotions that sculpt our imaginations. Few stories evoke a sense of place so hauntingly as to make me want to go there. This one did.

Born in the Midwest, which he insists is by far the weirdest part of this country, Gahan Wilson emigrated to New York City and has lived in various locations on the East Coast, ranging from Key West to Boston ever since.

Gahan Wilson's cartoons may be what he's most famous for but he's a master of macabre writing as well. His cartoons, which presently appear mostly in *Playboy* and *The New Yorker*, have been gathered in something over twenty book collections through the years. He has written and illustrated a number of children's books, a couple of odd mystery novels, several anthologies, and a collection of short stories that have appeared in a variety of magazines and in books such as this one. He has been and (if fortune smiles) will continue to be active in various film and television enterprises.

THE DEAD GHOST

GAHAN WILSON

SINCE WE'RE TELLING ghost stories, I do have one I've kept to myself so far, except for the lawyers and so on, but there's nothing in the agreements I signed that says I can't pass it on to you as long as I don't use the names of any specific corporations, so here goes.

You remember I got banged up pretty badly last year. I can't go into details for security reasons, but it happened during a search-and-destroy op for the Organization which ended with a nut-case scientist blowing up his underground lab instead of the Senate Building. They rushed me to the hospital, where I was very efficiently diagnosed, then operated on, and by the time dusk came around, I was lying on a nice little bed in a nice little room, all skillfully reassembled with most of me wrapped into various bandages and the rest of me tucked into high-tech casts.

I have only the blurriest memories of eating some bland meal and then fading into a deep sleep. But I have a very clear recollection of waking in the dead of night, staring up at the ceiling dimly lit by streetlamps from floors below, and becoming more and more aware that something in the environment about me was sending out urgent danger signals.

Through the years I've learned the best reaction to such signals is to carefully try and track them down sense by sense, so I started by lying still and listening. From outside, there came only the harmless murmur of distant traffic and from inside, muted monitors gently beeping and the soft rustling of nurses—just those comforting sounds that let you know you're being cared for and looked after.

But then I switched to the tactile and immediately figured out what was raising the little hairs on the back of my neck. Ever so subtly, but very surely, the bed felt different from the way it had the last time I'd been aware of it. A moment of continued reflection and I realized that the mattress was now tilting a tiny more deeply to my right than it had before.

I turned my head very carefully and saw what appeared to be the corpse of a very large and decidedly overweight middle-aged man. The body was in an advanced state of rigor mortis and lay stiff and straight as a log, its bulging eyes staring upward, with the back of its thick neck propped on the headboard, and the heels of its large, rather froglike feet dug into the mattress.

It was naked but its flesh was pierced and adorned with the quaint little decorations hospitals like to affix to their more serious patients. Here and there were stuck the needles and torn-off ends of plastic IV tubes; scattered over the chest were the white suction cups with their trails of thin, broken wiring that once led to various monitoring devices, and taped to the back of one hand was the standard plastic tap conveniently connected to the venous system. As a final touch, there was a curving, neatly stitched little slash running across the thing's paunch to indicate the general location of the operation, which had apparently failed.

The most bothersome thing about this corpse, however, was that it wasn't made up of opaque flesh, but of translucent and glistening stuff you could see through, bones and all, like a jellyfish. It looked to be not a corpse, but the ghost of a corpse.

In spite of its semitransparency, it was not ephemeral or misty; by no means was it the sort of ghost that floats in the air and wavers when breezed upon. I knew this because I'd noted, when it first drew my attention, that it was, after all, heavy enough to tilt a mattress.

This line of speculative meditation was disrupted very effectively when something in the arrangement of the grisly thing slipped and the spectral cadaver suddenly lost its purchase on the headboard, spun round to face me, then flopped heavily on its side with a great thump, close enough to me so that I would have felt its breath had it breathed. As it was, I had the full advantage of a great puff of corpse stink that blew up from it when it struck the mattress.

I watched it carefully as it settled into its new position and for the first time, I began to speculate seriously on the possibility that this thing beside me might be just a bit more sentient than the usual corpse. If it was indeed a ghost, I reasoned, then the usual rules might not apply.

As the sinister implications of this possibility sank in I regretted even more than before the freshly broken bones, newly torn tendons, divers wounds, and highly encumbering space-age wrappings that prevented me from quietly quitting the bed, and perhaps even the room, as I ordinarily would have certainly done.

I looked around for the dangly emergency button that I dimly recalled the nurse had pointed out just before leaving, and I confess I let a deep sigh escape me when I located the thing at last and saw, through the transparent flesh of my repellent phantom companion, that it hung from the headboard on the far side of the ghost.

Gingerly, with the greatest possible care, I attempted to reach over the great mountain of spectral flesh beside me to grasp the device but found that my near arm—fortunately, the lesser injured of the two—far too short for the job.

I pursed my lips thoughtfully, then reached out to prod the bluely gleaming chest of the thing with, I suppose, some notion of rolling it off the bed, but my eyes widened when I realized that plan would not work for the simple reason that my fingers had not pushed against the horror's loathsome flesh, but sunk into it.

I took several deep and—I confess it—shaky breaths, clenched my teeth, and continued to press my fingers into the rotund front of the translucent apparition, pausing occasionally to wiggle the tips of my fingers in order to estimate the solidity of the phantom's corporeality. I learned that my theory was correct: the thing did indeed have a kind of gelatinous solidity.

I kept up the pressure and admit I shuddered when my living flesh penetrated the creature's ghostly fat and entered its oddly stringy muscles. A bit further along, I encountered the being's ectoplasmic bones and observed that though they offered more resistance, they were still penetrable, if gritty.

By now it had begun to truly dawn on me that by far the worst was still to come, for now I was faced with the job of plunging not merely my fingers and my hand, but *my whole, entire arm* through the guts of this truly detestable apparition if I was to get to its other side and grasp the signal button.

I am afraid there is absolutely no way at all to adequately convey in words the sensations produced by pushing one's arm through the entrails of a phantom cadaver. Though each eerie bit of it was vastly less solid than any equivalent part of our anatomy, still, every organ of the enormous specter lying so grotesquely by my side did its ghostly best to resist my determined penetrations.

Each vein and artery, large or small, made determined efforts to resist my probings with its protective membranes; the tiny walled caves in each organ encountered tried to block the appalled groping of my fingers as well as they could—I recall the heart with particular clarity—but I persisted, and though my hand grew terrifyingly dimmer as it worked its way through the specter's monstrous entrails, it crept ever closer to the thing's other side and finally, with a popping burst that I can hear to this day, it broke through and I felt my fingers clutch the buzzer and depress its blessed button!

Almost immediately I heard the soft padding of the nurse's shoes quickly nearing; then the door opened and there she was, staring first at me and then at the thing next to me.

Calmly she leaned over my side of the bed to take the pulse in my neck and study my face intently. She asked me if I was all right and when I managed an affirmative croak, she spoke one of those unintelligible hospital acronyms the medical profession is so fond of into the receiver pinned to the shoulder of her uniform, and in no time at all, I heard the swift approach of soft, rolling wheels as two attendants navigated a strange-looking gurney into the room.

It differed from any gurney I'd previously seen in that save for its shiny metal parts, it was painted a deep, funereal black, and instead of being a relatively simple cot, its framework supported a kind of casket bearing an ominous collection of efficient-looking locks and straps.

Without a word, the attendants pulled on heavy black gloves and smoothly hoisted the ghost corpse into the casket, which they then speedily locked and strapped shut with practiced motions. They then double-checked their work, gave both the nurse and myself a brief nod, and were gone.

The next day, I was approached by agents of the hospital bearing papers, and after a brief discussion with my lawyers, an extremely generous remuneration was arranged to prevent my pressing any charges.

Two final points: the efficiency of the hospital's legal follow-up very strongly suggests that my little adventure was not at all that unusual, and far more personally disturbing, as the ghost corpse was being loaded into the gurney's casket, its head turned—note it did not flop—and its bulging eyes glared down at me with very conscious malice. I suddenly realized it was my great good fortune that only then had the abominable thing managed to stir itself into full awakening.

And that's my ghost story.

AFTERWORD

Asked for a favorite ghost story, he says, "Obviously an impossible choice, and if you asked me yesterday or tomorrow, it might have been another one, but for today it's Oliver Onion's 'The Beckoning Fair One,' since it has (very appropriately) haunted me ever since I first read it. With no mercy whatsoever, the story shows how overwhelming and profoundly disruptive a genuine ghostly intrusion would be. I have never been able to shake off the impact of the story's climax, with its victim helplessly blinking in the sunlight, and I suppose I probably never will."

JACK CADY has been a truck driver, high-tree climber, teacher, and philosopher, as well as the author of eleven novels, five story collections, and the history *The American Writer*. He is emeritus writer in residence from Pacific Lutheran University. His novella, *The Night We Buried Road Dog*, won the Nebula Award and the Bram Stoker Award. His collection, *The Sons of Noah*, won the World Fantasy Award, and his novel, *Inagehi*, won the Philip K. Dick Award. He also received a Distinguished Teaching Award from his university. His most recent collection, *Ghosts of Yesterday*, was published in 2002, and 2003 should see the publication of a novel, *The Rules of '48*. He lives in Port Townsend, Washington, which is situated on that little lump of land where the Strait of Juan de Fuca meets Puget Sound.

SEVEN SISTERS

JACK CADY

I

IN THIS WORN town on the Washington coast, rain seeps through darkness and turns silver on fir needles when dawn rises gray as tired spirits. Rain washes thick clumps of black moss from decaying cedar roofs. On the edge of town stand the Seven Sisters, mansions once gay with lights and finery, now silent and nigh lightless except when sounds of rain are overcome by sounds of weeping.

To understand Seven Sisters, one need know somewhat of the town. In the long ago, back in the 1890s, buildings along our main street rose as elegant as Victorian architects could contrive. Turrets soared, ornamented. Lamplight gleamed through stained-glass windows. Our wharves bustled with offloading of goods from the Far East, including bond slaves and opium. Money flowed with the abundance of rain.

Harlotry, shanghai, and murder were common. Yet, though many people died, at the time no specters were reported. It has taken a bit over a century for haunted figures to congregate in group portraits of anguish.

Some of us see these creatures during gray dawns, and in gray sunsets when black clouds cover the sky but leave a streak of blue along the horizon. As the sun sinks and blue sky turns orange, long shadows cross our streets. Faces appear through mist; whorish faces, bookish faces, and a few young girls. Some of the faces seem fragmented, as if these spirits have pieces ripped away. Others hover and seem to be howling, their fear beyond our imagining, their gathering power a dread force.

And to further understand the town, one need know something of Gentleman Julian ("King Julie") Babcock, who was a renegade religionist, a renegade showman, a business mogul, and a scamp. During the meetings of this town's Historical Society—there are three of us: I, Peter Green, once haberdasher to gentlemen, and costumer; the Barrister Jabez Johnson, who once sat on the bench; and our female member, Catherine "Cat" Peterson, actress, who in her age has become less scandalous—we find ourselves still musing over Gentleman Julie.

"A finer tomkitty never yowled from the top of a fence. A more randy houndpup never bayed at the moon." This from Cat, who, though old, cannot help being beautiful, if bawdy. It is true she will not capture the eye of youth, but experienced men find themselves reassured. She proves to them that they could still make fools of themselves over a woman. Her silver hair gleams more brightly than our silver mist. Her face is creased rather than wrinkled, and her gray eyes are alight with potent life. She dresses in ornamental silks, long skirts sweeping to occasionally display a well-turned ankle. She remembers King Julie well, as do I and the Barrister.

"A silver tongue had Julie. He was a charmer. A spellbinder." The Barrister, like Julie, also strode the speaker's platform in his day. He was once a powerful orator. "We can thank every star in the firmament that Julie never went into politics." The Barrister's voice seems bigger than his body. Age has shrunk him to a mite of a man, although he remains formal in dress. In the days when he was on the bench, he was strict. He was known for his standard statement to the guilty: "For you, sir, a spot of jail will be instructional." In fairness, it can be said that if he was firm with miscreants, he has always been equally firm with himself. People joke that he wears suit and tie when he sleeps.

"We can also thank every star in the firmament," Cat adds, "that our Julie was sterile. Otherwise, we'd be up to our eyelids in third-generation Julies. And," she shudders, "Tomkitty."

"He made my fortune," I am forced to admit. "He dressed like a star of moving pictures, and the demand for costumes was endless."

"Costumes that still hang in place, and in darkness," the Barrister mutters. "One is loath to think of it."

He refers to closets and dressing rooms in Number Five of the Seven Sisters, known as *Thespia*. Julie, who built Seven Sisters, had a fondness for highflown names.

When Julie came to our town, the town was surprised into shaking off its infancy. The story of the town is not unlike the story of King Julie, who entered the frontier just as the Klondike gold rush opened in the 1880s. He did not own one plugged nickel. Equally, at the time, this town was a dismal settlement, wet and gray.

Julie began his career in Seattle, which was then a small town clinging to the shores of Puget Sound. Seattle rapidly turned into a frontier city where money flowed like wind in the sails of clipper ships. Seattle supplied adventurers who headed for the gold fields of Alaska.

Julie started building his fortune with cats and chickens. No vessel left for Alaska without a shipment of felines, because the gold camps were alive with rats. No vessel left for Alaska without cages of chickens, because on the Klondike a single egg sold for as high as five dollars.

Julie quickly widened his vision. During weekday evenings, Julie offered lectures on *Phrenology*, *Women of the Bible*, *Modern Prophecy*, and *The Secrets of Egyptian Immortality*. On Saturdays, outside of taverns, he sold snake oil (Dr. Julian's Elixir and Miracle Tonic).

On Sundays, he preached.

"A wonder he wasn't hanged," the Barrister murmurs. "And buried under the jail."

"It was frontier," I suggest. "The frontier allows wide margins."

"No it doesn't." Cat always smiles when she offers a flat contradiction . . . part of her charm. "The frontier is only liberal about murder and whoring."

Julie preached an early form of sexual permissiveness and community. He spoke with passion of a new Zion where each belonged to all, and all to each. His message was not completely new, because communes were then a feature of the Northwest Territory.

What made Julie's message different was its emphasis on immortality achieved through communion of bodies. Although young at the time, he seemed particularly tied to notions of immortality. Strangely (or perhaps not), most of Julie's congregation were women.

"Can you imagine," Cat muses, "being Julie, and alive, for all eternity having to feed his awful hungers and that godawful ego? Gives a girl a bellyache just thinking of it."

I understand Cat. I would not even wish to be me for all eternity, because I think I can do better. But, bellyache or not, there is no denying that Julie was obsessed with not dying. The obsession would become nigh maniacal as he aged.

"He sold stock in a railroad that was never built." The Barrister tends to lay one finger alongside his nose, and sniff in the face of rascality. The Barrister cares naught for life-everlasting.

"And then he started a bank." I pause, thinking of my own rise in fortune because of Julie.

"He had the gift of business," the Barrister mutters. "Dirty business. He was not political, but he bought politicians."

"And then," Cat murmurs, "he discovered Romance, big 'R.' And then he discovered Art, big 'A.' " She sounds uncertain, ready to sigh, or giggle. "Bloody fool," she says. "I'd be the last to keep a man from chasing a skirt, but there are limits."

Art. Big A. In ten years, Julie became scandalously rich. He entered this town while freely spreading money, and when it came to sex, he was as wanton as a mink.

And, like a mink, he was small and slim. I remember his body well, having tailored to it for years. He had a large head, a high rump, and thin legs. His shoulders were narrow, but his arms heavy. His Scots-blue eyes could cut like razors, and his thin lips curled with power. And yet, Julie was not first-of-all mean, only, perhaps, desperate. He dressed as meticulously as Beau Brummel, but had not the suaveness of that English gent.

II

THE TERRORS IN our streets ebb and flow from Seven Sisters. Spirits manifest when mist embraces mansions and hovels, or when shadows from the setting sun darken the land. In darkness some spirits weep, but others howl. We cannot hear the howling, but we see faces as they drift toward Seven Sisters. Along our streets pass more than sorrow, because while some weep, others seem intent on violence. Vengeance is as vital here, and as real, as rain.

When he arrived in our town, Julie was thirty-two, rich as Croesus, and enamored of a modern dancer named Gabrielle. She brought her dance company with her, a company described by the famous dancer Isadora Duncan as "crazed but beautiful ladies." Gabrielle, more practical than kiln-dried boards, gave her *all* to Julie. Nor did she mind when Julie bedded her entire troupe. It is not known if Gabrielle adhered to Julie's religion, but it is known that Gabrielle knew how to play her fish once he was hooked. Gabrielle had tested the frontier's crude halls, found them wanting, and wished for a permanent stage where audiences would come to her, and not she to them. Seven Sisters began as Julie built a mansion to house his harem; a mansion named *Forte.*

We, of the Historical Society, do not remember the early years. The Barrister was born in 1913, I in 1914, and Cat? No gentleman speculates on a lady's age.

By the time we matured, Julie was old: seventy-two in 1930, filthy rich, disgustingly active, and too vital; plus (it was rumored) at his age, obscene. Gabrielle had long since ceased to play the part of mistress. She called herself "artistic director;" but in truth, she was a procurer for Julie. Gabrielle's troupe, some of them, had remained but were no longer seen. It was as if they danced their way into smoke or mist. By the time we, of the Historical Society, reached working age, Seven Sisters stood at its height.

I must tell what it was then, before saying what it is now.

In my youth, Seven Sisters stood in a semicircle surrounded by rolling lawns and cascading fountains. A dark forest of fir and cedar framed the background. The houses were massive, three and four stories, and in their prime were masterpieces of Victorian architecture. From left to right, they were:

> ***Forte***, four stories bracketed with four turrets and painted in lilac with royal-purple trim. The first floor held a thrust stage for dancers, the top floors held apartments.
>
> ***Muse***, a brooding mansion with small windows of crystal, the windows lodged in walls painted black, and ornamented in gray. It rose into our gray skies like dark poetry.
>
> ***Maestro***, a concert hall with a ceiling forty feet high, and with practice rooms and living quarters. It stood three and a half stories, the colors bluegrass and teal.
>
> ***Gaudens***, the tallest and narrowest of the seven, it stood more like a tower than a house, and was itself a sculpture in marble-pink. Its balconies displayed busts of the famous, but in chaotic order . . . Socrates beside Mendelssohn.
>
> ***Thespia***, a theater lodged in the largest of the mansions. By 1920, gas lights had been replaced by electricity. The massive stage, and seating for a thousand, carried paint of red and black; was colored auburn and black inside, with rose-colored stage curtains. The mansion stood four stories and included small practice stages, closets of costumes, and, of course, living quarters with many beds.
>
> ***Greco***, more neoclassical than Victorian, stood brilliant and unornamented in white behind massive pillars. At three stories, it was the smallest of the mansions. Its architectural statement posed simplicity among mansions ornamented with Victorian roses.
>
> ***Michelangelo***, was a museum, and was thought by those whose business it is to know such things, an architectural failure. Natural light in the northwest runs to gray more than gold. The enormous windows of the mansion helped illuminate its display galleries and studios. Had the builder allowed the structure to remain plain, what a success might have been had. Instead, where clear glass was not needed, stained glass was added. The mansion stood like a patchwork quilt of color, sporting unneeded turrets and widows' walks.

When we of the Historical Society were young, we strolled the well-tended lawns. We watched beautifully dressed ladies and gentlemen pause as they chatted before fountains. In the mansions, craftsmen and artists worked. The place seemed a small city and we, young and untested, could not imagine the dread force hovering above the silver crash of water from the fountains.

"I surely believe," Cat says, "that we appeared on the scene just as decline began." She shifts lightly in her chair. In this old library, there are now musty smells as books begin turning liquid. Frames of windows have long since lost their paint and are swollen with northwest rain. Beyond the windows, decaying houses are themselves like a congregation of ghosts adrift against the gray sky. Those that still have paint have been repainted. Nothing original and bright remains. Only here and there, from a distant chimney, smoke from woodstove or fireplace rises above narrow streets.

Cat looks askance at the Barrister. She almost does not want to say what she is about to say. "One of the Popes, long ago, grew old. He tried to stay alive by suckling the breasts of women."

The Barrister sits stunned and does not see the relevance. He is not surprised, because the Barrister reads history. Mostly, he is shocked because someone, even someone as scandalous as Cat, would speak of such a thing. "Pope Innocent the Eighth," he murmurs, and his blush is vivid.

"Because," Cat says, "if we talk about Julie, let's cut the guff."

"Men live by symbols," I say. Better to say something innocuous than put up with this shocked silence.

PERHAPS CAT IS correct. Decline may well have started in the 1930s. Seven Sisters took decades to fade. The houses had been too well built. Many artists lingered. They made livings by working in this town, even as the town faded. And, with passing years, many lived to old age and died. The town, however, has no record of the deaths of Gabrielle or Julie.

"And yet, we were certain they died," I told the others. "I recall the rumors. Some said that Julie was murdered by an angry husband. Some said that he traveled to the Orient and never returned. The most likely rumor claimed that he stepped into eternity attended by the best physicians in the nation, and that the body was embalmed with rich spices and oils."

"Artists died as well," the Barrister said. "As did others."

"It's the manner in which people died." Cat allows herself a shudder. "Think of the deaths, then think of the mansions."

"Few deaths were normal." I am uneasy admitting what is so obviously true. "Most were not. Bodies did not develop dread disease. They withered from within. Something siphoned life. Life seemed purloined."

TODAY, AT THE beginning of a new century, Seven Sisters stand like crazed echoes. Our townspeople do not go there because of fear. The decaying mansions are now immersed in a forest of young fir and cedar, as untended lawns allowed forest to reclaim the land. The darkest and ugliest and completely broken mansion is *Muse*, its black paint washed away so that remaining boards are sodden and gray. Chimneys have tumbled, and the crystal windows have been shattered by vagrants, or, even more likely, by storm. Bare rafters decay in the rain.

The others are in great disrepair. *Gaudens* has scattered its busts of the famous. One steps cautiously through young forest and is sometimes surprised by a marble face staring upward. Busts lie on the ground, Rembrandt and Beethoven.

Perhaps the strangest is *Michelangelo*. Its large windows hang cracked and crazy before its galleries, and its stained-glass windows are now clear. Color, for over a century, has drained from those windows. In the galleries hang empty frames, or sometimes frames holding canvas that is blank. The frames no longer retain their gilt. A stark place, it is devoid of color, form, and even, some would say, perspective.

The only sister that still shows color is *Thespia*. Perhaps the color comes only because of rusting iron railings. At any rate, *Thespia* stands intact and stained. On the darkest nights, lamplight still shines from the high rooms of *Thespia*, and for a generation now, people have assumed that vagrants camp there.

Of late, however, we are no longer sure. Our qualms are the reason for the meeting of the Historical Society.

"Because," Cat says, "we are still alive." She shrugs. "No big deal, because lots of people live long lives. But we are too active. We move like fifty-year-olds, and you gents are approaching ninety."

I am not happy, thinking what I'm thinking. "We are the last people alive," I say, "who not only knew Julie, but who had intimate dealings with him."

"My accomplishments with men are private. My accomplishments with theater are sufficient. I have played alongside the Barrymores." Cat speaks with quiet dignity. "I trod his stage, but Julie never came within a country mile." She turns to the Barrister, and Cat is ready for a scrap.

"I," says the Barrister, "handled much of his legal work, but none of his dirty work."

"And I," I tell them, "never cut a corner, never compromised a task, never substituted cheaper material, and never padded the account." Since it sounds like bragging, I add, "It would have been poor business."

WHEN I WAKE in gray mornings, it is always with a surge of untoward energy, like the twinge of static electricity. Or worse, it is like a false stimulus, the kick of concentrated caffeine or some other drug. It is not normal, this I know.

When I step into our narrow streets, the town stands slanted, crazy and askew. One does not know whether to admit that this is a ghost town, or, more likely, a town profoundly under the control of spirits. Victorian houses stand like colorful ghosts. New paint peels, but wood is silver, and not the muddy gray of Seven Sisters. No original color remains.

Municipal buildings show a few lights. The town still owns a working fire truck. An aging policeman monitors our streets. The mayor runs the general store, which sees fewer customers each year. Perhaps the town survives because of eternal mist. Perhaps gray coastlines are most amenable to tormented and tormenting spirits.

And, approaching the library, one's heart cannot help but sadden. Weeds rise high around the windows. Library hours, these days, are from ten to two, Tuesdays. A volunteer librarian fights her losing battle against moisture, mold, and rot.

"We find ourselves in a pickle," the Barrister muses. "I had not realized we were the only ones left who had close dealings with Julie."

"Julie was morally venereal. Fully corrupt," Cat tells the Barrister. "We have just confessed that we were not. Something to think about."

"It is true that I am too spry for my age," the Barrister says. "Since we are granted this energy, let's use it. I'll research records at the courthouse. There'll be no answer, but there may be clues."

"I will research sunsets," Cat says, and I am not sure what she means.

"I will walk the night," I tell her. "I'm far too old to be playing it safe."

"Think of the arts," Cat whispers, and I am certain she is talking to herself. "Think of sex, or rather, its reasons."

III

IN A LAND of tormented spirits, it's easy to be cowardly. I walk through twilight and admit to cowardice that has kept me from watching haunted movements. As twilight fades and darkness thickens our streets, whispers become palpable. Perhaps the whispers have always been there, and we have not listened. While turning away from soundless screams, we have ignored the whispers.

Black moves against black. Beneath a shrouded moon, and far away, dark figures manifest, then fade to black. In yellow light from street lamps, movement appears where light melds to darkness. Something in our streets is not dead. Or, if that *something* is dead, it is propelled.

Faces congregate, but seem separate from the black-on-black movement. I sorrow to think that I am used to faces of horror, of shocked children viewing injuries they cannot believe belong to them, of the faces of the murdered or the raped.

And through the years, too many faces have been costumed: Pilgrims and

Plantagenets, Harlequins and Hamlets. Faces fanciful, but crippled: a belled cap invisibly jingling above blind eyes, or stern eyes staring from beneath eyebrows above which the skull is broken and missing. These forms have appeared and rapidly faded. Perhaps their transience is why we ignored them.

But it comes to me, walking our nighttime streets, that I may ignore them no longer. Survival of the body is not the question here. The question is survival of the soul. Their souls, if they still have them. Mine.

"Think of the arts and sex," Cat had said, "or think of their reasons."

"Better yet," I murmur to the night, "think of a bad pope, plus a corrupt opportunist. What had they in common?"

And, I answer, "They wanted to live past their natural span."

Our streets meander, but all eventually wend to Seven Sisters. When I stand among young trees and look at the mansions, it is almost always beneath a shrouded moon. Mist rises with the night. Clouds that form in the Aleutians roll down our coastline, sometimes bringing storm and wind.

Whispers in the forest rarely assert. Instead, they consult. Movements that earlier seemed random, I now understand are direct and with purpose. It has taken two weeks of nights to understand that this town is the site of a ghastly war.

Vengeance rides the wind, but it is not vengeance only. The dead make direct assaults on Seven Sisters. The assaults have something to do with survival. Survival of whom? Survival of what?

I only know that as darkness seals the forest, movement focuses on Seven Sisters. While some apparitions momentarily appear, I now know it is necessary to follow whispers and murmurs; not apparitions. And, slightly distant, but always present, dark forms move like jet-black ink scrawled across the night.

Whispers encircle Seven Sisters and wage a war of attrition, of surrounding, of gnawing. I was stunned at first, because I quickly understood that the collective army of whispers can actually direct the wind. Wind rises above treetops and concentrates on a single mansion. The concentration doubles the force of the wind, so that glass panes crack and shingles fly. Young tree branches are torn by wind. They are hurled against the mansion; a bombardment.

Equally impressive, during nights of rain I huddle in my waterproof and watch funnels of rain whirl crazily through the darkness, to crash precisely on weak points of a mansion. Rain centers on cracks in windows, siding, roofs. Having no other weapons, the army of whispers directs weather like a conductor before a symphony.

"MAYBE IT ISN'T war," Cat says. "Maybe it's theater." She sits again in the library as the three of us consult.

"You're joking."

"Maybe," Cat says, ". . . but theater is involved, so maybe not."

She is particularly beautiful on this gray day, and hers is an unconscious beauty. There's witchery in her smile. Her flowing gown of greens might seem showy on other women, but on Cat it seems only casual. It occurs to me that I have lived a passive life. What might it have been had it been lived beside a woman like Cat?

"I'll ask you to explain that theater business soon enough." The Barrister studies notes on a yellow pad. "I have interesting information. It seems Julie once had plans, and his plans went astray."

The Barrister has never owned a reputation for vengeance. He owns a reputation for being just. Now, though, he smiles, and his smile is not kind. His small and wrinkled face seems as formal as his suit and starched white shirt. His dark tie is held in place with a diamond stickpin. The diamond glitters only a little sharper than the Barrister's eyes. "That old saying . . . 'You can't take it with you' . . . Julie tried. What he didn't count on were other men just like himself."

The Barrister explains that Julie set up a foundation to administer his great fortune. The mission of the foundation was "to maintain and advance the aims of Seven Sisters in perpetuity." As the twentieth century rolled past, ambitious men contrived to load the foundation's board and directorship. They stole the fortune.

"Not a drop left," the Barrister says with some satisfaction. "Not a dram. In his grave, Julie lies as a pauper."

"If," Cat says, "he is buried. Because if one is buried, it pays to be dead."

It is the second time she has shocked the Barrister. Of course, the Barrister has not been walking our midnight streets. He has not stood in sunrise and sunset.

"If alive," Cat murmurs, "he would be a desperate, desperate man. If alive, then what's happening is both theater and war."

"If alive," the Barrister whispers, "he would be more than a hundred and forty years old. Do not make jokes." The Barrister knows full well that no one is joking.

"You don't get it," Cat tells the Barrister. "The arts are not simple entertainment. They are life itself. You don't get that, do you?" Cat is angry, though managing to seem only annoyed. She turns to me. "If there's a war, there are two sides. What is the other side doing?"

"I don't know. The notion never occurred." I know that Cat is going somewhere with this, but it lies beyond comprehension.

"Find out," Cat tells me, "because what's alive at Seven Sisters is after us. At least part of it is." Her anger still lives, but is now subdued. "The war is now our war," she says quietly. "It is defensive. Julie is still alive. He is suckling symbolic breasts." To the Barrister, she says, "Did you think the arts are male?"

The Barrister sits confused, as I do. Why this anger?

"After us?"

"In dawn and sunset, the horrors of this town appear." Cat sounds like a grade-school teacher. "There is not a rape, a murder, a disemboweling, or a lynching that is not recalled. Those are most of the broken faces we see. That kind of manifestation no doubt happens in other places, places beyond the town. Manifestation probably happens in any place where the past is as dark as hate." She shifts in her chair, pauses, and I can tell that she still controls anger. "Apparitions are all around us. Call them ghosts. Call them history. Makes no difference. But what happens at night *is* different."

"He is after us?" The Barrister, for perhaps the first time in his life, actually sounds fearful. "After us?"

"Shakespeare had it right." Cat once more muses to herself while ignoring the Barrister. "Storm and winds, thunder and Lear. War."

"I'll find out what the other side is doing," I tell her.

IN DARKEST NIGHT, spirits may, or may not, endorse my movements. One thing is certain. The wind drops. Night is as still as glass, but like glass, it may shatter. Mist flows away from the forest and the sky. Stars appear like streams of cold fire. In this depth of darkness, Seven Sisters sit like hulks thrown on a rocky shore. Candlelight, or lamplight, glows on the fourth floor of *Thespia*. It is small illumination, but increases during an approach through the forest. Someone, or something, wields light.

Forte stands at the edge of the semicircle. It is the oldest of the mansions. Starlight reveals broad and broken steps, and one can only pass up them by use of a flashlight. Covered porches encircle the mansion, and, in olden days, served as a promenade for beautifully coiffed ladies and tailored gents. It is on these porches that an intuition arrives.

The living have power here. It would be possible to step inside and strike a match. Words from an ancient book seem to echo along the porches, something on the order of "What's born in fire belongs to fire, so I fear hell's certain."

Whispers surround, question, hesitate. Fire is an option, but the whispers wonder to each other, debate.

On the other hand, one does not casually destroy the past, even those parts that are toad-ugly. At least one does not do so on a whim. It is wrong to destroy without knowing what is being destroyed.

From the porches, the main doorway leads into a foyer. The foyer leads to the auditorium and long, thrust stage where Gabrielle and her troupe once danced. My flashlight illumes furnishings now turning to dust. Upholstered chairs are pale as mist. Color has left or been stolen. A simple touch on the arm of a chair, and the thing crumbles. Overhead, ormolu roses hang like thin ice as copper alloy turns to dust. The very floors are without color. Missing, even, is any hint of carpet or varnish.

Drapery fragile as cold breath divides the foyer from the auditorium. And, in the auditorium, the mind goes numb.

On the huge stage, a single figure dances, ghostly as mist in dark forest. The stage dwarfs the figure, so that she seems no more than a child. Slow and rhythmic, she moves against paleness. There is no music here, except in her movement, which suggests music. It seems, though one cannot swear to it, that as she dances, she weeps.

And so, it would seem, fire is out of the question.

After five more nights, I am able to report that with the exception of *Thespia*, figures inhabit each mansion. I have not yet found the courage to enter *Thespia*.

In *Muse*, the figure is dark. It slumps over a desk, quill in hand, but the pen does not move. In *Maestro*, fingers caress a harp that holds no strings. *Gaudens* carries the sound of gentle tapping, like chisel and hammer, but the echo says that it is not marble being worked, only brick. *Greco* is perhaps most fearsome, because figures clothed in Athenian style seem in pursuit of philosophy, and the figures murmur: "Gordian knots of ice cream," and, "When the Jersey-moo arrives, the point lies proved."; and thus are the figures insane.

And *Michelangelo*, I doubt not, is most bizarre. In all the mansions, there has been no life, but *Michelangelo* hosts a mouse. One walks the galleries where pale walls stand empty, except where an occasional frame still hangs. The frames are stripped of gilt, and are gnawed.

As one strolls through the galleries, the mouse scurries ahead like a guide telling the story of each empty frame. There is only one mouse. Perhaps it is an incarnation of some sad spirit, condemned to gnaw until *Michelangelo* falls to dust.

"DESPERATION," CAT SAYS, and she talks about Julie. We once more sit in the library and look at moldering books and look through windows beyond which Victorian houses lean crazily against the sky. "Madness. What awful, awful hunger."

The Barrister whispers, "I have lived here all my life. A man ought to be allowed to die where he has lived."

I listen to the Barrister. Does his mind wander? He was in strong mental control only last week. Is he now senile?

"I'm beginning to think the same thing," Cat tells him. "It may be half past time to get the deuce out of town." She turns to me. "Run or stay?"

"We are duty bound to see this through." The Barrister still whispers. He does not look well. His small frame, already shrunken, seems like fragile sticks clinging to the inside of his suit. He is only a trellis for clothing. "My energies," he apologizes, "are not what they were."

Cat and I look at each other, and our looks ask the same question.

Trust Cat to choose honesty. "You are the first of us to be attacked," she tells the Barrister, and her voice is gentle. "You are physically smallest. The thing that was Julie, or maybe *is* Julie, is running out of options." She again looks through the windows. "There's nothing left of the original colors out there. Surely those were stolen first."

Sometimes, even in my great age, I am reckless to the point of stupidity. "I'll confront him," I tell them.

"We'll confront him." Cat turns to me. "You still don't 'get it.' I expect you'll be needing help." To the Barrister, she says, "Keep close to home. Rest. One way or other, this is soon over."

DEATH IS A fearful problem for the young, but people who are truly old do not fear it. We fear other things. I think about this as I wait for Cat. I stand at the edge of the young forest.

We, who are old, fear the death of our worlds. Each of us has known the world in a particular manner. As we grow old, the world gets revised. We, who are old, mourn the passing of ways that sustained us in youth. In my case, I mourn loss of formality and custom and honor. The Barrister, who is admittedly starchy, is one of the last men alive whom I truly admire.

Cat approaches through gathering darkness, and there's magic in her movements. No one, and certainly not the young, move with such grace. The approaching night seems to fall away like a discarded cloak. She moves through the dusk as a small essence of light.

"*Forte*", she says, and leads in that direction. As she moves, whispers from the forest congregate. They no longer question. If anything, the whispers endorse. Mostly, though, they seem excited in ways that only belong to the living. But, a whisper can't be alive . . . how can a whisper be alive?

"Do you hear?" I feel like a young kid tagging behind an older sister.

"Shush," Cat says. She is focused.

I follow in silence. When we stand in the foyer, dusk lingers in the windows. Sunset seems unwilling to fade. The last time I was here, the foyer was viewed by flashlight. In this gray light, it stretches long and wide and barren.

Cat looks at crumbling furnishings and muddy-gray walls. "Tomb of lost dreams." Her voice is quiet. Whispers surround us. On my first visit, the whispers stayed on the porches. Now they have moved inside. "Lost dreams," Cat repeats. "Let's see if we can find 'em."

I follow her to the auditorium, which has no windows. It is darker, even, than most of our nights. In the darkness, gray figures move. They are the same figures that moved black-on-black through streets and forest.

"It's been a while," Cat murmurs to herself. She watches the enormous stage, where a pale figure dances, ghostly, slow; dancing with its own silent rhythm. "I never was much one to hoof it," Cat whispers, "but since we're here . . ."

When she ascends the stage and joins the dancer, pale light trembles on the edge of darkness. If there is music in the air, it lives on the edge of hearing. And if it is music, it is in three-quarter time. One thinks of Mozart.

The living figure bows, the phantom curtseys. Both the bow and the curtsy are as delicate as music that now reaches to surround, but not touch the dancers.

"Quick study," Cat says in a soft voice, "I was always a quick study. So show me."

And they dance, slowly, in classic minuet, Cat learning as she goes. And as they dance, the specter no longer weeps, although Cat does. And she smiles. And dances.

Gray figures turn luminous. Light attends the stage. Whispers become murmurs, and I feel separated from Cat, from the phantoms, and from the luminous shadows. Something is alive here, and beyond my understanding. All around, murmurs speak of form, color, sound.

". . . a bit more light . . . blue filter . . . make it soft."

". . . that snare drum's in front, not back of the music. Get it where it belongs . . ."

The figures on stage gradually meld. What was once a specter fades toward Cat, and it is impossible to tell whether it becomes part of her, or simply disappears. Cat stands on the stage, transfixed like one seeing visions.

"If those two were trying to impress me," one murmur says, "they've done it."

"The drum should have gone to a deep tom-tom," a second murmur insists. "The snare was too sharp."

It seems a private discussion held in public, but I do not understand. When Cat speaks, it is not as I expected, which is to say, gently.

"Act two," she says, her voice brisk. "And it's only a two-acter. Let us proceed." And—by the Lord Harry—she giggles. To me, she says, "If you still don't get it, watch what happens next."

What happens next is that we leave *Forte* accompanied by murmurs from luminous shadows. In growing night, the shadows gain color. I feel sure that they will soon materialize.

Once clear of *Forte*, we turn and watch. It does not, like a house of legend, sink into the tarn. There is little spectacle in the death of *Forte*, although it is interesting. The four high turrets bend slowly inward, like dancers bowing to each other; but unlike real dancers, the turrets continue to fall. Dust raises its smoke above walls no stronger than paper. Destruction takes its time. It is methodical. The building shrieks as rusted nails pull from worn boards and as walls collapse inward. By the time of complete collapse, not a salvageable piece remains.

"I'd be the last," Cat murmurs, "to keep a man from chasing a skirt, but there are limits." To me, she says, "Julie never made the connection. All that this meant to him was a roll in the hay."

"And Gabrielle?"

"There's art," Cat says grimly, "and then, there's bad art. Those who can't dance well can always dance on their backs." She turns and heads for *Thespia*.

IV

NIGHTMARE LAY AHEAD. No grotesque vision of Hell ever burned more brightly. I write this record on yellow legal pads as I sit in the library. My writing instrument is a black marker: wide, dark lines against the soft glow of the paper. The lines seem thicker than my fingers. My sight fades, and the vivid ink seems insubstantial. The Barrister has died in peace, and I am soon to follow.

When Cat turned toward *Thespia*, I could feel tension gather as shadows gained substance and wind began to rise. The Harlequins and Pilgrims and Plantagenets who strode stages in other days now showed no blinded eyes or ravaged skulls. Their murmurs were alive, and they seemed alive as well. As we strode forward, I found myself in company with a band of costumed men and women. They were not yet corporeal, but they were no longer creatures of shadow. "I've saved, your Grace, a pocket full of wind . . ."

". . . warriors or cartoonists." Cat spoke to the forest, or to the company, but not to me. "I expect we'll have to decide which."

Thespia seemed to gather night as it loomed into darkness. It was always too massive for a house, too massive even for a theater. In many ways, it resembled a castle, but one of wood more than stone. True, the widely sweeping steps were of marble, and the foundation was of granite, but all else was wood. I did not then know that marble and granite can burn.

Gaiety accompanied our approach. Cat hummed, and seemed ready to whistle, or break into song. She moved with such grace that I did not at first realize what else was happening.

From the other mansions, black shadows emerged. They staggered, fumbled, and gradually gained strength. As they grew stronger, black turned to gray, and gray to luminosity. We walked in light as freed spirits congregated.

Thespia loomed so huge I could only feel intimidation. As wind began to bend trees, light from the fourth floor of *Thespia* brightened. The first three floors then illumed with glow like electric storms against clouds. As light grew, wind became stronger above the forest. It blew through my clothing and chilled my spine.

When we entered, Cat paused. "Welcome back," Cat murmured, probably to herself. After all, she had once walked the stage that opened before us. Cat looked around the immense auditorium, which contained not one shred of color.

"No wonder it attacked the Barrister." Cat finally spoke directly to me. "It's so hard up that life is even being drawn from the place where it lives."

"It?"

"Julie was always an 'it,' " Cat says. She reconsiders. "Maybe not always, but that's what he became." She sees that I do not understand. "My dear man. Wake up. You once fashioned cloth into beautiful things."

All around us, spirits hovered silent but poised. Those crippled spirits that had joined us from the buildings remained shadowy, but Cat's company of materialized spirits gained even greater substance.

"Black and white must buy color, or steal. Thus do I give you Julie." Cat turned to ascend broad stairs.

Wind thumped against *Thespia*. The building did not shake, but from upstairs rooms came moans as wind poured through broken windows. Wails rose as wind probed cracks between boards and window frames.

Second floor displayed dressing rooms, and a shock. In closets were products of my own hands. Costumes hung in tidy and colorful rows; costumes to bring forth aviators and princesses, churls, beggars, merry wives, or Spanish dancers.

"Their colors have survived," I whispered to Cat.

"I think," she said, "that they have been preserved. I think I'm beginning to understand this."

The second floor was also used as storage: coils of cables, dry and decaying manila rope, tools and other appurtenances of stagecraft. Below us, down in the theater, echoes sounded. They were not whispers. The echoes spoke in large, outstanding terms, proclaiming the awakening of dreams. Cat listened. Smiled.

As we climbed, color became more than a suggestion. It had not completely drained from walls where fading white had turned to yellow, and where ormolu held traces of pastels. Third floor was given over to private chambers, and it was on third floor that one knew that first taste of absolute fear. The fear is not so terrible one cannot bear it, but it lives like copper on the tongue.

Some of the doors to private chambers stood open. And what lay in them might have once lived. Wind swept the rooms and rustled faded gowns.

And less fearful, though like echoes, walls carried notations and graffiti; a record of what had once been positive about *Thespia.* "H.R.H in Hamlet, Spring, 1897." "Ferrill, 1918, the armistice just announced. We're playing a George Ade." "E. Barrymore, ah, Cassandra, 1932." The notations were normally faded, yet still seemed alive.

"Think on't, m'lord," Cat muttered, "Think ye longish and well." Around her, materialized spirits became more physical. Murmurs turned to soft speech; not confused, but questioning.

"We are stronger, are we strong enough?"

"The lion in its cage now mews," Cat said to the company. "Let's bait the lion." To me, she said, "He built his own cage. Let's see what the fool has done with immortality."

Steps to fourth floor wound crazily, as if the builder had grown tired of symmetry. They were broad, solid, and burnished with soft light that at other times might have seemed seductive. At the head of the steps, a massive door stood open.

"The play's the thing," Cat said to the spirits. "Improv emptiness and wind."

"That," said a cultured male voice, "is a quite well-studied role." The fully manifested speaker stood beside Cat, and he was costumed as a strolling minstrel. His hair curled dark, and his brown eyes flashed. Jerkin in cloth of green.

We entered and I stood amazed. I looked at a throne room, and two massive thrones. I saw gold roses in the gilded ceiling, and draperies of royal purple. I saw cloth of gold. Tapestry in rich reds ornamented walls, and yellow and violet rugs of Arabian design covered russet floors. Sculptures guarded corners and doors, forms of naked warriors and women, only some of them obscene.

"Engage him," Cat whispered to me. "We'll handle the rest." Her confidence served well because I have no great reputation for courage.

It seemed impossible to talk to the thing before me. Julie sat enthroned, the throne tall and chaotic with color. Paint did not chip or fade. Every color that could come from a pallet twisted and curled, the effect demented.

I looked upward. Julie's blue eyes peered peevish through lids heavy with bloat. The once-narrow frame had expanded beyond possibility of fitted clothing. A light and transparent robe covered pendulous breasts, and fingers were so enlarged they seemed all of a piece. Arms looked thick as rolled rugs, and legs were swollen like fleshy balloons. This was not fat, but bloat.

On the second throne sat a corpse. Gabrielle had mummified and seemed no more weighty than tissue paper; her once strong frame dwindled to thin twigs. When she spoke, her voice echoed from elsewhere, because her lips did not move. She had been drained of life, but not of speech. "Betrayed." The echo ran the ranges of despair like a chromatic scale. "Betrayed."

In this high place, northwest wind gained strength. It buffeted the walls.

I heard Cat's voice. It sounded loud or faint, depending on where she moved in the huge room. " 'Tis here, 'tis there, 'tis ever-where; but nowhere do I see it."

"What seek ye, mistress? Wither we away?" A male voice boomed, and I nearly turned from Julie.

"A sack of moonlight. Possibly a poem." Cat's voice sounded distant. "A wreath of music and a flight of bird."

"Peter," Julie said. "You're looking well." His voice remained the only thin thing about him. The voice issued from swollen lips. The snideness that was always his had increased. It held contempt, but it also held a hint of fear. He turned his massive head as much as he was able. "For that, you'd better thank me."

Cat had skipped beyond his vision. I saw her standing in a far corner, arms akimbo, and her gaze enraptured as she watched a man in green cloth cavort. "Buds of May 'neath pale winds dance, and on yon hill fair lambkins prance. Hey nonny nonny."

Wind crashed against *Thespia*, and now the building trembled. From the forest, branches of young trees were cast. They hit with ballistic force.

"Better explain that," I said to Julie. "Before thanking people, I like to know what the conversation's about." Oddly enough, my voice remained calm.

"I've stored life in you," Julie said. "You're nothing but storage, and you, I don't need." He listened for Cat. "But at least you brought the woman." Julie turned to look at Gabrielle. His lips were too bloated to curl, but scorn filled his voice. "This one has become a burden."

An ornamental suaveness had always been Julie's trademark, but now it was replaced by something savage. He sat enthroned, too bloated to walk, and he sat beside a corpse. Color whirled crazily around us as, far across the room, Cat and a company of spirits cavorted. The spirits were now as substantial as when they were alive.

"Betrayed." Gabrielle's voice seemed made of dust. It faded as a last rustle of her being departed.

"Betrayed." The word dwindled, and the mouth that had until then not moved, gaped. If Gabrielle was not free, at least she had been released.

"You were always a milksop," Julie told me, "thus useful. I control vitality here. I control life. If I invest in you, and keep you vital, I persuade myself that you're insurance."

And finally, after nearly ninety years of life, I began to catch on.

I made connections. Vitality was stored with us for use in keeping Julie alive. That was the reason for the Barrister's decline. Julie was feeding on his capital.

Poor fool. I finally understood, then understood something more. Cat was not scandalous. I was, or had been. I had played it safe, not knowing that poverty of spirit is defensive, but life isn't. Poverty of spirit only shapes more poverty. Creation shapes the world.

"I believe," I told Julie, "that your policy just lapsed." Beyond the mummified figure of Gabrielle, a ring of dancers circled a Maypole. Cat skipped nimble as a child.

"Give way," I told him. "The woman behind you has lived more in any five minutes of her life than you have in a hundred and forty years."

A sneer. And yet, the bloated figure above me moved uneasily. "Behind me?"

"My mistake," I told him. "You're way behind. She does not give two snips about you."

"Soupçon, of breeze, a stir of air, and rises lordly wind." Cat's voice sounded like a child at play. Dancers began to flow around the room, and from the first crack in the walls of Julie's bastion, there entered a movement of air. It was but a breath at first, but definitely a breach. Dancers pantomimed the wind, swooping, eddying, while laughter deepened.

"She'll care soon enough. What I can give, I can take away." Julie watched the actors as they danced. "I took what I needed from them once, I'll take again. You idiots have done a favor."

"Release the Barrister."

"Already done," Julie told me. "There's fatter game here."

"And a fatter hunter." I thought myself mad to bait him. Then I thought that he was the one who was mad. For a century, he had run roughshod. Now, with a breeze ruffling that tentlike and transparent robe, he could not imagine his hazard.

He was like a man trying to pick up a stone that he thought was a prop, an imitation made of paper, but instead, had turned out to be a real stone. He paused, perplexed. He concentrated, strained, and his eyes were portraits of fear.

"What cruel revenge they are taking," I said about Cat and her company. "It is the revenge of unimportance. They tell you that you were, and are, king of nothing, nothing more." In defiance, I wet my finger and held it aloft to determine the direction of the breeze. "Observe as they create the wind, because you look your last."

I thought I could not care about Julie, and yet as his struggle began, I felt small sadness. "If you were truly evil, I would rejoice," I told him. "But you're only arrogant. What you do is evil, but to be truly evil . . . you're not man enough."

Now the actors formed a cortege behind a casket borne on a donkey cart. They were costumed as clowns, and they cast flowers in the air; and flowers threw petals into the wind. A shower of petals blew toward us. Actors near the coffin sang a funereal song, although they smiled and their clown shoes flippity-flopped. At the end of the procession, like mischievous children, actors pranced.

"The king is dead," I told Julie, "and he was only king of a room that is about to disappear."

Fear, like none I have ever known, now lived on Julie's face. I doubted not that fear lived more vibrantly than any other emotion Julie had ever felt. At first I thought he was trying to steal life, then realized he was in a struggle to hold onto what he had already stolen. "You could offer help," he choked. "You owe."

"Nothing I can do." I thought of a hundred years of theft and exploitation. I thought of our dying town and the murder of people and the murder of dreams. "Nothing I want to do. No one owes anything, not even simple courtesy."

"I'll pay. I offer life."

I think he believed he spoke the truth. For all his many years he had fed, and fed. He had controlled. He could not then grasp that his control was gone.

He began to wither. At first he only seemed to shrink, and for a moment, I did not understand that the lives and colors he had hoarded were escaping. The bloat decreased. In the distance, actors postured, declaimed, and their play was grimly comic.

"A little life. Save a little." The plea was to me, or to fate, or to some god unknown; and it was frantic.

It was then I became cruel. "None," I told him. "You're not important enough for Hell, and so you simply disappear. You will not even be a bug, a mote, or any incarnation. Neither Earth nor Heaven will know you more." I had no notion whether I spoke true, but it seemed true. Mine were the last words Julie heard before succumbing to fear.

He did not shrink, but, like *Forte*, folded in on himself. As the bloat disappeared, and as blue eyes grew wild with insanity, Julie appeared as he had once been. His thin-legged, high-rumped form writhed on a throne now devoid of color; and as color departed, he screamed. He was momentarily young, and in torment.

As he departed, he aged: faded hair, faded but tortured eyes, creases beginning, then deepening. His fingers grasped uncontrolled as he screamed. When dismemberment started its slow and bloody progress, I had seen enough.

Cat took me by the arm. "At the very outside," she told me. "We have ten minutes." She tugged, and I was not loath to follow. My last memory of the place is of screams and the stench of decay.

We moved quickly and without speaking. Cat's band of actors accompanied us, and I could not for the moment believe that they were spirits. They trod the stairs, and the stairs drummed beneath their feet.

Past dusty rooms, past fragile bones, while we were chased by wind that scoured hallways. We moved quickly, but slowed as we left the building and stepped into young forest that danced in the wind. I felt age begin to creep upon me. Life was not stolen, but the vitality Julie had invested was now leaving. Soon I would be weak and tottering.

Cat stood beside me, sisterly and protective. Actors gathered about as we watched a consummation.

Fire started in a hundred or a thousand places from small torches of light. Wind wrapped around the building. An actor's voice muttered. " 'Blow winds, blow and crack your cheeks.' "

"I mourn its passing," Cat murmured to the actors, or possibly to me. "The theater couldn't help who owned it." Then she brightened. "But then, one does not need a building. The street is a stage."

It is a formidable sight to watch any large building burn. When the building is nigh the size of a castle, the sight inspires awe. The small torches of light appeared when lives trapped in that building flared in their escapes. Wind fanned the tiny fires, so that in only moments, the entire mansion alighted with flame. Wind flared around fourth floor, where if Julie still existed, he lay in an immense crematory. Fire illumed clouds and mist flowing from the forest. Wind searched, expanded, and the burning of *Thespia* was like a dry stick dropped into a blast furnace.

"Time to leave," Cat whispered to me. "Good job you did in there."

I turned to her. In the fire-glow, her face seemed young as a girl's, although age crept across her body. Her hands trembled. She smiled, happy as an excited child, and reached to touch my cheek. Beside her, spirits faded as they began to move into the forest. "I leave with them," Cat said. "It's where I belong. But you, I'll miss." And then she turned, walking slowly, and disappeared into the forest.

There is little more to tell. I had enough remaining strength to leave the forest. Our town's policeman found me trudging the road to town, and took me home. It was a week before I ventured out.

It seemed that with the passing of *Forte* and *Thespia*, any fear that locals owned was gone. When I stepped back into our streets, the remaining mansions had been raided, with little of value recovered. The buildings ood stripped and bare. A constant wind guaranteed their passing. The story was over, but the record still needed to be made.

The library is a cool, sometimes cold place, but I must close the record here. I want nothing of Julie, not even a notation, to enter my own rooms.

I note the passing of the Barrister. He died in peace, and in a hospital bed. He was conscious and only a little ill, but his illness was not Julie. He was his own man.

And I proudly note that I am mine. In nigh ninety years, I learned trade, and craft, and even artfulness; but never art. It took Cat to teach me. One need not regret lost years when one has learned great things.

AFTERWORD

My favorite ghost story is Peter Beagle's *Tamsin*, which, besides being beautifully written, deals in most of the things I enjoy about fantastical writing. It has Good and Evil, plus lots of well-researched history, and the characters are near perfect. The good kids are innocent, but not dumb. The bad guy (Judge Jeffries) is the most scary kind of monster, one of those quiet, nasty types; and when punishing forces cruise the world, you can actually feel winds pick up.

Joyce Carol Oates is one of the most prolific and respected writers in the United States today. Oates has written fiction in almost every genre and medium. Her keen interest in the Gothic and psychological horror has spurred her to write dark suspense novels under the name Rosamond Smith, to have written enough stories in the genre to have published four collections of dark fiction, and to edit *American Gothic Tales*. Oates's short novel *Zombie* won the Bram Stoker Award for Superior Achievement in the Novel, and she has been honored with a Life Achievement Award given by the Horror Writers Association. Her most recent titles are *Middle Age: A Romance* and *I'll Take You There*. She has been living in Princeton, New Jersey, since 1978, where she teaches creative writing. She and her husband Raymond J. Smith run the small press and literary magazine *The Ontario Review*.

SUBWAY

JOYCE CAROL OATES

PLEASE LOVE ME my eyes beg. My need is so raw, I can't blame you for looking quickly away.

Not you, not you, and you—none of you I can blame. *Only just love me, can't you? Love me. . . .*

THAT SUNDAY NIGHT, desperate not to be late! I had to change trains at Times Square, and the subway was jammed, both trains were crowded, always I knew it would happen soon, my destiny would happen within the hour, except I had to be at the precise position, when he lifted his eyes to mine casual-seeming or by chance turned to face me. I must be there, or the precious moment would pass, and then, and then—so lonely! In that swarm of strangers departing a train, pushing onto the next train, pushing to the stairs, breathless and trying not to turn my ankle in my spike-heeled spaghetti-strap shoes, my hair that's so sexy-black you'd suspect it must be dyed but *my hair is not dyed, this is my natural color*, and my skin white, exquisite moist-looking white like the face of a ceramic doll, and I'm wearing a black-suede mini-skirt and black diamond-patterned stockings (not pantyhose, but stockings, with a black-satin garter belt you can catch a glimpse of when I'm seated, when I cross my shapely legs in just the right way), and a white-lace see-through camisole with straps thin as threads, and beneath the camisole a black-satin C-cup bra that grips my breasts tight, lifting them in mute appeal. *Please love me, please look at me, how can you look away? Here I am.* My black hair I have ratted with a steel comb to three times its natural size, my mouth that's small and hurt like a snail in its shell I have outlined in crimson, a high-gloss lipstick applied to the outside of the lips enlarging them so I'm smiling breathless making my way to the other side of the track being pushed against, collided with, rudely touched by—who?—sometimes I'm to blame, these damned high heels, catching the heel in a wad of chewed gum, absolutely disgusting, sometimes I let myself be brushed against, it's an accident, or almost an accident, some leather-jacket swarthy-skinned guy swerving toward me staring at me chewing his mustache, hot dark-veiled eyes, I see him coming, headed in my direction, I can step aside if I make the effort, if I'm quick enough, but a strange lassitude comes over me, this one isn't the one and yet!—sometimes the jolt hurts, the force of him colliding with me as he hurries past, doesn't slow his pace or pause, doesn't apologize of course, not even a murmur of greeting, the touch is like an electric shock, half-pleasurable, though meant to hurt. As if he knows, this stranger, he isn't the one, not my destiny.

That Sunday night, not late—not yet 10:00 P.M. And not so crowded as the previous nights, those wild weekend nights, but still plenty crowded at Times Square, you can be sure. And I was desperate hurrying to make the downtown train. Before the doors closed. Stumbling in my high-heeled shoes so if you saw me you might've thought there was something wrong with me, some strange glisten of excitement in my black-mascara eyes and panting crimson mouth, and maybe you'd have wanted to help me, offer me your seat at least. And maybe, just maybe I would have accepted.

Always in the subway I think *On this train, in this car is my destiny: who?* Trembling with excitement. Anticipation! Contemplating through my lowered eyelashes the possibilities. Mostly men of course but (sometimes) women also. Young men, middle-aged men, occasionally even older men. Young women, with a certain sign. But not middle-aged, or older women. Never. I tried not even to look at them. Resented feeling sorry for them, their raddled faces and tired eyes. And sometimes in these eyes a look of hope, I despised. And sometimes out of loneliness one of these women might smile at me, move over inviting me to sit beside her, like hell I will sit beside some old bag like she's my mother.

On the train that night a woman of maybe forty-five took note of me as soon as I hurried into the car, out of breath and laughing to myself, my hair in my face. She was in some kind of green uniform, and ugly dirty-white nurse's shoes they looked like, and her gray-brown hair flat against her head in a hairnet, staring at me disapproving I thought, prissy fish-mouth I tried not to look at, I hate that type of person observing me, judging me. Not to the hairnet woman was I pleading *Look at me, love me! Hey: here I am.*

In the subway the trains move so fast you never can catch your breath. Outside the window that's a reflecting surface like a mirror mostly there are the rushing walls of the tunnel, then the train slows for a station, and the doors open, and people lurch off, and new people lurch on, and you lift your eyes hopeful and yearning *Who will be my destiny? Which one of you?* At 34th Street a man came on, sat near me, I was flattered to think he chose that seat deliberately the way his eyes trailed over me, my crossed legs in the patterned black stockings, my mouth in almost a smile, like I am expecting to recognize someone, like a child I am prepared to be pleasantly surprised, I am not a cynical person by nature. He stared at me, and his mouth moved in a twitchy way you might interpret as a smile. He was in his late thirties maybe, pale coarse pitted skin but still good-looking in that battered way some men look, sandy hair crimped and wavy over his head and shaved up the sides you could see it was no wig, and in his right ear lobe there was a glittering red stone I believed must be a ruby. The sign was he was wearing suede, like my skirt: sexy black jacket with chrome studs. He was wearing tight designer jeans, and ostrich-skin boots. On his wrist, a heavy I.D. bracelet. When he opened his mouth to smile, a gleaming tongue-ring winking at me. Like he knew me he said a name, maybe it was a name he'd invented at that moment or maybe it was a name known to him, he said this name, and I smiled at him in puzzlement saying no that isn't my name, I am not that girl, and he asked which girl was I then, and I told him Rosellen, and he repeated: Ros-ellen and said it was a beautiful name for a beautiful girl. In his eyes I saw that he was impressed with me, and he began talking about himself in a rapid low voice so other people couldn't hear, he said he was a lonely pilgrim searching for something he could not name, he'd been searching for all of his life, would I like to have coffee with him, would I like to have a drink with him, and all this time I was quietly observing him, through my eyelashes I was observing him, his eyes that were intelligent eyes though bloodshot and pouchy, and the truth came to me as if from a great distance *No: he is not the one.* So I told him politely I could not go with him. I told him politely I was meeting someone else. And he stared at me not so friendly now, his smile exposing his glittering tongue-ring not so friendly now, and he spoke to me in a soft crude voice not so friendly now, called me Ros-ellen like he didn't think so much of my name now, or of me. Others passengers close enough to hear him pretended not to hear, the hairnet woman who'd been listening to our conversation pretended now not to hear, at the next stop the tongue-ring man lurched to his feet and exited and was gone; and I checked my makeup in my little gold mirror compact feeling like I had almost made a mistake. . . . *He was a test. In your ignorance you might have chosen him.*

For my life at that time was a continual testing. That in ignorance or desperation I would make a terrible blunder, and would not realize my destiny.

Slamming into the car from the car ahead was a girl of about thirty with no eyelashes, no eyebrows like she'd pulled them all out or shaved them as a statement, and she'd shaved her head so these platinum blond quills were growing out, so striking!—everybody in the car stared at her even those who were nodding off woke to take in such a sight. The girl's face was glowing and shiny as if made of some synthetic material like a flesh-plastic, without pores, and her lips were big and pouty, and her mouth was moving as if she was talking to herself. Seeing me, eyes snatching onto mine, she stopped in mid-stride and stood above me holding the rail about two feet from me, observing me this slow smile breaking over her face like ice melting. A husky girl six feet tall in chinos and tight-fitting black T-shirt with DRAGO FREK in green letters. Her eyes on me were restless as minnows. She leaned down to ask did I know what time it was and I said I didn't know exactly, it was sometime after 10:00 P.M. I thought. Next she asked didn't I wear a watch and I shook my head no, she asked was I the kind of girl who didn't give a shit about the time, I laughed flattered saying I guess I must be. All this while Plastic Girl was leaning over me and her smile was widening and her big chunky plastic teeth were gleaming wetly at me. Plastic Girl said next, You're a girl who knows her own mind, I guess. That's fucking cool.

The hairnet woman was really listening to this conversation. Her prissy snail-mouth sucked in upon itself in concentration.

Raising her voice to be heard over the racket of the train Plastic Girl started telling me next about this place she was expected to be, some kind of fucking residence she wasn't going back to, except somebody there owed her, had some clothes and CDs of hers so she'd have to go back except not by any fucking front entrance she'd be going back through a window and it wouldn't be fucking broad daylight it would be night. I listened to Plastic Girl's voice like it was a radio voice. Her actual words were lost to me. I was distracted too by her heavy breasts with no bra, swaying inside the T-shirt, nipples hard as little pebbles. And her belly above the zipper-crotch of the chinos pushing out round and hard like a drum. I was wondering *Is this the one?* I had a feeling about Plastic Girl. . . .

At the next station a man pushed into the car, pushed between us like Plastic Girl didn't exist. Kind of rude behavior I thought but he was smiling sidelong at me like he knew me, or was pretending to know me, this was a game we'd played before. A woman seated beside me decided to move to another seat, uncomfortable with Plastic Girl and this new guy hanging above her, and right away the guy took her place before Plastic Girl could act. You could see Plastic Girl was angry. Baring her teeth like she'd like to tear at somebody with her teeth. I looked up appealing with my eyes, sorry! I was sorry!—but Plastic Girl turned and moved off, took a seat farther down the car that had just opened up. As the train lurched I could see her shaved head glowing like a bulb and her big lips pouting.

The man beside me nudged me asking did I remember him. Huh?

Did I remember him? Dunk's the name.

Oh God I realized then yes I had met Dunk before. Why I felt sort of familiar with him, sort of protected-by him the way you do with some men, instantly, though not most men, ever. A few weeks before we'd gotten to talking in the subway, and Dunk had taken me for a coffee (at Union Square). Possibly on this exact train. Possibly at this time of evening. Possibly I'd been wearing my patterned stockings, my suede skirt and see-through lace camisole that would've been a new purchase then, post-Christmas sale at Strawberry. Possibly Dunk had been wearing the dirt-stiffened jeans and fake buckskin jacket he was wearing now, and his steely-gray hair had been pulled back as it was now in a little pigtail at the nape of his neck. (You had to smile at this pigtail. You knew that Dunk thought it was comical, too. For he was nearly bald. All the hair Dunk had was growing in a narrow band around his head, he'd let grow long to fix into the pigtail.) There was something so old and comfortable about Dunk, like somebody you'd been seeing all your life on TV, this old pothead hippie from long ago you knew you could trust. Dunk said he remembered me, certainly he remembered Rosellen, did I know I'd broken his heart? Dunk made a weepy jocular sound like his heart was broken but mostly he needed to blow his nose which he did in a tissue, now making a honking sound so I laughed. That was Dunk's power, I recalled: the power to make you laugh. He'd been a psychiatric social worker with the city he said. He'd had to quit after twenty-three years and take disability pay which wasn't much. In the coffee shop he'd told me of his life lapsing into a monotone. He was one of those individuals who come on strong, make you laugh and intrigue you, then they settle in their usual mode, you discover they are boring though well-intentioned maybe, and kind-hearted as Dunk appeared to be kind-hearted, though his skin exuded heat like a radiator, and it was weird how his right eye kept drifting out of focus while his left eye had me pinned. In the coffee shop Dunk had told me one of his patients had threatened to kill him and he'd said what difference did it make, we are all going to die anyway aren't we. He'd been so depressed. He was better now but he'd been depressed as hell then. I didn't know what to say. I drank my coffee in silence. I'd realized by that time that Dunk was not my destiny. I didn't want to hurt his feelings but there was no mistaking, Dunk was not my destiny. He'd asked would I like to get a bite to eat with him? He was thinking, he said, Chinese.

Thank you, I said, dabbing at my lips with a napkin, but I can't.

I had not called him Dunk in the coffee shop. I had not wished to send a false signal of intimacy, or the promise of intimacy.

Nor did I say Dunk now. Saying I was sorry, this was my stop, I was meeting somebody and I was late, and goodbye.

WHO IS MY *destiny? You?*

WHOEVER IT WAS, I didn't see. Never saw his face. Never saw but a shadow in the corner of my eye. A giant bird spreading his wings. (I guess it was a man. Had to be. But even that fact, I can't be one hundred percent certain of.) It was the 14th Street Station. I'd gotten out, to change trains. My plan was to take the uptown to 57th Street. Past Times Square, I'd been disappointed in Times Square too often lately. I was standing at the edge of the platform just a little apart from the crowd. A few yards maybe. Not far. I didn't believe that I was standing dangerously close to the edge. Something was on my shoe, something sticky and disgusting like a big wad of gum, I was trying to scrape off my shoe when I saw, or half-saw, the shadow in the corner of my eye, advancing upon me from the left. The thought came to me swift and yearning *Please touch me* because it was so familiar a thought, never did I believe I was in danger. *Touch me even if you hurt me. Oh please.*

Then I was falling. I was screaming, and I was falling. It happened fast. Much faster than I can recall. Though even then I was thinking *He touched me, it was a human touch. He chose me because I am beautiful and desirable. He chose me over all others.* But already I am on the track. Out of nowhere out of the tunnel the train is speeding. My body is a big boneless rag doll flopping and being crushed by the train. The emergency brakes are thrown on, there's a deafening shriek as the train stops but it's too late, it was too late as soon as he pushed me from behind, the palms of both his hands flat against my back between my shoulder blades as if he'd planned the act, he'd rehearsed the act numerous times to perfection. My body is caught up inside the wheels, both my legs severed at the knees, my left arm torn off, my skull crushed as you'd crush a bird's egg beneath your feet, scarcely noticing you've crushed it. On the platform people are screaming. People have stopped dead in the tracks and some of them, mostly women, are screaming. I want to cry, these strangers care for me. In that instant they care for me. The hairnet woman had left the train when I did, maybe she'd followed me, the woman I'd believed had disapproved of me was now crying Help! Get help! Oh God get help! And there's Plastic Girl running to the edge of the platform like she's mesmerized, she can't see me because my body is hidden by the train skidding to a stop, Plastic Girl hasn't seen where my assailant has gone, where he has run to, she's stunned as if thinking *We could be sisters. That might have been . . .*

And there's Dunk, slack-mouthed in horror. Dunk with his bald-hippie pigtail gone gray. Dunk stunned and sick with grief he has lost me for the final time.

And others, who never knew me except to glimpse a girl pushed in front of a speeding train to her death, these others grieving for me, too. Never knew me in life but will never never forget me.

PLEASE LOVE ME? my eyes beg. Glancing uneasily at the window beside your seat, the uptown train is flying through the tunnel, or possibly it's the downtown, lights in the car so bright you can't see outside, only just your own reflection in the grimy window, your own face, and sometimes you don't recognize that face.

Please love me? I love you.

AFTERWORD

My favorite ghost story is Henry James's *The Turn of the Screw*, a brilliantly enigmatic and endlessly evocative tale of obsession.

STEPHEN GALLAGHER was born in Salford, Lancashire, England, in 1954. After working for a TV company for four years, his frustrations with the limitations of the job spurred him to write, learning the basic craft in radio and then moving into novels and screenplays.

With the sale of his first book, *Chimera*, he quit his job and headed to the United States with the intention of staying there until the money ran out. He toured extensively and settled for the longest period in Phoenix, Arizona, the setting for his later police procedural/supernatural horror novel *Valley of Lights*. He moved back to England in 1981 but later returned to the United States to write *Red, Red Robin*, set in Philadelphia.

Gallagher has written over a dozen novels, sold lots of film options, and written numerous screenplays and teleplays, including an adaptation of *Chimera*. In 1998 he wrote and directed a miniseries based on his novel *Oktober*. *White Bizango*, a short novel, was recently published.

His short stories have been published in *Shadows, The Magazine of Fantasy and Science Fiction, Asimov's SF Magazine, Weird Tales*, and in various anthologies.

DOCTOR HOOD

STEPHEN GALLAGHER

AT THE TOP of the narrow garden, Miranda climbed the steps to the front door of her childhood home and rang the bell. Then she waited.

No lights were showing in any of the windows. The lane on which the big house stood was a pocket of old-fashioned stillness in the city, tucked-away behind the cathedral and especially quiet at this hour of the night. You turned in through a gated opening half-hidden from the main road and seemed to enter an older, gentler, and more tranquil world. The lane was narrow and tree-lined. It wasn't maintained by the city but by the residents, who mostly left it alone.

She gave it a minute before producing her key and letting herself in.

"Dad?"

Now she stood in the hallway, and waited for an answer that didn't come. She set her overnight bag down on the floor. There was light somewhere upstairs but none down here at all, apart from the watery street lighting that shone in through the windows.

Miranda started to ascend, calling to her father as she went.

There was apprehension in her, but she wouldn't acknowledge it. She'd come here to establish that nothing was wrong. Not to flirt with dread. Dread's day would come regardless, she'd learned. Why spoil other days by anticipating it?

The next floor was also dark. The light came from the one above, where her old room had been. She stood on the landing and looked up the stairs.

"Dad?"

Something moved in the darkness behind her.

She spun around. In the space of an instant, she felt her heart rate spike and a cold shockwave pass through her. It seemed to take the breath from her body while lifting every fine hair on her skin.

"God Almighty," Alan Hood said, no less taken aback.

He was a pale and insubstantial shape in the darkness, but as he moved forward into the light, she could see him better. He had some sort of technical device in his hand that he glanced at and then shoved into his pocket.

"Where did *you* appear from?" he said. "You frightened the life out of me."

"I let myself in," Miranda said. "What was I supposed to do? You didn't answer when I rang the bell, and that was after I'd been trying all night to phone."

"Well, why not just call me tomorrow?"

"Well, why do you *think*?"

It came out a little more stridently than she'd intended, but it gave him an accurate snapshot of her mood. What could he expect? That she shouldn't worry? Her father lived alone in this enormous empty house, and she lived a hundred miles away.

He ran a hand through his uncombed hair and glanced all around him, in an attitude that was somewhere between distraction and embarrassment.

"I suppose I can see what you mean," he said, and then, "Why don't we go downstairs?"

She couldn't help looking at him critically as he moved past her. His clothes were clean, but didn't match and looked as if they'd been slept in. He was turned out the way a man might dress for gardening.

As she followed him down, the thought in her head was both an uninvited and an unwelcome one. *He's doing his best, but he's looking old.*

He apologised for the state of the kitchen, as well he might.

"I'm due a tidy up," he explained.

Miranda looked through towers of pans and dishes at the phone extension on the wall. This was the message phone. No wonder there'd been no answer when she'd called.

"Why's it unplugged?" she said.

Her father had to move some of the dirty stuff in the sink just to get the kettle underneath the tap.

"I was working on something," he told her as it filled. "I needed to concentrate."

If he'd disconnected the bedroom phones as well, her attempts to raise him must have rung out unheard in the basement.

There were no clean mugs, but he rinsed a couple and set them on the kitchen table. As he was pulling out a chair, she said to him, "Your head of department called me. He got my number from your doctor. He wanted to talk about something."

He looked at her in puzzlement as he sat. "What, exactly?"

"He didn't say. Just left me a message."

"And you couldn't leave it until the morning?"

"No."

"You didn't have to race over. Everything's fine."

"It doesn't look it," she said, and waited.

He looked around and past her, anywhere but at her. He clearly didn't have a ready or an easy answer to her concern.

"I don't know how to say this," he said. "Which is why I haven't tried. But since you've come all this way and you're obviously worried, I'd better tell you. I've been aware of your mother."

"That's no surprise," she said. "There can't be a thing in this house that doesn't remind you of her."

"More than that."

His gaze was on her and steady now, and she didn't like the way it was making her feel.

"What are you saying?"

"It's a perception thing," he said. "You want the science of it? There's no obvious cause but there can be a definite physical effect. The temperature falls. The electromagnetic potential at a given point changes. I can measure it. I'm not about to start believing in ghosts," he added quickly. "But maybe this is what makes people fall for the idea."

"Ghosts? Jesus, Dad . . ."

"That's exactly my point."

"So being you, of course you've got to study it."

"I can't dismiss any of it, can I?" he said. "It's firsthand experience. The alternative is to pretend it didn't happen. How professional would *that* be?"

What she really wanted was for him to stop right there, to change the subject, or even better, to tell her that he wasn't really being serious.

Anything that meant she wouldn't have to deal with this.

She said, "What form does the awareness take?"

"Mental certainty," he said. "For no apparent reason. Nothing seen, nothing heard, I just know she's there. While I fully accept that she isn't."

"All the time?"

"No."

"Okay. Right."

There was an awkward silence.

"So how's everything at your end?" he said.

PAUSING ON THE way to collect some bedding from the half-landing cupboard, Miranda trudged up the stairs that had once been so familiar to her. Most of her childhood and all of her teenaged years had been spent in this house. She'd never imagined there could be a day when it wouldn't feel like home. But the day had come nonetheless.

The suite of attic rooms had been her exclusive territory. The Independent Republic of Miranda. They'd redecorated the one room she'd painted black, but otherwise they'd left everything pretty much as it was. Now she saw cables on the upper landing and boxes in some of the rooms. They were like the boxes that computers came in.

So what was the purpose of all this? When she elbowed open the door to her old bedroom, a sudden flash half-blinded her and she almost dropped the linen right there.

On a tripod in the middle of the room, a Polaroid camera spat out a print.

"Oh, for fuck's *sake*!" she said, and when she'd tossed the linen onto the bed, she lifted the entire apparatus, tripod and all, and shoved it out onto the landing. There were microphones in the corners of the room, and they followed the camera along with their cables.

Lying in her old bed, in her underpants because she'd forgotten to bring nightwear, too exhausted to stay awake, too upset to go to sleep, her mind wandered a little and then settled into its well-worn small-hours track. The one she never chose, but couldn't avoid.

Just like tonight, for her it had started with a phone call. She'd made the same long drive, although she remembered nothing of it. At the hospital she'd found her father waiting, rudderless and dazed; Miranda had more or less had to take over, talking to the medical staff and then repeating their words for her father, who wasn't listening. She was, she realized, playing a part in a sad and sorry spectacle. The great Doctor Hood, major figure of international science, one-time Nobel co-nominee, the Northern Hemisphere's leading authority on dark matter, rendered almost childlike by personal disaster.

He'd discovered his wife at the bottom of the stairs, where she'd been lying for some time. But it wasn't a simple matter of a fall. For a week or more, she'd been suffering from persistent headaches and had been sleeping for as many as twenty hours out of the twenty-four. The best guess was that she'd woken alone in the house and been unsteady or disoriented. Further investigation showed an unsuspected brain tumor that had already grown to inoperable size.

Over the next few weeks, they moved her from ward to ward and tried different combinations of drugs to reduce the cerebral swelling and raise her from the coma she'd fallen into. It had worked for a few days, and for a while they'd had her back, lucid and aware even though her thinking had been a little strange. But then she'd relapsed and died. It had been a rapid decline, but at the time, it had seemed to take forever.

Now this. With her mother gone, her father was falling apart. It didn't seem fair. So much that she'd always taken for granted was no longer there. Much of the pain she felt was that of a lifetime's support system being kicked away. When she tried to explain it to Dan, his idea of sympathy was to match her troubles with competing ones of his own.

She'd been pressed into membership of a melancholy club where the options were limited. One either died young, or eventually one joined it.

Like it or not, she was the grownup now.

SHE WAS FIRST downstairs the next morning. The day was a bright one. After loading the dishwasher and switching it on, she went into the basement and did the same with the laundry.

He hadn't quite been letting himself go. Most of his clothes were clean, and had been hung to dry on fold-out racks. Miranda suspected that they'd probably stay there until he came to wear them, skipping the need for an iron to press them with or a closet to put them in.

The mail arrived, and she went back up to get it. Her father appeared then, bleary and tousled, in a paisley bathrobe knotted over mismatched pajamas. He followed her into the kitchen.

"This place is a mess," she told him.

"I know."

"Then why don't you do something about it? Where's Mrs. Llewellyn?"

He settled back into the place where he'd been sitting the night before.

"I let her go," he said.

"Why?" Miranda said. "You've had her for years."

"She kept offering to stay late and cook me a meal. And I don't think that feeding was all she had in mind. You know what I mean? I'm not up for that."

"If I mark up the Yellow Pages for you, will you promise to sort out a replacement?"

"Yes, miss."

"I'm serious, Dad. It's such a big place. You don't want it turning into a sty. Once it gets past a certain point, you'll be like one of these old guys the council sends a hit squad to fumigate."

"Thanks very much."

"You know what I mean."

"When I'm done with the observations I'm making, then I'll get a housekeeper in. I don't want someone fussing around and messing up the data."

Miranda set coffee in front of him while he looked through the day's letters. He glanced at each and then laid them aside without opening any.

She waited until he'd gone for a shower before letting herself out of the house and heading over to the university.

THE PHYSICS BLOCK was way out at the back end of the campus, the last major building before the playing fields and the sports center. It had won architectural prizes in the seventies and was hideous beyond belief.

Duncan Dalby was neither as senior nor as well-qualified as Miranda's father, but even Doctor Hood would have to agree that Dalby was a better choice for department head. He might have been a mediocre scientist, but he was a born administrator.

Informed of her presence, Dalby came out of a budget meeting to see her.

"Do you have any influence with your father?" he said.

"Why?" she said.

"Because, to be frank with you, he's giving me problems I can't handle."

"So you're asking me, can I tell him what to do? You're talking about the infamous Doctor Hood."

"Thanks to whom we've got a physics department that's on a par with the best in Europe. But for how long? Someone needs to make him aware of what will happen if his behavior doesn't change. I can't get through to him. I was hoping that you might. The only times he ever makes an appearance, it's to help himself to equipment that he doesn't account for. He's done no teaching. He's got five postgraduate students who've been getting no supervision. Our participation in the Dark Matter Project has fallen through and I can't pin him down to discuss it."

The Dark Matter Project was an EU-funded venture to build a specialized particle detector at the Bern underground laboratory in Switzerland. Alan Hood had been one of its most active lobbyists, and had been an obvious choice to chair the project's governing committee.

"Look," Dalby said, "I know he's had a tough time. But it's been nearly a year."

"He isn't losing his mind," Miranda said. "He's coping."

"Not professionally, he isn't."

"I'll talk to him," she said. "I'll see what I can do."

Five people were waiting for her in the building's smart but drafty foyer. Three young men, two young women. They were all older than the average undergraduate, but not by much. Their spokesman looked as if he was at least part Chinese.

"Are you Miranda Hood?" he said.

She was wary. "Yes?"

"Can we speak to you?" he said. "We're your father's research students." They all went over to the Union bar. The lunchtime rush hadn't started yet and they had their pick of the circular tables. One of the researchers brought teas and coffees from a machine on the counter, where you fed it a plastic sachet and it peed you a drink.

The part-Chinese boy's name was Peter Lee. He told her, "We're all just marking time with our own research. Duncan Dalby wants us to inventory everything in the labs for a full picture of what's gone missing."

"We daren't tell him exactly what's involved," added a young woman named Kelly. "There's a thermal imager alone gone missing that's worth fifty thousand. Have you any idea what he's doing with it all?"

"If I were a scientist," Miranda said, "I might be able to tell you. As it is . . ."

She was hesitating because her natural instinct was to defend her father, but she couldn't come up with any account of his activities that didn't put him in a bad light. Poor old Doctor Hood. Poor old man. Those whom the gods would destroy, they first soften up with a whiff of the occult.

She was still hesitating when the time alarm on her phone went off.

"Oh, shit," she said as something dawned on her.

Peter Lee made a polite face. "Something wrong?"

"Can you excuse me for a second?"

She left them talking amongst themselves and moved to an empty table, where she took out her organizer and ran through her schedule for the rest of that day. Miranda made her living as a private singing teacher, mostly coaching teenaged sopranos through the ABRSM grades. She wasn't going to make it back in time to take any of her lessons, it was as simple as that. She'd have to be on the road within the hour, and that clearly wasn't going to happen.

By the time she'd finished making calls and leaving messages, the bar was filling up. Of the physics department party, only Peter Lee was left.

"Sorry," Miranda said as she rejoined him, and he shrugged and smiled as if to say, not that it didn't matter, more that it did and he'd be lying if he pretended otherwise.

Miranda said, "What's the chance of getting a list of the missing gear?"

"Tricky," he said. "Nobody knows exactly what's gone. We've spent many an hour trying to work out what he might be using it for. Why?"

She was thinking of the cardboard cartons up in the attic. She'd peeked into some of them, and they hadn't even been unpacked. "Maybe we can get some of it back to where it came from."

"The gear's not really the main issue for us. It's more about the academic ground we're losing."

"But it's a place to start."

SHE WALKED OUTSIDE for a while, wondering what best to do. She was hardly up to this. She felt like a person charged with stopping a rock slide, armed only with a couple of sticks and a handkerchief.

When she finally got back to the house, the day was all but over and there was a note waiting for her on the door.

Experiment in progress, it read. *Enter via back door.*

In no mood to be messed around, she used her key and walked straight in.

The first thing that she noticed was a deep bass *wub-wub-wub* sound permeating the entire building and pitched so deep that she mainly felt it through the soles of her feet and in the pit of her stomach. The neighbors were probably watching their furniture walking around on its own and asking themselves what the hell was happening. As Miranda moved toward the foot of the stairs, there was another flash, just like the one she'd experienced the night before, but this time from a different camera. This one had a motor drive. It was aimed at the spot where her mother had fallen.

The throbbing noise stopped abruptly. She could hear him heading down. She didn't wait, but went up the stairs to meet him.

"Didn't you see the note?" he called out.

"Yes," she shot back, "I saw the note. You want to carry on like Professor Branestawm, fine. Just don't expect me to pretend this is normal and play along with you."

They met up on the middle landing, where there now stood a loudspeaker that wouldn't have been out of place at a Grateful Dead concert.

"What do you mean?" he said.

She looked at the speaker, and wondered how he'd managed to get it up the stairs without help. Her mental picture of his struggle didn't help his case.

"I'm not going to humor you in this," she said. "You are seriously making an idiot of yourself while your students' careers are going down the toilet."

"What have *they* got to do with anything?"

"Given the consideration you've shown them, nothing! That's my point!"

"Who've you been talking to?"

She took a deep breath and steadied herself and then she said, "I can imagine what it's like for you. It almost made sense when you explained it to me last night. But to everyone else, you're coming over as a . . . a . . ."

"A nutcase?" he suggested.

It was as good a word as any, and more polite than most of the ones she'd been thinking of.

"They're making plans, Dad," she said. "Everything you spent your life putting together, you're losing it all."

To her irritation, right at that moment her phone timer went off again. Or did it? As she pulled her phone out, her father searched around and produced an identical one of his own.

"It's mine," he said, killing the beeper. "I have to be somewhere." He slid past her without touching her and started to make his way down the stairs.

"That's right," she called after him in exasperation. "Walk away."

From down at the rack in the hallway, shrugging into his big overcoat, he looked back up at her and said, "Walk with me, then."

WHAT HAD ONCE been a densely settled part of town was now a wasteland. Some of the old pubs had been left standing, only to turn rough and then die in their isolation. Now they stood amidst blown litter and weeds, bereft, boarded and vandalized.

Hood said, "Your grandfather used to look at the houses and say he could remember when all this was fields. I wonder what he'd say now."

Miranda walked on with her head down, and didn't respond.

Without changing his tone, her father said, "I do know what you're thinking. The simple fact of it is that I can't deal with anything if I don't deal with this."

"Can't you deal with it outside office hours?"

"If it's any consolation, I find it all as ridiculous as you do. I'd love just to nail it and get back to normal."

Not quite everything had been razed. A post box here, an old church up ahead. Miranda was taking her father's words on board when she realized that not only was the old church not deserted, but it was their destination.

Some cars stood on the street. Bodies were getting out of them and one or two elderly-looking people were already going into the building. One of them waved, briefly.

Her father raised a hand in acknowledgment.

Miranda's heart sank.

On the pavement outside the door, as her father was making his way in, she stood and looked up at the hand-lettered board above the entranceway.

It had been nailed over the original church sign. It was in Gothic script, painted by a nonprofessional with only an approximate idea of what Gothic script ought to look like.

It read LANE ENDS SPRITULIST CHURCH and underneath, in smaller letters, *Healing, Open Evenings and Sunday Services.*

Someone behind her said, "Don't be shy!" and a batty-looking woman just inside the doorway called out, "You must be Miranda! Come in! Come in!"

And before she knew it, she'd been swept inside.

The building was in bad shape but it was still recognizably a church, albeit a peeling and crumbling one. The congregation numbered about thirty, and Miranda was the youngest amongst them. Everyone was in a group at the end of the nave, chatting enthusiastically. The woman who'd greeted her by name made something of a fuss of her and offered to take her coat, urging her to have a seat by one of the pillars with a radiator.

"They're the most popular spots," she explained. "They always go first." The woman was wearing a blue cardigan and had a lazy eye. Miranda had to make an effort not to glance back over her shoulder to see who she was talking to.

Her father was a few yards away, in the middle of the group. It was obvious that he was some kind of a regular here. As soon as she could, Miranda disengaged herself and moved to his side.

"I'm not staying," she said in a low voice when she had his attention. "I'll see you back at the house."

"Don't leave now," he said. "You might learn something."

"*Dad . . .*" she said, but was unable to continue as an excited murmur rose up at the appearance of a late arrival. He was standing in the doorway, and a couple of senior members of the congregation broke away to greet him. He was one of the worst-dressed men that Miranda had ever seen.

"That'll be Doctor Arthur Anderson," her father murmured to her. "He's come over from Leeds."

Anderson was a shrunken-looking homunculus in a brown-checked suit that looked as if it had once been put through the wash with him inside it. The points of his waistcoat were curling up even more than the tips of his shirt collar. With this costume and his wispy mustache and a chin that almost vanished into his neck, he'd have passed for Ratty in a low-rent theatrical production of *The Wind in the Willows*. He was declining a cup of tea, rubbing his hands together, expressing a wish to be getting on with it.

"Doctor of what?" Miranda said.

Her father mimed clicking a mouse. It was an old family joke. Click "Print" to download your diploma.

Miranda realized with an even further sinking heart that she'd left it too late to escape, because the street doors had been closed and everyone was moving to the pews to be seated. As predicted, the seats around the radiators filled up first.

Her father ushered her to a side bench. From here they could observe while sitting some way apart from the others.

"It's a clairvoyance evening," he said as the babble was quietening down. "They have them every now and again to raise funds."

She was still eyeing the exit as the service began, but one of the elderly men had set a chair beside it. Someone started to sing an unaccompanied hymn and after a bar or so, thirty reedy voices all joined in. It wasn't any tune that she knew.

Then Doctor Arthur Anderson, the man in the flood-salvage suit, took the floor and began to speak. He didn't use the pulpit, and he didn't use notes. This was clearly a speech that he'd made many times on similar occasions.

He said, "The spirits are all around us, they say. Well, it's true. And I know that because when the moment's right and the will is there, I can see them as plainly as I can see you. And people say to me, Arthur, they say, you've described them to me just as they were in life, but how does that work? How come Uncle Bert's still got his glass eye on the other side? How come Mum's still in her favorite cardigan, did that pass over, too? Because I thought we gave it to Oxfam. And what I say to them is this. I don't know. Because I don't. I just see what I see."

He paused for a moment and looked aside at the floor, as if to gather his thoughts, and then he went on. "Do I see the spirits? I believe I do, but I don't *know* that I do. It's a much-abused word, is spirit. We can't hear it without thinking of ghosts and spooks. The whole point of a spirit is, it isn't a thing. It's the essence of something without the form it comes in. But that's a bit deep for most of us, which is why we can't think of God the Father without making him into an old man. And in the same way, we can't think of the dead without making them into the people we knew. So what I think happens is, the spirits decide, I think I'll go and talk to old Arthur. And what Arthur's going to see will be something that looks like the form that spirit left behind, because poor Arthur's only human and his mind needs something to fasten onto."

Miranda cast another look in the direction of the exit, where the elderly man on the chair was nodding in agreement.

"Daisy," the visiting speaker said with a sudden change of tone. "Who's Daisy? Whoever you are, it's not your real name, it's your nickname, I know. I know you're here somewhere, put your hand up, love."

Nothing happened for a few moments but then, almost masked to Miranda by one of the church pillars, a tentative hand was raised.

"Someone used to call you Daisy, didn't he?" Anderson said. "And it's a name you've not heard for a long time. We're talking about someone who's passed over."

Miranda couldn't quite hear the response but it sounded like, "My brother." She tried to lean out a little way to see more, but it didn't help.

She knew how these things worked. He'd start fishing now, building on the woman's responses, shaking plausible-sounding information out of the tiny cues she'd be giving him.

"Just a minute, love . . ." Anderson said, and then he turned and spoke to the empty air beside him. Spoke to it as if there was a person standing there.

And Miranda thought, *Oh, come on.*

She thought, *They may be old and they may be credulous, but don't treat them as if they're stupid.*

"What are you telling me?" Anderson was asking the air. "It wasn't just Daisy, it was Daisy May?" He turned his attention back to the woman in the audience. "Is that right?"

"I had an Auntie May," the woman said, her voice barely audible even though she'd raised it.

"*That's* what he's trying to tell you," Anderson said with the triumph of a hard-won discovery. "That's who he's bringing the message from."

The message was something about the fears surrounding a medical procedure. The drift of it was that all would be well in the end. He went on like this, working his way through the audience, picking people out and talking to the spirits that he insisted were at their shoulders, sometimes bantering or making a friendly argument out of his dialogue with the invisibles.

It was fascinating, in its way. Even though she found it ludicrous, Miranda didn't move or try to escape. She didn't want to do anything that might draw the speaker's attention. She sat tight, like someone scared of making an erroneous bid at an auction.

When she caught a movement from the corner of her eye, she looked and saw that her father was studying the handheld device that he'd been using the previous night. It was about the size of a TV remote and showed its information on a liquid crystal screen. He was holding it low, so it would be concealed from the—what could she call them? Congregation? Audience?—by the empty bench in front.

It didn't end until more than two hours later. Anderson had talked himself hoarse, but looked as if he was game to go on indefinitely. The man who'd introduced him moved a vote of thanks, and everyone applauded. Miranda joined in, enthused by the prospect of unpeeling her rear end from the woodwork. After the time she'd spent seated, it was as if she had nothing beneath her but thin flesh pinned to the bench by the pointed ends of her pelvic bones.

There was a bucket collection for the roof fund, and then there was an announcement of a small spread in the vestry, consisting of tea and packet cakes and buttered malt bread.

"I'm not staying," Miranda warned her father.

"Neither am I," he said. "Just give me one minute."

She was assuming that her father wanted to talk to the speaker, but Hood ignored him and exchanged words with some of the others. They crowded around him, all but neglecting their guest. One woman had brought along a magazine that she produced and now pressed on him.

"I saved this for you, Doctor Hood," Miranda heard her say.

"*Did* you, Mrs. Lord?" Hood said. "Thank you."

"They've got a psychic's page where people write in. One of the letters is just like the experience you told us about."

"I shall read it. Thank you."

And even though Miranda was trying her best to find it all too ridiculous for words, she couldn't help feeling a twinge of envy at the genuine warmth that surrounded her father in this unlikely place.

He'd promised her a minute. They were out in just under twenty.

They walked some of the way home in silence. But then Miranda couldn't help herself.

"Please don't tell me you were taken in by any of that," she said.

"Not the slightest danger," he told her. "Don't worry."

"He was a total fraud."

"Ah," Hood said. "You can be wrong without being a fraud. Just as you can be sincere without being right."

"What were you measuring?"

He showed her the instrument. "It's called a tri-field natural EM meter. They were developed to measure the activity in electromagnetic storms. Ghosthunters use them."

"And what did you pick up tonight?"

"Nothing at all."

The main road was ahead. There were no cars to be seen, but the traffic lights changed and then changed back.

As they crossed, Miranda said, "They treated you like one of the family."

"I'm their pet skeptic," her father said. "They appreciate me. I give them open-minded attention without prejudice."

As they made the turn through the gateway that led into the private lane, she said, "I don't know where I stand with you. One minute I'm convinced you're off your trolley. Then I can see a kind of sense in what you're doing. Then suddenly I'm in the middle of a freak show and I don't know *what* to think."

"Don't think, then," he told her. "Just observe. I'm not going insane, however it looks. You could say that I'm just finding ways of preserving my sanity in the face of pressure. You should leave me to it."

"Don't think I wouldn't, if I could."

"Miranda, my problems are not your problems. I'm bright enough and old enough and ugly enough to sort them out for myself."

"Well," she said, "two out of three isn't bad."

When they got near to the house, she paused in the lane to check on her car. She couldn't remember locking it earlier, but it turned out that she had. Looking up from the vehicle, she saw that her father had gone ahead and was at the top of the house steps with his key already in the door. He seemed to hesitate, and then he pushed the door open and went inside.

It had only been a moment, but in that hesitation she believed that she could read him exactly. It wasn't as if he'd paused in apprehension of what he might find.

It was more as if he was bracing himself for the disappointment of finding nothing.

THE NEXT MORNING, Miranda slept late, but was still up and about before her father. She'd spoken to Dan for half an hour the night before and given him a list of people to call. She could get away with a week's absence, she reckoned. In one week, she'd lose only money. More than a week, and she might begin to lose students. Two canceled lessons in a row might not bother her less committed pupils, but with the more competitive ones, it would start to count against her.

She filled a dish with boiling water to steam her vocal cords, and made a pot of tea with the rest. Then she poured herself a mug without milk and took it into the dining room, ready to run her voice exercises.

She'd always found this room a little bit intimidating. It had a clubby, Edwardian billiards-hall look, dark and high-ceilinged, done out in maroons and greens with dado rails and paneling. A low chandelier hung over the dining table. A hundred or more family pictures hung on the walls.

And there was the piano, of course.

Her mother's upright Bechstein. Her father had offered to let her take it, but where would it go? The most that her own tiny lounge could run to was a Yamaha keyboard stowed off its legs in the space behind the sofa. And besides . . . moving in with Dan had been one of those try-it-and-see decisions, not the whole starry-eyed hog. She suspected that moving in and bringing a piano would have been rather more than their tentative relationship could take.

She raised the lid to play herself a starting note, and was appalled at the thickness of the dust that had been allowed to gather on it. There was more on the lid than on anywhere else, and her fingers left marks where she touched it. The sooner he found a replacement for Mrs. Llewellyn, the better.

Then she frowned. She rubbed her fingers together and felt the texture of the powder that clung to them. Silky. Then she sniffed. Lavender.

Lavender?

It wasn't dust at all. It was talcum powder.

He'd dusted the piano lid with her mother's talc.

For what? Ghost prints?

She felt helpless.

Fortunately, he hadn't dusted the keys as well, possibly out of a scientist's respect for their underlying machinery. She struck a C and began her scales.

Few people had any idea of the sheer physical technique involved in producing vocal sound. After all, they probably reckoned, who taught the birds to sing? She heard plenty who believed that you just stood there and did it, and who stood there and did it down their noses, in whiny fake accents, off-key, off-note, off the beat, and with their voices full of breath and strain.

Miranda's mother had taught her in this very room. She'd coaxed her through the grades and driven her to the festivals. Miranda could remember running up to her father's study to show him her prizes: second, third in the class, the occasional first . . . and always the same reaction. He'd look over his reading glasses and say something along the lines of, *That's very good, Miranda. You'll have to sing something for me later.*

Always later. And somehow he was always occupied elsewhere when she sang.

Miranda sensed that she was not alone.

She became aware of him standing there in the doorway. She didn't have to turn. She saw his reflection move in the glass of the photo frames, broken up and repeated like an image in an insect's eye.

"This is where it happened to me," he said.

She looked at him. He'd drawn a mug of tea from the pot and was there with it in his hand.

"How?" she said.

"The piano lid was open. I tried to pick out a scale. You know how much musical ability I've got. For once, it just came. And I had an overwhelming certainty that I wasn't alone."

"But you didn't actually see her."

"I saw nothing. I'm talking about awareness. Something I realized I had no definition for. Utter conviction without sensory evidence. I took my own pulse, and it was racing for no reason."

Mug in hand, he moved around the room. This side of the house got the worst of the morning light, and was often gloomy. As now.

He said, "I looked for some kind of explanation. Because something here required one. It's said that sometimes you can get a sense of presence or foreboding caused by a low-frequency standing wave from a fan or a vibrating object. But I tested the entire room and found nothing. Or stimulation of a certain part of the brain can induce a sense of formless apprehension, like there's someone standing uncomfortably close to you." He stopped by the enormous fireplace. There was a firescreen in the empty grate, and a basket of dried, dead flowers before it.

He said, "I had an encephalogram check over at the psych department and there's nothing to that, either. All I know . . . is that for a moment, I knew she was here. It happened again a week later, in one of the rooms upstairs. I don't know what triggered it that time. Something did, I'm sure. Something must."

He was behind her now. He leaned past her to reach the dusty piano and started to pick out a scale with one finger.

Five notes into it, he went wrong.

The bad note jarred, and a mood was broken.

"Don't hang around here," he said. "Time's not for wasting. Get on with your life."

She hoped he wouldn't look at her. But of course, he did.

He seemed bewildered. "What did I say?"

But all she could do by way of an answer was to turn away from him and run from the room.

LATER THAT MORNING, she met up with Peter Lee in the university library. He'd told her that with his own work on hold, he was making a little extra money researching old science journals for one of the other professors.

The library was an eighties addition, and such a monolith of a building that it looked as if it ought to have Stalin's picture hanging down the side of it. From there, they walked across the campus to the visitor parking where Miranda had left her car. She'd asked Peter Lee to go to the house with her to see how much of the borrowed equipment could be spirited back to its rightful place. She was hoping that her father would be out when they got there. But he wasn't.

They could hear voices coming from the kitchen. When Miranda went through, she found her father sitting at the kitchen table with a woman that she didn't immediately recognize. Both looked up at her. Peter Lee hung back in the hallway, but Hood spotted him and called him in and then made the introductions.

The woman's name was Yvonne. Yvonne Lord. She was the woman who'd saved a magazine to give to Miranda's father the previous evening.

"Yvonne's been describing her experience for me," Hood explained. "It makes quite a story."

"I'm sure it does," Miranda said.

"Tell it again," he suggested, and at that point he cast a look in Miranda's direction. "We're all open-minded, here," he said. "Aren't we?"

"Well, I don't know what you'll make of it," Yvonne Lord said. "I'm afraid it might sound stupid." She was a broad-shouldered, blonde-rinsed, quite handsome-looking woman of around fifty or fifty-five.

Peter Lee was pulling out a chair and sitting down, so Miranda reluctantly did likewise as the visitor began.

"It's happened to me five times in the past three weeks," she said. "Always when I'm just drifting off to sleep."

Yvonne Lord was a widow. Her husband, much older than she, had been dead for almost three years. Even though she was a believer, she'd had no paranormal experience during most of that time. It was only when she'd had the bedroom redecorated that the apparitions had started.

"I see him in the room with me, over by the wall," she said. It didn't matter whether the light was on or not, she could see him whatever. He seemed to be calling to her but making no sound, reaching for her but making no progress. It was as if he was pulling against something, like a man harnessed to a big sled with weights that he could barely move.

The first couple of times it had happened, she'd been unable to react or speak. The third time, she said his name and believed that he responded by renewing his efforts. It was then that she became aware of other presences. These were much vaguer, and without faces, and they came right out of the wall. These, she realized, were the forces that were holding him back. As she watched, their strength overcame his and they pulled him away. Though he fought them every inch, he eventually vanished, silently screaming, into the new Sanderson vinyl that she'd picked out to match the carpet.

She was doing fine until the screaming part. Then her voice betrayed an unsteadiness that gave Miranda a moment's feeling of guilt.

After that, she fell silent. Doctor Hood, who'd been taking notes, laid down his pen and said, "Is that everything?"

Yvonne Lord nodded.

"Right," Hood said. "Thank you. I think we can dismiss the idea of a poltergeist outbreak, because it has none of the features. And it's not a crisis apparition, because they only happen once, at a time closely related to the moment of death. Which leaves us with a residual or an intelligent haunting."

Peter Lee said, "What's the difference?"

"A residual haunting is just imprinted, usually on a location. Something triggers it and it plays back without variations. There's no life or actual presence involved. An intelligent haunting is more interesting because it implies the existence of life after death. The apparition can vary its behavior and interact with the observer. On what I've heard so far, this could make a claim to fall into either category. Everything depends on whether the apparition was merely following a pattern, or whether it really did alter its actions when you called your husband's name."

Peter Lee looked at the woman. "What do you think, Mrs. Lord?" he said. "Can you say for sure that there was a response involved?"

Yvonne Lord spoke carefully. "I think there's some part of my husband that's still with us," she said. "I think he's aware and in distress. The very thought of that is very hard for me to bear. I'll do whatever it takes to get him out of it."

"Dad . . ." Miranda said then. "There's something I need to ask you. Can we . . . ?"

She left the question hanging, and Hood got to his feet. Leaving the graduate student and Yvonne Lord together, they moved through into the dining room.

Hood got in first, saying, "Where did you meet Peter Lee?"

"He's helping me to sort out the mess you've got into. I bring him home, and what do I find? Tales from the Frigging Crypt in our own frigging kitchen! How embarrassing is that?"

She couldn't help her voice escalating in intensity, but she did manage to keep its volume down. The effect was that she could barely prevent it from turning into an indignant squeak.

"Separate this out," Hood said, dropping his voice and almost matching her tone. "There's what she saw, and what she thought she saw. The distinction between the two is exactly the area I'm interested in."

"Yeah, well give some thought to what *she* might be interested in."

"Oh, for God's *sake*, Miranda!"

"You were quick enough to spot the glad eye from Mrs. Llewellyn when there was no hocus-pocus involved!"

"Do you really not know someone's genuine pain when you see it?"

She wanted to say that the reality of the pain didn't prove the authenticity of its supposed cause, that maybe the mind just cut and shaped its own expression where the distress had no ready form . . . until she realized that she was getting perilously close to quoting the dubious wisdom of Doctor Arthur Anderson, at which point she broke off the argument and went to haul Peter Lee out of the kitchen. He and Yvonne Lord were making polite conversation, but he got to his feet and came at her command.

"We're going out," she called back over her shoulder.

She took Peter Lee to a corner pub a couple of streets away.

"Sorry about that," she said as they walked toward it. "Had to get away. I've heard more intelligent noises coming out of a colostomy bag."

The pub was city-center cod-Victorian in an authentic Victorian shell, open at both ends and filled with a lunchtime business crowd. She managed to catch someone's eye and got herself a pint of Jennings and the grapefruit juice that Peter Lee had asked for.

"Is that all you drink?" she said as she put the glasses down on the half-a-table that he'd managed to bag while she was at the bar.

"In the middle of the day, it is," he said. "Anything stronger puts me to sleep."

"Me too," she said, and knocked back a third of the beer in one go. "God," she said when she'd set the glass down again, "I just don't know what to do with him. All those years, he was like a giant to me. Now it's like . . ."

Whoa. She was beginning to hear how she must be sounding.

"I'm sorry," she said. "You've got your career on the line. You don't want to be hearing my problems."

Peter Lee shrugged. "Sokay," he said.

"What do you make of all that, though? How can an educated person even start to entertain such a notion?"

"Sometimes it takes an educated person to know enough to say, 'I don't know.' "

She looked at him, eyebrows raised. "That's deep," she said, suddenly realizing that thanks to the beer, she was getting the first warning signals from a low-down and dangerous-feeling belch.

Peter Lee started picking the ice out of his grapefruit juice and dropping it into the ashtray.

"I had a strange experience of my own once," he said.

Which he then went on to tell her about.

MIRANDA WOKE UP on the sofa in the ballroom-sized lounge a few hours later, living proof that she and daytime drinking were necessary strangers. Her head felt bad, in the way that fruit goes bad. Soft, rotten, ready to split.

She went up to the bathroom to look for some aspirin. It was a room that she rarely saw when she visited, having a bathroom of her own on the attic level. When she opened the door of the wall cabinet, it was to find all of her mother's toiletries lined up on the shelves. The bottles, the lotions, the perfumed bath cubes that people bought each other as presents but no one ever used. The home-color kit, the highlighting shampoo, the lavender talcum powder.

She knew that most of her mother's clothes were in the wardrobes, still. He'd told her as much. He was waiting until the time felt right to let them go, he said.

She found some soluble aspirin, but nothing to dissolve them in. On her way down to the kitchen, she was vaguely aware that something was different, without immediately being certain of what . . . and then she realized that not only was the enormous speaker gone from the landing, but also the wiring that had hung down the stairwell. All removed. Various cameras and other ghost-busting items appeared to have been stripped out as well.

That brightened her, a little.

In the kitchen, sipping from a clean glass out of the dishwasher, she picked up Yvonne Lord's magazine and leafed through it until she found the page of readers' letters to Rita the Psychic. The first was from a woman whose husband had died and who was now being visited regularly by a pigeon that stood on her bedroom windowsill and tapped at the glass with its beak. Could this be my husband, Rita, the reader wanted to know, returning with a message for me? Yes, replied Psychic Rita, I believe it almost certainly is, which caused Miranda to blow soluble aspirin down her nose.

The phone started ringing then, and she was still choking when she picked up the receiver. It was a real effort just to manage "Hello?"

"You're awake, then," she heard Peter Lee's voice say.

"What makes you think I was asleep?"

"The sounds you were making when I left you at the house."

"Did you move some of the gear back to the lab?"

"We're not at the lab," he said. "Are you fit to drive? There's something going on here that you maybe need to see."

IT WAS A suburban Close of modern houses, none of them more than ten years old. They'd been crammed onto the available land like penguins on a rock. Each had a one-car garage and a driveway and an immaculate Brazilian strip of garden, and the convenience of being able to step straight out of your front door and into your neighbor's face.

The horseshoe-end of the Close had turning space for one car, and there were seven non-resident vehicles in it with their wheels up on the pavement. The biggest of these was a white university service van. There was no mistaking the house Miranda needed; the kids from the department were all over it.

She parked the car as near as she could. Two of them were up ladders, fixing plastic blackout sheeting over the upper-story windows. Down below them she recognized one of the graduate students hooking up a heavy-duty generator cable between the house and the van. Others were stepping over it with boxes, taking care not to trip. Some of the boxes looked familiar.

Miranda followed the students in. No one challenged her. The front door was pinned back, the house opened up to the world as if for surgery. A boy in the hallway was fixing up an array of six Pentax cameras in a framework. She heard her father's voice somewhere upstairs saying, *Check the walls for buried wires. Anything that conducts. Start at the manifestation point and work outward.*

Hard to tell for sure from down here, but it sounded as if he was enjoying his evening.

The stairs were impassible for the moment and so she made her way through the house, looking for someone she might recognize. She found Peter Lee in the glazed conservatory on the back of the building. The invading party had taken over the space, and Peter Lee was setting up a command center here. At this moment, he was down on the floor trying to link up four portable TVs with the outputs of four separate video recorders, which in turn had to be matched with switchable input from somewhere near a dozen cameras.

She stood over him for a while, watching without being noticed, and then to get his attention, said, "When did all this get underway?"

He looked up, squinting with one eye because of the bright tungsten working light behind her shoulder.

"While you were sleeping," he said. "We brought all the gear from the house and a vanload more from the lab." Then he grinned. "Duncan Dalby's going to hit the roof."

"Nobody seems worried."

"It's a ghost-hunt!" he said.

She gave up on Peter Lee and moved back into the main part of the house, where her father was now in the hallway. As soon as he spotted her, he broke off his conversation and said, "Miranda! Don't just stand there, make yourself useful."

Someone bumped past her with a laser printer.

"Doing what?" she said.

"Help Mrs. Lord with the coffee."

As she took a breath to tell him what she thought of that idea, there was an approving chorus of voices from all the rooms around her. So instead of responding, she clamped her lips shut and went through into the kitchen.

By late evening, everything was in place. Video cameras were tested and running. The house had a complete new nervous system and a brain room to drive it. Devices in the upstairs rooms ranged from a state-of-the-art ion cloud detector to an array of cheap motion sensors from the home security section of a DIY store. Spot-temperature observation, infrared profiling, electromagnetic field detection . . . in the midst of directing the installation, Doctor Hood had taken the time to liaise with anxious or indignant neighbors out in the Close. She'd heard him soothe them, reassure them, convince them that the work here was crucial and without any attendant dangers to the surrounding property. . . .

And all without ever once mentioning the "g" word.

Everyone gathered in the sitting room to hear Mrs. Lord tell her story once again and to discuss a strategy for the evening's observations. It had been impossible for Miranda to get a head count before this, because everyone had been constantly on the move and there had been some people who'd turned up with gear, worked for a while, and then hadn't been seen again.

Now she counted nine, including Peter Lee and three of the graduate students she'd met back at the physics department. All listened intently as Yvonne Lord went through the story that Miranda had heard earlier on in the day. Miranda had the worst spot, right at the back of the crowd, almost pushed out into the hallway, trying to see over everybody's heads.

When Yvonne Lord's story was done, Hood sent her upstairs to take a Valium and get herself ready for bed before the cameras went live. Once she was out of earshot, he opened the matter up for discussion.

Someone said, "What if we're looking at something purely psychological?"

"You mean, is it only in her imagination?" Doctor Hood said. "That's entirely possible, but we're not going to start with a conclusion and then cherrypick our evidence to fit. I know that's a bit radical for this profession, but let's give it a try for once. As long as ghosts wear clothes, I'm inclined to be convinced that the psychological is a major element. But let's not be closed to the possibility of the actual existence of some underlying physical trigger here. So-called spirit photographs often show a ball of fog where a live observer sees a human form. That factor alone is of serious interest to me."

Everyone was assigned to a post. Nobody said as much out loud, but Miranda's role was to keep out of the way. Yasmin, the medical technician, went up to attach a pulse monitor to Mrs. Lord, and on returning, gave Doctor Hood the go-ahead to send all the cameras and monitoring equipment live.

Miranda felt herself prickle all over as the ghost house went on-line.

EVERYONE FELL SILENT and tried to settle. There was no way of knowing how long they'd have to wait for something to happen. Maybe nothing would. Maybe their presence would be enough to upset the conditions that had caused the phenomenon. Or maybe ghosts just didn't like a crowd. As far as was possible, they'd confined their wiring and mess to the downstairs rooms and kept the upstairs looking normal. That meant a lot of gear hidden behind furniture, in the loft, and even in the wall cavity.

Under these bizarre conditions, artificially relaxed by the Valium, Yvonne Lord had undertaken to lie in her own bed with a pulse meter taped to one hand and a signaling device adapted from a Playstation joystick in the other, and in that unnatural state to wait for her dead husband to make his nightly appearance.

In a creaky cane chair at the back of the conservatory, Miranda let out a long breath and felt much of her energy following it. Her main view was of the backs of her father and Peter Lee, watching over all the monitors and readouts, observing, tweaking, calibrating, swapping theories in the lowest of low voices.

Looked at from any angle, it was a joke, wasn't it? Spook-hunting was for the oddball, the damaged, the credulous. Bobble-hat people. Not bright kids like these.

And yet . . .

Under more normal academic circumstances, under the tutelage of the world-famous Doctor Hood, these same bright kids would be exercising their intellects in the search for and study of dark matter. And what was dark matter? Miranda was no scientist but she was a scientist's daughter, and knew that her father's regular field of study involved a material of unknown composition that had never been seen, measured, nor even proven to exist, and yet was reckoned to comprise more than ninety percent of the known universe. The strongest argument for its existence was that without it, the heavens would fall. Spiral galaxies would fly apart, and the light from distant stars would bend without reason.

Despite nobody knowing what it was or what it was made of, dark matter had to exist in *some* form, because otherwise certain phenomena lacked any rationale.

Which of course had no parallel in anything that was going on here.

She could hear Yvonne Lord's breathing over an intercom-sized speaker on the main desk. Every now and again, there'd be a rustle of sheets as the woman shifted her position.

Everyone waited, and nothing much happened.

Miranda was looking at Peter Lee.

I had a strange experience of my own once.

He'd been walking home late one night, he'd told her. This had been some years before, when he'd been a second-year student. He'd had a lot on his mind and had only been vaguely aware of a figure walking ahead of him. When he thought about it later, he realized that the figure had been dressed in very old-fashioned garb, gaslight-era clothing, but the fact hadn't struck him as anything remarkable at that moment. All that he'd registered was the presence of a man in front of him, heading in the same direction as himself.

When the man reached the house where Peter Lee was living at the time, he stopped as if to enter. Peter Lee registered this, and took an interest. The gap between them was closing as Peter Lee approached. The man met his eyes, smiled . . . and then walked right through the closed and locked door.

That was it, and that was how he'd told it. His only such experience, ever. The significant element to Peter Lee's mind was not that he'd seen a ghost, but that the ghost had so obviously seen him.

Miranda's father was looking pensive.

"Nothing much happening here," he said. "Let's run some juice through the wall. See if we can start something rolling."

Peter Lee got up and moved out of the conservatory and into the main part of the house. Yasmin the medic, half-hidden by monitor screens, said, "How do you record an observation when your observer's asleep on the job?"

"Already?" Doctor Hood said. "Are you sure?"

"I'm on sound. Her pulse has slowed and she's making z's."

Miranda turned her attention toward the intercom speaker and, yes, she could hear a faint snoring coming out of it as well.

"I don't want her *that* relaxed," Doctor Hood said.

"Does she do Valium every night?" Miranda ventured. "Maybe the whole thing's no more than a recurring dream."

"Ion surge," someone said then, with an edge of excitement that everyone immediately picked up on. Other voices chipped in with further observations, some called through from the adjacent room.

"I'm picking up an EM field by the wall."

"Temperature down two degrees."

Doctor Hood looked at all the TV monitors and switched cameras on a couple of them. Miranda looked over his shoulder and saw the same thing that he did. Nothing. Empty stairs, empty landing, empty bedroom apart from the half-visible figure of Yvonne Lord in one corner of a screen, nothing happening in the boxroom on the other side of the bedroom wall. All in grainy digicam nightshot vision, images magically pulled out of the darkness.

"How closely did that coincide with the voltage?" Hood said.

Peter Lee stuck his head around the door.

"I hadn't started the voltage yet," he said.

"High, high activity," said the boy who'd reported the ion surge. "I've got levels jumping all over the place."

"Sound?"

"Woman in a room breathing," the girl said. "Slow breathing, slow pulse, same as before."

"Is she reacting to anything?"

"Nope."

"Is she even aware?"

"Doesn't look like it. We've got an independent phenomenon. It isn't coming from her."

Then there was a sound that made everybody gasp and jump at the same time as six Pentax cameras fired off all at once, and only inches from the room microphone. The switchblade sound of the shutters was followed by a chorus of motor drives as the film rolls advanced.

On the monitors, there was nothing to see. Yvonne Lord stirred a little.

Responding to movement within the range of their infrared trigger, the reset cameras fired off yet again.

And still, in the room, there was nothing.

Doctor Hood was on his feet. "For God's sake, woman! What do you think we're here for? Wake up and look!"

"Live body on the stairs," somebody said then. "Moving."

There was a whimper from one of the students nearby. A few heads turned in the direction of the hallway. Miranda realized that her fists were bunched up so tight that her nails were hurting her hands. Those all around her were focused on the work they had to do, but she could sense without looking that in this little chintzy house, on its quick-build middle-income suburban dormitory estate, there was a sudden and shared terror in the air. The theoretical had suddenly become all too real.

She glanced at those students she could see from where she was seated. One was flushed, another bloodless, one was actually shaking.

"Moving up or down?" Hood said.

"Up."

Miranda said, "It's Peter Lee."

She'd just spotted him on one of the screens, crossing the upper landing. As he entered the bedroom, he passed from one screen and onto another in a different part of the array. Grayed-out, featureless, and leaving a streaky trail of fading pixels as he moved, on the screens he looked as convincing a ghost as any spirit footage.

"He's compromising the experiment," someone said.

"Quiet, there," Doctor Hood said. "Stick with your observations."

She saw Peter Lee cross the room and crouch by the bed, just his shoulder in shot and nothing visible at the wall where the apparitions were supposed to take place.

"He's talking," the girl on sound reported.

"Put it on the speaker?"

"He's on it," she said. "The mike's barely picking him up. I don't know why. He ought to be coming through loud and clear."

Doctor Hood bent to listen more closely. But most of what Miranda could hear was just loud static hiss with the odd, formless surge of sound pushing up through it without actually breaking into clarity, like bad shortwave after midnight. And on that same soundtrack, the cameras kept firing, winding, firing again . . .

"Whoever's there, he can see them," Hood said.

. . . and still the video monitors showed an all-but-empty view of a suburban bedroom where Peter Lee, seen from above and behind, stood and faced a cleared space before a blank and newly decorated wall.

And yes, he seemed to be talking to someone that the cameras couldn't see.

"The needles are dancing off the scale," someone said, and then, "Oh, my God. I think they're answering him."

And someone else said, "She's waking up."

And then there was a real, honest-to-God, firsthand sound as a muffled cry was heard through the fabric of the house; the awakened Yvonne Lord had sat up in bed and was shouting out her husband's name at the top of her voice.

Scientific discipline finally cracked. Everyone rose to their feet. Someone screamed and it sounded as if someone else in the next room was throwing up. In the turmoil, Doctor Hood pushed his way through the clutter of people and equipment and disappeared into the hallway. Miranda could see him on the monitor then, making his way up the stairs two at a time.

"Temperature up two degrees," called a lone, conscientious voice, but no one else was paying any attention. At least one person was in tears. Everyone was talking at once and somebody was saying, over and over, *I want to go, I want to go. . . .*

Miranda followed her father.

When she reached the upper landing, she could still hear the racket going on downstairs, like a noisy party where the music suddenly stops. No one had tried to come after her.

The room lights were on. They were so bright, they hurt. Yvonne Lord was sitting up and crying uncontrollably, and her father was at the side of the bed with his arm around her shoulders. Peter Lee stood a few feet away, his features drained and shocked-looking, his stance a little unsteady. The cameras were silent now, their rolls of film all used up.

Miranda said, "What did you see?"

Peter Lee said, "It's not what she thinks."

"Did you interact with the manifestation?" Hood said. "Did he answer you?"

"He wasn't aware of me. All he can see is her. He doesn't even know he's died, yet. The others answered for him."

"What others?"

"I don't know who they are. They're trying to help him over." He looked at Yvonne Lord. "But it's her. She probably doesn't even realize it, but in her heart, she can't let him go. She'll keep his spirit entangled here until she does. Which means that every night he'll try to get back to her, and every night they'll have to pull him away. He fights them. Sometimes she sees what's happening. Whether she sees it or not, it still goes on."

Miranda looked at her father. He was still holding Yvonne Lord, rocking her for comfort, but absently. He didn't appear to be listening.

"You'll see nothing on the film," Peter Lee said, and wiped his dry lips with the back of a shaking hand. "It's not like he's haunting her. It's more like *she* won't stop haunting *him*."

SHE DROVE HER father home. He sat beside her in the car and said almost nothing.

Yvonne Lord had gone to relatives, and a couple of the more iron-nerved of the graduate students had made the equipment secure in the house for the night. They'd done it on the condition that all the others wait right outside, and they worked with all the lights on. Angry neighbors tried to make a scene, but nobody would talk to them. The Close was silent now. The vehicles were gone and the house stood empty.

It was well after midnight when they turned into the quiet lane of big houses behind the cathedral. Someone was walking a dog, pausing under a streetlamp down at the far end while the animal stopped to sniff and pee, but that was the only life around.

She followed her father into the house. There was a vague sense of deja vu about the moment, and she knew why.

This was exactly the way that it had felt, coming back to the house from the hospital on the night that her mother had finally died.

She'd always had the guilty feeling that her mother's death had never hit her as hard as it should. She'd rationalized this in various ways, telling herself that she'd channeled her own grief into concern for her father. But she wondered if instead she'd merely used him as a buffer, hiding behind him while he took the full brunt of the hurt.

Just as they'd done that night, he switched on lights and she went to make tea. Little rituals. Little comforts.

As she was swilling out the pot, she heard him in the dining room. She heard the sound of the piano lid being raised and then she heard him playing a halting scale on the keys.

Just a simple one. Do, re, me, fa . . .

And then a wrong note.

He didn't try again. She heard him close the lid and then she heard him going upstairs. Slowly, as if in defeat.

She felt her heart lurch, momentarily overcome with a weight of love mixed with self-pity. He'd always been able to lessen her sorrows just by being there, but she felt that she could offer nothing that would lessen his. And she could no longer pretend or imagine that he'd be there forever. When he was gone for good, who would she hide behind then?

The night beyond the kitchen window was blacker than black. There was a blind, but they never drew it down. Her reflection looked back at her, a creature drawn with a neon wand in liquid crude. The water on the stove made a sound like a jetliner streaming ice vapor from its wings. It was as if all of her senses had edges. This was how she could remember feeling sometimes as a little girl, when she'd stayed up too long and too late but wouldn't admit that she was tired.

A thought crossed her mind, and made her skin prickle.

She went through into the dining room and gently, so as not to announce it with a sound, lifted the lid on the piano. As she settled onto the stool, she inhaled the deep scent of lavender and it was as if she felt her heart flood.

Delicately, walking her hand up the keyboard, she played a chromatic scale. Then triads in various keys. Then a melodic and a harmonic minor. Though she played them softly, they broke the silence like pistol shots. These were the patterns of notes underlying the vocal exercises that her mother had taught her to warm up with. How many times must they have been heard in this room?

Not often, of late. But once, long ago . . .

But nothing.

It wasn't working.

The notes were just notes. They brought no sense of presence. Not beyond anything she might be imagining, anyway. For a moment, she'd thought that it might have been within reach, but already she could feel the magic leaking away.

Until she heard her father's voice upstairs.

They were alone in the house. But that wasn't how it sounded.

She couldn't hear words, just the low rumble of his speech. She held her breath, the better to hear. Held it for so long that she was getting light-headed. Although she couldn't be sure of exactly what was being said, it sounded like some kind of a question, or perhaps an entreaty. Was he on the phone? Could it be something as stupid and obvious as that?

But in the moment that Miranda finally let go of her breath and exhaled, she could almost have sworn that she heard a woman's voice replying.

Her head snapped up and she looked at the ceiling, as if by sheer intensity of will she might be able to look right through it and on into the rooms above. She could have cursed herself for her timing. She listened even harder, but now she heard nothing.

If there had been a response, it had been a brief one. One word, two words, no more. Maybe just an echo in her head. Maybe just the blood pounding in her brain.

She wanted to run upstairs. But her finger was still holding down the last key on the piano. Even though the note had long faded, the action was not yet closed.

Close it, and the moment would be over.

Which it was anyway, as she heard the heavy tread of her father descending the stairs.

SHE FOUND HIM in the kitchen, finishing what she'd started. Steam from the kettle had fogged the kitchen window. His back was to her and as he sensed her, he turned his head to look over his shoulder.

Something was different.

Miranda said, "Was it her?"

He winked at her and smiled, as fathers do at their little girls when life's in order and much as it should be, and returned to his task.

He didn't acknowledge her again.

Back in the dining room, she lowered the lid on the piano. What had originally been an even dusting of talc had become well messed-up. Any apparition that now cared to leave its mark would have to take its chances at passing unseen.

Miranda paused, staring at something she hadn't noticed before. Had her father done this? She was certain it hadn't been her.

Scrawled in the powder, lightly drawn with an idle fingertip, all but faded and blurred, there were two words.

Release me.

Nothing else.

Miranda leaned forward, her face only inches from the lid. She could see every trace, contor, and swirl of the letters, every grain of the powder. The grains on the lacquer like stars in empty space. She took a deep breath, pursed her lips, and blew. Not hard like someone trying to blow out a flame, but gently, steadily, like someone cooling an angry patch of skin.

As she blew, the words faded. After only a few seconds, they were all but gone. And when they really were gone, gone for good, she sat back and felt a peace like nothing she'd ever experienced before.

From the kitchen, she heard her father call her name.

Nothing here was anything that she could explain.

"Coming, Dad," she said.

Knowing that, for this moment at least, all was well.

AFTERWORD

My favorite ghost story . . . doesn't actually have a ghost in it, but H. G. Wells's "The Door in the Wall" is a powerful and universal tale about what it is to be haunted. That unreachable garden of childhood, those lost playmates who still wait for us, somewhere . . . if only we could remember that road we once took, the place where we turned.

DANIEL ABRAHAM is a native of New Mexico, born in Albuquerque in the last months of the 1960s. While he's spent brief periods living on both coasts, he has found himself well suited to the high desert. He graduated from the University of New Mexico with a B.S. in biology (magna cum laude) and was accepted into Phi Beta Kappa, both of which embarrass him slightly. He went on to a brief and soul-destroying career in retail sales before taking a job as technical support at a local ISP.

He has been selling short fiction steadily since 1998 and has appeared in *Asimov's Science Fiction Magazine* and *Realms of Fantasy* as well as several anthologies, including *Vanishing Acts*. This is his first horror story, and was initially named "Henrietta Pfeffernus and the Amicable Divorce" because it seemed a sufficiently perverse title. With Henrietta's reduced presence in the actual writing, the title was shortened. It is also the first story he's sold that he's unlikely to tell his grandmother about. He thinks it might unease her.

AN AMICABLE DIVORCE

DANIEL ABRAHAM

"SOMETHING'S GETTING IN the house," his ex-wife said, her velvet Southern drawl pressed flat by the cell phone. "I don't know what to do."

"How do you mean?"

"Little things keep moving around. Like I went to bed last night and I swear the remote was by the chair where I always put it, but in the morning, it was on the floor."

"Ah."

Claire's voice was soft, conversational, familiar. Ian lay back on the couch, crossing his ankles on one armrest. A headache pressed at the back of his eyes. He called them his Claire headaches and hadn't mentioned them to her. When they hung up, it would go away or else intensify and add nausea to the pain.

"And sometimes at night, I hear scratching, like fingernails on the table."

"Rats?"

"Oh Christ, I hope not. I was thinking that maybe there's a neighborhood cat getting in Henrietta's door."

"Should nail it shut," he said, the absent pronoun shaping it almost as an offer that he might do the work.

"I know. But I keep hoping she'll come home. Whenever I pick up the hammer and nails, I think of her coming back after being locked in a basement somewhere or getting lost and finding her way home like they do in the movies, and then there she'd be, locked out of her own house, just crying and meowing, and what if I didn't hear?"

"It's been three weeks," he said, trying to keep his voice gentle.

"I know," she said. "I just keep hoping."

The fact was that fat, irascible Henrietta hadn't been his cat for months. In her disappearance, her death, something else irreversible had happened, and the time when he had been whole ratcheted one notch farther into the past.

He must have been quiet too long, because Claire spoke again, changing the subject.

"So, how are you? What's happening?"

I want my son back, he thought, *I want my wife back. And everything I touch turns to shit. But hey, thanks for asking.* He swallowed and forced himself to smile, even though she couldn't see it.

"I'm fine," he said. "Work's too busy, but better that than too slow. I can't complain."

"Good. I'm glad to hear that. I'm really glad that, with everything that happened . . . I mean . . . I'm glad this isn't awkward."

"I know what you mean."

"I should probably . . ."

"Same time next week?"

"That'd be great."

"Take care," Ian said, waited the span of two breaths to see whether she would speak again, just the way he had when they had first met and couldn't stand to be apart. The line clicked and went dead. He didn't return the phone to his pocket. The dial pad glowed green, each number like the pupil of an animal looking at him from the dark. He punched out Little Dave's number with his thumb.

"Dave here," Little Dave said instead of hello.

"It's Ian. I need to get drunk."

"Must be Friday."

"Pick me up?"

"Always do. It's my sunny personality. An hour. Be downstairs."

Ian killed the connection. The silence washed in. Sunset pulled out the shadows and reddened anything it touched—the day bleeding out. He could smell the faint pong of his own sweat, and his mouth was sticky and foul. Another week done, another weekend starting.

And Claire. She was probably sitting in the house that had been theirs, watching TV, talking on the phone. He imagined her the way she had been, before the world turned to ashes and shit. Her eyes almost closing when she laughed, the sound of her feet rubbing together when she was on the edge of sleep, the smell of her perfume on the pillows. The loneliness of his little apartment pressed him down.

He still had a picture of the three of them—husband, wife, and child—on his coffee table, though he'd gouged the eyes from Claire's image with a penknife one night when he'd had too much to drink. He was ashamed of the petty vandalism now, but it was his only picture of the three of them, and he couldn't bring himself to get rid of it.

The phone rang, startling him.

"Hello?"

"I thought I told you to be downstairs," Little Dave said.

"Sorry," he said. "On my way."

Downtown glittered with bars and nightclubs, police cars and lowriders, college kids scamming their way past the door with faked I.D.s and pert tits. Little Dave pretended to love it.

"I'm telling you," Little Dave said, smoothing back his thinning hair. "Just like old times."

"Just about."

Little Dave parked on the fourth floor of a structure right by the river, clicked the security club over the steering wheel, and set the alarm while Ian leaned against the retaining wall and looked down into the slow, black water, wider than a highway. They fell into step as they walked toward the stairs and the street.

"You talked to her again, didn't you?"

"Yeah. We're trying to be in contact once a week."

"Ian. Mon ami."

"It's just something we're trying. You feel like Jake's? Shoot some pool?"

Little Dave shrugged agreement. Two blocks down, they turned at the mouth of the alley, and the darkness swallowed them. The door to Jake's was lit by its red neon sign and guarded by a nameless bouncer, large and impassive as a prison, his face and arm scarred by some ancient fire. Inside, a jukebox mindlessly spooled through hits from the Billboard college charts, and lamps squatted over pool tables. Ian considered the cues, looking for the one least bent, while Little Dave got a couple of beers from the bar.

"You should give yourselves more time," Little Dave said.

"Hmm?"

"You and Claire. It's too early to be looking at matching back up."

"We aren't. We talked about that."

"Oh. Talked about it, did you? Well, that just clears it all up then," Little Dave said, sarcasm in his tone. "Come on. I can smell a man on a jones like a fart in a car."

"We're just trying to maintain contact."

"Whatever. All I'm saying is, losing a kid is tough, and she's got to feel kind of responsible for it, you know? You shouldn't push things, man. Take time. Let shit find its own space."

Ian took the bottle of beer from Little Dave's thick-fingered hand and drank. It tasted vile—cheap and bitter. He took another drink.

"We don't talk about that."

"You guys don't talk about Austen?"

"No. I mean you and I don't," Ian said, his voice gone cold. "Rack 'em."

ANOTHER WEEKEND PISSED away, another week started. The Monday-morning office grind was as much an escape from Sunday midnight as Friday night had been from Friday. Only change made breathing bearable; only change gave hope of change, even if the redemptions all failed.

It was just past midnight, Thursday morning by less than an hour, and he was dreaming of Austen—the pale lips, the blood-wet hair, the ragged edge of skin seen side-on again, again, again—when his phone went off. He thrashed in the darkness, the dream still riding him. In the twisted logic of nightmare, he knew that if he reached the phone in time, if he could get to the phone, only Claire's Austen would die, not his.

He could hear *his* boy shrieking in the next room. If he could get the phone . . . The feel of cool, hard plastic in his hand and the glow of the buttons began to undercut the dream. He pressed to accept the call.

"H'lo?" he managed.

"Ian! It's in here," she hissed, her voice so tense and close he could feel her lips brush his ear. "It's been in here. While I was asleep. It got in the *bed*—"

"Claire? What's the matter?"

"I don't know what it is. I thought it was her, I thought it was Henrietta."

Shut the fuck up and tell me what happened. He bit his lip and took a deep breath.

"Claire, sweetie," he said. "I don't know what happened. You need to tell me."

She took three long, ragged breaths. Ian fumbled for the bedside light, suddenly dreading the darkness. The light turned his windows into mirrors, staring blankly back at him.

"I was asleep," Claire said, her voice calmer. "And when I tried to turn over, there was something against my leg. Right where Henrietta used to sleep. You remember?"

Ian rubbed the back of his own knee, recalling the warm, familiar weight of cat.

"Yeah," he said. "I remember."

"There was this noise. I thought it was Henri licking herself. I wasn't awake. When I moved, it got up and jumped off the bed. I heard it. Hearing it land was what woke me up."

"It was probably just a dream."

"It wasn't. In the kitchen. It might be blood, I don't know," she said, and then, "I'm scared."

He hesitated, wanting to ask, hoping but afraid.

"Do you want me to come over?"

"Yes," she said, and her tone made the word sound like *of course* and *please* at the same time.

"Hang tight. I'm on my way."

The drive out to the house took twenty minutes. Pulling into their street, he saw the porch light glowing over his door, the only light burning on the block. A wave of vertigo washed him. To be coming down this street again, to this house, to this woman. It felt unreal, like being in a long nightmare, but on the edge of waking.

Claire opened the door before he could ring the bell. Her housecoat was wearing through at the elbows. Her hair was pulled back, and it seemed more white than blonde. She looked frail.

"Thanks for coming," she said and stood aside. Her voice seemed fuller, richer, softer than he was used to. He'd been hearing it so much through the phone.

"You bet," he said and stepped in.

Nothing had changed. The same pale carpet, the same old sofa where he'd taken naps Sundays after church. The ceiling fan in the living room that still clicked while it sliced the air. Only the smell was wrong. Claire closed the door behind him.

"Back this way," she said and walked toward the kitchen. He resisted the urge to put his hand on her shoulder or her hip. The tacit permissions between husband and wife had been suspended. All that was left was the impulse.

"When I woke up, I went looking. I thought maybe it was Henri."

The kitchen was a mess from the waist down. Above the countertops, everything was fine, clean, normal. Below, at the height a two-year-old or a small animal might reach, it was ruined. White gouges marked where claws dug through the cheap veneer of the cabinet doors. The garbage can was knocked over, old food spilling out of its mouth. A pile of what must have been feces—brown and yellow and white—reeked in the middle of the room. And smeared over all of it were swaths of blood.

Claire stood in the doorway, her arms across her breasts, her lips pressed thin.

"You slept through this?" Ian said, regretting the disbelief in his tone as he heard it. Claire didn't take offense.

"I've been taking pills. Insomnia."

"Oh."

"I went through the house. I didn't see anything at first, but after this . . ."

"There's more?"

"A little here and there. Some blood or a scratch."

Ian squatted at the refrigerator, looking at the smear of blood running across it. Whatever did this had been angry.

"A raccoon?" he suggested.

"There's handprints, though. See? Like right there."

"Raccoons have fingers like that."

"That thick?"

"It's smeared, sweetie. That's all. It probably tore a claw coming through the cat door. Raccoon. Or maybe a badger."

"It felt like a cat," she said. "It felt like Henri."

Ian stood and brushed his palms together, though he hadn't touched anything. His reflection in the window above the sink looked calm, competent, sane. Like someone she could rely on when she needed him, someone she could trust.

"You're working on your own wild kingdom, sweet," he said, dismissing the mess lightly to reassure her. "That's all. Are there still those boards out back? I'll just nail that cat door shut."

"I'll get you a hammer and some nails."

"I know where they are."

Claire managed a rueful smile—*of course you would*—and started straightening the damaged kitchen. The backyard was night-dark. Out of her sight, a sense of unease pricked at him. He kept looking for the glow of animal eyes in the blackness beyond the circle of light around the door. Nothing appeared.

He found the boards—old lengths of weathered two-by-fours that he'd always meant to oil and use to build forms for her flower garden. The wood was rotting a little, splintering. He started the nails first, then propped the back door open and braced it. The white-plastic cat door set in the wood was marked gray where Henri's back had brushed against it over the course of years.

He lay a board across it diagonally and drove the nail home. Each blow sounded like a pistol shot in the still night, and the door bounced at each shock. What should have taken four blows took eight. He secured the other end and then took another board to the inside face, laying it in the other diagonal in an X.

Claire stood in the doorway, blocking his light. Backlit, her housecoat was almost transparent, and the familiar lines of her thighs hurt a little to look at.

"You'll want to be careful. I don't want to bend the nails down—it'll make them hard to take out. There'll be some sharp points sticking out."

"She's really gone, then, isn't she?" Claire said.

"It's been a long time."

"I know. You remember when we got her? She was tiny. Hardly even weaned."

"Yeah. She used to climb up on the bed and try to suck my earlobes."

Claire laughed and leaned against the doorway, looking out past him at the darkness. He started the last nail, but found himself striking more softly, drawing out the task for those few extra seconds. Claire scratched absently under her right breast. Ian felt his cock start to shift and harden, and he turned back to the job.

"She was such a good kitty," Claire said. "I mean, she was always so . . . I don't know."

"Yeah. She was."

"What do you think happened to her?"

"Probably got a better offer at some other house," he said, hoping she could believe it and knowing she wouldn't.

She was weeping now. No sobs shook her, but her tears flowed down her cheeks, and her eyes reddened. Ian put down the hammer and reached out, his fingers touching her bare foot. She looked down, a pained half-smile thin on her lips.

"I hate this," she said. "I think of my kitty dead in a gutter someplace, and I hate the whole fucking world."

She's talking about Austen, he thought, and felt his own sorrow rise to meet hers. He unblocked the door, stood and folded her into his arms. She pressed her head against his breast and pulled him in, letting the door swing closed behind them. In the silence of the kitchen, he stroked her hair, her shoulder, her back, while she cried, her sobs—soft and infrequent—the only sound. Ian felt his breath coming shorter at the smell of her. Her hands slid around him, fingertips pressing against his shoulder blades, her breasts against his ribs. Tears washed his own eyes. His hands shook. When he felt her lips against his neck, kissing him, he caught his breath.

Her mouth moved against him slowly, her hands pulling him close, pressing his cock against the soft flesh of her thigh. He didn't move for fear that he might break the moment.

"Ian," she murmured, her voice low and rich, "don't go home tonight."

I am home, he thought. *Where besides here could ever be home?*

"No," he said. She guided his hand to her breast, slid her fingers down over the cloth of his pants, brushing against his prick. She leaned back to look at him, her face soft, the ravages of years and of all their sorrows washed away by the warmth of lust, or else by some other need so close he couldn't make out a difference.

"Come to bed with me," she said.

"Christ. Yes."

Naked and between his old sheets, between her legs, pressing his cock into her, Ian almost cried. Her gasps, her gaze locked on his and fierce with hunger, her fingernails scoring his back when he came inside her—it felt almost like being saved.

"YOU LOOK LIKE shit," Little Dave said, sliding into the chair across from him. The lunch rush packed the café. The thick scent of searing meat lay over the perfume and sweat smell of too many bodies in not enough space. The din of chewing and conversations, cell phones and laptops, built a white noise and gave them something like solitude.

"Feel perfect," he said.

"You order yet?"

"Yeah. You're having a burger, medium rare, fries and a coke."

"You're cool. So what's the story?"

Ian tried to look innocent, but the corners of his mouth twitched up. Little Dave grinned and nodded, urging him on.

"Talked to Claire last night. I think things are starting to . . . you know . . . improve."

"Really? Fucked up. I mean, I'm glad and all, but who guessed, you know?"

A harried waitress pushed in beside them and dropped plastic baskets of food in front of them, her expression glassy and dislocated.

"Well, its not like things were bad before," Ian said, leaning around the waitress' reach. "In the end, a tragedy like this makes you closer. As bad as it is, it's something we have together."

"She said that?"

"Sort of. And she's lost so much, you know. I went over because Henrietta went missing and the other neighborhood cats were coming in and messing the place up."

"Cats?"

"Or something. And I think being together just kind of woke her up, you know?"

"And what about you?" Little Dave said, gesturing with a french fry.

Ian smiled, shook his head, and bit into the burger. The meat was rarer than he usually liked it—almost bloody.

"What about me?"

"You know. What did she have to say about how you're dealing?"

Ian shrugged, tilted his head like he was hearing something in a language so close to English he could almost divine the meaning.

"The anger, the guilt," Dave said airily. "All that shit."

"Anger and guilt about what?"

Little Dave blinked and his chewing slowed. Ian's food sat abandoned in its cheerful basket.

"What anger and guilt, Dave?"

"Forget about it."

"No, I think I'd like you to explain that comment. You think I blame her for Austen? Well . . . well, I don't, okay? I *don't*. It was an *accident*. The problem is that Claire can't fucking deal with the grief!"

"But you're fine."

"No. I want my family back. But once I get them, yeah, I'll be fine!"

"Them?"

"Her."

"Okay, then. You don't have to yell about it," Little Dave said. He took a bite of his lunch and looked over Ian's shoulder, not making eye contact.

"What?" Ian demanded.

"What 'what'? You say that's the problem, I say okay. It's your fucking life, mon ami. You know better than I do."

The afternoon seemed darker when Ian got back to the office. The normal stresses of the day—the constant ringing of the phones, the angry or demanding e-mails glowering on his computer screen, the buzz of the fluorescent lights, the way his tie chafed the side of his neck—all seemed worse. He told himself he was just tired, that after all, he hadn't gotten much rest last night. The memory of waking up in his bed, Claire naked beside him, made him smile for a moment and forget his growing sense of being picked at.

Stepping into his apartment was a relief. The bulb of the living-room light glowed against the daylight, still burning from the night before. He pulled off his tie and dropped it on the floor, then lowered himself to the couch. His arms felt leaden. He was getting old if one long night left him exhausted. He pulled his legs up, lay back, stretched.

It wasn't, he decided, a bad place. The peeling linoleum in the kitchen, the mildew creeping along the edges of the bathtub, the trashcan filled with empty bottles of beer and whiskey. This wasn't him. This wasn't his home. It was a cell where he served out his sentence. It was temporary, and the fact that it would end—that it had begun to end when Claire had put her lips against him—forgave it. It was almost over. He had to play his cards right, and he'd have his life back soon. He could feel it.

He let his eyes close, let the weight of his body draw him down. He didn't know he'd fallen asleep until his phone rang. The sunlight was warm and low, the night coming up. He wiped his eyes with the back of his hand and pulled the phone out of his pocket.

"Hello?"

A pause, the familiar catch of breath in the back of her throat.

"Ian?"

He closed his eyes and smiled.

"Claire."

"Hi. How are you?"

"A little sleepy. Long night."

"Yes. Well. I was thinking . . . I think we should talk. Face-to-face. I don't want to do this over the phone."

"I think you're right," he said. "I'll be right over."

"I was thinking dinner, actually. I have a table for us at Amanda's Grill in an hour. If you can, I mean. I know it's not much notice, but I was . . ."

"Amanda's is good. I love you, Claire. I've always loved you."

From the pause, he knew he'd shaken her, taken her breath away for a moment.

"I love you, too," she said at last, her voice a whisper.

Amanda's lay against a curve in the river, the patio bent to look over the black water. He'd arrived first and been shown to his seat by a pale woman with seal-dark hair. He'd ordered a vodka-and-tonic, but changed his mind and got coffee. From his seat, he could see the 8th Street bridge, old stonework with downtown traffic flowing above, dark water flowing below, the two streams at an angle to each other, like an X.

The coffee came before Claire did. He was on his second cup before she came walking across the patio toward him with a rueful, exhausted smile.

"Are you late, or was I early?" he asked, and she sat across from him.

"I got halfway here and turned back. Nerve failed."

The dark-haired girl appeared again and took Claire's order. Across the water, Ian made out a couple walking down the riverwalk, hand in hand.

"So," Ian said after the waitress had gone.

"Yeah. You want to start, or do you want me to?"

"No chit-chat?"

"I'm way past chit-chat," she said, and a slow smile played across her lips, the way she looked late at night, trying not to fall asleep even when she was weary to the bone.

"Take it away, then."

She looked out, considering the city, and crossed her legs. After a moment, she sighed.

"I think we made a mistake," she said.

His heart leapt, and the night was glorious, romantic as Paris. The rush of the river could barely cover the sound of angels' wings.

"I do, too," he said. "We were messed up, though. Divorce seemed like the answer."

Bird-quick, she looked over to him, surprise in her eyes melting to sadness in the space of a breath. Ian's heart died.

"Oh," he said.

"Ian? You didn't think this was a reconciliation. Did you?"

"I thought last night . . . Jesus. That didn't mean anything to you, did it?"

"I was lonely and scared." She leaned toward him, her eyes seeking his. Her hands were little fists on the table. "I love you—shit, I even want you—

but not like we were before. I'm confused. I don't know who I am anymore, but I know I'm not her."

"What do you mean *her*. Her who? There's only two of us here."

"I know," she said. "Baby's not making three anymore."

Ian heard the rage, felt it flowing up into him, heating his face.

"That isn't what I meant. Don't you ever fucking joke about that. Don't you fucking dare make a joke about *that*."

"Some nights I'm almost okay," she went on, as if he hadn't spoken. "Some nights all I can do is cry. It feels like too much trouble to breathe. It's like I remember your wife, but she didn't have this many scars. And she had a baby boy."

"This isn't about him!"

"Don't shout."

"This isn't about him," he said in a lower voice. "You've got to let go of that, you've got to get past the grief. *I've* forgiven you. You need to forgive yourself."

"Did you really?" she asked, her tone quiet and bleak. "And what about Austen? You think he forgives me?"

"You need to move on, Claire."

"I am moving on, though. I hate it. But I'm doing it."

Tears welled up in her eyes, but her expression didn't change.

"Claire. Sweetheart. Don't do this. I need you."

Please, this is my life you're fucking with. Please don't do this to me again, he thought. *There's got to be some point when I start to matter.* But he didn't say it, fear-sick of her reply.

"I'm sorry," was all she said.

THE APARTMENT LAUGHED at him. He lay in his bed in the dark, sweating and listened to its amusement. The ticks and creaks of the building made words. What an idiot, mistaking a nostalgia trip for redemption. What a sorry prick for wanting his ex-wife back.

He got up just after midnight and paced from the kitchen through the living room to the front door and back. His whole new, degraded, shitheap life bounded in seven steps. Outside his window, the city glowed and the sky was dark, like the stars had been brought down, screwed into shining over parking lots and needle parks and whore houses.

A false dawn mocked in the east when he finally fell asleep, curled up awkwardly on the couch. He dreamed of Austen, a little boy barely out of diapers. He dreamed of the smile—trusting, open, joyous—and then he dreamed *her* child a hundred deaths. Endless variations of the same story spooled through him, pricked at him, delighted in his pain. And at the end of each scenario, the pale lips, the blood-wet hair, the ragged skin of the wound, and the horror, the insistence that it wasn't his perfect baby who'd died. *His* boy would never do that; *his* boy was *alive*. And from there, back into the dream from the start.

His phone woke him an hour after he should have been at work. He explained to his manager that he was ill, terribly ill, then sat on the couch, head in his hands. The couch had kinked his back, and he was sticky with sweat. He went to the toilet, vomited until his belly ached, and crawled into bed.

In his next dream, he had found a way to move backward in time by fucking Claire. The past was receding, flowing away behind him like a river, but he was between her legs, pumping into her, clawing his way against the black water. Her cunt was loose and rubbery, but he kept pressing himself into her. Henrietta came back, fat and demanding. His wedding ring slid onto his finger. His back ached, and his thighs felt sticky. He reached almost all the way back. He could see the moment, could see his baby—the blood, the wound, the lips—like seeing someone just underwater. Claire's pale fish-flesh shuddered under him.

If he could come, if he could just come, he could get back, he could reach back in time and everything would be right again. Austen would come to life, his wife would never have left, and he could be himself again, a whole man instead of the splintered creature half love, half rage. If he could just get off. He slammed his cock into her, fast and hard, but there was no pleasure in it, only the feeling of being rubbed raw, abraded. He was so close, if he could just *come*.

He woke himself sobbing. Even awake, he wept uncontrollably, smothering his own screams in his pillow, clawing at the sheets, bent double in pain. It seemed to go on for years, but exhaustion took him, and he lay silent, staring at the random pattern of cracks in the ceiling. Sweat sheened his skin, like the aftermath of a broken fever.

His mind felt blank, sandblasted. He got up, went to the bathroom and pissed sitting down, resting his head against the cracked tile of the wall. His legs trembled like he'd been running, and his back still ached from sleeping on the couch.

He wasn't hungry, but habit took him to the kitchen. He fried some bacon, and then, while the fat drained off the crisped meat, some eggs in the grease. A cup of coffee, half an apple that had been in the fridge, the brown surface cut off and the white flesh showing. He sat at his table, eating breakfast and watching the sun go down. Another day pissed away. Another chance for something—anything—good to happen gone, and he could no more get it back than pull the sun up over the western horizon.

He was in the shower when the phone rang, the rushing water almost drowning it out. He killed the water, grabbed a towel and got to the phone by the fourth or fifth ring.

"Hello?"

"Ian?"

Claire's voice was wrong. Even the single word was enough to tell him that, slow but desperate, like she was fighting to speak and only just succeeding.

"Claire? What's the matter?"

"It's . . . in the house. I don't know what . . . it is. I can hear it . . . ripping something."

"Where are you? Are you okay? What's wrong?"

"Pills. Couldn't sleep . . . last night. After we talked. I took three . . . so I could rest. I'm scared, Ian. It's in the house. How did it get in the house?"

In the background, past her pained drawl and the static of the cell phone, he heard something shriek, high and angry.

"Where are you?" he shouted.

"Bedroom."

"Can you shut the door? Claire? Can you shut the bedroom door?"

A long pause, something like rustling in the background.

"No," she said at last, tears in her voice.

"Okay, just stay calm. Stay calm."

"It's *saying* something, Ian. There's words. Please. Please come. I need you."

He thought of her, lying in bed, thought of her bare, familiar flesh and the warm press of her mouth on his. Of her blank stare across the restaurant table as she said it was a mistake. Austen—lips, hair, skin. The dream of pressing himself into her cunt half in anger, half in regret.

There was a silence on the line, then another shriek closer and louder, and then he spoke.

"Claire?"

"Yes," her voice was barely a breath.

"Please don't call me again."

"No, no, no. Ian, please," she whispered, and then, "Oh, *Jesus*."

He thumbed off the phone and pulled on pants, took a shirt from the closet—white button-down—and a good vest. His hair was slicked back wet against his scalp. He stopped to comb it, brushed his teeth. He looked all right. Not young anymore, and not innocent. He was starting to get a tiny patch of gray at the temples. Gravitas, he told himself, and tried smiling. He only looked numb. He wondered whether Claire was screaming yet. Would his boy go for her eyes?

He picked up the phone again and dialed with his thumb.

"Dave here."

"Dave. It's Ian."

"Mon ami! What're you doing?"

"It's Friday. I need to get drunk," he said. The apartment seemed to settle back into itself after the day's sunlight and heat, preparing itself for night.

AFTERWORD

When I was young, my father used to read me stories by Enrique Anderson Imbert. Being fluent in Spanish (which I'm not), he'd translate them on the fly. I still remember one scene where a child watched a wave of nothingness move through his father's eye, and another where a man sunk under the ground reached up to touch the sole of his lover's shoe. It was years before I understood that these were stories about political disappearances in Argentina. For me, they were just ghost stories.

✠

RAMSEY CAMPBELL was born in Liverpool, and still lives on Merseyside with his wife Jenny. He has been described by the *London Times* as "the nearest thing to an heir to M. R. James." He was presented with the World Horror Convention's Grand Master Award and the World Horror Association's Bram Stoker Award for Life Achievement in 1999. His most recent novels are *The Darkest Part of the Woods* and *The Overnight*, and his nonfiction is collected in *Ramsey Campbell, Probably*. An expanded edition of his erotic horror stories, *Scared Stiff* was published in 2002. His forthcoming novel is *Spanked by Nuns*. He asserts that he's had no significant supernatural experiences and has little inclination to believe in them—but he finds the supernatural imaginatively appealing.

FEELING REMAINS

RAMSEY CAMPBELL

I'M WATCHING MRS Hammond's empty house while I try to think of anything interesting about myself to write for my English homework when I see my mother. She's walking down the street with two people in track suits, a woman and a boy. I know my mother says you have to see the spirit inside everyone, but any time there are track suits in our part of town it means trouble. The other night a gang of girls in them kept jumping on the cars in our street, but by the time the police came and my parents finished discussing whose fault it was the girls behaved like that, they'd gone. I hope my mother's showing the people the way out of our suburb, but she holds the front gate open and the boy in roller boots clumps under the rosy arch. I save my homework on the screen and wait till she unlocks the front door and calls "Jeremy, come and say hello."

I go to the top of the stairs. When she gives me her look that says she trusts me not to disappoint her, I have to go down. "Jane and Brad, I told you about Jeremy. He'll be a friend for you, Brad," she says. "Jane's one of my students, Jeremy."

That needn't mean she's an addict like the women my mother brought home from the refuge where she used to work. I thought Brad was bald and my mother would expect me to be sorry about that, but he's only shaved so he'll have even less hair than his mother. Mine is saying "I should take off your boots in the house, Brad. I expect we can find you some old Christmas slippers of Jeremy's."

Brad makes his mouth thinner, but Jane grabs his shoulder when he starts clumping out of the porch into the hall. "Do what Willa tells you. Act like you deserve to be let in a house like this."

"You'll have to pay for new ones if they're nicked," he tells my mother.

"We promise they'll be safe, don't we, Jeremy? We understand if people who haven't been as lucky as us value what they have. Of course you're making your own luck now, Jane, by coming to night class."

"They should have made me stay at school when I was these ones' ages. The advice centre says I should be able to sue the education."

"Will you look after your new friend, Jeremy, while Jane and I work out what schedule's best for her?"

"I was doing my English."

"I'm certain Brad wishes he had homework. You don't want him and Jane to think we've no time for people who need us."

I can't see why they'd think that or feel entitled either. Brad sits on the doormat and yanks his boots off and jumps up to shove past me and sprint upstairs. "Show him your room, Jeremy," my mother says. "Perhaps he can give you some ideas to write."

At least he isn't wearing any shoes. When he's finished using the toilet without shutting the door or flushing he steps in the bath and the bidet and then the shower stall in the guest room. He looks around my parents' room as if he's memorising everything and runs into mine. I knew he'd head for the computer, but he sticks two fingers up at it when he sees there's only writing on the screen. He holds onto my desk to poke his face at the window. "There's the house your mam said some old twat lived in."

"It's where an old lady used to live."

"Where's she now?"

"Gone."

"Where? She live by herself?" Brad says and starts typing on my keyboard. All the words have four letters, and some of them are spelt right. "Leave it alone," I shout, hoping they can hear me downstairs. "That's for school."

"Your mam said you had to let me do some." He rests a thumb on the power button and watches me nearly get to him before he switches the computer off. He dodges me and runs downstairs yelling "He won't tell me about the old woman and he won't let me go on his pee see."

I switch it back on and wait for it to scan the drives. I'd pray if I knew what to pray to. When the screen shows I haven't lost anything I shut down properly, because my mother's calling "Come and talk to us, Jeremy. We don't hide from our guests."

They're in the front room. Mother and Jane are drinking coffee out of Empowered Woman mugs while Brad wanders about picking things up. "You'll break that," Jane keeps saying as if she wants him to prove she's right, and he nearly drops the carving of a goddess my father bought at the African craft shop.

"You're supposed to be paying attention to your guest, Jeremy. You're thirteen and he's not even at secondary school."

"He nearly wrecked my computer."

"Things are only things and we shouldn't get attached to them," my mother says, though she doesn't seem too happy with Brad handling her Muslim pictures on the mantelpiece. "People are what matters. Why wouldn't you tell Brad about Mrs Hammond? I'm sure he'd enjoy hearing how you took care of her."

"He likes to know about people," Jane said. "He never knew his dad before the scum went off and left us."

"Tell Brad how you were Mrs Hammond's little helper after Mr Hammond died."

Suddenly Brad's interested. "How'd he die?"

"Fluid retention," my mother tells Jane as if she's the only one that's listening. "His heart gave up."

"Too much booze, you mean? Sounds like a man."

I'm remembering how Mr Hammond's legs swelled up till they were twice as wide—I used to think they were like balloons and the ankles were knots you could untie to let everything out. "I don't think his wife ever recovered from," my mother stops saying, "it took him most of a year. But you did everything you could for her, didn't you, Jeremy?"

Brad is opening and shutting the doors of an icon as if he hopes it'll change into something better than a Greek saint with gold around his head. "Just you listen, you," Jane says. "This is how you're meant to behave. What did he do, Willa?"

My mother opens her eyes wide at me to make me answer and looks disappointed when I can't. "Shopping and housework and just sitting and talking to her," she says.

That was the worst part—listening to her and feeling how afraid she was. It felt as if all the dimness of her house had crawled inside my head and started filling up my chest as well. Maybe the dark was meant to help her stop seeing herself, but I thought it made things worse. I'm willing my mother not to go on about Mrs Hammond, and surely Jane and Brad have to leave soon, because I can smell dinner, lentils again. But my mother says "Our guests are dining with us, Jeremy, and then I said you'd keep Brad with you while Jane and I go to my class."

"I haven't finished my homework."

"You didn't seem too busy when we came along. You seemed to be concentrating on Mrs Hammond's house."

Maybe Brad will be so rude about dinner she won't want him to stay. He stares at his chunk of her lentil loaf and says he wants a burger. Jane isn't too impressed either when she hears how we never eat anything that injures the rainforest or puts us higher up the food chain than anybody else or with additives in. She tells Brad to be grateful and get on with eating, though she doesn't do too much of that herself. When he won't, my mother makes him a sandwich of the ham my father says he needs for a balanced diet, but Brad hasn't finished his first bite when he starts wanting to watch television and not sit at the table. My mother persuades him to take his plate with him and sends me after him without mine. I'm watching him spill crumbs from his plate and his mouth while he plays with the remote control and keeps asking why we've got no sex channels when my father comes in.

He gives Brad the kind of blink he's started giving anyone my mother brings home, the kind that says he's tired and now he'll be more so. She meets him in the hall and just about puts a kiss on his cheek, as if she doesn't want Jane to see. "Jane, this is Leslie," she says, and tells him "Plenty left for you in the oven. We're off to my class now and the boys are staying here."

"There aren't likely to be ructions, are there? Only I've brought home quite a wodge of work."

"I'm certain you're man enough for everything," she says with a wink at Jane. "Are we ready? The boys can wash up."

"You do what Leslie says since they've let you in their nice house," Jane tells Brad.

"What does Jane stand for?" my mother asks her as they walk arm in arm along the hall.

"I don't stand for anything."

"Darn right, and what does your name stand for?"

"Justice Against Naked Exploitation."

"That's what we need. I got all my students to empower their names," my mother tells my father as she leaves.

I wonder if he's thinking they're all women when he comes to frown at me and Brad at the kitchen sink. The second time Brad drops a plate in it to see how much noise it makes if it won't smash, my father hurries to him. "Please, allow me."

Brad flinches out of the way in case he's touched. "Willa said I could watch your telly."

"Then you must, of course," my father says and helps me finish washing up. By then Brad is turning the sound up and down and changing channels as fast as he can. My father goes in the office, where his desk is smaller than my mother's, but soon he opens the door and calls me. "Do you think you might take your friend along to the play area for a while?"

"I didn't want to stay here anyway," Brad shouts and runs out of the house.

"Go with him, Jeremy," my father says with even more of his usual worried look. "He's our responsibility."

I don't see why he has to be, but if I say I'll get a disappointed lecture and a worse one from my mother. I go after Brad as my father shuts himself in the office. Brad's across the road in Mrs Hammond's front garden. "You can't go in there," I tell him.

"You mean you can't, soft twat," he says and dodges round the back.

There's nothing to be afraid of, I try and think. There never really was for Mrs Hammond, so how can there be for me? I don't want Brad doing anything I'll be blamed for not stopping. I hurry down the path with weeds sticking out of all its cracks into the back garden, where the hedge hides me and Brad from the neighbours. He's trying to see into the kitchen. "Dirty cow, was she?" he says.

He means the way the windows look black with grime, though they aren't. He points at the top of the kitchen window, at a gap big enough for him to put his skinny arm through. "Give us a step up."

"You mustn't go inside."

"Give us one or I'll say your dad kept feeling me and that's why I ran off."

"Nobody'd believe you."

His face squashes itself thinner at me, and then he sees a lawnmower lying on its back in the long grass. He tips it up and drags it to the house and wedges the handle under the windowsill. There's a bar under the handle, and he stands one foot on that. "If I fall through the glass I'll say you pushed me," he says.

I'm almost sure nobody will believe him except maybe Jane, but being so close to Mrs Hammond's house is making me nervous. He levers himself up and grabs the top of the sash and plants his other grubby foot on the windowsill. He wobbles as he shoves his arm through the gap, and I wonder whether he'll say I felt him if I hold onto him. Then he twists the catch and the sash rattles down. He steps over and lands with a clang in the sink and pokes his head out of the window. "What are you going to do now, soft twat?"

There's nothing to be afraid of in there except what he might do. I know that's what I'm most afraid of when he jumps down onto the kitchen floor. "Wait," I plead. "I'll come."

I'm not as used to getting into other people's houses as him. I haul myself up to the sill from the bar of the mower and swing one leg through the window to try and stand in the sink. It's further down than I like, and when I drag my other leg over the sash I nearly lose my balance. I feel as if I'm falling into somewhere deep and dark. I manage to grab hold of the taps, and when I'm steady I shut the window and fix the catch. Brad is staring at the windows painted black inside as high as Mrs Hammond could reach. "Mad old bitch then, was she?" he says.

"Just didn't like seeing herself in anything."

"Mad old bitch," he says as though I agreed with him. He stares at the scratches she made all over the metal sink with a fork, and then I have to chase after him into the hall. He touches the switch for the jangly chandelier and leaves it alone in case people see he's in the house. He scowls at the walls—at the patches that look painted with darkness. "Who got all her pictures?" he says as if it should have been him.

"They weren't pictures, they were mirrors. She took them down."

I remember them lying on their faces on one of her spare beds that was covered with broken glass. Brad's throwing all the doors open. The rooms sound too big and empty, though they've still got furniture that looks fat and sagging out of shape with the dimness the black windows make. "Be a good fire," Brad mutters to himself, but then he runs upstairs.

The bathroom mirrors are smashed in the bath. "Said she was a dirty cow," Brad sniggers, and I can't tell him it was where she was most afraid to see herself. He probably wouldn't listen anyway. He's too busy heading for her room, where I used to hear her begging and praying when I had to let myself into the house with the keys she gave my parents. She wasn't answering the doorbell any more, and she didn't answer when I called up the stairs—maybe she didn't hear me for talking, or maybe she couldn't stop. "That's some sponge that's gone bad," I heard once. "That's a stick with some old rubber round it. That's a claw, I don't know what it belongs to. That's a nasty mask someone's wearing. It's not me. It's not me."

She hadn't smashed the bedroom mirrors then. She'd wedged the wardrobe door open with some shoes to hide the glass on it, and she'd covered up the dressing-table mirror with a dress. Now they're just bare wood that makes me think bits of a coffin have got into the room. "Feels squelchy," Brad says, and I think he's imitating Mrs Hammond somehow till I see he means the carpet under his bare feet. "Nothing worth a turd in here," he complains and runs to push up the painted-over window.

He kneels on the floor and squints through the slit at the backs of the houses across the garden. "Bet they've got stuff we ought to have," he mumbles. As he's getting up he points at the bed. "Is that her?"

I feel as if the dimness is a crawling lump of soot that fills my head. I'm not just afraid to look, I can't even see. Then Brad picks up what he was talking about—Mrs Hammond's photograph album that was shoved under the pillow. A photograph of her being not much older than me falls out and he treads on it while he turns the pages, not caring if he tears them. "It's just her old pictures," I say to make him stop.

I wish I hadn't said it. Surely Mrs Hammond couldn't hear me, but I feel guilty anyway, because it was the album she held onto when she was trying to hide from herself in the bed. "Which one do I look like?" she kept pleading the last time I let myself into the house. "Do I still look like this?" Now Brad picks up the photograph she was talking about and throws it in the album. "Got any matches?" he says.

"I never have any."

"Sad soft twat then, aren't you?" he says and runs downstairs.

I'd leave the album if I didn't think he might come back and use it to set fire to the house. I tuck it under my arm and go after him. When he sidles out of the front door I copy him and shut it so gently it feels as if it's turned into rubber. Brad sneaks out of the gate but waits to mutter "If you say we went in there I'll say you made me go in so you could have a feel of me."

I won't be saying we went in. I'd take Mrs Hammond's album to my room if I didn't have to follow him while he spies on houses. More than once he wants me to keep watch while he prowls into someone's garden or round the back of their house, but I won't do that however many names he calls me. We go through the whole suburb that way in the dark till we come round again to my house.

I let myself in and have to let Brad in as well. I'm glad he goes straight to the television, because it means he doesn't see me putting the album under my bed. I'm hurrying to tell him to turn the television down when mother and Jane come in. "Jane wrote nearly a whole paragraph," my mother tells anyone who's listening, "didn't you, Jane? You'll be wearing a white collar at your factory at this rate, if you even stay. I know you'll do everything you can for your workmates."

Jane doesn't seem to like being talked about so much. "Have you been behaving?" she shouts at Brad over the television. "Get home now and turn that off. You can't take it with you even if it's bigger than ours."

"He hasn't been much trouble, has he, Jeremy?" my father wants me to agree.

"He didn't stop you working."

"Luckier than me, then," Jane tells my father.

Brad switches off the television and sprints to pick his boots up. He's sitting on the doorstep to pull them on when my father says "Excuse me, young man, but could that be our remote control that's slipped into your pocket by mistake?"

"Give it here," Jane yells at Brad, and nearly hits him across the head with it except he ducks. She jabs it at my mother and says "I'm sorry that's all you get for helping."

"You've given me and more importantly yourself a lot more than that."

As Jane drags Brad out of the gate my mother calls "Looking forward to next week."

My father makes a noise like humming a question and says "Bedtime for our youngest member unless he wants to finish his homework."

That's all they say till I'm out of the bathroom and in bed, but the silence feels like my mother getting ready to tramp into the office and start. "So the best you can offer one of my students is calling her child a thief."

"Well, hold on, I don't think we can honestly say I quite—"

"Diet's all that's wrong with him, the kind the multinationals won't be happy until everybody's eating. That and wanting to be a man. Couldn't you and Jeremy deal with him for even a couple of hours? His mother has to all the time."

"I wonder if we saw much evidence that she—"

"There's lots of evidence anybody but a man could see that she's as brave as every one of my mature students. They need to be, not having the gender advantage. They work as hard as I do, but perhaps you don't think that's hard enough."

"Of course I do. I really wish you wouldn't teach at night if it leaves you on edge like this."

"You'd rather we both left all the people we've failed to sink further, would you?"

"I'm not sure you can say it's us who've failed—"

"Our whole class has," my mother cries, and a lot more as well.

When my parents come upstairs at last I still can't sleep. My father says we always have to leave our bedroom windows open at night so the central heating doesn't make us vulnerable to all the germs that are developing or being developed. The gap must be letting a wind in my room, because there's a noise under the bed as if something's got hold of Mrs Hammond's album but can't quite open it. I'm not going to look. I'm almost asleep when I hear the fumbling creep away, and then I am.

In the morning my parents aren't speaking much to each other, more at me instead. I'm almost glad to head for the school I have to go to because everyone else is as deserving of an education as I am and it wouldn't be fair to the others to put all the best children together. I don't think I'm one of them even if my dad does, just one of the few that go in uniform. Shaun's been sniffing glue again and starts dancing on his desk, and Cindy keeps screaming at people because she says they're staring at her, till they do to make her scream. Only those aren't the main reasons I can't do my work properly. Even when the teacher gets Shaun and Cindy taken off to the disruption room I can't stop trying to think what to do with Mrs Hammond's album.

I don't want to hear something moving in my room at night again. I never have before even when there was a wind. There's nowhere to put the album except back where I found it—if my parents see it they'll know I sneaked into Mrs Hammond's house. Only we gave her keys to her son after she died even though he hadn't been visiting her, so how can I get back in? I nearly think of asking Brad, though there are plenty of children at my school who'd be the same kind of help. I'll have to climb up to her bedroom window he left open at the bottom if I can carry the album and a ladder across the road without being seen. Maybe I can climb without a ladder. I'm trying to remember the back of her house as I walk home with the homework half the class never bothers doing. By the time I reach my street I'm sure there's a drainpipe close to her window. But there's no drainpipe—there isn't even a house.

All that's left is a huge lump of black smoke squirming every way as if it wants to dodge the water three fire engines are squirting at it. The house has fallen in with just some bricks of the ground floor and half a window left standing. It looks as if the house has been pulled out of shape by the smoke that's black as tonight will be. I'm watching it and feeling Mrs Hammond's nightmare is holding me there when my parents drive up in my mother's car.

When she climbs out her head goes up as if her open mouth is pulling it till her chin points at where the house was. "How on earth has that managed to happen?" she says as if whoever's responsible is listening, and I do my best not to.

"At least Mrs Hammond's gone, thank heaven," says my father.

"The late owner," my mother tells a fireman. "We did think she might cause a fire when there's so little care for the elderly in their own homes, but do you know what actually happened here?"

"The lady who reported it said some boys were seen going in there recently," the fireman says, rubbing some black onto his forehead with the back of his hand.

"That's the least we can expect when child care for single parents is so inadequate."

He gives her quite a look and says "You'll have to excuse me" as he strides off to his engine. Maybe he doesn't realise that leaves my mother with an argument still to have, or maybe that's what he's avoiding. I watch the smoke trying to stand up as if it's desperate to find the shape the house used to be. When my mother says "Come along, Jeremy, we don't stare" I hurry after her.

All the way through our Indian dinner that's mostly rice so we remember how other people have to eat, I'm afraid someone will ask me if the boys were me and Brad. Instead she talks about her students so hard I can tell my father doesn't dare to mention the children at his school. I wonder if she can't let herself believe I got into Mrs Hammond's house, but I think it's more she won't believe Brad did. As soon as all the dinner's eaten my father says to me "I'll see to the washing up and I should be about your homework."

I can't open my window in case the smoke that's left gets in. It feels as if its dark is trying to—I keep feeling its dark has crept behind me. Whenever I look round there's nothing I haven't always seen except Mrs Hammond's album lying under the bed. I push it further under to make sure my parents won't see it, but when I try and concentrate on my homework I can't help seeing bits of the smoke heaving themselves about and turning into the night. As soon as I've finished my work, which isn't much good, I go to the bathroom again and make myself switch off the light and get in bed.

I seem to wake up more often than I sleep, but I suppose I do some of that as well, because I keep thinking something wants to catch hold of me in the dark. I try to stay close to the side of the bed near the window, but that means the dark is behind me. Before I came to bed I must have pushed Mrs Hammond's album too hard, because in the morning I see a picture of her when she was a few years older than me has come out on the far side. It's crumpled up as if someone tried to get hold of it, and most of its yellow has turned black—it looks as if the blackness is turning her into a shape I'd rather not see. I pinch the photograph between my nails and wriggle it into the album and drop the album in my schoolbag.

I just want the only thing that's left of Mrs Hammond's to go somewhere it'll be safe. I'd ask my parents to give it to her son if I wouldn't have to tell them I was keeping it away from Brad—I'd ask where the son lives if they wouldn't make me tell them why I want to know. I can't eat much breakfast for being afraid they'll see the album before I can leave, and my father has to eat what I don't or my mother would tell us how many people could live on it for a week. I try not to look as if I'm carrying anything I shouldn't in my bag when my mother puts her mouth on my forehead and my father shakes my hand before I can run out of the house.

I wonder if I'll have to keep the album away from people, but the girls and boys who might add it to the litter everybody drops at school are after anyone who doesn't look English because the papers say the country's letting too many asylum seekers in. At lunchtime I go upstairs to the library, where I often hide though there aren't many books I want to read or many I don't either. The librarian who's always blinking and patting her foggy hair as if she's making sure nothing has jumped into it off anyone is at the desk. "Hello, er," she says when I start taking out the album. "Did you enjoy it?"

"It's an old lady's photos I wondered if you'd want to have."

"Oh," she says the way people sigh at babies, "er. Is she your grandma?"

I haven't seen either of my grandmothers for years, because my mother argues with them about everything, which she says means they're victims of their class. "She was just a lady who lived near us," I say.

"And how did it come your way, er?"

"She died. She didn't want anything to happen to it," I say and wonder if that's true—I somehow think it is.

"I don't see it as material for us," the librarian says without even looking inside it. "I expect you should give it to a parent or whoever you live with to look after, er."

"Jeremy," I tell her, but she's at her hair again as if I might have brought her more than a book.

There's a history lesson after lunch, and I try to give the album to the teacher. "That's not the kind of history we teach," he says without looking in it, and lifts his top lip with his bottom one as if he'd like to plug his nose up, "even if any of you little charmers wanted to learn." He oughtn't to mean me, and it's so unfair I don't think about the album for the rest of the afternoon. I don't start feeling nervous till I'm halfway home, but when I let myself in there's another reason. My mother's waiting with something to say and a blank face.

The longer she doesn't say it, the worse I think it's going to be. I'm sure I'm being blamed but I don't know for what. I hide in my room and try to work till my father comes home. At first she only sends him up to tell me dinner's ready. She ladles out her carrot casserole before she dumps herself on her chair. "Well, I hope everyone's satisfied," she says to the ceiling.

"It's quite tasty and filling, thank you, dear."

If I were my father I wouldn't have said that. I can tell she wasn't talking about dinner. She makes us wait for her to say "My student Jane's son has been arrested."

"No great surprise, perhaps. What's the offence?"

"Supposedly he was found in a house up the street, and the couple who live next door to it are claiming he robbed them. I don't know how someone his size would be capable of taking everything they say he took."

"Perhaps it was inevitable. You shouldn't blame yourself."

She lets her eyes and then her face down to him. "They're saying they saw him near their house the night before last. Presumably nobody who hasn't had their advantages is allowed near."

I see my father wants to think she's stopped accusing us, but he doesn't dare. "You were taking him to the park, weren't you, Jeremy?" he says.

"I said I would."

If she asks whether I did I'll tell them everything. Maybe that will stop me feeling that it's getting darker inside me than it is yet outside. But all my mother says is "I'm going to Jane's to see what I can do for her. I've no idea when I'll be back."

"I've got my parents' evening at school," my father tells me. "I'll try not to be too late. You won't mind being on your own, will you?"

"There's nothing round here to be scared of," my mother says. "You aren't a woman living by herself."

I know she means most of her students, but I feel as if she's talking about Mrs Hammond. I don't want to remember how being alone in her house filled Mrs Hammond up with fear. I pretend I don't mind being left by myself at night. I keep on trying to pretend once my parents leave.

I spend all the time I can at washing up the dinner things till the window shows me it'll soon be dark. I start watching television, but there's nothing on that can reach inside my head. Running through the channels twice makes me feel I'm trying to be like Brad, and I think how my mother would blame me but not him. I know I ought to be doing my homework, though when so many people at my school don't, sometimes I wonder why I should. My mother would make me feel guilty for wasting my advantages, that's mostly why. There's no reason for me to be scared of going in my room.

I switch on the light and the one on my desk as well before I take my books out of my bag and shut Mrs Hammond's album in it. Even when I turn the computer on I feel there isn't enough light in the room. Outside the window it looks as if the dark is spreading out of the black place where Mrs Hammond used to live. When I start thinking the blackness or something in it wants to get hold of me I pull the curtains together.

For history we have to write what it was like to live in England in the years leading up to the Second World War. I take everything I can find in my schoolbooks and type it on the screen, but it doesn't feel as if it was ever alive. Mrs Hammond would have been about my age at the beginning of the thirties, and I try to think if she told me about them. I can't remember anything she said, but my thoughts seem to start using her voice. I keep thinking I ought to look in her album.

I'm not sure I want to while I'm by myself, even if it helps me do the kind of homework my mother always says I can. I do my best to let the stuff I've copied tell me more to write, but trying makes the inside of my head feel as if it's turning black. I almost type the only thing that's in there, which is "See my pictures," even if it sounds like Mrs Hammond's voice that's left its mouth somewhere. I don't want to hear it. I jump up and pull the album out and put it on my desk.

It falls open, and a photograph tries to stand up. It's the one I found crumpled on the floor, which must be why it's moving, only it looks as if someone's trying to get hold of it without much of a hand. I squash it between the cover and the first cardboardy page, which doesn't have strips cut out of it to hold photographs. I wish I'd shut the album instead, because I don't like the look of any of the photographs at all.

They're in the order of how old Mrs Hammond was. The baby ones are nearly black like fruit that's shrunk—all you can see are little eyes trying to peer out of the blackness. I start hoping they've all gone like that, because the bits of her as a girl that the blackness hasn't covered up look so thin I think it's taken their flesh off. But those aren't as bad as the ones where she's grown up. Maybe the blackness is some kind of mould, because the parts of her it's left white look swollen like toadstools that burst if you poke them. I get as far as a picture of her and Mr Hammond with their eyes staring out of two fat raw white blobs. I shut the album tight, which feels as if I'm not squashing only pictures. I don't want it in my room.

I don't even want it in the house, not when it's keeping Mrs Hammond's voice inside my head. "See the rest," I think she's pleading. "See all of me." I'd leave the album outside and wait till tomorrow to think what to do if I wasn't afraid it might rain. I find three plastic bags in a kitchen cupboard and put the album inside one and the others too. There's a wind, and if I leave the album behind the house my parents may hear the plastic rustling and find out what it is. I hurry out the front instead, across the road.

Half Mrs Hammond's front door is lying on its back beyond some coaly bricks. Bits of burnt wood flake off and grit under my nails when I lift the door enough to slide the album under. Tomorrow I'll pretend to find the album on my way to school and give it to my parents to pass on to Mrs Hammond's son. I try to imagine her voice being muffled by the door when I drop it, except that's like imagining her trapped in her coffin, not able to see. The wind stirs up the patch where she lived, and the choking smell feels as if the dark is rising up to wall me in. I dash across the road into not enough light, but I'm only at the gate when I hear our phone ringing.

I have to get the key out of my pocket and push it in the lock the right way up and turn it, and all the while I'm afraid the phone will stop or won't. I shut the dark out and run to grab the phone out of its plastic nest on the wall. "Hello?" I call louder than the voice in my head.

"Are you there at last? I was starting to think you were doing a Brad. Don't tell Willa I said that. Were you asleep?"

"Not yet."

"Glad I didn't wake you, then, but time for bed all the same. I'm just in discussion with some colleagues."

I can hear the kind they're having and the other noises of the pub. "Will you be home soon?" I plead.

"Not while you're conscious, I shouldn't think. I do need to relax occasionally, you know. Just get your head on the pillow and before you know it you'll be gone. Willa and her women may have got themselves some strength, but that doesn't have to mean they've taken ours away." I don't think he meant me to hear the last part, or maybe he doesn't care. "See you in the morning, Jeremy," he says.

I ram the phone into its nest and run upstairs to the bathroom. I stay in there till I realise I'm staring at my face in the mirror. That reminds me how Mrs Hammond couldn't look in one. I'm afraid something like her face will wobble up over the edge, trying to see me instead of itself. I'd rather be in my room than think about that, and I dash across the landing.

There's too much of a mirror in my room. I keep my back to it while I undress for bed and hurry to the switch by the door. I turn the light off and on again at once. I've never seen my room so dark. I run over to the window and open the curtains without looking at the glass that might as well be a mirror. Either the streetlamp outside Mrs Hammond's garden isn't working—maybe somebody like Brad has broken it—or the blackness from where she lived has caught it somehow, because when I switch the light off it's as dark as it was. It's so dark I'm afraid switching the light back on won't make any difference. But it does, and I leave it on and hide in my bed.

At least I've stopped having thoughts that sound like Mrs Hammond. Maybe it's too light for her, that's if I ever really heard her. I don't mind when it starts getting dark inside my eyelids, since that means I'm falling asleep and I know it's light in the room. Then I'm asleep, and I don't like it, because I'm groping about in a place with no light till I stick my fingers in a toadstool. That feels so bad it jerks my eyes open and me awake.

I'm still in the dark, and my hand feels the same. I hope I've only dreamed I'm awake, but then I feel how I'm lying at the edge of the bed with one arm hanging nearly to the floor. I hear something dragging on the carpet, and there's a tug at my arm. What I thought was a toadstool I'd poked my hand into are fingers holding mine.

My thoughts start talking in Mrs Hammond's voice. There's nothing in my head except them and terror, and I don't even know how much of that is hers. "Touch more of me," I think or hear. "I can't feel like this. This can't be me. It's just all this dark making me worse."

I'm desperate to get free, but I'm afraid if I tear myself loose her hand will come with me, or some of it will. I make myself roll closer to the edge and reach down with my other hand. I touch hers that's holding mine and run my fingers up her arm. "That's it," her voice says in my head. "Find my face."

I think I'd stop living if I did that. The rest is bad enough. Her hand is too big for the arm that feels thinner than its bones used to and made of spongy putty. There's just one thing I can think of to do if my mouth will work. I push my tongue between my lips to open them and oil them. "I can feel you're all right," I say, though my words don't want to leave my mouth. "You're like your favourite photo when you weren't much older than me."

"Am I really?" I think her voice is going away and then I hear it's only sunk. I stop touching her arm and inch back onto the bed and pray she'll let go of my hand before I have to pull it out of her squashy one. But I'm leaning off the edge of the bed as if I may fall instead of creeping out of reach when she says "See me, then" not in my head but in the room and not using much I'd call a voice.

I'm not sure what comes then. Maybe it isn't light even if I can see by it—maybe it's her hope. For however long it takes me to start seeing her I can't breathe. I see her arm first, then how it stretches all the way across the room to the rest of her. She's the lumpy white heap against the wall, because I can just make out a thing on top like a soft balloon with hardly any face. I don't know if she's lost her eyes or if what it's made of has swollen over them.

I feel a tug at my hand. There's a noise like a stuffed wet sack dragging along the wall as she tries to get up and come across the room to let me see her clearer. I wrench myself loose and press my back and my head against the wall above the pillow, and rub my hands together in case any of her has stuck to them. Squeezing my eyes shut doesn't feel safe enough, so I grip my hands over them. In case it helps keep her off I scream.

I'm doing all that when my parents get home. My mother must have picked my father up on the way, because I hear her car and then they both come into the house. "That's never Jeremy, is it?" my father doesn't quite shout.

"I hope you won't try to suggest it's my fault if it is."

They have a competition over who'll be upstairs first, and my father wins. "Whatever's the matter, Jeremy?" he says in his pub voice, and clicks the switch a few times. "Why is it so dark in here?"

I want to be taken out of the room into the light where Mrs Hammond will be afraid to come and see herself. "Too dark," I try to say. When hands take hold of me I scream louder till I'm sure they aren't hers. I keep mine over my eyes as my parents argue while they lead me out. I don't know when I'll dare to open my eyes again, and even if I do I know the darkest place will be inside my head. Maybe Mrs Hammond will wait in there for me to see her. Maybe I'll have to till I'm afraid to see myself, and then I'll be on my way to her place. Maybe till then I won't really know what screaming is.

AFTERWORD

My favorite ghost story, and in my view the greatest ever, is *The Haunting of Hill House*. I know of no other writer in the field who conveys paranoia and spectral dread with more delicacy than Shirley Jackson. Who else could terrify with the sight of a picnic on a lawn? Robert Wise's film *The Haunting* captures some of the psychology and attendant terrors of the novel, though in its insistence on how much is left unseen, it sometimes recalls Lovecraft at his least restrained. As for the remake, I shall say only that the press release claimed it was faithful to Shirley Jackson. We must hope it put nobody off the book. No less affecting than the reticence of the novel is its extraordinary poignancy. They are qualities I should like to see rediscovered by the field, and soon.

✠

SHARYN McCRUMB, an award-winning Appalachian writer, is best known for her *Ballad* novels, set in the North Carolina/Tennessee mountains. The latest of these is *Rank Strangers*, an account of the Civil War in western North Carolina, and its echoes today. Her novels include the *New York Times* Best Sellers, *She Walks These Hills* and *The Rosewood Casket*, which deal with the issue of the vanishing wilderness. Other *Ballad* novels include *If Ever I Return, Pretty Peggy-O*; *The Hangman's Beautiful Daughter*; *The Ballad of Frankie Silver*; and *The Songcatcher*.

McCrumb has been honored with the Outstanding Contribution to Appalachian Literature Award, the Chaffin Award for Achievement in Southern Literature, the Plattner Award for Short Story, the St. Andrews Flora MacDonald Award for Achievement in the Arts by a Woman of Scots Heritage, and the Sherwood Anderson Short Story Award. She lives and works in the Virginia Blue Ridge.

In a surprising shift, "The Gallows Necklace" has nothing to do with her Appalachian novels.

THE GALLOWS NECKLACE

SHARYN MCCRUMB

WHEN NEVILLE GORDON realized that the elderly man by the window was his old schoolmate Edward Seeley, he felt as if he had seen a ghost. Surely, he thought, given the date and the purpose of his journey, this encounter could not be coincidence. Gordon stood in the doorway of the first-class railway compartment still staring at the car's only other occupant, a leathery old man gazing out the window of the train, watching the green lawns and hedgerows flash past. After the lawns of outer London would come clumps of woodland and stretches of golden fields and then a more exalted group of gray buildings as the train pulled into the station at Oxford.

The train rocked a bit as it rounded a curve, and as Gordon put out a hand to steady himself, his newspaper slid to the floor, but he made no move to retrieve it. He was still staring at the man beside the window. He had the weathered look of an old soldier, now retired from some tropical Empire outpost but still fit and military in his bearing. His clothes were not new, but they were well-cut and of good material. Despite the patina of age that had seamed his face, he still had the look of that earnest schoolboy Gordon had known in his youth. *So,* he thought, *Seeley went abroad after the tragedy. He prospered, and now, after all these years, he has come back to England in his retirement. How extraordinary to meet him today.*

"It's Seeley, isn't it?" he said aloud, settling himself in the opposite seat. "Mungo?"

Upon hearing that old school nickname of so many decades past, the gray head turned, and the man's look of wariness changed to a hesitant smile. "Why, it's Neville. Neville Gordon!" he said. "Good heavens, it's been a long time, hasn't it? But I'd have known you anywhere, anywhere at all. You haven't changed—well, of course you have—not a lad of twelve anymore, but all the same . . . know you anywhere."

They shook hands. In a few moments of staccato conversation, Gordon filled in the gaps of a lifetime. After their school days at Winchester, Seeley prepared for his military career by attending Sandhurst, while Gordon had gone on to Oxford to read law. Now he had been a solicitor in the family firm for more years than he cared to count. He had married an earl's daughter, dead these ten years now, and there had been one son, a fine, bright lad, destined to follow his father into the firm, but it was not to be. The boy had died on the Somme. In his lawyerly way, Gordon had endeavored to convey the bare bones of his life story with a flat recitation of facts, but his voice shook a little when he spoke of the death of his son. He was still practicing law, he said. Work was all he had really. No reason to stop now. Gave him an interest in life. Gordon kept too busy to dwell upon the aches and pains of his advancing age, but now, seeing the change the years had wrought in Mungo Seeley, he felt the full weight of the decades pressing down upon him.

"And what about you, Seeley?" he said. "You were a soldier, from the look of you. You must have been in the war as well?"

"No. I was posted in India. I was too old for any real fighting, I'm afraid, so they left me out there to see to things while better men carried on the fight in Europe."

Gordon nodded. "And have you a family as well?"

Seeley looked away. "No . . . no. I never married. Not after—no, I never did."

Not after the tragedy, he had been about to say. His face twisted with the effort of suppressed emotion, and Gordon knew that courtesy required that he change the subject to something less painful for Seeley to discuss, but he could think of nothing else. They had been schoolmates, but after so many years, they had nothing in common. Any reminiscences would invariably lead up the same path and therefore back to Sarah. Today of all days he must think of Sarah. Surely this meeting of old acquaintances on the 11:25 to Oxford—surely this could not be coincidence?

"Have you kept in touch with Sarah?" asked Gordon, looking away from that stricken countenance. "Perhaps a card at Christmas?"

"No," Seeley whispered. "I went right away. Wanted to forget all of it. Couldn't." He glanced down at the newspaper, still on the floor of the compartment. "The date! Gordon, it was *today*."

"Yes, of course it was. Surely you remembered. Are you not on your way to Oxford to see her?"

Seeley looked pale. "No. I had no idea she was there. Last place in the world . . . No. I wanted to do a bit of research in the Bodleian. Project of mine . . . Got the idea while I was out in India, don't you know . . . a history of Hindu superstition. Saw some amazing things out there. Saw a dagger once with a curse on it that—"

"I am going to see Sarah," said Gordon, stemming the tide of explanations. "I am her solicitor, you see."

Seeley mouthed the words to himself. He leaned forward with a look of timid eagerness and said, "So you see her still?"

Gordon nodded. "From time to time."

"How extraordinary!" said Seeley. "What became of her? What is she like now? Still beautiful, of course?"

Gordon permitted himself a tight, lawyerly smile. "Well, she is a handsome woman still, though at sixty-three I should hardly call her beautiful. Her hair is silver now, instead of gold, and her face is lined, but when she is exceptionally pleased or angry, those incredible blue eyes of hers can still pierce you heart. She married, you know."

Seeley's eyes widened and he gasped. "I . . . I never thought she would. Not after—"

"Oh, yes. Ages ago. She is a grandmother now."

"I cannot imagine it," said Seeley, shaking his head.

"No, I suppose not," said Gordon. "It's odd, isn't it, how people we have not seen for a long time remain unchanged in our imaginings. We know the years pass. We see time's effect on our own countenances in the mirror, but still we picture absent friends as if they were immune to time. Why, seeing you was a bit of a shock, Seeley, for you have been twenty in my mind's eye lo these many years."

Seeley scarcely seemed to be listening. "So she is old now," he murmured.

"Up in years, but not frail. Why don't you come along and see for yourself, Seeley? I'm sure she'd be delighted to have you turn up. I am here on a matter of business, but our meeting will not take a great deal of time, and she always has me stay to supper afterward. Do say you'll come along. It's always pleasant to meet old friends. I know she would agree."

"I might bring back unpleasant memories . . ."

"You can hardly think she needs reminding of them. And there have been more horrors since then. The War, you know . . . she lost her son and I lost mine. We will talk of happier days."

"I will come," said Seeley. "If you are certain that my visit will not be a burden to her in any way. Er . . . perhaps I ought to dine elsewhere?"

Gordon laughed. "Sarah will hardly grudge you your cutlet, Seeley. She is rather well-off, even in these uncertain times. There was an inheritance from her mother's family, and then she married well—an older man of private means. He was wealthy enough to do whatever he fancied in life, and he chose to pursue his muse, which was poetry, at the university. He was, as I said, a good bit older than she, and he died three years ago, but Sarah has been fortunate enough to keep her health, and there is sufficient money to keep her in comfort, so I should not call her life a tragic one at all—mindful of course of what the Greeks said."

"Eh—the Greeks?"

"The ancient ones, Seeley. They said: *Call no man happy until he is dead.* We learnt that in old Brunson's class at Winchester, you know."

"Oh, that. 'Course we did. Couldn't think what you meant at first." Seeley gave him a tentative smile. "Imagine Sarah still being at Oxford. Been there all her life then."

"Well . . . she went away for a bit, you know, after the inquest. I believe it was during her stay with relatives in Cornwall that she met Sir Alfred. She is Lady Beldon now. I'm afraid people made rather a joke of the name at first. One of the picture papers printed her photograph with the caption *The Beldon Sans Merci* . . . They were still angry, of course."

"Angry?"

"That she had not been hanged."

RIPARIAN, THE HOME of the widowed Lady Beldon, lay well beyond the outskirts of Oxford, amid wide lawns and well-tended gardens that sloped down to a grove of trees on the banks of the Thames itself. From the low wall that separated the property from the lane, one could see an expanse of lush green grass, and on a rise beyond that stood the long, low Queen Anne house of mellowed rose brick, its rows of French windows opening out on to a flagstone terrace. The windows caught the light of the early afternoon sun, and the old bricks shone in the heat of the September afternoon, giving the scene a warm and drowsy air. Just beyond the property, the road ended in a dusty circle at the edge of a wood.

"End of the lane," said the taxi driver, nodding toward the house. "Lovely place, innit? Looks right out over the river at the back, lucky souls. Enjoy the day while you may, gentlemen. Clouds coming in afore dark."

"Yes, indeed," said Gordon, counting the coins out into the driver's outstretched hand. "I don't doubt you're right." He was relieved to know that the local people had forgotten the Darcy tragedy, as the case was called then. It was natural enough, he supposed. The taxi man had not even been born when those events occurred. But Sarah herself had not forgotten. The windows of her sitting room on the back of the house were heavily curtained, and even in high summer they were never open to the view of the river. He turned to Seeley. "Let's go along in," he said. "And, Mungo, do try to be cheerful."

Seeley wondered later just what he had been expecting when he met Sarah Darcy after all these years. Despite what he had said about being unable to imagine her old, he had imagined being ushered into the presence of a stooped and gaunt old woman, wreathed in black mourning clothes, and somber with the weight of that old tragedy bearing down upon her spirit. But he had been wrong.

As soon as Gordon and Seeley set foot upon the checkered marble floor of the entrance hall, they were met by a smiling woman whose hair seemed more blonde than gray, and whose elfin manner was as sunny as the primrose tea gown she wore with such careless elegance. The years had indeed been kind to Sarah Darcy. She was no longer a girl of nineteen, it was true, but she carried the decades lightly with no trace of sorrow for herself . . . or for anyone else. Before Seeley could dwell on that last thought, she had enveloped him in a brisk hostessy hug, brushing his cheek with her lips, and exclaiming, "But it's dear old Mungo! I cannot believe it. Neville, you are an absolute wizard! Where on earth did you find him?"

Gordon smiled. "I can take no credit for that conjuring trick, I'm afraid. He turned up in my compartment on the train, and I insisted that he come along with me. I knew you'd be pleased."

Her smile flickered only for an instant. "Why, of course!" she said. "I'm too delighted to see you both, and you must promise that you will stay to dinner and tell me every single thing that you have been doing since I last saw you."

Mungo's tanned face turned a deeper shade of red. "That shouldn't take long to tell," he said gruffly. "Been a soldier for most of the time. Knocked about the world a bit. Never married, y'know. Just me now."

Sarah nodded. "*Just me*," she said with a trace of sadness in her voice. "It all comes down to that in the end, perhaps." She turned back to Gordon. "You mustn't mind me," she sad, tapping him playfully on the arm. "Just a sad moment. But we have things to attend to, and it will be better to have it over with, so that I can enjoy your visit."

Gordon nodded. "We shan't be long."

"Well, perhaps a bit longer than usual," said Sarah. "I have some papers for you to look over, concerning the Beldon properties in London."

Gordon nodded. "Of course. We must go over those as well as . . . the other. Perhaps Mr. Seeley will excuse us for a bit."

"Yes, that would be best," said Sarah, tugging at a bell pull. "Cunningham will show you into the library, Mungo. I know how much you've always loved poring over musty old books. And we shall be out to take tea with you before you know it."

A tall, sepulchral manservant arrived as if on cue to conduct Seeley away to the library. As they left the marble entrance hall, he heard the drawing-room doors close behind Gordon and Sarah. It occurred to him then that the lawyer had not carried a briefcase with him. "He hasn't got any papers with him," Seeley said aloud. "How can they be conducting legal business?"

Cunningham permitted himself a discreet cough. "It is not my place to comment upon the mistress' affairs," he said. "But perhaps Sir knows about the ritual imposed upon her ladyship many years ago at the . . . er . . . um . . . the trial."

Seeley stared. "The trial. Of course. I remember . . . but that was forty years ago. Surely they abandoned all that ages ago?"

"Oh, no, Sir," Cunningham intoned. He had stopped in front of a carved oak door, almost black with age. "The judge's instructions were quite specific on that point. Miss Sarah must always wear the hangman's noose about her neck, and upon the anniversary of the tragedy, her compliance with the order must be witnessed by an officer of the court. If she should ever have neglected to carry out this directive, she was to be hanged." He paused and flung open the door. "The library, Sir."

SEELEY SAT IN the leather armchair beside the unlit fireplace, sunk in the gloom of the dimly lit room, with its musty smell of unread books. Apparently the library had been her husband's refuge, and no one had taken an interest in it since his death. Above the mantel hung a full-length portrait of the young Sarah, resplendent in a low-cut blue gown whose color matched her eyes. It had been painted before the tragedy, then, for she was never to wear low-cut gowns thereafter. The painted image of her loomed over him, flaxen-haired and impishly smiling, with the gold necklace of Burmese turquoise shining against her pale throat.

They had found the necklace clutched in Jack Rhys-Taylor's clenched fist.

Seeley glanced up at the portrait for a moment, repressing a shudder, and then at random he pulled a volume of Tacitus' histories off the shelf and began thumbing through it, scarcely taking in the sense of the words on the page. He had not looked at a line of Roman history since his school days, but still, it was something to keep him occupied while Gordon and Sarah performed the bizarre ritual that had saved Sarah from the gallows. It had been so many years now that he had nearly forgotten the details of the judge's edict: the hangman's noose perpetually worn. The peculiar penance in lieu of execution or a prison sentence had been much remarked upon at the time. Some people had approved of the mercy implicit in the sparing of the prisoner's life, but there were newspaper editorials questioning the mental fitness of the judge, who had indeed retired before the year's end, but despite the comments, his curious ruling was left to stand. The consensus was that the deaths caused by the accused were the result of folly, not deliberate malice, and that Sarah would never be a danger to society. The authorities seemed to think that as a well-born young woman, she would suffer as much from the prolonged symbolic punishment as a lesser mortal might feel at the gallows itself. In his later years, Seeley might have questioned the arrogance of such a verdict, but at the time, his own regard for the defendant had made him grateful that her life was spared.

He wondered what it had been like all these years—to wear the hangman's noose about her throat. Because of her rank—the granddaughter of a duke—rather than out of consideration for the fact that she was a woman, Sarah was permitted to wear a silken rope instead of the coarse hemp actually used in hangings, and she was permitted to conceal the silken rope beneath her clothing. The court had not deemed it necessary for the rope to be visible to all and sundry, but Sarah had been made to give her word that she would wear it always. Because she was a member of the aristocracy, the authorities assumed that she would be honor-bound by that promise, and presumably she was.

Seeley recalled that Sarah had taken to wearing blouses of high-collared lace, or brightly covered scarves about her throat, to conceal the ever-present gallows necklet. Unless people knew who she was and what had been her penance, they might never suspect that she wore the rope at all. Seeley supposed that the punishment was gentle enough, and the judge's trust had been repaid, for indeed Sarah had led a blameless life ever since. Seeley had been away from England for many years, but the newspapers and society gossip followed the British armies to the most far-flung outposts of the Empire, and had there been a breath of scandal connected to Sarah's name, he would have heard.

"Hello! I'm sorry. Did I startle you?" The young woman in the doorway seemed at first an apparition to Seeley.

When she appeared in front of his chair, he gave a cry of alarm, and the copy of Tacitus tumbled from his lap and lay facedown and forgotten upon the hearth rug.

I am dreaming, he thought. *I had nodded off in this chair, waiting for Sarah and Gordon, and now I find myself transported back before the war*. Or perhaps he had dreamed everything that had transpired since those days of his youth. How wonderful it would be to wake up and find himself still young and Sarah untouched by tragedy after all, to find that the Great War that had been such a nightmare for the world had in fact been only a private nightmare of his own. . . . In the time it took to form those wistful thoughts, Seeley's mind righted itself to full alertness, and he realized the war and the present were unchanged, and that the fair-haired young woman in the doorway was not a ghost, nor was she Sarah. The resemblance was familial, not phantasmal.

"I am sorry," she said. "I've startled you. I had not realized that anyone was in here."

Seeley struggled to his feet and stammered a hasty introduction. "I am an old friend of your . . . of . . . of Lady Beldon. . . ."

The vision of the young Sarah smiled at him. "I am Lady Beldon's granddaughter. My name is Marguerite, and so of course everyone calls me Daisy." She nodded toward the portrait. "I look rather like her, don't I? I can see that it must have given you a shock to wake up and find me standing over you. It must have been some time since you had last seen her."

"Ages," said Seeley. "How ever did you know?"

"Well, your reaction, for one thing. You still think of my grandmother looking as I do now, and that has been quite a while ago. Besides, I have been living here for several years now, ever since my mother died of influenza at the end of the war. I should have recognized you if you had visited us since then. I do hope you'll join me for tea?"

Seeley nodded. "I should be delighted," he stammered.

"Oh, good. Grandmere's lawyer has come down for his annual visit. They shut themselves up for ages, talking business, I suppose. They emerge in time to change for dinner, but hardly ever in time for tea. So I am glad that they provided me with company for a change. I can't think what is taking them so long!—Well, I can. Grandmere said that she had some questions about the London properties to put to Mr. Gordon, but still, it is tiresome of them."

She does not know, thought Seeley. He was shocked that this should be the case, but a moment's thought told him why this should be so. Of course the secret of her grandmother's tragedy would have been kept from a small child, and the girl's parents had died before they thought her old enough to be told the story. She must be now about the same age that Sarah was when the whole thing happened. It did not seem long ago at all.

There had been a party in Oxford that September evening. . . . Seeley could no longer remember the details of that. Later events had swept the memories of the early part of the evening right out of his mind. Seeley had taken the train up from Sandhurst, on the pretext of visiting old school chums, but really to see Sarah. They had all been moths hovering around the flame that was Sarah Darcy. She was a golden girl, as elusive and insubstantial as a will-o'-the-wisp, and they were all in love with her, or at least infatuated beyond all reason.

In those days, Mungo Seeley was a tall, awkward boy from a Glasgow military family, bound from the cradle for a soldier's life, and he knew that Sarah Darcy would never consent to be an army wife in some outpost of the Empire, but from the moment he met her, Seeley had refused to consider the impossibility of a match between them. Willingly he had joined the throng of her admirers.

How had he met her?

Through Jack Rhys-Taylor, he supposed. Or perhaps it was Albert Candler or Tom Spenser. He had been at school with all of them, and when they went up to Oxford, he often visited them, allowing himself to be hauled along to dances and party suppers with that careless, laughing crowd of young people, and the beautiful Sarah Darcy was foremost among them. She was not a student, of course, but her father was the dean of one of the colleges, and she had drifted into the world of the revelers as naturally as a bee finds a rose garden.

That fateful night, after the early evening dance had become too tame for them, they had all converged on the riverbank for a late evening of punting on the Thames. The party consisted only of Sarah and her swains. Surely her prospective suitors had danced with other girls that evening, but if so, the ladies were overshadowed by Sarah's golden radiance, and they were left behind in the headlong dash to the river's edge. Amid laughter and shouts of encouragement, the boys and Sarah had piled into three of the small punts belonging to the nearest college—not that they asked anyone's permission to take them. They cast off in the moonlight, a flotilla of boisterous, drunken youths, determined to impress their fair lady with song or seamanship, according to their lights.

Sarah had been in the boat with Jack, Tom, and two fellows from Trinity—Robbie Graham and Arthur Laurie. Arthur poled the first punt up river, while Sarah leaned back against the bow, trailing her hand in the water and smiling lazily at her fleet of admirers. From time to time, she would call out to the other boats, or join them in the chorus of a song as they drifted along the dark ribbon of water. Neville Gordon, who was steering the second craft, kept shouting to his two passengers to pipe down and stop rocking the boat before they all ended up in the river. Seeley, the visitor from Sandhurst, rode in the third punt with a shy and spotty divinity student from Merton. They took turns poling the craft, and Seeley was regretting that he had not had more to drink, because he felt suddenly cold on the dark river, and the raucous singing of the others only served to remind him that he was an outsider. The boat had drifted along well astern of the other two punts, perhaps because neither he nor the Merton chap had been industrious in their poling. They knew that they stood little chance of being noticed by Sarah, and now the whole idea of the expedition had begun to seem silly.

Seeley was just thinking to himself that he would asked to be put ashore so that he could walk back to his lodgings, when he heard a great splash and then shouting.

"Anything wrong?" someone called out.

"Only Jack being a hero!" someone called out in the darkness. "Sarah has dropped her necklace in the water, and he's gone over the side to fetch it!"

"What, in the river?" said the divinity student. "It's pitch-black down there. He'll not find it."

"No, I shouldn't think he would," Seeley agreed. "The weeds seem quite thick here as well. It's like poling through a hedgerow. Perhaps it's clear where the others are."

They heard Sarah's voice drifting over the water. "But I mustn't lose it!" she cried. "Mummy will kill me. It was my grandmother's necklace. Oh, please do find it! I shall . . . I shall give a kiss for it. . . ."

More laughter. Then another splash and more voices calling out, "Arthur, you fool! It's quite deep here!"

Seeley peered ahead at the dark shapes adrift on the river, but he could not make out any faces. One of the boats rocked as its occupants peered over the sides, and there were more splashes and shouts of, "Steady now!"

A minute or more passed, and Seeley took up the pole and began to maneuver the punt toward the other boats, where all had suddenly gone quiet.

He had been wrong, though. When he returned some twenty minutes later with some men from the nearby cottages, they found that no rescues had been effected, and the shouts to the divers had ceased in the face of their certain death. The only sound was Sarah Darcy's soft, persistent weeping, and no one was bothering to comfort her.

The rescuers worked with boat hooks by lantern light, but the sky was already turning gray with the first light of dawn when the first of the bodies broke the surface of the dark river. Three of the revelers had drowned—Arthur, Jack, and the divinity student from Merton, who had gone in to try and save the first two. Robbie Graham had also dived in to attempt a rescue, but the others had managed to pull him back aboard before he, too, became trapped in the weeds.

Seeley wondered later if he should have insisted on taking Sarah away with him, but he doubted that she would have gone, and although he was ashamed to admit it, the thought had not even occurred to him at the time. Perhaps he had wanted to get away from her screams as much as he had wanted to help, but he pushed that thought out of his mind.

He had stayed for the inquest, come back for the funerals, and back again for Sarah's trial, though his testimony had hardly mattered. Both he and Gordon had testified that it was all a dreadful accident, that Sarah had meant no harm when she dropped the necklace, but the jury had listened stone-faced to their protestations. What was a young lady doing out on the river late at night, unchaperoned with a gang of varsity students, they wanted to know. No better than she should be, their stern faces said. Perhaps she did want to be rid of at least one of the young gentlemen. Who's to say she didn't? There was no mercy to be had from them. Sarah's position was made all the worse by the fact that Jack Rhys-Taylor had been the heir to a baronetcy. His people were said to be distraught by his untimely death, and at the time of the trial there were whispers that their influence had been brought to bear on the case to ensure that the foolish young woman did not get off scot-free. And indeed she had not.

Now a lifetime had passed, and Seeley found himself looking again at the necklace that had caused the tragedy. It sparkled around the neck of another lovely girl, almost the image of the young Sarah herself, and the sight of that necklace made him shiver. The young woman sat there at his elbow, pouring tea and smiling, and he made replies to her conversation, with what words he scarcely knew, and all the while his mind roared with the memories of those cold, pale bodies stretched out on the riverbank, wreathed in the tendrils of water weeds.

It seemed strange to him somehow that Sarah had gone on to have a life, and that those three young men had not. He had never got over the uneasiness of having survived the incident. Everyone had said that Seeley did the correct thing by going for help, but he could not overcome the fact that he had risked nothing, while his friends were drowning. He might not have been able to save them, might even have died himself, but he had never quite escaped the guilt of not having tried. In the long army career that followed for Seeley, no act of valor had ever quite compensated for his inglorious prudence that night on the river.

And what did Sarah feel after all these years? He wondered if she ever thought of those who were drowned. She recalled the tragedy, of course. How could she not? But did she ever think of those three young men as bright and happy individuals, or were they now simply the authors of her discomfiture?

DAISY BELDON STOOD up. "Have you finished your tea, Mr. Seeley? I have. And it's such a lovely warm evening for September. The mist is coming up, but there's still a bit of daylight left, and it seems a pity to stay cooped up inside all day. Would you like to go out and see the garden? The roses are gone, but we have autumn flowers in the borders, and of course the herb garden."

It was precisely the sort of reasonable suggestion that a well-bred hostess might make to a visitor to the house, and Seeley, who was quite tired of sitting anyhow, got up without a moment's thought and followed her down the passageway and through the curtained French windows that led to the garden . . . that led to the river.

He saw that the twilight had deepened the sky to the color of pewter, and skeins of darker clouds now hung in the air. There couldn't be more than half an hour's light left, for although the afternoon weather had been perfect, it was late September and the days were short. On the river, a mist was rising.

"It's so peaceful in the garden," said Daisy, wending her way around a stand of rosebushes. "I love to look out over the flowers and to watch the river drift by. Grandmere never comes out here, though. I pick the flowers and take them in to her so that she can arrange them in vases. She does lovely flower arrangements. It's the sort of thing that girls in her day had to learn."

Seeley smiled. "I remember those days," he said. "I remember your grandmother carrying a nosegay that she had made herself. We were at a dance. She was wearing that very necklace, as I recall."

Daisy reached up and touched the necklace at her throat. "You remember seeing her wear this necklace? How odd. I've never seen her put it on. Once, when we were searching for a pair of earrings for me to wear to a dinner party, I saw the necklace tucked away in her jewelry box, and I asked her why she never wore it. The stone matches her eyes, don't you think?"

Seeley nodded. "I always thought so," he said. "And now they match yours as well."

Daisy Beldon prattled on with the assurance of a pretty young girl who thinks that all the world looks kindly on her and takes an interest in the minutiae of her existence. "It's curious," she said. "When I asked Grandmere about the necklace, she said she didn't care for it. Then she said I'd better have it, because when she was nearly my age, she had got it as a gift from her own grandmother."

"A family heirloom. Yes, I do recall that," said Seeley politely.

"I'm fond of it. In fact, I wear it all the time," she said with an uneasy titter of laughter. "I only wish I could stop dreaming about it."

Seeley turned to stare at her. "I beg your pardon. Did you say that you dream about this necklace?"

"Yes. I shouldn't have mentioned it, really. I know it's very silly of me, but it is beginning to worry me a bit. I got the necklace only last spring, and since then I'd had the dream a time or two, but just lately it has happened nearly every night."

Seeley stared out at the river now swirling in evening mist. After a moment, he said, "Would you think it terribly impertinent of me, Miss Beldon, if I asked you to describe your dream for me?"

"I shouldn't mind telling you about it, Mr. Seeley, only you must promise not to tell my grandmother. I mustn't worry her." She waited for his nod of assent before she continued. "I see the necklace tangled in a clump of weeds . . . not a garden, exactly. They are strange, willowy plants that seem to float as if the wind were blowing them, but I feel no wind. I reach out my hand to grasp the necklace, and suddenly I cannot breathe. I try to run, but I cannot. I wake up choking and gasping for air."

Seeley felt the sudden chill of the evening. The darkness had deepened now, draining the color from the garden, and when he turned to look at the river, he found it completely swathed in mist. The sky was growing darker now, giving him the sensation that a silver cover had been placed over the house and grounds, blotting out the world outside. He found himself longing for the comforting sight of the paneled library, with a fire in the grate and a decanter of whiskey on the tray before the armchair.

"A most unusual dream," he said. "Perhaps you ought to put the necklace away for a while."

"I know. I've tried." Her voice dropped to a whisper. "A few days ago, I began to take it off before I went to bed, but in the morning when I awoke, I found I was wearing it again! I suppose that I am so attached to the necklace that I cannot bear to be without it."

"Perhaps if you asked that it be locked away in the safe, that would settle the matter," said Seeley. "Rum thing, your dreaming like that. Puts me in mind of India . . . tales I heard. We should go in now. It's getting dark."

She turned to look at him. "It is chilly, isn't it? The dark comes so quickly in autumn, I always think. Why don't you go back inside, Mr. Seeley? I just want to pick a few flowers for my room in case a rain tonight spoils them, but I won't be long. I'll join you shortly."

With some misgivings, Seeley turned and went back into the house. Although he was concerned about the young lady, he was not sorry to leave the garden, beautiful though it might be. He found that he no longer wanted to be within sight of the river, especially not in the presence of that infernal necklace which was the origin of that long-ago tragedy. He had almost reached the library when he heard Gordon calling out to him.

"There you are, Seeley! We couldn't think where you'd got to. Will you join us for a drink before dinner?"

Gordon and Sarah bore down upon him, smiling with relief that the yearly ordeal was over, but despite their gaiety, the feeling of oppression did not leave him. "I was just walking in the garden with Miss Daisy," he told them. "A most charming girl. She is outside still, gathering flowers. Perhaps we might call her." He gestured toward the drawn curtains covering the French windows.

Sarah shivered. "Daisy is always mooning about in that garden," she said. "Let us go in to dinner. I'll send Cunningham to fetch her."

"No," said Seeley. "She's just outside. Let me go." Even as he said it, he felt a stab of misgiving, and he suddenly realized that he did not want to go back out into that dark garden, but he knew that he must. Perhaps this feeling of dread was only an old man's fancy, or the oppression of a coming storm, but what was he to make of the dream? His years in India had taught him not to dismiss such things lightly.

Before Gordon and Sarah could argue further, Seeley fumbled with the curtained French windows and jerked at the catch, then plunged out into the deepening twilight. He stood there on the flagstone terrace, blinking as his eyes became accustomed to the dim light.

"Miss Beldon?" he called out. He had not spoken loudly because he thought she would be close by, but his voice echoed in the darkness, and no one answered.

Seeley did not see her at first. He had expected to find her still cutting flowers in the borders of the terrace, but when he perceived that she was not there, he scanned the expanse of lawn, and saw a dark figure walking toward the river. He called out again, but when there was no response, he began to run toward her.

He was only yards away from Daisy Beldon and the river when he saw that she was not alone. Standing at the water's edge beside Daisy Beldon was a taller figure, his head bent as if the two of them were in conversation. Seeley hurried on. There was something familiar about the silhouette before him.

As he drew near, he heard the lazy drawl of a man's voice saying, "We're just going punting down the river for a bit . . . won't you come?"

Seeley stepped out of the mist and clasped the girl by the arm. "Hello, Jack," he said softly.

Jack Rhys-Taylor looked just as he had on that other night on the river so long ago. He was still dark-eyed and handsome, regally slender, and wearing a look of well-bred coolness that was the antithesis of fear. He was still twenty. At the sound of his name, he turned to look at Seeley, puzzled, perhaps, by the sight of this old man who seemed acquainted with him.

"It's me, Jack," said Seeley in answer to the unspoken question. "It's Mungo."

"Hello, Mungo," said Jack, in the same jaunty tone he had always used. "We're just going out on the river. I say, doesn't Sarah look lovely in her necklace?"

Seeley turned to look at Daisy. She stood at Jack's side, dazed and silent, like a sleepwalker. In the faint light, her resemblance to her grandmother was remarkable. Beyond her, Seeley could see the shadowy form of a punt, just beyond the reeds at the water's edge. More dark shapes sat in the boat—waiting.

Words hovered on Seeley's lips, but he had the absurd thought that it would be discourteous to remind Jack of the fact that he was dead. "It has been a long time," he said at last.

"Not a bit," said Jack softly. "We only just left the party a little while ago. Lovely evening for punting. I know Sarah is keen to go along. And we mean to take her with us."

Seeley wondered if his fear at seeing the apparition had caused him to imagine the undercurrent of menace in Jack's voice. The lights from the house caught in the gold of the necklace, making it shine in the darkness. Without thinking, Seeley snatched at the pendant, tearing the chain from Daisy Beldon's throat. "This damned necklace! It has done enough," he said, and he threw it far out into the river.

Daisy seemed to come to then, with a cry of alarm. "Grandmere's necklace!" she cried. "Oh, I can't lose it!" With the toe of one slipper, she began to kick at the heel of the other, struggling to get them off. "I must go after it!"

Seeley looked back at the old woman, standing in the glow of light on the terrace. He wondered if she could see them—and if it would matter to her. She made no move toward them, as she had made none on that other night on the river.

Seeley pushed his way past Daisy Beldon, who now stood alone on the bank of the river. He waded into the dark current that swirled about the reeds. "No, my dear, I'll go in and get it," said Seeley quietly. "You go back to the house now. I shan't be long."

AFTERWORD

My favorite fictional ghost story is called "The Green Scarf" by A. M. Burrage, in which a newly discovered relic calls up ghosts from the English Civil War. My favorite true ghost story is "Clara's Ring," an experience in the childhood of the real Nora Bonesteel.

CHARLES L. GRANT started out writing science fiction and won awards for his short stories in that genre. However, he's better known these days for his horror and is the author of numerous novels, most recently *Redmoor: Strange Fruit*, an historical horror novel, and *There's A Red Moon Tonight*, published under the pseudonym Talbot Clark. His short fiction has been collected in *A Glow of Candles and Other Stories*, *Tales from the Nightside*, *Nightmare Seasons*, and *The Black Carousel*, and reprinted in *Best New Horror* and *The Year's Best Fantasy and Horror*. He is also an award-winning editor of over twenty-five anthologies, including the critically acclaimed *Shadows* series.

BROWNIE, AND ME

CHARLES L. GRANT

I THINK IT'S going to rain.

Not that it matters, I guess. Everything is packed, I've made sure all the lamps and appliances are unplugged, and all the windows are locked.

It didn't take long, though. And it didn't take long at all for the house to begin smelling as if no one had lived there in a while. I have to admit, it kind of took the wind from my sails. I had hoped there'd be something of me left, after I left; I had hoped me and the house had had more than that. That the years, the decades, had counted for something.

The funny thing is, I hadn't planned on leaving.

The idea was, they'd wonder where I was, down at the Brass Rail or over at the Cock's Crow, and someone would get a little worried, someone else would either call the police or get into his car and drive over. They'd knock on the front door, knock on the back door, walk around the house a couple of times, and finally ask the neighbors if they'd seen me. Nobody would have. Not for days. So they'd break a window, probably the one in the kitchen, off the back porch. They'd climb in, they'd wander through the first floor calling my name, feeling a little foolish and maybe a little scared.

They'd be thinking about murder.

They'd be thinking about killers.

And then, one of them would find me.

In bed maybe, or in my reading chair.

Nothing quite so dramatic as a knife across my throat or a decapitation. Just me.

That's the way I was going to go. No fuss, no bother. Good old Richard, he always knew how to treat his friends right. He even died right. No fuss, no bother.

I hadn't planned on leaving this way at all.

But that Wednesday when it started had been pretty nice, the sun warm enough to let me take off my coat, walk around the streets a little and stretch my bones. The gardens were mostly already in bloom, or looking as if all that green-held color would explode any second. The dogs were out, sniffing the earth. The kids were out, playing ball in the street, playing baseball in the park. The women were out, legs finally showing after so many months of cold, faces up, eyes bright.

I don't know if they knew I was watching.

I don't know if they cared.

It didn't matter.

The fact that I knew, the fact that I could still look and smile, told me I had made it through another winter without dying.

By Thursday, the warm had settled in, and I took the car out of the garage, drove over to the train station and parked behind it. There were no other cars. Just me. And dead leaves on the blacktop.

Hands in my pockets, I walked around to the platform and stood on the edge, breathing deep, my eyes partly closed. I could smell it then, and not just the spring air.

The tracks.

I could smell the tracks.

It sounds silly, I suppose, but then, folks as old as me remember too much, I think. Remember the feel of the wheels beneath your feet, the sound of them, the call of them; remember the sway of the cars, the people who sat there, waiting for me to take their ticket, talking to the young ones, reminding them of their stops as they looked out the window, saw the world passing, and dozed.

Remember how glad I was when we finally left the city—Hartford, New Haven, New York, they're all the damn same—and headed back to a place where I actually cared about the folks I saw every day.

Leaning out of the car, checking the platforms, checking the tracks, signaling the engineer, and hanging there for a few seconds while the train lurched away from the station. Not quite flying, but as close as I'd ever get.

Smelling the tracks.

Wet, hot, cold, they had a smell that let me know they would carry me this way at least one more day.

So on that Thursday I climbed down off the platform—using the steps, of course; I can get around, but I can't jump around—and started walking along the bed, checking the rails, kicking the gravel, eyeing the spots where rust might be a problem.

Habits never die, never break—you can only forget them, except in your dreams.

That's when I saw Brownie.

I was half a mile, maybe more, from the depot when he stepped out of the woods that lined the route in both directions. He wore a white shirt with thin blue stripes, suspenders that held up a baggy pair of corduroy trousers, and thick-soled shoes. A thin green cardigan, the buttons undone. A chewed pencil behind one ear. A dead cigar in his left hand. One thing about Brownie, he didn't have a lick of hair on his scalp; when he went gray, only his eyebrows changed.

He didn't see me at first, but he must've heard me. He turned suddenly, shaded his eyes, and hurried back into the trees before I could call out.

Now, I'm not an agile man anymore, but I can move when I have to, and I moved. By the time I reached the spot where he ducked into the woods, I was puffing, sweating, and my face was probably red and shiny.

But I didn't see him.

I called a few times, and maybe I should have gone into the woods after him.

But the other thing about Brownie is, he's been dead nine years.

"So what are you saying, Rich?" Putter asked me later, in the bar. "You saw a ghost or what?" His face was ready to smile.

"I don't know. I guess."

He shook his head thoughtfully, staring into his beer. He was shorter than me, a lot heavier, his name from golfing and from just puttering around. It was the way he passed what was left of his time, and it made him happy, I guess. It would have driven me nuts.

"No such thing as ghosts," he finally said.

"I know that."

"So what did you see?"

"Beats the hell out of me."

In the other chair of the three-chair table, Vera Hallow knitted her umpteenth sweater of the season. That's all she did. Putter putted, Vera knitted. She lived at home with her daughter, hated the woman, and spent as much time in the Brass Rail as she could. Her daughter scolded her, yelled at her, demanding her mother consider her reputation. Vera, at just a spit over seventy, reminded her that a woman her age would kill for a reputation.

Her daughter didn't think that was very funny.

"Angel," Vera said.

I looked at her. No purple hair for her, or shapeless print dresses, or clunky shoes. She went to the beauty parlor every two weeks, always wore a skirt suit and low heels. Age had tap-danced on my skinny face; age waltzed across hers, barely leaving a mark.

She nodded without looking up, needles clicking. "Brownie was a good man. He's probably an angel."

Putter snorted. "No wings, Vera. Hell, he wore what he had on when he died, for God's sake."

"So? Who says angels have to have wings and white robes? You ever see one?"

He snorted again. "I'm not crazy."

"Thanks," I muttered.

He grinned. "Rich, for God's sake, it wasn't an angel, it wasn't a ghost. It's warm, you were walking too much, you were thinking about them dumping you off the railroad." He spread his hands. "Easy."

Maybe it was. Maybe he was right.

But it bothered me, seeing Brownie, and it made me wonder if there was something going on that I ought to know. I've heard lots of folks my age talking about "knowing when it's time," but I never believed it. The way I figured it, when the end came, you were probably going to be damn surprised.

Surprised it took so long.

Surprised it came so soon.

The thing is, Brownie and I weren't exactly best friends. We nodded to each other on the street, once in a great while had a beer together, but we never spent any private time in each other's company. When I was kid, he was a Negro; now he's a black man. Didn't make any difference to me one way or the other, we just didn't hit it off well enough to be friends. And I hadn't thought about him in years. If this was a sign, or an angel, or an omen, it would have made more sense to show up as my wife. Or my son.

"Stop thinking about it," Vera scolded. "You'll have nightmares."

I had another beer and went home, taking my time, taking the long way, just in case.

Nothing happened except I got a cramp in my leg.

I didn't have a nightmare, but I didn't sleep very well either. Or the next night. Or the night after that.

After a week, I grumbled over to see Doc Wolton. Putter didn't like her, said a woman had no business messing around with his privates and asking him foolish questions. I liked her. She was young enough to make me remember, and old enough that I figured she knew what she was talking about.

"Go away," she said when the exam was done. "I can't make any money off healthy people like you."

Direct, too.

I laughed, and didn't argue when she gave me a prescription for something to help me sleep.

"It happens," she said, walking me to the door. "You've got a bee, Rich, and you're going to have to get rid of it."

I had told her about Brownie. She listened, nodding in all the right places, and suggested I was having one of my periodic bouts of guilt about my family. They came on me every so often, although never like this.

It's hard when a man outlives those he loves.

He can't help thinking the wrong one was taken.

He can't help thinking there had been a horrid mistake.

I saw Brownie again a few days later. I was on the platform, he was on the tracks a hundred yards or so away. He watched me, then waved slowly. I waved back, and looked away. I didn't check to see how long it took before he left; I stayed a little while and went home, took a beer from the refrigerator and drank it standing up.

A few days after that, he was back. No closer. He waved, I waved, and that was that.

By the end of the month, I was getting used to it.

"So," Putter said, "how's Brownie today?" He laughed, drank, ordered another.

"Leave him alone," Vera snapped. Knitting another sweater. "He's got things on his mind."

Putter belched. "Sure. Ghosts and angels."

Something was wrong. Putter was still Putter, maybe a little heavy on the booze, but Vera was nearly breaking speed records with that knitting of hers. She barely said a word except to defend me or swear at the Democrats, and when I couldn't stand to see the blur in her hands anymore, I reached over and did the unthinkable—I grabbed the needles.

She gaped.

"What?" I asked.

She pulled away angrily. "Nothing. Now you've made me lose count."

"An earthquake couldn't make you lose count," I said.

Putter had his glass in front of his face, but I could see his eyes, and they were scared.

I looked from one to the other, trying to figure it out, but didn't have the chance. Vera crammed her knitting into her bag, threw a bill onto the table, and left without saying good-bye. I watched in astonishment, too stunned to go after her.

Then Putter tapped my arm, made me turn around. "She saw him, Rich."

I must have looked stupid, because he said it again: "She saw him. Brownie, I mean." He stared into his beer; his left hand was trembling. "Last night. He was in her yard. She said it was like he was just passing through."

I stared at the door, half tempted to go after her, but I didn't.

"Me, too," he added, not quite choking. He shoved himself to his feet, the glass tottering until I grabbed it. Then he leaned over and said, very quietly, full of rage, "What the hell are you doing to us, Rich? What the hell are you doing?"

He left, making it clear by the rod up his spine that he didn't want me to follow.

I sat for a while, turning his glass around in my hands, ignoring the others, feeling like somehow I had been dropped into a ball of cotton. Everything was muffled, my breathing came hard, and when I finally moved to go home, I felt pressure around my ribs and lead in my arms and legs.

I had done something to my closest friends, and I hadn't the vaguest idea what it was.

That scared me.

I've seen a lot all these years, been shot at, been near dying more than once what with this and that falling part, but I was never really scared.

Now I was.

The lights stayed on, and I stayed away from the windows, didn't get much sleep thanks to some godawful heartburn and some just as godawful crap I had to drink to drive it away, and the next morning I cleaned up, ate something for breakfast, I don't remember what, and walked across town to Vera's place. A small house, a Cape Cod with a hedge and flowers and always something hanging on the front door, depending on the season.

She wouldn't answer.

I rang the bell, I knocked front and back, but she wouldn't answer.

Putter wasn't home either, or he wasn't answering the door.

By this time, I was getting angry. But I didn't know where the anger should go. At them, for being so old and foolish as to listen to an old idiot like me; or at me, for being a big mouth and telling them about Brownie.

I wandered a little, I sat, I wandered, I think I ate, I'm not sure, and finally ended up back at the depot, sitting on the platform's edge, swinging my legs, waiting for that son of a bitch to show himself again.

He did.

Just about dusk.

He came out of the woods across the way, hands in his pockets, that damn cigar in his mouth. He stayed far enough away that I couldn't see him very clearly, the speckled dark almost blending him into the trees behind.

"What the hell do you want?" I finally said, feeling like a jerk. Talking to a dead man; I must have been out of my mind.

Brownie shrugged one shoulder.

"You're scaring us half to death, you know," I complained. "We don't need it." I spat onto the tracks. "Vera's got that goddamn daughter of hers, Putter's got nothing, and I got . . ." I looked up.

Who did I have?

I had a wife who had left me thirty-two years ago, and the memory of a son who hadn't talked to me for twenty. They died within a year of each other five years ago; I only found out when Putter told me. I found out, and I got drunk, and didn't sober up for months, punching walls, throwing chairs, playing the *if I had only* game, the one that assumes you can foretell the future and rearrange the past.

Vera and Putter saved me.

But even now, on the TV when a man hugs his children, I have to look away.

"I don't get it," I said, almost whispering.

Brownie took the cigar from his mouth and examined the unlit tip.

A quartet of leaves bounced across the tracks toward me.

I watched them tumble and scratch until the base of the platform stopped them, just below my feet.

When I looked up, Brownie was gone.

No surprise.

What did surprise me was the kid who came scooting around the station house on his bike. Scared the hell out of me. Scared him, too, by the look on his face when he spotted me. He damn near fell off, and when I raised a slow hand to show him I wasn't going to hurt him, he wheeled around abruptly and was gone, like a ghost.

I laughed a bit then.

It showed I still had it—the power, maybe even the Look. I had used it often, that Look, to keep my trains in order. No rowdies on my routes, that's for sure; no troublemakers, no drunks, no arguments, no fights. I was tall enough to loom a little, and there was, I've been told, something in my face that somehow stopped folks from causing trouble.

My wife had told me that more than once, as a matter of fact. I never had to spank my son, or even raise my voice. It was the Look, and the loom, that kept him in line. Until she took him away. After that, I don't know. All I had left was the train.

So I went back home, ate a little, slept a little, and decided the next morning that Putter and Vera would come around, sooner or later. I wouldn't tell them about Brownie again; and if they asked, I would lie.

Meanwhile, the weather staying as nice as it was, I set about cleaning the house, opening the windows to let the winter out, dusting, vacuuming, all the things that take up time when time was all you had. I did it deliberately slowly, making sure I didn't miss a speck of dust, a wrinkle in the carpets, a burned-out bulb in the hall closet. Then I plunked myself down on my favorite porch chair to read the paper, thinking that maybe I'd head for the Brass Rail that night to see how my friends were doing.

The photograph on the front page almost passed me by.

It was the kid on the bike. He had been hit by a pickup on his way back from wherever, and had died in the King Street Hospital only the day before. Internal injuries. The driver of the pickup claimed the kid had swerved in front of him, not giving him a chance to do anything but close his eyes.

That, I thought, was a hell of a thing. A whole life gone before the life began.

It didn't occur to me for another hour that the accident was my fault. I had scared the kid, and he'd run off, pedaling as fast as he could, not paying attention to anything but getting away.

Another hour of just sitting there, wondering if I should say something, wondering if I was just making something out of nothing.

When daylight left me, I got up and went inside, went to the phone and called Putter, who, when he heard my voice, hung up.

I started for the Rail anyway, to have a beer or two, changed my mind and walked very slowly over to the park. The gates were still open, and I followed the tarmac path for a while, then veered to the right and followed a dirt path until I reached the bandstand.

Vera was on the steps, knitting beneath the lights that circled the bandstand's conical roof. The season's first concert was to start at nine; some folks were already setting up their chairs and blankets.

"Hey," I said, coming up alongside her.

She turned away quickly, not missing a stitch or whatever they're called.

"Damnit, Vera, what's the matter?"

She didn't answer for a long time. Then, her voice trembling a little: "They took Putter away this morning."

"What?" I moved to get in front of her, but her spine went rigid, and I stopped. "What the hell you talking about, Vera? Who took him away? Why?"

"That last day he saw you," she answered, needles flying, nearly making sparks, "he went home, never came out. They found him sitting in the kitchen, filthy, starving, staring at the phone, mumbling to himself." Her shoulders sagged a bit, her head bowed, the needles flew. "Didn't even know his own name, Richard. He didn't even know his own name."

A bunch of little kids raced and whooped across the grass, arms and legs at odds with each other. Three men with worn instrument cases climbed the bandstand steps, excusing themselves to Vera, ignoring me completely.

When they began tuning their horns, Vera put her knitting away. Precisely. Each movement painfully, tearfully, slow.

"Go away, Rich," she said as she stood, her back still toward me. "Go away."

She walked off without looking back once.

I walked off myself and looked back a hundred times, until I couldn't see her anymore, until I couldn't see anyone.

Putter.

Putter was gone.

And Vera might as well be.

Who did I have left?

Brownie was on my porch when I finally got home. He was in my chair. The cigar was in his mouth. One thumb was hooked into his suspenders.

The plan was to ignore him, but when I opened the door, I couldn't help but turn around. "You know, you're causing me more trouble than you were ever worth, you son of a bitch."

He didn't answer; he watched the street.

"I mean, for God's sake, you're dead!"

"So are you," he answered, took out the cigar, and grinned until he vanished.

Well, of course, I thought as I went inside. That explains everything. I'm dead and I don't know it. Vera didn't know it either, nor the driver who nearly clipped me with his convertible when I stepped off the curb by the park, or the dog that barked at me when I passed his territory.

Jesus, how stupid did Brownie, whatever the hell he was, think I was?

I woke up just before dawn.

Go away, Rich.

She hadn't looked at me.

The driver hadn't either, even though I'd questioned his lineage at the top of my voice.

Be damned, I thought, but I didn't believe it.

I dressed and went to the corner grocery to pick up some bread, wasted five minutes trying to get one of the pimple-faced clerks to pay me some attention, and later, nearly got run over by a shrieking pack of little kids on some kind of outing, and not one of them apologized, not even the teacher who herded them along.

Be damned.

I guess it wasn't heartburn after all.

So I packed, and I closed up the house, and I brought my suitcase to the porch and locked the front door one last time before slipping the keys under the welcome mat. Down the steps, then, and to the sidewalk, where I checked the house that smelled as if no one had ever lived there.

No one had.

Just me.

The living had left that place decades ago.

It was nearly dark when I reached the tracks. A ghost moon above the trees. Birds settling in the depot eaves. Something small and quick moving in the trees.

And my moonshadow leading me south along the tracks, toward New York City.

Lots of people down that way.

They see Brownie, or someone like him, they'll figure it's their time, even if no one believes it, and they'll either fight it or accept it, while Brownie moves on.

But when those people see me, when I want them to see me, when they look me in the eye, when they see the Look and the loom, and maybe a little smile, they're going to know damn well there's no such thing as "someone's time."

So who do I have left?

That's easy . . .

Everybody.

AFTERWORD

Sweetheart, Sweetheart by Bernard Taylor is my favorite ghost story. A novel that at once manages to be both moving and extremely unsettling. Someone, I forget who, called it a "typical English ghost story," but believe me, it's anything but typical. For me, anyway, there isn't anything that beats it.

Some of KATHE KOJA's best work explores the borderline between madness and art, in which her characters are infused with a passion bordering on obsession. Koja is a gifted stylist. Her understated prose creates powerful images and brings to life the most difficult of characters.

Kathe Koja is a Detroit-area native and lives there with her husband, artist Rick Lieder, and her son Aaron. She has been a full-time freelancer since 1984, after attending the Clarion Workshop at Michigan State University (thanks to the Susan C. Petrey scholarship), but has been a writer since she was four years old. Among her novels are *The Cipher*, *Skin*, *Kink*, and *Straydog*; some of her short fiction is collected in *Extremities*. Her most recent novel is *Buddha Boy*. *The Blue Mirror* will follow in 2004.

VELOCITY

KATHE KOJA

LINDEN; ASPEN; MAPLE; ash. A postcard setting, slant light and falling leaves, gravel switchback leading to a KEEP OUT gate, more sentry trees, a clustering clot of outbuildings—spare metal sheds, an emptied four-car garage. At the heart of the property, alone in bloody maple drift, stands an incongruous house, a hard-edged, sumptuous folly that at first glance seems neglected: dusty windows, drawn blinds, heavy bicycle chain hung across the door, front door. The chain is old; the locks—two locks—are bright and new.

Everywhere, broken bicycles.

Q: So what you're saying is that the process is equal to the art produced? That *how* is, essentially, *why*?

A: No, I . . . *no*. I'm saying the way I make my art can't be separated out from what I make, like a, like an egg white, OK? Christ, where do they find you people? I'm *saying* that when I aim a bike at a tree and crash it, that that's *part* of what the piece is about. The velocity, where it hits, how it fragments—every time it's different, none of them end up the same—

Q: Yet the process is identical. Are you willing to discuss what informs the process itself?

A: Give me a hand here. (His right arm is in a sling. He needs help to light another cigarette.) I have no idea what you just said.

Q: More simply, then: Why do you make art by running bicycles into trees? What . . . drives your particular mode of self-expression?

(No answer)

Q: Are you at all willing to discuss—

A: I thought you wanted to talk about my work. I thought this was—

Q: But art is a product of a human imagination, a human mind, a human body; especially your art, Mr. Vukovich. You shattered your arm while making this latest sculpture, you—

A: I don't have to listen to this shit.

(Break.)

THE HOUSE WAS built in the early 1970s, an austere and "modern" fantasia of brushed metal and glass block. It has eight rooms, three of them very large: the living or reception room, which takes up most of the first floor; the dining room, and the master bedroom; the rest are markedly, almost painfully, small. All are spare, as in a monastery or zendo: low teak tables, white futons, stainless-steel appliances. All the windows have identical white-paper blinds. All the walls are red. The dining table is laid with service for nine.

Q: Were you pleased with the Ortega installation?

A: Sure. Mary was great. She always does a great job.

Q: She's been your dealer for quite some time now, correct? Since you . . . returned from Arizona?

(No answer.)

Q: Mary Ortega is well-known—almost notorious—for her attraction to, let's say, a certain type of painful art. Art that expresses hurtful or violent emotions, art that specifically—

A: Jesus Christ, you're not going to get off it, are you? You didn't come here to talk about my work at all, all you want is to talk about my goddamned father, isn't that right? (He needs help to light his cigarette. His uninjured arm is trembling badly, almost theatrically.) There are plenty of articles about him, why don't you go read them? Why don't you do a search online? You'll be fucking buried in—

Q: Your father was a famous man. And since his death—

A: He didn't *die*, he killed himself.

Q:—forgive me, since his suicide, you've lived here alone in the house that he designed and commissioned, making art that graphically recalls the manner of his death. Mr. Vukovich, I don't mean to be unkind or impertinent, but when a father commits suicide by driving into a tree, and his son's art does nothing but recreate that moment, one cannot help but speculate that these things are intimately related. One cannot—

A: You think it's some kind of, of *tribute*, is that it? Jesus! You think that I—

Q: What I think is unimportant. What matters are your thoughts, your ideas about the—

A: I think you better pack up your little briefcase and go. That's what I think.

THE RED HOUSE, as it is called, is a kind of singularity, and as such, there was for a time a great demand for tours: from architecture and design professionals, professors and students, historians interested in its provenance, cultural anthropologists, as well as all the lesser hordes that treasure celebrity and wealth. After the owner's spectacular and graphic suicide, the estate fell hostage to legal squabbles between his first wife and current partner; the dispute was eventually resolved in the wife's favor, but by that time she herself had died, in a fire at her horse farm in Truro. The couple's only surviving relative, a son, himself an artist, came into possession of the house, and immediately discontinued all public tours. It was believed that he was living on the property, but his attorney's office would not confirm that this was true.

Q: Perhaps it would—perhaps we might talk a little about your early work. In Switzerland, you—

A: If you want to talk about him, I don't care. No, really. Let's do it. I don't give a fuck. (Speech today is slurred. He seems to have difficulty sitting upright. The cast has been removed from his arm, but he is still wearing a sling.)

Q: You're sure? I don't want to—All right, then. Your father, Edwin Vukovich—

A: The Prince of Darkness. Ed, to his friends. Of which he had none. Not even my mother. My mother used to warn me not to tell him anything: where I lived, what I was doing. If you tell him, he can use it, she always said. Don't give him anything he can use.

Q: He was an architect—

A: Architect manqué. Everyone thinks he designed the Red House, you know, but that's not true. He got this kid from RISD to make some drawings, and then he—Anyway, when I was at school, everyone thought he was like some big influence on me. Influence! He never even saw one of my installations, not one.

Q: And yet perhaps his influence was felt in other ways—?

A: Yeah. Like cancer. When I was in Berlin—fuck Berlin, when I was in *Sedona*, these people would show up out of the blue, these—sideshow freaks—Once, at one of my openings, this woman came up to me, she had all these pictures she wanted me to look at. Pictures of him, you know, him and her and—He was like an insect, you know? A praying mantis or a scorpion or something. He had no idea what it was like to be human and he didn't care.

Q: Yet he was quoted more than once as saying how proud he was of your work. He even tried to purchase one of your—

A: Right. *Heresy*, it was one of the first things I did at Mary's. It was like a ski run, with these little—You've seen it, right?

Q: Photographs of it, yes. It was an extraordinary installation. The almost insane sense of speed, of uncontrolled velocity—

A: Yeah. A good piece.—But Mary's smart, you know. She gave him a lot of sweet talk, but she wouldn't let him have the piece. Just like my mother said. Like voodoo. Skin cells, little bits of bone . . . They didn't tell you how he used to beat my mother, did they? He'd go through her closet, take out one of her little chain belts, Gucci, whatever, and just go to town. I used to try to get between them, make him stop. . . . When I got older, I bought a gun. I actually thought it would help! But I didn't need a gun, what I needed was, was silver bullets—

Q: Mr. Vukovich—

A:—or a stake through his heart. Right? Isn't that how you kill the devil? But that's the thing, you know? That's the whole fucking problem, because you can't kill the devil, not ever. Not with stakes or crosses or lawyers or—

Q: Mr. Vukovich, if this is distressing you, we—

A: *Christ*, my arm hurts.

(Break.)

IN THE ROOM that was formerly used as the laundry, the appliances have been removed and a small living space constructed, a scruffy human patch on the glass and steel. The items inside—a blue down sleeping bag, worn and leaking feathers; a Coleman stove; a bed tray; a scuffed plastic washtub—suggest an extended habitation. A shelf has been affixed three feet from the floor, just above the bundled sleeping bag, in easy reach of anyone lying below. On this shelf is a pink drugstore flashlight, an inhaler, an ashtray, a Remington automatic shotgun, its barrel sheared almost to the nub, and a copy of *Art in America*. Above the shelf is a crucifix, olivewood, immensely old. The corpus has been replaced with two bent roofing nails.

A: When I was working on *Acrimony*, I kept getting these phone calls. At first I thought it was just crank stuff, some dumbshit breathing on the phone; once or twice I even talked to him. Just, you know, Are you having fun, asshole? Mary said it was creepy and that I ought to call the cops, or the phone company, or something, but I didn't. I thought it was kind of funny. . . . But then he started calling me at home.

Q: You were staying—?

A: At home. At the Red House.

Q: I don't—the number is unlisted?

A: There're no phones in the house. No phone jacks, even. But I'd hear it ring, and ring, and ring; it'd go on for fucking hours. Sometimes I'd go sit outside just to get away from the sound. Sometimes I'd sleep outside. . . . Then I started sleeping at the gallery, in Mary's office. Which helped.—You should see your face. You look like the cat that just ate shit.

Q: (Silence.)

A: When I finally got the show up, the calls stopped. Like he was trying to fuck me over, right? Get me to stop working—

A: Who?

Q: Who do you think? Mary said I was working too hard, you know, or taking too much speed.—Wait, erase that. But if it was the speed then how come I never heard it unless I was working? The phone, and the knocking on the windows—I had them come and trim the branches, just hack them away from the house. I mean, I knew what it was but I wanted to be sure, right? And I was right. It wasn't trees or shrubs or branches, it was goddamn *knocking* and it was him. Just like the phone was him. Just like the guy at the bike shop, the one I always use, right? Now he won't sell me any more bikes, he says it's too dangerous. Dangerous! To *him*, he means. Because he knows. Because he gets into people's heads, like poison gas, or something—like he did to my mother, I watched him do it. She used to be, she was so . . . And then he killed her. I know it was him, there's no way that barn burned by itself. And he got Teo, too—

Q: Teo?

A: Her horse. They found them together, she was all—And then he tried to do it to me. In Sedona, Berlin, where-the-fuck-ever, doesn't matter, never did. You think being dead is a *problem* for him? Hell, no! It just makes it *easier*, you know? It just makes everything easier.

Q: Mr. Vukovich—Mr. Vukovich, when you were working on *Calefaction*, Mary Ortega was quoted as—

A: Don't change the subject! Don't change the subject! You said you wanted to talk about him, well that's what we're talking about! Are you afraid? Is that it? "Speak of the devil and the devil appears"? But he's already here. He's already right—

Q: Mr. Vukovich—

A: Stop *saying* that.

(Break.)

AS PER THE trust, the Red House and its grounds are serviced on a seasonal schedule. Mowing, raking, bundling brush, blowing snow; repairing the depredations of weather; replacing the furnace filter, caulking the cracks; there is a lavish budget set aside for these things and they are always faithfully performed.

The former laundry room is rigorously avoided, unless there is actual damage within it needing repair. When the lawn crews arrive the broken and discarded bicycles are carefully removed to the garage; before the crews leave, the parts are restored to their earlier approximate positions. This is not part of the trust's directions, but there is a sizable rider to the maintenance contract to ensure that these things are done, or not done. Money, as always, is neutral, and efficient in its demands.

Q: You have a new show opening soon?

A: I'm not—Yeah. I guess. I don't know the dates, you better ask Mary.

Q: It's titled *The Erl King*, is that right?

A: Yeah. Mary doesn't like it, the title, but that's just too fucking bad. I know what I'm doing.

Q: Mr. Vukovich, you—would you rather not continue today? You seem very—

A: I don't *seem* like anything. I *am*. You would be too. Maybe you will be. He doesn't like me to talk to you, you know. So I was up all fucking night last night, listening to him crawl through the pipes. I was afraid to, to take a shit, you know? Because what if he decided to crawl inside me? I wouldn't put it past him. I wouldn't put anything past him.

Q: Perhaps we ought to reschedule our—

A: Perhaps you ought to shut the fuck up and listen to what I'm telling you . . . listen . . . did you hear that?

Q: Hear what? I didn't—

A: Oh yes you did. You wanted to know all about my art, my homage to his suicide or whatever you called it—

Q: I—

A:—like it's some weird oedipal thing, but the fact is, I just have to keep doing it, you know, until it sticks. Until it *works*. Man, you think I like to keep doing the same piece over and over? Think I like hurting myself? breaking my arm? *and* my shin, and my fucking heel bone, which still hurts, they never did set it right—But I have to. I don't need that guy at the bike shop, I can order anything I want, they don't even have to know it's me. Because if he's in the pipes today, where will he be tomorrow? Huh? Up my ass, that's where, and crawling out of my mouth! You think I need that? I'd rather break my neck on a bike! I'd rather—

Q: Mr. Vukovich, you're very upset. We'd better stop this now, we'd better just—

A: You see this gun?

Q: I—oh my God. Look, I'm, I'm leaving now. I can't—

A: No, take it. Take it! And hold it on me. Like this. Like this! *Hold* it! . . . that's right. You sit there and you hold it. And if he crawls out of my mouth, you shoot him. Hear me? Shoot the motherfucker in the head.

BECAUSE OF THE way the Red House is constructed, because of its placement on the grounds, and the arrangement of the trees and shrubs around it, it owns a peculiar radiance in the early evening sun, a deep and affecting glow as if the house were lit from within, like fire in the depths of a jewel.

Visitors are not always aware of this phenomenon, and are sometimes confused by the house's name, seeing only its gunmetal-gray-and-glass exterior. But if one arrives at almanac sundown, the house will indeed be glowing, its inner nature made proudly manifest, as hot and red and chambered as a beating heart.

AFTERWORD

Favorite ghost story? Short form, Charlotte Perkins Gilman's "The Yellow Wallpaper," a masterpiece of understated dread. Long form is *The Haunting of Hill House*, by the incomparable Shirley Jackson, who, as Stephen King so wonderfully notes, "never needed to raise her voice."

LUCIUS SHEPARD was born in Lynchburg, Virginia, grew up in Daytona Beach, Florida, and lives in Vancouver, Washington. His short fiction has won the Nebula Award, the Hugo Award, The International Horror Writers Award, The National Magazine Award, the Locus Award, The Theodore Sturgeon Award, and the World Fantasy Award. His short novel, *Louisiana Breakdown*, was recently published; forthcoming are a novella collection and a collection of mixed nonfiction and fiction, *Two Trains Running*.

LIMBO

LUCIUS SHEPARD

"*. . . limbo, limbo, limbo like me . . .*"
—TRADITIONAL

THE FIRST WEEK in September, Detroit started feeling like a bad fit to Shellane. It was as if the city had tightened around him, as if the streets of the drab working-class suburb that had afforded him anonymity for nearly two years had become irritated by the presence of a foreign body in its midst. There was no change he could point to, no sudden rash of hostile stares, no outbreak of snarling dogs, just a sense that something had turned. A similar feeling had often come over him when he lived back East, and he had learned to recognize it for a portent of trouble, but he wasn't sure he could trust it now. He suspected it might be a flashback of sorts, a mental spasm produced by boredom and spiritual disquiet. Nevertheless, he chose to play it safe, checked into a motel and staked out his apartment. When he noticed a Lincoln Town Car across the street from the apartment, he trained his binoculars on it. In the driver's seat was a young man with short black hair and a pugilist's flattened nose. Beside him, an enormous sour-looking man with bushy gray sideburns and a bald scalp, his face vaguely fishlike. Thick lips and popped eyes. Marty Gerbasi. Shellane had no doubt as to what had brought Gerbasi to Detroit. A half hour later, after doing some banking, he picked up a green Toyota that had been purchased under a different name and kept parked in a downtown garage for the past twenty-nine months, and drove north toward the Upper Peninsula.

At forty-six, Shellane was a thick-chested slab of a man with muscular forearms, large hands, and a squarish homely face. His whitish-blond hair had gone gray at the temples, and his blue eyes were surprisingly vital by contrast to the seamed country in which they were the only ornament. He customarily dressed in jeans and windbreakers, a wardrobe designed to reinforce the impression that he might be a retired cop or military man—he had learned that this pretense served to keep strangers at a distance. His gestures were carefully managed, restrained, all in keeping with his methodical approach to life, and he did not rattle easily. Realizing that assassins had found him in Detroit merely caused him to make an adjustment and set in motion a contingency plan that he had prepared for just such an occasion.

When he reached the Upper Peninsula, he headed west toward Iron Mountain, intending to catch a ferry across to Canada; but an hour out of Marquette, just past the little town of Champion, he came to a dirt road leading away into an evergreen forest, and a sign that read: LAKESIDE CABINS—OFF-SEASON RATES. On impulse, he swung the Toyota onto the road and went swerving along a winding track between ranks of spruce. The day was sunny and cool, and the lake, an elongated oval of dark mineral blue, reminded Shellane of an antique lapis lazuli brooch that had belonged to his mother. The lake was surrounded by forested hills and bordered by rocky banks and narrow stretches of brownish-gray sand. Under the cloudless sky, the place generated a soothing stillness. A quarter-mile in from the highway stood a fishing cabin with a screen porch, peeling white paint, a tar-paper roof, and a phone line—it had an air of cozy dilapidation that spoke of evenings around a table with cards and whiskey, children lying awake in bunk beds listening for splashes and the cries of loons. Several other cabins were scattered along the shore, the closest about a hundred yards distant. Shellane walked in the woods, enjoying the crisp, resin-scented air, scuffing the fallen needles, thinking he could stand it there a couple of weeks. It would take that long to set up a new identity. This time, he intended to bury himself. Asia, maybe.

A placard on the cabin door instructed anyone interested in renting to contact Avery Broillard at the Gas 'n Guzzle in Champion. Through a window Shellane saw throw rugs on a stained spruce floor. Wood stove (there was a cord of wood stacked out back); a funky-looking refrigerator speckled with decals; sofa covered with a Mexican blanket. A wooden table and chairs. Bare bones, but it suited both his needs and his notion of comfort.

The Gas 'n Guzzle proved to be a log cabin with pumps out front and a grocery inside. Hand-lettered signs in the windows declared that fishing licenses were for sale within, also home-baked pies and bait, testifying by their humorous misspellings to a cutesy self-effacing attitude on the part of ownership. The manager, Avery Broillard, was lanky, thirtyish, with shoulder-length black hair and rockabilly sideburns; he had one of those long, faintly dish-shaped Cajun faces with features so prominent they seemed caricatures of good looks. He said the cabin had been cleaned, the phone line was functional, and quoted a reasonable weekly rate. When Shellane paid for two weeks, cash in advance, Avery peered at him suspiciously.

"You prefer plastic?" Shellane asked, hauling out his wallet. "I don't like using it, but some people won't deal with cash."

"Cash is good." Avery folded the bills and tucked them in his shirt pocket.

Shellane grabbed a shopping basket and stocked up on cold cuts, frozen meat and vegetables, soup, bread, cooking and cleaning necessities, and at the last moment, a home-baked apple pie that must have weighed close to four pounds. He promised himself to eat no more than one small slice a day and be faithful with his push-ups.

"Get these pies made special," Avery said as he shoveled it into a plastic bag. "They're real tasty."

Shellane smiled politely.

"Might as well give you one of these here." Avery handed him a leaflet advertising the fact that the Endless Blue Stars were playing each and every weekend at Roscoe's Tavern.

"That's my band," Avery said. "Endless Blue Stars."

"Rock and roll?"

"Yeah." Then, defensively, "We got quite a following around here. You oughta drop in and give a listen. Ain't a helluva lot else to do."

Shellane forked over three twenties and said he would be sure to drop in.

"If you're looking to fish," said Avery, continuing to bag the groceries, "they taking some pike outa the lake. I can show you the good spots."

"I'm no fisherman," Shellane told him. "I came up here to work on a book."

"You a writer, huh? Anything I might of read?"

Shellane resisted an impulse to say something sarcastic. Broillard's manner, now turned ingratiating, was patently false. There was a sly undertone to every word he spoke and Shellane had the impression that he considered himself a superior being, that the Gas 'n Guzzle was to his mind a pit stop on the road to world domination, and as a consequence, he affected a faux yokelish manner toward his patrons that failed to mask a fundamental condescension. He had bad-luck eyes. Watered-down blue; irises marked by hairline darknesses, like fractures in a glaze.

"This one's my first," said Shellane. "I just retired. Did my twenty, and I always wanted to try a book. So . . ."

"What's it about?" Avery asked. "Your book."

"Crime," said Shellane, and tried to put an edge on his smile. "Like they say—write what you know."

IT TOOK HIM until after dark to settle into the cabin, to order an Internet hook-up, to prepare and eat his dinner. Once he'd finished dessert, he poured a fresh cup of coffee, switched on his laptop and sent an e-mail that prevented a file from being sent to the U.S. Justice Department. The file contained a history of Shellane's twenty years as a thief, details of robberies perpetrated, murders witnessed, and various other details whose revelation might result in the indictment of several prominent members of Boston's criminal society. It was not that effective an insurance policy. The men who wanted to kill him were too arrogant to believe that he could bring them down, and perhaps their judgment was accurate; but knowing about the file had slowed their reactions sufficiently to allow his escape. He was confident that he would continue to stay ahead of them. However, this confidence did not afford him the satisfaction that once it had. It had been many years since Shellane had derived much pleasure from life. Survival had become less a passion than a game he was adept at playing. Lately the game had lost its savor. Apart from the desire to thwart his pursuers, he was no longer certain why he persevered.

He was about to shut down the computer when he heard a noise outside. He went into the bedroom, took the nine millimeter from his suitcase, and holding it behind him, went out onto the porch and nudged open the screen door. A slim figure, silhouetted against the moonstruck surface of the water, was moving briskly away from the cabin. Shellane called out, and the figure stopped short.

"I'm sorry," a woman's voice said. "I was out for a walk. The lights . . . I didn't know the cabin was rented."

"It's okay." Shellane stuck the gun into his belt behind his back and pulled his sweater down over it. "I thought it was an animal or something."

"Aren't many animals around anymore," said the woman as she came into the light. "Just squirrels and raccoons. People say we've still got a few wolverines in the woods, but I've never seen one."

She was slender and tall, most of her height in her legs, with long red hair gathered in a ponytail, wearing jeans and a plaid wool jacket. Early thirties, he guessed. A pale Irish country face with a pointy chin and wide cheekbones. Pretty as a morning prayer. Faint laughlines showed at the corners of her olive-green eyes. Yet she had a subdued air and he suspected that she had not laughed in a while.

"I'm Grace," she said.

"Michael," said Shellane, remembering to use his temporary identity. "Guess you're my neighbor, huh?"

She gestured toward the lake. "Three cabins down."

Being accustomed to city paranoia, it surprised him that an attractive woman—any woman, for that matter—would tell a stranger where she lived. He had assumed that following the introduction, she would retreat, but she stood there, smiling nervously.

"How about some coffee?" he asked. "I was going to make another pot."

Once again she surprised him by accepting the invitation. As he fixed the coffee, she moved about the cabin, keeping away from the center of the room, touching things and stopping suddenly, like a cat exploring new territory. Now and then she would glance at him and flash a nervous smile, as if to assure him she meant no harm. She possessed a jittery vitality that drew his eye, alerted him to her every gesture. He set a cup of coffee on the table and she sat on the edge of her chair, ready to take flight.

"I didn't really want coffee," she said. "It's just living out here, I don't get to meet many people."

"You're not renting?"

"No, I . . . no."

Her mouth thinned, as if she was keeping something back.

"What are you doing up here?" she asked. "Vacation?"

He told the retirement story. Her attention wandered and he had the idea that she knew he was lying. He asked what she did.

"I . . . nothing, really. I take a lot of walks." She came to her feet. "I should go."

Maybe, he thought, paranoia just took a while to develop in the Upper Peninsula. He followed her to the door, watched her start toward the lake. She turned, walking backwards, and said brightly, "I'm sure we'll run into each other again."

"Hope so," he said.

He stood in the doorway until she was out of sight, sorting through his impressions of her, trying to distinguish the real from the imagined. "Trouble," he said, addressing himself to the shadows along the shore, and went back inside.

HIS BRIEF ENCOUNTER with Grace stayed with Shellane all the next day. She had been interested in him, he believed. Because he was interested in her, he questioned whether he might be flattering himself; he was not given to assuming that every woman with whom he spoke was attracted to him. He trusted his instincts. She had to be fifteen years younger than he. It would be foolish to get involved with her—under the best of circumstances, she would be a problem, and these were far from the best of circumstances.

That evening, however, he went for a walk along the dirt road that followed the shore, half in hopes of running into her. Her cabin, set among the trees high on the bank, was more house than cabin. A deck out back. Satellite dish on the roof. Light sprayed from a picture window, and Grace was standing at it, wearing jeans and a cableknit white sweater. Curious about her, wanting to get closer, he climbed the bank to the right of the window. Her head was down, arms folded. She looked miserable. He had an urge to knock, to say he was passing by and had spotted her, but before he could debate the wisdom of obeying this urge, headlights slashed across the front of the house. Rattling and grumbling, a big blue Cadillac at least thirty-five years old pulled up beside the house and the reason—Shellane suspected—for Grace's misery climbed out. Avery Broillard. He clumped to the door, knocked his boots clean, and went inside. Grace had apparently retreated into the rear of the house. Broillard stood in the front room, hands on hips. "Fuck!" he shouted, and made a flailing gesture. Then he stomped off along a hallway.

As Shellane headed for home, a bank of fog moved toward him across the lake, like the ghost of a crumbling city melting up from the past. He was furious with himself. That he had been on the verge of coming between husband and wife, boyfriend-girlfriend, whatever . . . it spoke to a breakdown in judgment. All it would take to bring the cops nosing around was some asshole like Broillard getting his wind up, and though Shellane could handle the cops, it would be wiser to avoid them. Agitated, unable to calm down, he drove into town, thinking he would eat at a diner; but when he saw the lights of Roscoe's, a low concrete building with a neon sign that sketched the green image of a snub-nosed pistol above the door, he turned into the parking lot. Inside, he grabbed a seat at the bar and ordered a cheeseburger plate. At the far end of the room was a stage furnished with amps and mike stands and a PA, backed by a sequined curtain. A bearded roadie was engaged in setting up the mikes. All the tables were occupied, and it appeared that more than half the crowd were women. The babble of laughter and talk outvoiced the jukebox, which was playing "Wheel in the Sky," a song emblematic to Shellane's mind of the most pernicious form of jingle rock. He nursed a draft and watched the place fill beyond its seating capacity. Apparently Broillard did have a following. People had packed in along the walls and were standing two-deep at the bar.

He had intended to leave before the live music started, but when the lights dimmed and a cheer went up, people massing closer to the stage, jamming the dance floor like a festival audience, curiosity got the better of him. Five shadows moved onstage from the wings. A spot pinned the central mike stand, where Broillard was strapping on a Telecaster with glittery blue stars dappling its black finish. He flashed a boyish grin and said, "How 'bout somebody bringing me a beer? I feel a thirst coming on." Then he turned his back on the crowd and the band kicked in.

At best, Shellane had expected to hear uninspired songs about beer and dangerous roadhouses and wild, wild women played with rough, energetic competence; because of his distaste for the band's front man, he hoped for worse. But the Endless Blue Stars had a lyrical sound that was way too big for Roscoe's, their style falling into a spectrum somewhere between Dire Straits and early Cream. Retro, yet glossed with millennial cynicism. The first song featured a long intro during which Broillard laid down sweetly melodic guitar lines over a four-four with a Brazilian feel that built gradually into a rock tempo. When he stepped to the mike, the crowd waved their arms and shouted.

> *"Walked out tonight, a frozen blue,*
> *the moon was dark and shooting stars were dying . . ."*

The bassist and drummer added harmony on the next line:

> *". . . with a cold white fire. . . ."*

Then Broillard's throaty baritone soared over the background:

> *". . . things ain't been the same*
> *since I fell in love with you,*
> *I've been so hypnotized . . ."*

The mood cast by the song—by all the songs—was irresistibly romantic, an invitation to join in a soothing blue dream of love and mystery, and Broillard's Byronic stage persona was so persuasive Shellane wondered if he might have misjudged him. But when the band went on break and Broillard came swaggering over to the bar, dispensing largesse to well-wishers, his arm about a pretty albeit slightly overstuffed brunette, caressing the underside of her right breast, Shellane decided this was the thing that made music—all art, for that matter—fundamentally suspect: that assholes could become proficient at it.

Broillard spotted him, dragged the girl over and said, "Needed a break from all that peace and quiet, eh?"

Shellane said, "Yeah, you were right," and then, though he was tempted to dishonesty, complimented him on the set.

"I didn't figure you for a music lover," said Broillard.

"That song, the one that went into a seven-four break after the second verse . . ."

" 'Three Fates.' " Broillard looked at him with renewed interest, "You play?"

"Used to," Shellane said. "I liked that song."

"Yeah, well," said Broillard dismissively. "Cool." He gave the brunette a squeeze. "Annie, this is . . ."

"Michael," Shellane said when Broillard couldn't dredge up the name.

"Right. Mister Michael is a writer. Crime novels."

Annie blinked vacantly up at Shellane, too blitzed to say "Hi."

Somebody caught Broillard's shoulder, claiming his attention. As he turned away, he smirked and said to Shellane, "Stick around, man. It gets better."

OVER THE NEXT two days, Shellane was kept busy in detailing a new passport, setting up bank accounts on-line. Twice he caught sight of Grace walking along the shingle and considered calling to her, but her air of distraction reinforced his belief that she was a woman with time on her hands. Such women had a need for drama in order to give weight to their lives—he did not intend to become the costar in her therapy. But he continued to speculate about who she was. He remembered no wedding ring, yet she displayed a kind of cloistered unhappiness that reminded him of married women he had known. Perhaps she removed the ring to give herself the illusion of freedom. Or to give someone else that same illusion.

Around noon on the third day, he took a couple of beers, a sandwich, the new James Lee Burke novel, and went down to the shore and sat with his back against a boulder that emerged from the bank, a granite stump scoured smooth by glaciers and warm from the sun. He read only ten or fifteen minutes before laying the book aside. If he had done crime in Louisiana, he thought he might have stayed with it. The crews there were more interesting than the Southie ratboys he'd worked with in Boston . . . at least if he were to trust the novel. Burke might be exaggerating. Crews were likely the same all over, just different accents. He stared out across the sunstruck lake, watched a motorboat cutting a white wake, too far away for the engine noise to carry over the sighing wind and the slop of the water. He half-believed nothing bad could happen here. That was ridiculous, he knew. Yet he felt serene, secure. He felt that the landscape had adjusted to him, reordered itself to accommodate his two hundred and twenty-six pounds and settled around him with the perfection of a tailored coat. No way he could hack it here for three years as he had in Detroit. But the fit was better here and he didn't understand why this was. He stuck out in Champion. There was no cover, no disguise he could successfully adopt.

He finished a beer, ate half the sandwich and went back to the book, but his attention wandered. Wind ruffled the shining reach of the water, raising wavelets that each caught a spoonful of dazzle and making it appear that a school of jeweled lives were surfacing from the depths. The trees stirred in dark green unison. The shingle was decorated with arrangements of twigs, matted feathers and bones, polished stones. Mysteries and signs. Shellane closed his eyes.

"Hello," said Grace, and his heart broke rhythm. He let out a squawk and sat up, knocking over his freshly opened beer.

"I'm sorry!" She put out a hand as if to repair the damage. A fearful gesture, and her face, too, reflected fear.

"I didn't hear you come up."

She relaxed her pose, but still seemed wary, and he had the idea that she was used to being frightened.

"It's okay," he said. "No big deal."

She had on jeans, the plaid jacket, and a T-shirt underneath—black with sequined blue stars. Her hair, loose about her shoulders, shone a coppery red under the sun. Even her skin seemed faintly luminous.

"Did you eat yet? I've got half a sandwich going to waste." He held out the baggie containing the sandwich.

She stared at it hungrily, but shook her head. The wind lifted the ends of her hair, fluttered the collar of her jacket

The depth of her timidity astonished him. Broillard might have a lot to answer for.

"What are you reading?" she asked.

He showed her the book.

"I don't know him," she said.

"It's detective fiction, but the writing's great."

She cast an anxious glance behind her, then sank to her knees. "I mostly read short stories. That's what I wanted to write . . . short stories."

"*Wanted* to write?"

"I just . . . he . . . I couldn't . . . I . . ."

She stalled out and Shellane resisted the impulse to touch her hand.

"I wasn't very good," she said.

"Who told you that?"

As he spoke, he recognized that he was casting aside his resolve and making a choice that could endanger him. Something about her, and it was not just her apparent hopelessness, pulled at him, made him want to take the risk. Her face serially mapped her emotions: surprise and alarm and fretfulness. Green eyes crystaled with reflected light.

"Your husband," Shellane said. "Right?"

"It's not . . ." She broke off and glanced off along the shore road. The blue Cadillac was slewing toward them from the direction of Broillard's cabin. Grace scooted behind the boulder. As the car turned onto the access road, Shellane saw that the brunette from the tavern occupied the passenger seat. The Cadillac skidded in the gravel, then sped off among the evergreens.

"Did he see me?" Grace emerged from behind the boulder. "I don't *think* he did."

He ignored the question. "He brings 'em home? His fucking bimbos? You're there, and he just brings 'em home?"

Her nod was almost imperceptible, hardly more than a tucking in of the chin.

"Why do you put up with it? What does he do? Does he hit you?"

"He never . . . no. Not for a long time."

"Not for a long time? Terrific!"

She opened her mouth but only shook her head again. Finally she said, "It's not entirely his fault."

"Sure, I can see that."

"You don't understand! He's very talented and he's been so frustrated. He . . ."

"So he takes his frustrations out on you. He makes you feel bad about yourself. He tells you you're worthless. He blames you for his failings."

Shellane reached for her hand. She looked startled when he touched her wrist, but let him pull her down onto her knees. "If that's how it is," he said, "you should leave him."

The boat that had been racing around at the far end of the lake swung close in along the shore, the sound of its engine carving a gash in the stillness. The driver and the woman with him waved. Neither Shellane nor Grace responded.

"He doesn't deserve you," Shellane said.

"You don't know me . . . and you don't know him."

"Twenty-five years ago, I used to *be* him."

"I doubt that. Avery's one of a kind."

"No he's not. I had a girlfriend who loved me. A beautiful girl. Smart. Doing great in grad school. But me, I couldn't get it together. I was too damn lazy. I thought because I was smart, the world was going to fall at my feet. Eventually she left me. But before she did, I did my best to make her feel as bad about herself as I felt about myself."

"Did you ever get it together?"

"I got by, but I never did what I wanted."

"What was that?"

"It's kind of a coincidence, actually. I wanted to be a musician. I wrote songs . . . or tried to. Screwed around in a garage band. But I settled for the next best thing."

She looked at him expectantly.

"Maybe I'll tell you sometime."

They sat without speaking. Shellane told himself it was time to pull back. This pause was the perfect opportunity. But instead, he said, "Have dinner with me tonight. We can drive into Marquette."

"I can't."

"Why not? He'll be playing tonight."

"He plays every night."

"Then why not have dinner? You afraid someone will see us?"

She gave no reply, and he said, "Come over to the cabin, then. I'll cook up some steaks."

"I might have to eat at home." She flattened her palms against her thighs. "I could come over after."

"Okay," he said.

"I don't want you to think . . . that . . ."

"I promise not to think."

That brought a wan smile. "We can just talk, if that's all right."

"Talk would be good."

She appeared to be growing uncomfortable, and watching her hands wrestle with one another, her eyes darting toward the lake, he timed her and said to himself, the instant before she spoke the same words, "I should go."

LATE THAT AFTERNOON, it seemed that deep November arrived at the lake in all its dank and gray displeasure, a cold wind pushing in a pewter overcast and spatterings of rain. As the dusk turned to dark, a fog rolled in, ghost-dressing the trees in whitish rags that clung to the boughs like relics of an ancient festival. Shellane, who had gone for a walk just as the fog began to accumulate, was forced to grope his way along, guided by the muffled slap of the waves. He had brought a flashlight, but all the beam illuminated were churning walls of fog. He must have been within a hundred yards of the cabin when he realized he could no longer hear the water. He kept going in what he assumed to be the direction of the shoreline, but after ten minutes he was still on solid ground. He must have gotten turned around, he thought. He shined the flashlight ahead. A momentary thinning of the mist, and he made out a building before him. If anyone was at home, he could ask directions. The visibility was so poor he couldn't see much until he was next to the wall. The boards were knotty, badly carpentered, set at irregular slants and coated with pitch. He ran his hand along one and picked up a splinter.

"Shit!" He examined his palm. Blood welled from a gouge and a toothpick-sized sliver of wood was visible beneath the skin. He shook his hand to ease the hurt and happened to glance upward. Protruding from the wall twenty feet overhead was a huge black fist, perfectly articulated, twice the circumference of an oil drum. From its clenched fingers hung a shred of rotting rope.

Shellane's heart seemed itself to close into a fist. Swirling fog hid the thing from view, but he could have sworn it was not affixed to the wall, but rather emerged from it, the boards flowing out into the shape, as if the building were angry and had extruded this symbol of its mood.

He heard movement behind him and spun about, caught his heel and fell. Knocked loose on impact, the flashlight rolled off, becoming a mounded yellowish radiance away in the fog. Panicked, he scrambled up, breathing hard. He could no longer see much of the building, just the partial outline of a roof.

A guttural noise; pounding footsteps.

"Hey!" Shellane called.

More footsteps and another voice, maybe the same one.

"Hey! Quit screwing around!" he shouted. The hairs on his neck prickled. Who would own a place like this? Pissant Goths. Rich kids who'd never gotten over The Cure. Another movement, this time on the left. Something heavy and ungainly.

Fuck directions, he told himself.

He started away from the building, walking fast and holding his arms out like Frankenstein's monster to ward off obstructions. Less than ten seconds later, he hit a drop-off and staggered into cold ankle-deep water. He overbalanced and toppled onto his side, raising a splash. He pushed up from the silty bottom, found his way to shore and stood shivering. Listening for voices. The only sound was that of the water dripping from his clothes onto the sand. He felt foolish at having been spooked by, probably, a bunch of twits who wore eye liner and drank wine out of silver cups and thought they were unique.

That fist, though. What a freak show!

If things were different, he thought, he'd give them a lesson in reality. Blow a couple of nine-millimeter holes in their point of view. But his annoyance faded quickly, and after squeezing and shaking the excess water from his clothes, he trudged off along the shore.

HE DOUBTED THAT Grace would show that evening. Truth be told, he wasn't sure he wanted her to. His experience in the fog had rekindled his caution and he thought it might be best for them both if she blew him off. He could be no help to her and she would only endanger him. At nine o'clock he switched on the laptop and called up his crime file. Seeing Marty Gerbasi in Detroit had made him realize it was time to add a more personal reminiscence. He'd been having a beer in the Antrim back in Southie, the winter of '83, when Marty had come in with Donnie Doyle, a pale twist of a kid with peroxided hair and a rabbity look who occasionally hooked on with a crew as a driver. Stupid as a stopped clock. They'd sat down next to Shellane and all three of them had tried to drink the bar out of Bushmills. Marty was buying, playing the grand fellow, laughing at Donnie's stories, most of them lies about his gambling prowess, and winking broadly at Shellane as if to say he knew the kid was bullshit. Around

1:00 A.M. they staggered out of the bar—at least Donnie staggered. Marty and Shellane could handle their liquor. No one ever saw Donnie Doyle after that night, and afterward Shellane understood that having Marty buy you drinks was not a good thing. Like so many of Shellane's associates, he lacked the necessary inch of conscience to qualify as human. Over the years, Shellane's recognition that he was involved with a company of affable sociopaths had grown more poignant, eventually causing him to rethink his future, to realize that sooner or later Marty would offer to buy him drinks. He never found out what Donnie Doyle had done to deserve his night out with good ol' Roy Shellane and the guinea angel of death, but he figured it was nothing more than some unfortunate behavior, maybe a tendency toward loquaciousness or—

A knock on the door. Ignoring his determination that he was better off without her, he jumped up to let Grace in. The plaid jacket and jeans again. Ponytail.

"Sorry I'm late," she said as he stood aside to allow her to pass.

"I didn't know if you'd make it at all, what with the fog."

She sat at the table, shrugged out of the jacket; she had on a green turtleneck underneath. "It's nice and warm in here," she said, then pointed to his hand, which he had bandaged after removing the splinter. "What happened?"

Her eyes widened when he told her about the black house.

"You know who owns the place?" he asked.

A shake of her head. "It's really old. Lots of people stay there."

"Have you met any of them?"

"They don't talk to me."

Shellane went into the kitchen and poured two fingers of bourbon. He glanced at her inquiringly, held up the bottle, expecting her to refuse.

"I'll try it," she said.

He poured, set the glass in front of her. She touched the rim with her forefinger, closed her hand around it, then had a sip. She sipped again and smiled. "It's good!"

She was easier around him than before, and this both elated and distressed him. What he felt for her, when he tried to isolate it, was less defined than what he felt toward her husband. He was attracted, but the basis of the attraction perplexed him. True, she was sexy, with her green eyes and expressive mouth and strong, slender body. Her vulnerability made him feel protective and this enhanced his other feelings. But he could not help thinking that a large part of the attraction was due to the danger she presented. For several years he had limited his contact with women to those he met through outcall services; now, alone with her in this secluded place, he wondered if he was not toying with fate, pretending there was something for them other than the moment. She finished her drink and asked for a refill. He doubted she was much of a drinker and thought this might be her way of signaling that she was ready to take a step. He did not believe her capable of discretion. Her spirit was so damaged, if Broillard were to get a whiff of another man and pressured her, she might confess everything. Broillard might no longer care about her, but in Shellane's experience, men who abused their women were extremely possessive of them.

She asked what he used the laptop for and he told her the lie about his book. She pressed him on the subject, inquiring as to his feelings about his work, and he fended off her questions by saying he didn't know enough about writing yet to be able to talk about it with any intelligence.

"You were a songwriter," she said.

"I was a wanna-be. That doesn't qualify me to talk about it."

"That's not true. If you want to do something, you think about it. Even if it's not conscious, you come to understand things about it. Techniques . . . strategies."

"Sounds like you should be telling me about *your* work," he said. When she demurred, he asked what she would write about if she regained her confidence.

"It's not my confidence that's the problem."

"Sure it is," he said. "Having enough confidence to fail is most of everything. So tell me. What would you write about?"

"The lake." She tugged at a strand of hair that had come loose from the ponytail, stretched it down beside her ear as if to contrive a sideburn. "It's all I know. My father and I lived here from the time I was four. My mother died when I was a baby."

"It's your father's house you're in now?"

She nodded. "After he died, Avery came along. He helped me with the business."

"The Gas 'n Guzzle?"

"Avery renamed it. It used to be Malloy's. I wanted to keep the name, but . . ." She gave another of those glum gestures that Shellane was beginning to interpret as emblematic of her attitude toward an entire spectrum of defeats.

"So Avery moved right in, did he?"

"I guess." She held out her empty glass again and he poured a stiffer drink.

"Looks like I'm going to have to call you a cab," he said

She giggled, lifted the glass and touched the liquid with the tip of her tongue. It was the first sign of happiness she had shown him, and it was so pure a thing, so innocently sexual expression, that Shellane, himself a little drunk, was moved to touch her cheek.

Startled, she pulled away. He apologized, but she said, "No, it's okay.

Really!" But she was flustered. At any minute, he thought, he would hear her say she had to go.

She stared into her glass for such a long time, Shellane grew uncomfortable. Then, her tone suddenly forceful, she said, "I could write a hundred stories about the lake. Every day it has a different mood. I never wanted to live anywhere else." She glanced up at him. "You like it here, too, don't you?"

"Yeah, but I couldn't live here."

"Why not?"

"It's complicated," he said after a pause.

She laid her palms flat on the table and studied their shapes against the dark wood; then she pushed up to her feet. "May I use your restroom?"

She was so long in the bathroom, Shellane began to worry. The water had been running ever since she went in. What could she be doing? Effecting an ornate suicide? Praying? Changing into animal form? He considered asking if she was okay, but decided this was too much solicitude.

Wind jiggled the latch, and a bough scraped the roof. He stretched out his legs, his eyelids drooped, and he pictured Grace with the glass raised to her lips, the tawny whiskey and the coppery color of her hair blended by lamplight. He failed to notice the sound of the bathroom door opening, but heard her step behind him. Her face was scrubbed and shining. She was holding a bath towel in front of her, but let it drop to the side. Her breasts were high and small, strawberry-tipped; the pearly arcs of her hips framing a tuft of coppery flame. Her eyes locked onto his.

"I'd like to stay," she said.

THERE CAME A point during the night, with the wind sharking through the trees, rattling the cabin as if it were a sackful of bones, knifing through the boards to sting Shellane's skin with cold . . . there came a point when he understood that he understood nothing, either of the world or the ways of women, not even the workings of his own heart. Or maybe understanding was not the key he had thought it was. Maybe it only functioned to a point, maybe it explained everything except the important things, and they were in themselves like the underside of a cloud, part of an overarching volume impossible to quantify from an earthbound perspective. Maybe everything was that simple and that complex. Whatever the architecture and rule of life, whatever chemistry was in play, whatever rituals of pain and loneliness had nourished the moment, it was clear they were not just fucking, they were making love. Grace was like a river running through his arms, supple and easy, moving with a sinewy eagerness, as if new to each bend and passage of their course. The wind drove away the clouds, the fog. Moonlight slipped between the curtains and she burned pale against the sheets, announcing her pleasure with musical breaths. Coming astride him, she appeared to hover in the dimness, lifting high and then her hips twisting cleverly down, face hidden by the fall of her hair. At times she spoke in a whisper so faint and diffuse, it seemed a ghostly sibilance arising from her skin. She would say his name, the name she thought was his, and he would want to tell her his true name, to reveal his secrets; but instead, he buried his mouth in her flesh, whispering endearments and promises that though he meant them, he could never keep. At last, near dawn, she fell asleep and he lay drifting, so exhausted he felt his soul was floating half out of his body, points of light flaring behind his lids, the afterimages of his intoxication.

He must have slept a while, for the next he recalled, she was stirring in his arms. The sun sliced through the curtains, painting a golden slant across the shadow of her face. Her eyelids fluttered and she made a small, indefinite noise.

"Morning," he said.

Anxiety surfaced in her face, but stayed only a moment. "I wasn't sure . . ." she murmured.

"Sure about what?"

"Nothing." After a second or two, she sat up, holding the sheet to her breasts, looking about the room in bewilderment, as if amazed to find herself there.

"You all right?" he asked.

She nodded, settled back onto the pillow. Her eyes, lit by the sun, were weirdly bright, like glowing coins. He turned her to face him, laying a hand on her hip. A tear formed at the corner of her left eye.

"What's this?" he asked, wiping it away.

Her expression was almost clownishly dolorous. She took his hand and placed it between her legs so he could feel the moistness there, then pushed into his fingers, letting him open her.

"Jesus, you'll be the death of me," he said.

AFTER SHE HAD gone, making another of her sudden exits, leaving before he could determine what she wanted or be reassured as to what she felt, Shellane went down to the shore and rested against the old glacial boulder. His thoughts were images of Grace. Her face close to his. How she had looked above him, her hair flipped all to one side in violent toss, like the flag of her pleasure, head turned and back arched as she came. A presentiment of trouble, of Broillard and what he might do, called for his attention, but he was not ready to consider that question. He believed he could handle Broillard—he had handled far worse. The Mitsubishi warehouse in Brooklyn. The New Haven bank job. He recalled a mansion they'd broken into in upstate New York, going after an art collection. An old Nathaniel Hawthorne sort of house with secret rooms and hidden passages. A billionaire's antique toy. The security system had been no problem, but the house was full of eighteenth-century perils they could never have anticipated, the most daunting being a subterranean maze. One man had been skewered by a booby trap, but Shellane had succeeded in unraveling the logic of the maze and they managed to escape with the art. If he could deal with that, he could take care of Mister Endless Fucking Blue Stars.

He chuckled at the brutal character of his nostalgia.

Memories.

He had been hoping Grace would return, but several hours passed and she did not. Around noon, the blue Cadillac roared past the cabin on its way toward Champion, Broillard off to spend the afternoon at the Gas 'n Guzzle, and Shellane headed along the shore toward Grace's house. He stood on the beach below the place for several minutes, uncertain about approaching. At length he climbed the slope and peeked through the picture window. She was sitting on the carpet with her back toward him, legs drawn up beneath her. Her shoulders were shaking, as with heavy sobs. He had not taken notice of the furniture before—ratty secondhand stuff in worse shape than the pieces in his cabin. Clothing strewn on the floor. A plate of dried pasta balanced on the arm of the sofa. Piles of compact discs and magazines. Empty pizza boxes, McDonald's cartons, condom wrappers. Your basic rock-and-roll decor. He went to the door and knocked. No answer. He pushed on in. She did not look up.

"It's me," he said.

She sat staring straight ahead, strands of coppery hair stuck to her damp cheeks.

"Come on." He extended a hand. "Let's get out of here."

She did not move; her expression did not change.

He dropped to his knees. "What's he say to you?" he asked. "That you're ugly . . . stupid? That you don't have a clue? You can't believe that."

A damp heat of despondency radiated from her. It was as if she were steeped in the emotion, submerged beneath it like a statue beneath a transparent lake.

"You're beautiful," he said. "You know things with your heart most people don't have names for. I can tell that of you . . . even after just one night." Though he did believe this of her, what he said rang false to his ears, as if it were a line he had learned to recite and had chosen to believe.

She began to cry again, silently, her shoulders heaving. Shellane felt incompetent in the face of her despair. He wanted to put an arm around her, but sensed she wouldn't want to be touched.

"Is it guilt you're feeling?" he asked. "About last night?"

He might not have been there for all the attention she gave him. He remained kneeling beside her for a short while and then asked if she wanted him to go.

It seemed that she nodded.

"All right." He got to his feet. "I'll be at the cabin." He crossed to the door, hesitated. "We can get past this, Grace."

Once outside, he recognized the idiocy of that statement. She was not going to leave with him—he knew that in his bones. Even if she would, he had no desire to drag her along through the shooting gallery of his life. Anger at Broillard grew large in him. Back at the cabin, he paced back and forth, then flung himself into the Toyota and drove toward town at an excessive rate of speed. He parked in the Gas 'n Guzzle lot and sat with his hands clamped to the wheel, telling himself that if he let go, he would charge into the place and play an endless blue tune on Broillard's head. Yet as he continued to sit there, he recognized that his battle to maintain control was pure method acting. He was conning himself. Playing human. If he let go of the wheel, he would do nothing. He might wish that he would act, that he would lose it and go roaring into the Gas 'n Guzzle and drop the hammer on Broillard in the name of love and honor. But he would never risk it. Twenty years in the cold ditches of the criminal classes had left him at a remove from the natural fevers of the heart. He supposed he had become, like his old crime partners, an affable sociopath who stood with one foot outside the world, a man whose emotions were smaller than the norm. And this being the case, wasn't what he felt for Grace equally undernourished and false?

His anger dimmed and without ever having left the car, he drove back to the cabin and sat on the steps, practicing calm, gazing out at the tranquil blue surface of the lake, the unwinded evergreens standing guard along the shadowy avenues leading off among them. Still as a postcard image. Soothing in its simple shapes and colors. He recalled how Grace had talked about it. He believed her view of the place to be romantic delusion, but wished he could share in it. The idea of sharing anything, after the years of solitude, filled him with yearning. But he knew he was incapable of it. Those shadows of Hiroshima burned onto stone, those parings of lives. That was him. A thin, dark urgency was all that remained.

MID-AFTERNOON, AND Grace had not appeared. Shellane started toward her house, but thought better of it and took himself in the opposite direction, hoping to walk off his gloom. The sun had sunk to the level of the treeline, and though a rich golden light spread throughout the air, the glaze of midday warmth had dissipated. His breath smoked; a chill cut through his windbreaker and hurried his step. He kept his eyes down, kicking at stones, at whatever minor obstructions came to view, manufacturing small goals such as kicking a fish head without breaking stride. He had gone almost a mile when he saw a figure standing among the trees about a hundred feet away. A naked man. Not wearing a stitch. Skinny and tall and pale. Judging by the man's stillness, Shellane thought he must be waiting for someone. His second impression, based on no clear evidence, was that the man was waiting for *him*. A pinprick of cold blossomed at the center of his chest and he peered at the man, trying to make out his particulars. He felt as if a channel had opened between them, a transparent tunnel in the air, and that along it flowed a palpable menace.

This, he thought, was a sign of how shaky the thing with Grace had made him. There were no grounds for fear. Yet he kept on his guard, uncertain whether to turn back or go forward, and when the man started toward him, moving with a purposeful stride, he felt a sting of panic that sent him scrambling up the shadowed, needle-covered slopes, in among the trees. After perhaps twenty seconds, he was overtaken by embarrassment—he did not consider himself the sort to panic for any reason, let alone the appearance of a skinny naked stranger whom he could snap in two. He stopped and looked around, but saw no one. He adjusted the windbreaker about his hips and shoulders. Drew a steadying breath and rested a palm against the trunk of a spruce; his palm came away sticky, smeared with reddish resin. He studied the marks—like a hexagram of tacky blood—and wiped the hand clean on his trousers.

"Fucking Christ," he said, and stepped out of hiding.

The man was standing no more than twenty-five feet away, his bony ass turned to Shellane, and he was staring down at the lake. He was bald, his skull knobby, bean-shaped, and his skin was bleached and grayish. Shellane eased behind the spruce trunk and turned sideways so as to be completely hidden. The wind built a faltering rush from the boughs, like the ragged issuance of a final breath. His heart felt hot and huge, less beating than pulsing rapidly. A scraping noise caused him to stiffen. The idea that he had nothing to fear wouldn't stick in his mind—he was terribly afraid, and for no reason he could fathom. Then the man came stalking past Shellane's hiding place, and a reason became apparent: his face had the glaring eyes and gashed mouth and mad fixity of a jack-o-lantern. Outsized features carved into the gray skin. He paused no more than a dozen feet away, his head tilted. Shellane noticed a ruff of flesh at the base of his neck . . . maybe it wasn't flesh. Rubber. The son of a bitch must be wearing one of those rubber Halloween masks. But if it was a mask, Shellane wasn't eager to learn what lay beneath. He held still, not allowing himself to breathe until the man's ground-eating stride carried him out of sight.

On his way home, he remembered the black house and thought that the man in the mask must be one of the freaks who lived there. The thing to do would be to check the house out. No. That wasn't it. The rational thing to do would be to put the lake in his rearview. This place was punching holes in him. Or maybe it wasn't the place. Maybe the years had worn him down to zero and he just happened to be here when it all started to fall apart, a sudden erosion like that of a man who'd been granted an extra century of life and on the day the term expired, he turned to dust? What if he was only walking around in his head, and in reality he was no more than two piles of gray dust in a pair of empty shoes?

"Bullshit," he said to himself, and picked up the pace. To be that way, to be the dust of a dead spell. He should be so lucky.

BY THE TIME Shellane reached the cabin, his desire to leave the lake had been subsumed by concern for Grace and a generalized depression that blunted the sharpness of his fears and muddied his thoughts. Feeling at loose ends, his energy low, he sat at his laptop playing solitaire. The darkness that soon began to gather seemed to compress the space around him, and he saw himself isolated in a little cube of brightness adrift in boundless night. A man holding digital aces, cards made of light, haunted by freaks and old crimes and a weeping woman. It was all bullshit, he realized. This poetry of self-pity leaking from him. He remembered the ridged and bloody hole in Donnie Doyle's forehead, and remembered a few seconds before the hole had appeared, Marty Gerbasi handing him the gun and saying, "You do it, Roy." And he had said, "What?" as if he didn't know what Marty meant. But he knew . . . he knew this was how he bought into the big game, this was the soul price of his profession. Gerbasi said, "I like you, Roy. But that don't mean shit. You need to do this now, understand?" He understood everything. The moral choices, the consequences attending each choice. And so he took the gun and wrote a song on Donnie Doyle's forehead, the only important song he had ever authored, a hole punched through the bone. . . .

The door latch rattled at Grace's knock, so light it might have been a puff of wind. He felt the pressure of her gloom brushing against his own, like two rain clouds merging. He let her in and sank to his knees before her, his face to her belly, the clean smell of wool soaking up and stilling the tumble of his thoughts. When he stood, his hands following the curve of her hips, slipping beneath the sweater to cup her breasts, he felt that his fingers were stained white by her flesh, that whiteness was spreading through him. Her lips grazed his ear and she said, "He hit me. In the stomach, where it wouldn't show. He told me I was ignorant. A fat Irish cow." She went on and on, cataloging Broillard's attacks, all in a husky tone doubtless influenced by Shellane's gentler assault, and yet the list of her husband's sins had an erotic value of its own, informing and encouraging his gentleness. Rage and desire partnered in his mind, and as he removed her clothing, it seemed he was removing as well the baffles that kept his anger contained, so that when they fell into the bed and made the mattress springs creak in a symphony of strain, it was as if anger were riding between his shoulderblades, spurring his exertions, inspiring him to pin her to the bed like a broken insect and fabricate a chorus of moans and cries. Though joined to her, part of his mind listened with almost critical acuteness as she whispered breathy endearments. Wind dance, meaningless love garbage. Garbled expressions of comic-book word-balloon passion, sounding one moment like she was strangling on oatmeal, the next emitting pretty snatches of hummed melody. She bucked and plunged, heels hooked behind his calves, the tendon strings of her thighs corded like wires. They were both fucking to win, he thought. To injure, to defile. Love . . . love . . . love . . . love. The chant of galley slaves stoking his mean-spirited rhythm. When he came, a cry spewing from his throat, he was aware of its rawness, its ugly finality, like that of a man gutted by a single stroke, shocked and beginning to die.

SHE LEFT HIM with her usual suddenness in the morning, returning, he assumed, to the befouled emptiness of her home. Scatters of rain tapdanced on the roof and he stood by the bed, staring down at the wet spot on the sheet that had dried into a shape reminiscent of a gray bird on the wing. The violence of their passion, its patina of furious artificiality, all inspired by her relation of Broillard's abuse—it unsettled him. He was still angry. Angry at her for trying to use him. That was what she had been doing. Trying to rouse his anger. And she had succeeded. He was angry at Broillard for having caused her to hate so powerfully, so obsessively, that she would use him, Shellane, as means of wreaking vengeance. But at this moment he didn't care if that was her intent. He was ready to be used.

He drove into town and parked off to the side of the Gas 'n Guzzle, then walked toward the entrance, moved by an almost casual animus, as if of a mind merely to offer a stern warning. It was no act of self-deception—not this time; it was a mask he wore to hide from others a dangerous mood. Thanks to Grace, he had at least reclaimed something of his old self, the purity of his anger. He pushed the door inward, jingling the bell atop it. A girl in a hooded gray sweatshirt was at the counter, buying cigarettes from Broillard, who offered him a careless wave. Shellane ambled along the aisles, picking up a can of soup, spaghetti, virgin olive oil. When the girl left, he waited at the counter while Broillard rang up the sale.

"Little pasta tonight, eh?" said Broillard, checking the price of the spaghetti. "How's it going out there?"

"Real great," Shellane said. "I'm fucking your wife."

The words sent a cold chemical flooding through him. His hands were like ice. Broillard gaped at him, an expression that—with his long hair and sideburns—lent him a hayseed look.

"I know how you treat her," Shellane went on. "But you lay a hand on her, you say an unkind word, I'll take you to the deep woods and leave you for the beasts."

"You nuts, man?" Broillard made a grab for something beneath the counter. Shellane caught his wrist and squeezed until the bones ground together. With his free hand, he fumbled about on the shelf. His fingers curled around a wooden shaft—a sawed-off baseball bat. He rapped Broillard with it on the side of his head, hard enough to provoke an outcry.

"Supposing I smash your fingers with this little guy," Shellane said. "There goes the ol' career, eh?"

He rapped Broillard again, harder this time, sending him to his knees, hands upheld to stave off another blow.

"I don't know who you're doing," Broillard said with whiny outrage, "but it ain't my wife!"

"Nice-looking redhead name of Grace. Beautiful green eyes, perky tits. Ass round as a teapot. Sound familiar?"

Broillard pushed himself into a corner, as far from Shellane as possible, and his voice unsteady, shrilled, "Get the fuck outa here!"

"Oh, I'll be going . . . soon as I'm certain you understand that I'm your daddy. From this point on, you don't even whimper unless I give you a kick."

Broillard summoned breath and shouted, "Help!"

Shellane leaned across the counter and clubbed him on the kneecap. While Broillard was busy absorbing the pain, he went to the door, locked it, and turned the "Closed" sign outward. He shut the blinds, throwing the interior of the store into a gray twilight.

"Now we can be intimate," he said, coming back over to the counter. "Now we can communicate."

"I swear to God," Broillard said. "If you—"

Shellane shouted, an inarticulate roar that caused Broillard to flatten against the wall.

"Grace told me a great deal about you," Shellane said, "but she didn't let on what a big pussy you are,"

"I don't know what the fuck you want, man, but this is crazy!"

"Crazy is hitting her in the stomach so it won't show. Telling her she's a fat cow and she fucks like a sick fish. Like a cat with the heaves. That was very inventive, Avery . . . that last. It has the feel of hateful observance."

Looking stricken, Broillard came to one knee. "Who told you?"

"Grace. She gave me chapter and verse on your sorry ass."

"She's dead." Broillard said it with bewilderment, then more vehemently: "She's dead! Somebody's feeding you a bunch of shit!"

"What do you mean, she's dead?"

"She's dead . . . she died! Two years ago!" Broillard's expression gave no indication that he was lying. "She's dead," he repeated with an air of maudlin distraction. "I . . . you can't—"

"Don't be playing with me."

"I'm not playing. It's the truth!" Broillard put his hands to his head as if fearful it might explode. "This is too weird, man. What're you trying to do?"

Shellane wondered if he had been tricked. "You have a picture of her?"

Broillard blinked at him. "Yeah . . . I think. Yeah."

"Let me see it!"

"I gotta—" Broillard pointed to the cash register.

"Get it!"

Broillard reached with two fingers between the cash register and a display case, extracted a dusty photograph with curled edges, and handed it to Shellane. In the picture, Broillard was standing in front of the blue Caddy, his arm around Grace, who was shielding her eyes against the sun. He was thinner. The shape of a sideburn barely sketched on his cheek. Grace looked the same as she had that morning. Both wore Endless Blue Stars T-shirts.

"That's not her," Broillard said with weak assurance. "She's not the woman you're banging, right?"

Shellane had a moment's dizziness, as if he'd stood up too quickly. He stared at the photograph, unable to gather all his emotions, aware only of dread and hopelessness.

"She's dead!" Broillard said with desperate insistence. "Go out to the cemetery and look, you don't believe me."

Shellane let the picture fall onto the counter. "We'll both go," he said.

THE LOCAL BONEYARD was quiet and neatly landscaped, and as they passed among the ranked stones, a few drops of rain still falling, Shellane was put off by the impacted piety of grandfather trees and green lawns. Death was quiet enough in its own right. He thought he would prefer to wind up in a Third World cemetery, someplace with a feeling of community, kids drooling taco juice on your plot, balloon salesmen, noisy families picnicking in front of their loved one's crypt. Grace's stone was a modest chunk of gray marble in a corner of the graveyard, close by an elderly maple, its crown of yellow leaves half denuded. What looked to be her college yearbook photo, a waist-up shot of a smiling girl in a dark blue sweater, a gold locket on a chain, was recessed in the marble beneath a transparent plastic square. Her legend read:

GRACE BROILLARD
1971–2000
Beloved Wife

No flowers were in evidence. The smell of leaf mold and a damp, darker odor.

Numb, uncomprehending, Shellane asked, "How did she die?"

"Natural causes," Broillard said.

"The hell does that mean? What's natural about the death of a twenty-nine-year-old woman?"

"She passed out. Some kinda trouble with her heart. We thought she drowned, 'cause she fell over at the edge of the lake. But the doctor told us her heart just stopped. She didn't have any water in her lungs."

Looking off at the sky, Shellane felt that his emotions had been eclipsed by a gray sun. "Lie down," he said.

Broillard tried to dart away, but Shellane caught his arm. "I want you to lie down on the grave."

When Broillard refused, Shellane swept his legs from beneath him, and he went sprawling atop the grave. He propped himself up on his elbows.

"Lie flat," Shellane told him. "Get familiar with the pose."

Reluctantly, Broillard obeyed. "What you gonna do?"

"You vile twist of shit! You drained the life out of her. You beat her down inch by fucking inch. You had her trapped. You took over her home, her business, and for her kindness, you hammered on her until she didn't care enough to live."

"You didn't know her! She was a liar! Anything she wanted, she'd lie to get it! She—"

Shellane kicked him in the side; Broillard gasped, clutching the injured area.

"You didn't know her," he said again, with a quaver

"If she lied, it was because you tormented her. You gave her no reason to be truthful." He nudged Broillard's leg. "Confess your sins, Avery. Cleanse your soul before you come face-to-face with the Creator."

Broillard's eyes were squeezed shut. "Please . . . please don't."

Shellane wanted to hurt him, but each time he contemplated doing so, he lost focus. The sky above had the look of a flat gray lid; a maple leaf skated sideways on the breeze, back and forth, settling to the ground. "Grace," he said, testing the truth of the name, finding that it provoked not dread, but desolation.

"I'm sorry . . . I." Broillard began to weep, his words fractured by sobs.

"Shut up," Shellane told him.

"I didn't want her to die!" Broillard said. "I was all fucked up, I just—"

Shellane put his foot on Broillard's stomach, a light pressure, and Broillard tensed, sucked in his breath.

"I want you to lie there for an hour," Shellane said. "One full hour. Maybe she'll come to you. Give you a kiss."

"No, man. I—"

Shellane pressed down harder.

"Tell her you were fucked up. Stoned. Drunk. Stressed out. Tell her you were crazy. Your creative spirit was suffocating. Buried under a rock of circumstance. And as you struggled to liberate your essence, you accidentally kicked her in the heart ten thousand times. I'm sure she'll be merciful." He kneeled beside Broillard. "A full hour. You leave before the hour's up, I'll find out. Do you know how?"

Eyes still shut, Broillard shook his head.

Shellane put his mouth close to man's ear and whispered very softly, "She'll tell me."

OF COURSE HE HAD doubts. Doubt assailed him as he drove back to the cabin. There must be an explanation other than the obvious. A twin sister, an actress hired to play a part. But that was ludicrous, soap opera-ish. The idea of a ghost was much more logical, and what did that say about the world? That the occult could seem more rational than the mundane. Yet he suspected that he must not believe it. If he did, he would be more frightened of returning to the lake; he would want to run into the cabin, scoop up his belongings and be gone. Or was he half a ghost himself? So diminished and deadened by his sins, he was accessible to death's creatures, immune to their terrors. This struck him with the force of truth and he tried to dredge up some awful fear hidden from sight, a mortal terror that would humanize him. He conjured new images of Grace. Imagined himself in bed with a corpse, a skull filled with maggots, saddled in a bone pelvis and sucking a mummified tongue. But she was none of those things. Whatever the physics of her substance, it was akin to his own. When he saw her, maybe then he'd be afraid. Now it was all speculative, but when he saw her . . . that would be the test of his humanity. Then he'd know if she was too real for him or if he was sufficiently unreal to be real for her.

The lake had gone a deep ocean blue under the prison sky, sluggish waves piling in to scour the shingle, and the boughs of the evergreens lifted with the hallucinatory slowness of undersea life. The cabin looked forlorn, a shabby relic. Grace was standing among the trees beside it, watching the road as he pulled up. Like a tiny figure placed in the corner of a landscape to lend perspective and a drop of color. He sat in the car, waiting for her to call out, but she remained silent. He stood with one foot on the ground, one on the floorboards, and stared at her across the roof of the car. In her jeans and plaid jacket, she looked entirely ordinary, and he wanted her to be real. Ghost or flesh-and-blood, it made no difference so long as she was real. As he walked toward her, she folded her arms and ducked her head. He stopped a few feet away, thinking that he would see death in her; but she was only herself. Mouth held tightly. Eyelids lowered. He started to frame a question, but could not come up with one that didn't sound absurd. Finally he said, "I know what happened to you."

"Do you?" She gave an unhappy laugh. "I'm not sure I do."

Coppery strands of hair drifted across her face—she did not bother to brush them aside.

"You died," he said. "Two years ago." Unable to speak for a second, he put a hand to his brow—his fingers trembled. "How's it possible . . . for you and me . . . ?"

"I'm not an expert on the subject," she said with irritation. "I've only done it the once."

"But we can touch each other. That doesn't make sense."

"When you put your hand on me, the first time, down by the water, I felt it. That's all I know." She shrugged. "I'm amazed you can even see me. No one else does, I don't think."

"You were worried about Broillard seeing you. The other day, on the beach."

"That's how I am with him. I don't go, 'Oh, he can't see me.' I just react the way I always have with him."

The wind poured through the trees, drowning out every other sound. Shellane turned up the collar of his jacket. He studied the edges of Grace's body, hoping to determine if they wavered or flickered or displayed any other sign of the uncanny. Which they did not. And yet there was something about her. That luminous quality he had first observed down by the water. With the gray sky above and trouble in the air, she should have looked pale and drawn; but she still had that glow, that eerie vitality, and he thought now this must be a symptom of her unnatural state. The desolation he'd felt beside the grave returned. He had an impulse to run for the car, but his feet were rooted.

"Avery told me," he said. "I had a talk with him about the way he treated you, and he told me."

"You must have frightened him. For all his bullying, Avery's a very frightened man."

"I was tempted to kill the son of a bitch."

She let out a despondent sigh. "I wanted you to. That's why I told you that stuff about him. For a long time, getting back at him was all I thought about."

Some ducks that had been floating by the margin of the shore flapped up from their rest and beat against the wind toward the far end of the lake.

Grace watched them go. “I’m sorry,” she said. “I just hated him so much.”

“And now you don’t?”

“No, I still hate him. But it doesn’t seem as important.”

She held out her hand and he drew back, both a fearful rejection and one of embittered practicality. If she was a ghost—and what else could she be?—he was not relating to her as such, but rather as he might to a woman with a problem he did not want to get involved in. Like a girlfriend with a drug habit. Fear nibbled at the edges of his awareness, an old Catholic reflex serving to remind him that she was an abomination, a foulness, a scrap of metaphysics. But he could not turn away.

“Why’d you think I’d kill Avery?” he asked.

“I knew things about you from the first moment. It was so weird. I knew who you were. Not your name or anything, but I had a sense of your character. I could tell you’d done violent things.”

“My name’s Roy Shellane.”

She repeated it. “I didn’t think you looked like a Michael.”

The wind came again and she hugged herself.

“I feel alive,” she said wonderingly. “Ever since you got here, it’s like I’m back in the world. I’ve never felt so alive.”

He studied her face, trying again to discern some taint of death, and she asked what was wrong.

“I keep expecting things to be different now I know,” he said. “That you’ll turn sideways and vanish . . . something like that.”

“Maybe I will.”

“I keep thinking I’m going to be afraid.”

“Are you?”

“Just that you’ll vanish,” he said. “And I guess it frightens me that I’m not more afraid.”

The way she was looking at him, he knew she wanted him to reassure her. With only the slightest hesitancy, he stepped forward, half-expecting his arms to pass through her, but she nestled against him, warm and vivid in her reality. He felt a stirring in his groin, the beginnings of arousal, and this caused him to question himself again, to speculate about what he had become.

“Roy,” she said, as if the name were a comfort.

He rested his chin on the top of her head and gazed out over the lake, at the heavy chop, the foot-high waves trundling toward shore, and felt a sudden brilliant carelessness regarding all his old compulsions.

“I know you can’t stay for long,” she said. “But a little while . . . maybe that would be all right.”

DURING THE DAYS that followed, it occurred to Shellane that theirs was a pure romance, free of biological imperatives, divorced from all natural considerations, and yet it seemed natural in all its particulars. They made love, they slept, they talked, they were at peace. Even knowing their time together would be brief, that was not so different from the sadness of more conventional lovers whose term of intimacy had been proscribed. Yet Grace's abrupt departures continued to trouble him. For one thing, he was never certain she would return; for another, he could not think where she went or into what condition she might have been reduced. If he asked, he knew she would tell him—if she herself knew—but he was afraid to hear the answer, imagining some horrid dissolution. Sometimes when he left her sleeping and was busy at his laptop or puttering in the kitchen, he would have the feeling that in his absence she ceased to exist and sprang back into being whenever he looked in on her. But these were minor discords in the music of those days. The most difficult thing for Shellane was an increasingly acute feeling that his ability to interact with her hinted either at madness or the imminence of some black onrushing fate. The similarity of his youthful behavior to that of Broillard seemed to tilt the scales of possibility toward the latter, to hint at a karmic synchronicity. Yet he was not prepared to give her up. Whenever he considered leaving, this thought would be pushed aside by more immediate concerns, and though he realized he would soon have to leave, he was unable to confront the fact.

Two days after he had learned the truth about her, while she lay sleeping, Broillard knocked at the door. He was in bad shape. Bloodshot eyes; disheveled; coked up, his sinuses mapped by hectic blotches. Like a vampire beginning to decompose in the strong sun. He wiped his nose and twitched, yet attempted to present a manly appearance by speaking in a stern voice and holding his shoulders square.

"You'n me need to work shit out," he said.

"Not a good time," Shellane told him. "I'm occupied."

"Yeah? Me, too. I'm occupied in figuring out why I shouldn't call the cops on your ass."

"Perhaps what stays your hand is the thought of having them go sniffing around your place, looking for drugs."

"You think I won't go to the cops? I'll call 'em right now."

"I'll wait inside, shall I? We'll have a chat when they get here."

Shellane started to close the door, but Broillard shouldered it open. Then, abandoning the tactics of machismo, he said with unvarnished desperation, "I need to talk to you, man!"

"It'll have to be another time."

"If you're fucking with me, that's cool. I don't care. I just wanna know!"

"I'm not fucking with you," said Shellane. "Grace is with me now."

Broillard stood on tiptoes, trying to see past Shellane into the cabin. "Where is she?"

Shellane flirted with the notion that this might all be a hustle involving a fake grave and a pretend ghost, a variation on the Hooker with an Outraged Husband. "Seems I'm the only one who can see her," he said.

"Oh, sure . . . yeah." Confidence soaring on chemical wings, Broillard made as though to push inside, but Shellane elbowed him back.

"You're more than a little thick, Avery. Where else do you think I learned the sordid facts of your life?"

"She mighta called you . . . or written you a letter. Like maybe you're a relative or something."

"Of course she did. 'Dear Uncle, the other night Avery sent me to the outlet store to buy him a pair of cashmere socks. He prefers to masturbate in cashmere. We haven't made love in four months—he says I'm too fat. But he's gone through dozens of socks.' Just the sort of thing she'd disclose to a relative."

Broillard gaped at him.

"We're all sad animals." Shellane gave him a gentler shove, moving him back from the door. "Some of us manage to rise above it."

"You think she's such a saint? Maybe it *was* me fucked her up, but she wasn't never a saint, man. She wanted something, she'd do whatever she needed to get it." Broillard bunched his fists, ready to be a soldier. "This is my fucking property and I got a right to inspect it. I'm coming in."

Shellane was about to repeat his original response, but then, thinking that Broillard might become a problem, he said, "All right. But you won't be able to see her."

Once inside, Broillard stood in the center of the room, turning his head this way and that. "Is she here?" He fixed Shellane with a terrified look. "Where is she?"

Shellane gestured at the refrigerator.

Broillard stared at it. "Grace?" he said, and then to Shellane: "What's she doing?"

"Watching you. She doesn't appear overjoyed."

Doubt and fear contended for control of Broillard's features. He sat heavily in a straight-backed chair beside the table. "Can she hear me?"

Shellane sat opposite him, facing away from the refrigerator. "Give it a try."

Broillard made an effort to compose his face. "Grace," he said. "I'm so sorry, baby. I was—"

"She doesn't like you calling her 'baby,'" Shellane said. "She never liked it."

Broillard nodded, swallowed. "I didn't want to hurt you, ba . . . Grace. It's like I was watching someone else do the things I did. I don't know what the fuck was going on." His voice cracked and he covered his eyes with his right hand. "I'm so sorry!"

Shellane glanced at the refrigerator. Grace was standing beside it, wearing only her panties. Tears cut down her cheeks. A cold pressure pushed upward from the base of Shellane's spine and he had the feeling that something very bad was about to happen.

Broillard's tone was urgent. "What's she doing?"

"Crying," Shellane said.

"Aw, Christ . . . Grace! I know I can't make things right. But I'm—" Broillard fumbled in his trouser pocket, pulled forth several folded sheets of notebook paper. "I wrote something. About you . . . about everything. You want to hear it?"

He looked to Shellane for guidance and Shellane shrugged, as if communicating Grace's indifference.

"I don't know how to talk to you, Grace," Broillard said in a plaintive voice. "This is the only way I got."

Her face empty, Grace had come halfway across the room and was standing to his left as he addressed himself to the refrigerator, reading from the sheets of paper, singing the words in a muted but obviously practiced delivery intended to convey anguish:

Never thought it could happen,
never saw the storm comin',
never once had a clue about
how much you were sufferin' . . .
It all was so damn easy,
I took love for nothin',
What I thought was us livin'
was the heart of your dyin',
and now all I remember is
Grace Under Pressure . . .

As he reached the chorus, Broillard built his reading to the level of a performance, half-shouting the words. Shellane could not decide whether his loathing was colored by pity, or if what he felt was embarrassment at seeing another man act with such unabashed stupidity and arrogance.

. . . forever and ever,
Grace Under Pressure . . .
It's all I can think of,
the way you just sat there,
with everything broken . . .
Grace Under Pressure . . .
Grace Under Pressure . . .
Grace Under Pressure . . .

He began a second verse, and Grace stepped behind him, gazing at the back of his head with dispassion.

> *Aw, I wish I could breathe you*
> *straight through until mornin',*
> *where a white dream arises*
> *from the bright flash of being . . .*

Grace trailed her fingers across his neck and Broillard broke off, stared at Shellane. "What just happened? She do something to me?"

"Did you feel something?"

"What'd she do? I got all cold."

Grace appeared to have lost interest in Broillard. She was weeping again, her shoulders hunched and shaking, and Shellane recalled how she had acted the afternoon when he had come to her house. Silent; tearful; unmindful of him. He wondered why her fingers never left him cold. "She touched you," he said.

Broillard scraped back his chair and stood, hands braced on the table. He seemed poised to run, but unable to take the first step. His eyes were bugged and he breathed through his mouth.

"I don't think she liked your song," said Shellane mildly.

"Is she close? Where the fuck is she?"

"I wouldn't move if I were you," said Shellane, though Grace had wandered back toward the refrigerator. "You'll bump into her."

He took Broillard by the elbow. "Let's go." He opened the door to the porch, admitting a glare of the lowering sun, and guided him through it. "You wouldn't want to piss her off. She gets pissed off, she does all that *Exorcist* shit."

Broillard shook free of Shellane's grasp. "You're fucking with me, man. You got my imagination playing tricks, but I know you're fucking with me. I'm calling the cops."

He started for the outer door, but stopped dead. The door stood open and framed there, barely visible against the light, a glowing silhouette had materialized. It was as if an invisible presence were drawing the light in order to shape a rippling golden figure with the swelling hips and breasts of a woman, limned by a pale corona that crumbled and reformed like superheated plasma. The figure was so faint, it seemed a trick of the light, similar to an eddy on the surface of a pond that briefly resembles a face. It brightened, acquiring the wavering substantiality of a mirage, and Shellane saw that the light within the outline was flowing outward in all directions, a brisk tide radiating from some central source.

Broillard made a squeaky noise in his throat.

"Grace?" Shellane said.

With a womanly shriek, Broillard sprang for the door and burst through the figure, briefly absorbed by its golden surface. He went sprawling over the bottom step, rolled up to his knees, and ran. The figure billowed like a curtain belling in a breeze, then winked out.

Shaken, unable to relate this apparition to what he knew of Grace, Shellane went back inside. The sheets of paper on which Broillard had scribbled his song lay on the floor. He picked them up and stood at the table, unable to think or to even choose a direction for thought. Finally he crossed to the bedroom door and opened it. Grace was still asleep, lying on her side, one pale shoulder exposed. He touched her hip and was so relieved by her solidity, he felt light-headed and sat down on the edge of the bed. She turned to face him, reached out with her eyes closed, groping until her fingers brushed his thigh.

"Grace?"

"I'm here," she said muzzily.

"Avery's gone."

"Avery?"

"Don't you remember? He was here . . . a minute ago."

"I'm glad you didn't wake me." She stretched, twisted onto her back and looked up at him. "What did he want?"

"He wrote you a song."

"Oh, God!"

"It really sucked." Shellane crumpled the pages in his hand. "You don't remember him being here?"

"I was asleep." Her brow furrowed. "What's the matter?"

He told her how she'd acted with Avery, how she acted the afternoon he had come inside her house—another occasion she did not recall—and about the apparition. She listened without speaking, sitting with her knees drawn up, and when he had done, she rested her head on her knees so he could not see her face and asked him if he loved her; then, before he could answer, she said, "I realize that's a difficult question, since it's not altogether clear what I am."

"It's not a difficult question," he said.

"Then why don't you answer it?"

"Every minute I stay here, I know I'm in danger. You don't understand that . . ."

"I do!"

"Not all of it, you don't. The fact remains I'm in danger and yet I feel at home. Easy with this place . . . with you. That frightens me. *You* frighten me. What you might mean frightens me."

Her injured expression hardened, but she continued to look at him.

"There's an old Catholic taint in me wants to deny it," he said. "It's telling me this is unnatural. Against God. But I love you. I just don't know what's to come of it."

She said nothing, fingering an imperfection in the blanket.

"And you?" he asked.

She shrugged, as if it were trivial. "Of course. But I wonder if I'd love you if you weren't my only option."

His face tightened as he parsed the meaning of the words.

"See how we hurt each other," she said. "We must be in love."

The light dimmed, clouds moving in from the south to shadow the lake. They started to speak at the same time. Shellane gestured for her to go on, but she said, "No . . . you."

"Where do you go when you leave?" he asked her. "What happens to you?"

"Limbo," she said.

The word had the sound of a stone dropped into a puddle. "That's where unshriven infants go after they die . . . right?"

"'Unshriven.'" She laughed palely. "You're way too Catholic, Roy. Limbo's what I call it. I don't know what it is." She touched the place on his palm where he had picked up the splinter. "You were there. You saw it."

"I did?"

"The black house. The one you asked me about."

He took this in. "You're saying the afterlife's a house on the lake?"

"Not on the lake. You could walk around the entire lake, you wouldn't find it."

"I found it," he said.

"You weren't walking anywhere near the lake."

All the half-formed suspicions he'd entertained regarding his fate seemed to mist up inside his head, merging into a dark shape. "Where was I?"

"I'll tell you what I know." She slid down in the bed, curled up in the way of a child getting cozy. "The night I died, Avery was off playing somewhere and I wasn't feeling well. My chest hurt . . . but I had an ache in my chest all the time, so I didn't think it was anything. I went outside to get some air and I was walking along the shore when I had a feeling of weakness. It came on so suddenly! I could tell something was really wrong and I tried to call for help, but I was too weak. I thought I'd fainted, because the next I knew, I was sitting up and a fog had gathered. I wasn't in pain anymore and I felt stronger, clearer. A little disoriented, but clear in the way I handled it, y'know. I kept walking and before long I came to the house. I was terrified, but there was nowhere else to go, so I went inside."

"What it's like in the house?" Shellane asked.

"When I'm there, I feel kind of how I did with Avery. Dejected. Faded. I'm always getting lost. The people there . . . nobody talks much. Maybe I'm projecting, but I get the idea everyone's like me. They're people who gave up and now they're just moping about. There are some others, though. Tall and really ugly. That's what I call them. The uglies. I don't think they're human. There aren't very many. Maybe twenty. They chase after us—it's like it's a game for them. They can't kill us, of course. But they hurt us. They use us. Men, women. It doesn't matter."

"They use you sexually?"

A nod. "They act like animals. They're incredibly stupid. But they're strong, and they know how to move around in the house without getting lost."

Shellane recalled the tall, naked man who had pursued him in the woods. "Ever see them around the lake?"

"Sometimes they follow me out, but they won't go far from the house."

"Why's it so difficult to get around inside the house?"

"It's not difficult, it's just you never know where the doors will take you. The house changes. You go through a door and it kind of sucks you in. Like . . . *whoosh!* and you're somewhere else. But you can't retrace your steps. If you go back through the same door, you won't wind up in the room you left. I try to figure it out, but I never have the energy. Or I'm too busy hiding from the uglies."

"But you return here. You learned how to do that."

"That's different. It's not like I understand what I'm doing. I get a strong feeling that I have to leave, so I head for the nearest door, and when I step through, I'm back at the lake. I think it's the same for the others. At least I've been in rooms when people suddenly space out. They get a blank expression and then they take off."

She tugged at him, drew him down beside her. He lay on his back, studying the water stains on the ceiling, appearing to map a rippled white country with a sketchily rendered brownish-orange coastline. His arm went about her, but his thoughts were elsewhere.

"What are you doing?" she asked.

"Thinking about the house."

"It doesn't do any good."

"Maybe not."

"But you're doing it anyway?"

"I'm good with problems. It's what I did for a living."

"I thought you were a thief."

"I wasn't a snatch-and-grab artist. I stole things that were hard to steal."

A gust of wind shuddered the bedroom window, and coming out of nowhere, a hard rain slanted against the panes.

"When you pass through the doors," he said, "you say it feels as if you're being sucked in. Anything else happen?"

"I get lights in my eyes. Like the sort that come when you're hit in the head. And right after that, I'll get a glimpse of other places. Just a flash. I can't always tell what it is I'm seeing, but they don't seem part of the house."

"What makes you think the ugly ones know how to get around in the house?"

"Because whenever they take me with them, we always go to the same places. They don't display any uncertainty. They know exactly where they're headed."

"Do they do anything to the doors before opening them? Do they touch anything . . . maybe turn something, push something?"

She closed her eyes. "When I'm with them, I'm afraid. I don't notice much."

"You said there are about twenty?"

"Uh-huh."

"What about the rest of you? How many?"

"The house is so big, it's impossible to tell. A lot, though. I hardly ever see anyone I've seen before."

"The house doesn't look so big."

"When you're standing outside, you don't really get the picture."

Shellane worried the problem, turning it this way and that, not trying to reach a conclusion, familiarizing himself with it, as if he were getting accustomed to the weight and balance of a stone he was about to throw. He heard a rustling, saw that Grace had picked up the sheets of paper on which Broillard had scrawled his lyrics and was reading them.

"God, this is delusional!"

"He's better when he writes about feelings he doesn't have," said Shellane. "Grandiose, beautiful feelings. He's got no talent for honesty."

"Not many do," said Grace.

WHEN SHE LEFT that afternoon, he did not follow her, though he intended to follow her soon. That was the one path available to him if he was to help her, and helping her was all he wanted now. He sat at his computer and accessed treatises on the afterlife written from a variety of religious perspectives. He made notes and organized them into thematic sections. Then he wrote lists, the way he did before every score he'd ever planned. Not coherent lists, merely a random assortment of things he knew about the situation. Avenues worth exploring. Under the word "Grace," he wrote:

> becomes a real woman in my company
> can taste things, drink, but doesn't eat
> lapses into ghostly state around others (once with me alone)
> endures a state of half-life at the house
> feels there is something she's supposed to do
> "knows" I can help her

He tapped the pen against the table, then added:

> is she telling me everything?
> if not, why?
> Duplicity? Fear? Something else?

It was not that he sensed duplicity in her, but her situation was of a kind that bred duplicity. Like a convict, wouldn't she be looking to play angles in order to improve her lot? Wouldn't that breed other forms of duplicity? It was not inconceivable that she might love him and at the same time be playing him.

Under the word "House," he wrote:

> In my Father's house, many mansions . . .
> philosophical speculations—particularized form
> of afterlife? For people who've given up. Who,
> failing to overcome problems, surrender to death.
> (Look up Limbo in Catholic dictionary)
> The uglies (men?). Demons. Instruments of
> God's justice. Forget Christianity. What if the
> afterlife is an anarchy? Lots of feudal groups
> controlled by a variety of beings who can cross
> back and forth between planes of existence.

Science fiction, he thought; but so was Jesus.

> A maze. Hallucination?
> Mutable reality?
> The doors. Core of the problem? Can they be
> manipulated?

He made several more notations under "House," then began a new list under the heading, "Me."

> Have passed over into the afterlife once
> Why?

He circled the word "Why"—it was an omnibus question. Why had he turned off the highway toward the lake? A whim? Had he been led? Was some ineffable force at work? Why had he, after years of caution, been moved to such drastic incaution? He wrote the word "Love" and then crossed it out. Love was the bait that had lured him, but he believed the hook was something else again.

The lists were skimpy. His preliminary lists for taking down a shopping-mall bank had been far more substantial. This would be, he thought, very much like the job in upstate New York, the house with the maze. He'd have to case the place while attempting to survive it . . . if survival was possible. And maybe that was the answer to all the "Whys?" He could feel his body preparing for danger, cooking up a fresh batch of adrenaline, putting an edge on his senses. It was the kick he'd always been a chump for, the thrill that writing songs could not provide, the seasoning he needed to become involved in the moment. And that, he realized, might be the answer to all the whys. He had caught the scent of danger, followed the scent to the lake, and there had taken it in his arms. Like Grace, for the first time in a very long while, he felt alive.

AFTER WAKING, GRACE liked to have a shower. It was not a cleanliness thing—or so Shellane believed—as much as a retreat. He assumed that she must have taken a lot of showers when she was in the world, hiding from Broillard behind the spray, deriving comfort from her warm solitude. Shellane usually let her shower alone, but the next afternoon he joined her and they made love with soapy abandon, her heels hooked behind his thighs, back pressed up against the thin metal wall, whose surface dimpled and popped when he thrust her against it. As they clung together afterward, he watched rivulets of water running over her shoulderblades toward the pale voluptuous curves of her ass, gleaming with a film of soap, dappled with bubbles. He saw nothing unusual to begin with—he wasn't looking for anything. But then he realized that the streams of water were not flowing true; they were curving away from the small of her back, as if repelled by a force emanating from that spot. Curving away, then scattering into separate drops, and the drops skittering off around the swells of her hips. Fear brushed his mind with a feathery touch, a lover's touch. Instead of recoiling, however, he moved his hand to cover the place that the water avoided, pressing his fingertips against the skin, and imagined that he felt a deep, slow pulse. This was the thing he most wanted, he thought. The seat of what he loved.

"I'm drowning," Grace said, and pushed him away. "There was a waterfall coming off your shoulder. I couldn't breathe."

Her smile lost wattage and he knew she must have understood the irony of her complaint. He cleared wet strands of hair from her face and kissed her forehead.

"This must be so awful for you," she said. "To feel comfortable with someone. Almost like normal. And to know it's anything but." Soapy water trickled into her left eye and she rubbed it. "It does feel like that sometimes, doesn't it?"

"Normal? Yeah, more or less."

She seemed disappointed by his response.

He put his hands on her waist. "All the craziness that goes on between men and women, 'normal' isn't the word I'd use to describe any relationship."

She slid past him out of the shower and began to dry herself. He had the feeling she was upset.

"You okay?" he asked.

"I'm cold," she said in a clipped tone, and briskly toweled her hair. Then, her voice muffled: "Are you always so analytical?"

"I try to be. Does it bother you?"

She left off drying and held the towel bunched in front of her breasts. "God knows, it shouldn't. I do understand how hard this—" She broke off and started drying her hair again, less vigorously.

Shellane turned off the water, stepped from the shower. The linoleum was sticky beneath his feet; his skin pebbled in the cool air. The back of his neck tingled and he had the feeling they were not alone, that an invisible presence was crammed into the bathroom with them.

"It's almost over, you know," Grace said. "One of these times soon, I won't come back. Or else you'll leave."

"We've got a while yet."

"You don't know that. You don't know anything about what's happening."

A noise came from the front of the house—a door closing. He threw open the bathroom door and peered out. Nobody in sight.

"Who is it?" asked Grace from behind him.

"Maybe the wind."

He wrapped a towel about his waist and went out into the living room. On the table next to his laptop was an envelope and a portable cassette recorder. The envelope was addressed to Grace. She came up beside him, wearing his bathrobe, and he offered the letter to her. She shook her head. He tore open the envelope and read from the enclosed sheet of paper.

"Once again Avery offers his apologies," he said. "He regrets everything." He read further. "He claims he wouldn't have treated you so badly if you weren't unfaithful."

"He never changes!" Grace folded her arms and scowled at the letter as if it were a live thing and could register disapproval. "He was unfaithful to me every day. With footwear! And then when I . . ." She made a spiteful sound. "We hardly ever made love after we got married. I was so desperate . . ."

"You don't have to explain," he said.

"It's habit. I used to have to explain it to Avery all the time. He liked hearing me explain it."

Shellane set the letter on the table and pressed the "Play" button on the recorder. Avery's voice, tinny and diminished, issued forth over a strummed guitar:

"Beauty, where do you sleep tonight?
In whose avid arms do you conspire . . . ?"

"Our boy's waxing Keatsian," said Shellane.

"Turn it off."

". . . beauty is everywhere they say,
but I just can't find a beauty like thine . . ."

"Please!" said Grace.

Shellane switched off the recorder. "Sure sounds like he loves you."

"I believe he did once. But you can't tell with Avery. He's adept at mimicry."

They stood without speaking for a time, then Grace pressed herself against him. "I shouldn't have pulled you into this," she said.

He wanted to reassure her, to tell her that he would not have forgone the experience of being with her. But though he believed this to be true, he no longer was certain of it. That he could accept her to the point he could dismiss, even dote upon, the symptoms of her strangeness—this fact had, almost without his notice, shredded the fabric of his emotions, and it had grown difficult for him to separate hope from desire.

After she had gone into the bedroom to become whatever she became without him, he dressed and sat at the table, studying his lists. They revealed no pattern, no truth other than the nonsensical and menacing truth that he was in love with a dead woman. In love, also, with her deathly condition, with her odd glow and the curious behavior of water on her skin. It was a splendid absurdity worthy of an Irish ballad. The trouble with such tunes, though, they tended to neglect the ordinary heart of things, things such as the commonplace mutuality that had developed between them, which was a matter truly worth commemorating in song. Nobody sat around scratching their ass or discussing the character of an ex-husband in an Irish ballad. They were all grand sadness and exquisite pain. Of course, sadness and pain were likely headed his way, and he had little doubt they would be grand and exquisite. As if anticipation were itself an affliction, his thoughts spun out of control, images and fragments of emotions whirling up and away, prelude to a despair so profound it left him hunched over the table, eyes fixed on the lists, like a troll turned to stone by an enchantment he had been tricked into reading.

THE LAST OF the gray light blended with the mist forming above the lake. Shellane stirred himself, went to the stove and heated a can of soup. He leaned against the counter, watching steam rise from the saucepan, remembering an interview he'd seen with a man who had directed a horror movie—the man said his film was optimistic because though its view of the afterlife was gruesome, the fact that it lent any credence whatsoever to the concept was hopeful. Shellane supposed this would be a healthy attitude for him to adopt. But the prospect was so completely daft. It had been a long while since his Catholic school days, and the ideas associated with the religion—virgin birth, the Assumption, the hierarchies of angels, and so forth—had lost their hold on him. Now he was being forced to confront an idea even less logical, one concerning which his knowledge was so fragmentary, any conjecture he made about it had the feeling of wild speculation.

Once his soup was done, he went on the Internet, accessed a Roman Catholic dictionary, and looked up "Limbo." According to doctrine, Limbo referred to a place in which unbaptized children, souls born before the advent of Christ, and prudent virgins awaited the Second Coming, at which point they would be assumed into Heaven. Grace did not appear to fit any of these categories; thus it followed that the church was a bit off-base in its comprehension of the afterlife. No surprise there. Yet the idea of a halfway house, an interim place where souls were parked for the duration, for some term pertinent to their lives—this accorded with what Grace had told him. The black house, however, seemed to incorporate an element of punishment, to be less a limbo than a state of purgatory. A kind of boutique hell targeting a select clientele?

"Fuck," he said, switching off the laptop, and stared at his uneaten soup.

Grace, fully dressed, came out of the bedroom. "I have to go," she said absently as she crossed the room. He watched her leave, sat a moment longer, then once again said, "Fuck," heaved up to his feet and grabbed his jacket off the peg beside the porch door and followed.

HE MOVED CAUTIOUSLY through the fog, listening, peering ahead, and thus he noticed the point at which he crossed over from the lakeshore into whatever plane it was that Grace had made her home. The wind suddenly died, the sounds of the spruce boughs swaying were sheared away, and his anxiety spiked. Despite the cold, a drop of sweat trickled down his back; he felt a pulse in his neck. Each step he took seemed the step of a condemned criminal walking toward the death chamber. Legs weak, mind bright with fear. When he came in sight of the black house, its gabled second story lifting from the murk, he did not think he could go on. Even without the motive force of the wind, the fog boiled around him, as if alive, and the notion that it might be a form of ectoplasmic life, tendrils and feelers plucking at his clothes, trailing across his skin, wanting to touch him . . . that got him moving again.

He paused at the door. The knob was of black iron and had the shape of an open hand. He would have to give it a shake in order to enter, and the dire symbolism inherent in this made him less eager to proceed. He had a memory of himself as an altar boy, kneeling, striking the bell as the priest intoned the litany, gazing up at the great gold cross mounted against crimson drapes, participating in the medieval magic of the mass. Whatever he had believed then, he wished he could believe it now. He wished he could take the power that had inspired his awe, all that glorious myth and promise, into his shaking heart. But if the house proved anything, it was that God was far more perverse than the church had dreamed. The unreal fingers of the fog traipsed across the back of his neck, and the fingers of the iron hand seemed to press into his wrist, trying to feel the hits of his heart. Before further doubts could enter in, he turned it.

White lights stabbed into his eyes. It was just as Grace had told him—like the actinic flashes caused by a blow to the head. Then he was drawn deep inside the room, rushed forward as if on a moving walkway. For an instant he thought he might have been transported to the ground floor of a parking garage. A dark, musty space with a strip of brilliant light to his left. Everything blurred and rippling. Either his vision steadied or the house settled on a form, and he saw that he was facing a row of large, round holes—perhaps forty or fifty in sum—piercing a wall of black boards. Yellow radiance spilling from them. He strained his ears, listening for signs of life. Hearing none, he walked toward the wall, then along it. The holes were of equal dimension, six feet wide and high, each opening onto a small cell, unfurnished except for a bowl set in the floor. The bowls were the radiant source, light spraying up from them. The first cell he came to was empty and littered with wastes. Shreds of a slick transparent membrane adhered to the edges of the hole; as far as he could tell, the membrane had not been affixed to the wall, but had been extruded from it, as though it were a natural production of the wood. The second hole was also empty. Shellane reached in to learn if the bowl could be lifted out and used to light his way. The radiance burned him, provoking a prickly, crawly sensation like that of an inflamed rash. In the third cell sat a figure that appeared to be made of dull, tarnished gold with the bulbous shape and pudgy face of an infant. But it was the size of a man. Swaddled head to foot in a golden robe that seemed of a piece with its flesh and left only the face exposed beneath a tightly fitted cowl. Its features had an Asiatic cast, and Shellane recalled photographs of Chinese babies clothed in similar fashion. He was so certain it was a statue, when the creature turned its head toward him, mouth open in what must have been—though Shellane could hear nothing—a full-throated scream, he fell back a step. He punched at the membrane, which was stretched tight across the entrance to the cell; although the shreds hanging from the entrances of the first two cells were flimsy, the surface of the intact membrane was rubbery and hard. The huge baby lowered its head, and a chubby hand, emerging from the sleeve of its robe, pawed in apparent agony at its face and gave another silent scream.

Horrified, Shellane continued on. Five other cells were occupied, three by ordinary men, all of them naked. The other two prisoners were extremely tall men, also naked, with grayish skin and deformed faces, similar to the man who had chased Shellane along the margin of the lake, though their deformities were not as severe as his had been. Sunken eyes; their mouths gashes with thin, ragged lips; flat noses, elongated skulls. The ruffs of flesh at the back of their necks caused Shellane to realize that his pursuer had not been wearing a mask. The chests of these two men displayed a peculiar articulation, as if they had too many bones. Their genital areas were hairless; their eyes so deeply recessed, shadowed by prominent ridges, they threw back not a glimmer of light. On seeing him, they reacted in fright, scrambling back against the rear of their cells and gaping.

One of the normal-looking men—scrawny, with a careworn face and stringy gray hair—seemed initially disinterested in him, but after Shellane had been standing in front of his cell for a minute or so, he pushed himself up against the membrane, pleading with his eyes and mouthing words that Shellane could not understand. He offered a helpless gesture and hurried along.

Beyond the cells lay a door taller and wider than the first; the doorknob was a clenched fist of black iron. Shellane was still afraid, but he was operating efficiently now. Fear had become a resource, a means of refining judgments. He searched the area beside it for projections, a declivity that might conceal a control, a switch. At about eye level, he found a patch of wormy ridges in the surface of the boards, like a cross between circuitry and varicose veins. He tried pushing at them and felt some give, but achieved no result. At length, he opened the door and was swept forward into a space full of shattering light. Like hundreds of flashbulbs being set off. For a second or two, he seemed to be in a place that he could make no sense of—all bright movement and crystalline geometry. Then he was standing on a balcony guarded by a swaybacked railing, gazing out onto a confusing perspective of other balconies and windows and doors and stairways, above and below and beyond, every structure fashioned of black wood. The scene was confusing partly because of the lack of variance in color, partly because the architecture had such a uniform character, an Escheresque repetitiveness of form. It reminded him of old wooden tenements in New Orleans with their courtyards and step-through windows and rickety stairs. These structures, with their sagging balconies and cockeyed doors and unevenly set windows, had that same arthritic crookedness, the same aura of age and disrepair. But unlike New Orleans, there were no planter boxes, no music, no bright curtains, no brightness of any kind apart from the white glare in which everything was bathed. The space was roofed with boards and massive beams, but it was unclear if what he saw was one enormous interconnected building or many separate ones. Several dozen people were in sight and whether on balconies, in the various rooms, or passing along the street of boards below, they went slowly, hesitantly, their movements suggesting infirmity or overmedication. He wasn't close enough to see their faces, but they all looked to be of ordinary human dimension.

A stairway led away from the balcony where he stood and he started down it, passing empty rooms, crossing other balconies. Three floors below his starting point, he encountered a pretty black-haired woman leaning against the railing. Her pale blue eyes flicked toward him—they matched the background color of her flowered summer dress. Though she was young, no more than seventeen or eighteen, a long term of disappointment was written in her kittenish face.

"I'm looking for a woman named Grace Broillard," he said.

"Good luck."

"You know her? Red hair, green eyes. About thirty."

She turned back to the crooked black distance. "Good-bye."

He was silent a moment. "Why won't you help me?"

"Help? That's a concept I'm not familiar with."

He closed the distance between them, rested a hand next to hers on the railing.

"I don't want to talk," she said. "I don't want to share your pain. I don't want to hear about your pitiful life. I've—"

"I'd like to ask you some questions, that's all."

"I've got my own pitiful life to think about. So fuck off."

He put his hand on her arm, and she looked up angrily, but anger faded, replaced by shock.

"Shit, man!" She placed a hand on his chest as though to feel his heartbeat.

"What?" he asked. "What is it?"

"You're alive." This, voiced in an astonished whisper, reminded him of how Grace had behaved toward him on the beach that first day.

"You didn't notice at first? That I was alive?"

"Un-uh." She touched his hair. "You're going to be very popular here . . . as long as you *stay* alive."

"Why's that?"

"Because of how you make me feel. I'm assuming the effect isn't specific to me." She smiled. "It's okay if it is."

"What did you see that made you aware I was alive."

"I don't know . . . nothing. I didn't notice, I guess."

Shellane thought about the gray-haired man in the cell. He had ascribed the man's delayed reaction to his presence to the fact of his being in pain; but that might not be the case.

"Maybe you can help me," she said. "And maybe I can help you find your friend. I bet the jerks have got her."

"The jerks?"

"Do you even know where you are? The freaks, the creeps. The tall, geeky fucks." She disengaged from him and retreated along the railing. "If you can't find her, she's probably with them."

"Why would you think that?"

"It's how things work here. If you know someone from outside the house, you never stray far from them inside it. So if you can't find her, she's probably with the jerks." She went back to staring out at the black tenements. "You're not going to help me, are you?"

Her shift in mood had the same abruptness as Grace's withdrawals, the same switched-off quality, and he wondered if this was a condition of the place or if the people who gravitated here were all prone to similar behavior.

"I don't know if I can help," he said. "But I need to find this woman before—"

"Yeah, I know. Grace. The love of your life or some shit. Gotta find her." She walked off several paces. "Keep going through the doors. You'll hook up eventually."

"You want to come with me?" he asked. "I don't know what's going to happen, but if you want to come . . ."

He eased up behind her, trying to see her face. She was weeping and appeared no longer to recognize that he was there.

Shellane abandoned the stairs, passing through a number of rooms in quick succession, all traditional in their configuration. One contained several items of furniture, notably a dusty standing mirror in which he glimpsed a haggard, rumpled version of himself, and in three of them he found a single person, two women and a man. They treated him much as had the black-haired woman. They did not recognize immediately that he was alive, and once they did, they answered a few questions, asked for his help, then lost interest. Based on their reactions and what they told him, he constructed a hypothesis.

Religious perspectives on the afterlife were, of course, inaccurate; but it might be that none were completely inaccurate. Perhaps the afterlife consisted of many planes, and these planes—or rather, a misapprehension of their nature—had inspired the rise of the various religions. Might it not be possible that one such plane had been appropriated by a sub-order of creatures whose power was slight, and who were capable of capturing a certain type of enfeebled soul? Perhaps they were themselves enfeebled. Creatures perceived as terrifying by the earthbound, but to those familiar with them, those whose fear was colored with contempt, they were jerks, creeps, geeks. The uglies. Metaphysical lowlifes. It seemed a ludicrous proposition until he compared it to the ludicrous propositions of the major religions. The salient difference between those propositions and his own was that his was based to a degree on personal observation.

Beside each door were little clusters of wormy ridges in the wood, similar to the one he had found beside the second door he'd tried. He pushed at the ridges in sequence, two at a time, in various combinations, but all to no avail. Then he gave the knob of one door a quarter turn, not sufficient to disengage the lock, and the ridged seams beside the door pulsed as if a charge or a fluid were passing through them. He was elated to find that an orderly process was involved. There must be a sequence—many sequences—of constrictions that affected the doors, causing them to take you to different quarters of the house. Either he was not strong enough to manipulate the ridges or there was some other contributing factor that he did not understand.

The last door he tried delivered him into a tunnel with walls of black boards. As with the fist that protruded from the exterior of the house, they had the irregular, roughened look of wood in a natural state, and this made it appear that he was walking along inside a huge hollow limb. Thin gaps between them glowed whitely, producing a dim light. The other portions of the house he had investigated—despite the people he'd encountered—had seemed sterile. Lifeless. Here, he sensed a vibe of animal presence and as he proceeded along the tunnel, he smelled a fecal odor and observed signs of rough occupancy. Gashes and indentations in the wood, boards that had been pried partly loose. Evidences, he thought, of rage or frustration, or of a vandal's idiot frenzy. The tunnel wound downward at a steep angle for approximately forty feet, then straightened and narrowed to the point that he could nearly touch both walls at once; after a stretch of about sixty feet, it widened by half, and as he rounded a bend, he spotted Grace standing a few yards ahead, her back pressed against a wall. When he called out, she turned her head and stared at him in alarm. He saw that she was imprisoned by two bands of black wood encircling her waist and neck, leaving her arms free.

"Roy!" She strained toward him, then slumped in her restraints as Shellane tugged at the restraining bands. There was no visible lock, no catch. They looked to have grown around her.

"They'll be back soon." Grace tried to push him away. "You have to go! I'll be all right! Just go!"

He studied the wall beside her.

"They'll kill you!" Grace said.

"Quiet. I'm working here."

Next to one end of the band encircling her waist was a single ridge, barely an inch long. Close by it, a board had been worked loose, leaving a half-inch aperture admitting a white radiance.

"You can't help me! This is just going to make things worse," she said. "Please! I want you to leave now!"

He unbuckled his belt, whipped it off and pried with the corner of the buckle at the loose board.

"What're you doing?"

"Trying to understand."

He managed to pry the board up sufficiently so that he could grip it with the tips of his fingers. He pulled it back farther and put an eye close to the gap he had made. A flash of white light, and he saw an unfamiliar night sky. Too many stars and a glowing red cloud occupying its southern quadrant. Hovering at an unguessable distance between him and the cloud was a dark wormlike structure, and he had the impression he was looking at something of immense proportions.

Another flash of light, then another, a third . . .

In the intervals between flashes, he was afforded glimpses of completely different scenes. Vistas; landscapes; complicated interiors. Many he was unable to quantify—their geography was too vast and bewildering to be comprehensible; even those that he was able to comprehend possessed the quality of immensity. Endless reaches containing strange, cosmically proportioned structures. By the time he pressed the board back into place, he thought he understood the house. A sketchy understanding, but the basic picture was clear. The doors were programmed (he could think of no better term) to admit you to different areas of the house; but before you settled into the room to which you had been directed, you saw the place through which you transited . . . or perhaps another place that you might have transited to. A place removed from or possibly inclusive of the house. There was a great deal he was unsure of, but he knew one thing for certain—the doors could be reprogrammed.

Grace continued to warn him away, but he refused to listen. Wishing it were sharper, he pushed the tongue of his belt buckle against the ridge beside her neck, denting it. He pushed harder, lodging the point in the dent and jamming it down with both hands. After nearly a minute's sustained effort, the seam writhed and abruptly deflated; the bands holding Grace retracted without a sound, appearing to flow back into the boards behind her. She let out a gasp and staggered away from the wall.

"The doors," he said. "They can be adjusted . . . calibrated to take you away from the house. I'm not sure what this place is, but it embodies mechanical principles. Maybe . . ."

Grace planted both hands on his chest and sent him reeling backward. "You're not hearing me!"

"Jesus, Grace! I'm trying to tell you how to escape!"

She tried to shove him again, but he caught her hands.

"You're not hearing *me*," he said angrily. "I'm trying to help you. The uglies . . . they manipulate the house. And they're stupid, right? Everyone I've talked to says that. So if they can do it, chances are you can, too."

Grace twisted away from him. "You don't know anything! You've only been here a little while. Most of us have been here for years!"

"Goddamn it! Why don't you take a second and listen to me?"

"Do you want to die? 'Cause that's what's going to happen!"

"Just listen and I'll go."

"I heard what you told me! I'll check the doors!"

"And watch the uglies. Whenever you're with them, watch what they do with the doors. I—"

She hurled herself at him, clawing his face, punching his chest, screaming at him to leave, driving him backward; but then she broke off her assault and stared at something over his shoulder with fierce concentration. There was no sign of fear in her face; though fear, Shellane understood on turning, must be responsible for her intensity.

Three of the uglies had come into view around a bend and were crouched as if in preparation for an attack, squeezed together by a narrowing of the walls. Two of them resembled the men imprisoned in the cells, but the third, the biggest, was identical to the man who had pursued Shellane through the woods. Severely deformed. Jagged orbits shadowing his eyes, a darkly crimson mouth visible behind a toothy jack-o'-lantern grimace. Shellane set himself for a fight. Despite Grace's assertion that they were strong, they looked spindly and frail. He thought he could do some damage. But rather than charging at him, they began to whimper like a chorus of terrified children, gaspy and quavering. The one on the right lifted its head to the ceiling, as if seeking divine assistance, and let forth a feeble ululation. Urine dribbled down its leg. The others hid their eyes, but peeked at him, as if not daring to turn away from the source of their terror.

They were afraid of *him*, Shellane realized. There was no other explanation. He took a step toward them—their whimpers rose in pitch and volume. Definitely afraid. He caught Grace's hand, tried to pull her away. But she yanked her hand free and dropped to her knees.

"Grace." He kneeled beside her. "Come on! Get up!"

She sank into a reclining position, her eyes averted, like a child who had been made aware of an inevitable punishment and sought refuge in collapse.

The uglies still seemed afraid, but Grace's surrender weakened Shellane's will and he had little confidence that he could handle all three of them. Nevertheless, he gathered himself and ran at them, waving his arms, shouting, hoping to drive them off. They scuttled away, but when he stopped his advance, they, too, stopped, huddling together, plucking and clutching at one another like fretful monkeys. He took a second run at them. Once again they fell back, but not so far this time. A touch of curiosity showed in their crudely drawn faces. He turned to Grace and thought he saw in her a glint of hope, but she looked away, as if she were trying to hide it from him.

A growl issued from behind him, bassy and articulated—a bleakly mechanical noise, like the idling of some beastly machine.

Two lesser growls joined in guttural disharmony with the first, and he spun about, his hands in a defensive posture, knowing he would have to fight.

But it was no fight.

They covered the distance separating them from Shellane in a few shambling strides and leaped with their hands clawed, a wave of bony edges and blunt, powerful teeth that carried him down, enveloping him in their bitter stench. He managed to land a single punch, striking the chest of the tallest. Like hitting a hardwood wall. Then he was tossed, kicked, slammed, worried, bitten, scratched, and kicked again until he lost consciousness. When he waked, when he managed to unscramble his senses, he found he was being dragged by the feet. Head bumping, arms flopping. Grace screamed and he struggled to wrench free, but the hands gripping his ankles were irresistible. He twisted about and caught a glimpse of her being borne aloft, held by the collar of her jacket in one long-fingered gray hand. Bile flushed into his throat. The effortful grunting breath of the creature dragging him was the sound of panic. He summoned his reserves, focusing, trying to fortify a central place in his mind from which he could observe and judge what might be done.

They came to a door. The creature released one of his ankles, and through slitted eyes, Shellane watched its free hand reach to the wall beside the door and press a forefinger in sequence against the raised seams clumped together there. The door opened and they were sucked inside. Flashing white lights disoriented Shellane and he thrashed about, kicking at his captor's leg. The ugly bent to him, its insult of a mouth—wide enough to swallow a ham—widened further in a smile, its tongue dark and thick like a turtle's. Beneath the ledges of its orbits, its eyes gleamed with a rotten sheen. It slashed at his face with its thumb, slicing his cheek with a thumbnail, and a warm wetness spread down over his jaw and neck. It tipped its head to one side and made a slurred, mocking noise. Then it seized him by the shirtfront and thrust him through the door, dangling him over a long drop. It looked as if something had come hurtling down from heaven or the heights or whatever place this was, something roughly circular—a meteorite, a boulder, Jehovah's fist—and smashed everything in its path, creating a central shaft in the building roughly twenty feet in diameter. The shaft fell away into shadow, walled by a broken honeycomb of exposed rooms and splintered black boards. Before Shellane could grasp what was happening, the creature swung him as easily as he himself might swing a cat and slung him through the air. The ruin pinwheeled. The pull of gravity and death took him at the top of his arc. Turning sideways as he started to fall, he saw a gaping darkness rush up at him, and the next instant he slammed into something that drove wind from his chest and light from his brain. Only after regaining consciousness a second time did he realize that he had been thrown across the gap and that the uglies, bearing Grace with them, had leaped across after him.

They passed through another door. Shellane was too groggy to register much about the room beyond, but he caught sight of a hearth in which a roaring fire had been built, and though he was not the most reliable of witnesses at the moment, he would have sworn he saw tiny homunculi playing in the flames, hopping from log to log. Grace was speaking, her tone urgent, the words unintelligible, but he had the impression that she was pleading.

Shellane's head had cleared to a degree, though his vision seemed to be blurred; but as he was dragged through yet another room, he recognized that the indistinctness of the large, shadowy figure sitting cross-legged in a corner was due not to an impairment, but to the fact that its black substance was in a state of flux, a whirling filmy shell encasing a human form. At the next door, the tallest of the uglies again manipulated a patch of ridges in the wood, and while the knowledge would do him no good, Shellane felt satisfaction in having been right about the operation of the doors.

The room into which the creature then dragged him was tiny, the ceiling so low that the uglies were forced to walk in a half crouch. It had a gabled roof and a shuttered window that extended up from the floor. Shellane was left to lie beside the window. One of the uglies threw the shutters open onto a foggy darkness and he saw a huge black fist jutting from the boards directly below. He was past fighting. His ribs ached, his left knee throbbed, and his mind worked sluggishly. Even when a rope was placed around his neck, he could not rouse himself, but only wondered how they were going to pass his body through the fist, a question answered when a second creature pressed a finger to a ridged patch beside the window and with terrible slowness, the fist uncurled as if to welcome him. Grace screamed. Shellane turned onto his back and spotted her at the door. Two of their captors were fondling her roughly, grabbing her breasts and buttocks. He started to tell her something, but forgot what he wanted to say. Then this became irrelevant as a foot nudged him out the window.

He dropped barely a foot or so, but the rope choked him and his feet kicked against the boards. In reflex, he grabbed the rope, tried to haul himself up; but he was being lowered and could make no progress. Overhead, the uglies were framed by the window, one embracing a still-struggling

Grace, whose face was pressed into its chest. The tallest was paying out the rope. Shellane's eyes darkened and he felt a tremendous heat inside his skull. His right foot bumped against the half-curled hand and then he was inside it, waist-deep in its loose grip. He caught at its upper edge, levering himself up with his elbows, refusing to be lowered farther. The surface of the uppermost finger was crusted with brownish stains. He puzzled over them, wondering what they might be. Then that question was answered as the hand began to close and he understood that some unfortunate enough to happen onto the house while they were alive had chosen to be crushed rather than hanged. Gasping, his throat constricted, he looked up to Grace, dimly moved to find her. The figures above appeared to be joined in a wobbling dance, pushing each another to gain a better view, communicating in grunts and growls. Then the smallest of the four, the shrillest, flung herself at the tallest, clawing at its eyes, and the rope came uncoiling down toward Shellane. He released his grip, allowed himself to fall, not so much because he recognized that he'd live if he did, more a sympathetic reaction to the rope's fall. His head struck the first joint of the fist's little finger and he dropped the last few feet, landing on his back with a jolting impact.

He did not black out and the recognition that he was free penetrated the clutter of his thoughts. Gritting his teeth against the pain in his ribs, he pushed up to a standing position and began a limping retreat. Grace screamed at him to run and he threw himself forward with his shoulders, dragging his left leg, moving blindly through the fog. He knew she must still be struggling with the uglies or else they would be on him—his pace was much too slow to outrun them—and this spurred him to limp faster. There was nothing he could do for her. The pragmatic view, however, did not sit well with him. Every step he took sparked a sense of shame and inadequacy. Wincing whenever he inadvertently planted his left foot, feeling the inception of a pain more difficult to ease than the one that crippled him, he kept on going until, after a short while, he heard wind sighing in the spruce, and water lightly slapping the shore, and knew that he was safe, an infinity removed from certain lesser demons and their rickety black hell, but utterly alone.

ONCE HE HAD bandaged his wounds, believing that Grace would not return, that she was lodged in a cell filled with burning light or enduring some crueler punishment, Shellane spent the remainder of the night hoping he was wrong. Whatever pain she was experiencing, he was to blame—he had insinuated himself into a situation that he had completely misjudged, and as a result, he had caused her already bleak outlook to worsen. Staying at the house would have served no purpose, yet he felt he had breached a bond implicit in the relationship, and he castigated himself for having abandoned her. The hours stretched and he felt once again how weak and attenuated his attachment to life had become. Without Grace, without the renewal of passion she had inspired, he could not conceive of going on as before, preparing a new identity, a new hiding place. What could any place offer other than the fundamentals of survival? And what good were they without a reason to survive? He sat at the table, breeding a dull fog of thought that was illuminated now and again by fits of memory. Her face, her laugh, her moods. Yet memory did not brighten him. All the commonplace instances that shone so extraordinarily bright in his mind were grayed with doubt. He knew almost nothing about her, and he suspected that if he were capable of analysis, he might discover that the things he knew were dross, not gold, that she was not at all extraordinary. She had simply fit a shape in his brain, perfect in some imponderable way. Every part of his body labored—heart slogging, lungs heaving. It seemed that something had been ripped out of him, some scrap of spirit necessary for existence.

To distract himself from grief, he wrote lists. Long lists this time, comprised chiefly of supposition. His knowledge of the house was limited, but he was certain about the doors—the uglies were able, thanks to their strength, to program their destinations. Though it was pointless, he couldn't keep from speculating on the nature of the place and the apparent infinity of locations to which it seemed connected. It was hard to accept that the afterlife possessed an instrumentality. Back in the days when he was a believer, his notion of heaven had been a bland, diffuse cloud country, and his vision of hell was informed by comic books. Spindly crags and bleak promontories atop which the greater demons perched, peering into the fires where their minions oversaw a barbecue of souls. The house was at odds with both conceptions, but he had no choice except to believe that beyond death lay a limitless and intricate plenum whose character was infinitely various, heavens and hells and everything in between. It was similar to the Tibetan view—souls attracted to destinations that accorded with what they had cherished in life, be it virtuous or injurious. Unlikely, though, that Tibetan cosmology contained anything comparable to the black house.

If he were trapped in the house, he thought, he'd first observe the ways in which the uglies manipulated the ridged seams beside the doors and try to devise a mechanism that would allow him to exert more force when pushing. It was a simple enough mechanical problem. And of course he would study the uglies' behavior, their habits. He wondered why they had been afraid of him. They had presumed him to be dead and had lost their fear after noticing he was alive, mortally vulnerable. As with everyone else he had met in the house, it took them a while to notice his vitality. But that didn't explain what they were afraid of. Perhaps they saw things people did not. Different wavelengths. Auras. Souls. Somehow he posed a threat. Because he had manipulated the doors? It was the most likely reason. If he were dead and in the house, they'd make his life—his afterlife—hell. Keep him penned up or too busy to interfere. At least they would try. Primitive as they were, they'd screw it up sooner or later and give him an opportunity. But he would have to endure a great deal of pain before such an opportunity arose.

He understood then that he was not thinking in the abstract; he was contemplating his own death, using the same methodical approach that he would use in developing a plan for a robbery. The idea that this even occurred to him was not shocking. He made a perfect candidate for the house. He no longer cared about life, and like Grace, who'd had Broillard to finish her off, his own killers were at hand. They would eventually track him down. All he had to do was wait. And what would he be giving up? Paranoia and solitude, hookers and barflies, no plans for the future except those of escape. A life without significant challenge, an emptiness that would be far emptier without Grace. He tried to weaken this argument with self-doubt. His belief that he could learn to manipulate the doors . . . Wouldn't death make of him, as it had of Grace and the others, a befuddled, energyless soul incapable of functioning? Then he recalled how he and Grace had interacted in the house. She had been angry, afraid, but full of vitality. Of life. The two of them together might form a battery that would generate sufficient strength to manage an escape. What if there were more than two? He had seen—what?—fifty or sixty people in the house, and there must be many more. He and Grace might infect the rest with their energy. They might be able to overpower the uglies.

He straightened in his chair and made a scoffing noise, dismayed that he could entertain these fantasies—a postmortem revolution, the democratic overthrow of minor-league demons. Next he'd be accepting Jesus as his personal savior. He went into the bedroom and pulled his suitcases from beneath the bed. Get out of here now. That was the only reasonable agenda. He began to pack, though not in his usual painstaking style. Balling up shirts, stuffing them in. But gradually his pace slowed. The sheets smelled of her. She was real. Nothing could change that. She was real, the house was real, and however frail the foundation supporting his guesswork, everything he had seen and done was real. He had followed a trail of intuitive decisions and they had led him here, to Grace, to this moment and to these speculations, which his instinct judged sound, and which, though the logic of the world prevailed against him, he was unable to refute.

Leaving his bags open, he returned to the front room. Trees and shrubs and shoreline were melting up from the half-dark, and as they sharpened, shadowy branches evolving into distinct sprays of needles, the margin of the lake defining itself in precise gray curves, the things of the world came to seem increasingly imprecise to Shellane. Their precision a poor reflection of the simpler, albeit more daunting, order he had detected in the house. As if death were a refinement of life. He settled back into his chair. Noon approached. Soon a blue Cadillac would come grumbling along the lake road. Soon he would cook breakfast, take a shower, make a plan, creating a structure that had no other purpose than to repeat itself. He saw himself as he had once been. Rock-and-roll days. Girlfriend sobbing in a corner of that dingy, brain-damaged apartment in Medford. Him yelling, shouting, because he had no self-justification that could be spoken in a quiet tone or a reasonable voice. The quick drug hit of a score, adrenaline rushes and gleefully desperate escapes, and afterward sitting in a nondescript bar with nondescript men, laughing madly over drink at the skill, guts, and brains required to risk everything for short money in the service of greater men who watched them like spiders watching trained flies and smiled at their ignorance. Walking like a ghost through Detroit. Brushing past the world, touching it just enough to envy its unreal brilliance. Was that it? A life like so many bits of rusty tin threaded onto a gray string? These days with Grace canceled out every moment of that heatless past. He put his hand on the telephone, let it rest there for several minutes before lifting the receiver and dialing, not because he was hesitant, but rather stalled, lost in a fugue from which he emerged diminished and uncaring.

A man's voice spoke in his ear. "Yeah, what?"

"You recording this?" Shellane asked.

A pause. "Who's asking?"

"If you're not recording, start the tape. I don't want to have to repeat myself."

Another pause. "You're on the tape, pal. Go for it."

"This is . . ." Shellane had a thought. A wicked thought, another addition to his Book of Sin. But damned once, damned twice . . . What did it matter?

"You still there?"

"My name is Avery Broillard," Shellane said. "I work at the Gas 'n Guzzle in Champion, Michigan. In the Upper Peninsula, about an hour's drive west of Marquette."

"No shit? How's the weather up there?"

"I can tell you how to find Roy Shellane."

Silence, and then the man said, "That would be very helpful, Avery. Why don'tcha go ahead and tell me?"

"It's tricky . . . the directions. I'll have to show you. I work until seven tonight. Can you have somebody up here by seven?"

"Oh, yeah. We can handle that. But, Avery . . . whoever the fuck you are. If this is bullshit, I'm gonna be upset with you."

"Just have somebody here by seven."

After hanging up, he had a moment's panic—a twinge of fear, an urge toward flight; but it found no purchase in his thoughts. He sat a while longer, then set about making breakfast. Fried eggs and ham, toast, and his last wedge of apple pie.

SHORTLY AFTER FIVE o'clock that afternoon, a dark-green Datsun parked about a hundred feet off along the access road. Shellane pictured Gerbasi crammed into the front seat—the rental-car options in Marquette must not have been to his liking. He considered going out to meet them, but though he was eager to be done with it, he was so enervated, worn down by depression, feelings of loss and anxiety, his eagerness did not rise to the level of action. At a quarter to seven, the doors of the Datsun opened and two shadows moved toward the cabin, one much bulkier than the other. They vanished behind trees, then reappeared larger, at a different angle to the cabin, like ghosts playing interdimensional tag. Shellane could have picked them off, no problem. He was in an odd mood. So lighthearted that he was tempted to hunt up the nine millimeter and destroy the men who were intending to do what he wished, just as a prank on himself; but he couldn't recall where he had put the gun. He heard whispers outside. Probably arguing over whether to shoot through the window. Gerbasi wouldn't go for it. He enjoyed the laying on of hands. That was his kink. The fat bag of poison wanted you to commune with him before he did the deed. Over thirty years of murdering people who had not necessarily required it, and life had been kind to him, except socially. For some years now, he had been in love with a woman who shared a house with a guy who claimed to be a gay political refugee from Cuba, a story that scored him few points in the neighborhood but lent his bond with the woman an innocence that placated Gerbasi, who remained oblivious to the fact that he was being cheated on in plain view. It was amazing, Shellane thought, what there was to know about people.

The door blew inward and Gerbasi's associate, an ex-pug, a light-heavy who had obviously taken a pounding during his days in the ring, ridges of scar tissue over his eyes, posed TV cop-style with his shiny gun and grunted something that Shellane did not catch but took for an admonition. Then Gerbasi hove into view. Spider veins were thick as jail tattoos on his jowls, and the bags beneath his eyes appeared to have been dipped in grape juice. His breathing was wet and wheezy, and his muted-plaid suit had the lumpish aspect of bad upholstery. The lamplight plated his scalp with an orange shine. He waddled three steps into the room and said, "This don't seem like you, Roy. Just sitting here waiting for it."

Shellane, his flame turned low, had no reply.

Gerbasi snapped at his helper, telling him to close the door. "What's going on with you?" he asked Shellane.

"I surrender," said Shellane.

"The guy Broillard, he claims he didn't call us." Gerbasi's eyes, heavy-lidded, big and brown like calfs' eyes, ranged the tabletop. "Know anything about that?"

"Broillard? The Gas 'n Guzzle guy? He called you about me?"

Gerbasi's stogie-sized forefinger prodded Shellane's laptop. "Somebody called. Broillard says it wasn't him."

"Maybe he had a change of heart," suggested Shellane.

"Maybe you set his ass up." Gerbasi gave him a doleful look.

"You didn't hurt him, did you?" Shellane failed to keep the amusement from his voice.

The light-heavy chuckled doltishly. "He ain't hurting no more."

"I figure you set him up," Gerbasi said. "But why would ya do that and still be hanging around here?"

"Don't think about it, Marty. You'll break your brain."

"Maybe he's got cancer," offered the light-heavy.

"Worse," said Shellane.

"What's worse than cancer?"

"Shut the fuck up," Gerbasi said to the light-heavy; he removed a long-barreled 22. from his shoulder holster.

"Truth," Shellane said.

"Y'know, you look way too satisfied for a man's gonna be wearing his brains in a coupla minutes," Gerbasi said. "You waiting for rescue, Roy? That it?"

"Just do your business."

"Guy's in a hurry," said the light-heavy. "Never seen one be in a hurry."

"Who cut your face?" Gerbasi asked Shellane.

"Do it, you fat fuck! I've got places I need to get to."

"Hear that shit?" said the light-heavy. "Motherfucker's crazy."

"Nah, he's got an angle. Man's always got an angle. Don'tcha, Roy?"

Shellane smiled. "I live in certain hope of the Resurrection."

Gerbasi gave his head a dubious shake. "Know what I useta say about you? I'd say Roy Shellane runs the best goddamn crews of anybody in the business, but he's too fucking smart for his own good. One of these days he's gonna outsmart himself." He seemed to be expecting a response; when none came, he said, "I think maybe that day's come."

A bough ticked the side of the cabin; the light-heavy twitched toward the door. Shellane understood why Gerbasi enjoyed playing these scenes—he wanted the fear to grow strong so he could smell it. But though Shellane was not free of fear, it was weak in him, and he thought that he must be proving a profound disappointment.

"I get the feeling you think you're holding a great stud hand, but you don't know you're sitting at the blackjack table," Gerbasi said.

The light-heavy looked confused.

Shellane rested his head in his hands. "Do I have to fucking beg you to shoot?"

"Hey." The light-heavy came up beside Gerbasi. "Maybe he's wearing a wire."

"He was, they'd be here already, dumbass! But something ain't kosher." Gerbasi let the gun dangle at his side. "Tell me what's going on, Roy, or I'm gonna hafta give ya some pain."

"I don't give a shit what you do. You understand?"

"No, explain it to me."

"You had a soul, I wouldn't need to explain."

"I told ya . . . the guy's crazy," said the light-heavy.

"You don't shut your goddamn mouth, swear to Christ I'm gonna put one in ya," Gerbasi said.

"Jeez! Fine. Fuck . . . whatever."

Gerbasi sucked at his teeth, studied Shellane, rocking slightly on his heels. "I think I got it," he said to the light-heavy. "Man's tired of living. That's all it is. Right, Roy?"

"Whatever you say."

"Remember Bobby Sheehan? Man looks at me and says, 'Fuck you, Marty.' Not like he was pissed off. Just weary. Just fed up with it all. I asked, man, I said, 'Fuck's wrong with you, Bobby? This how you wanna go out? Like a fucking sick dog?' And he says, 'A sick dog's got it all over me. A sick dog don't know what's making it sick.' " Gerbasi nodded. "It's kinda like that, ain't it?"

"Fuck you, Marty."

Gerbasi stepped around behind Shellane, and a weakness spread from the center of Shellane's chest outward. He fixed his eyes on the door, but he seemed to see everything in the room and sensed his isolation, the gulf of the surrounding dark with its trillion instances of life. Spiders, beetles, roosting birds, serpents, badgers, moles, fish streaming through the dim forests of the lake bottom. Every least scrap of vitality enviable to him now. He managed to summon the image of Grace's face, and her olivine eyes struck deep into him, filling him with acceptance. This was the end to which he had come. This woman, this unstable chair, this badly hung door, this shabby room drenched in orangey lamplight. He felt he was falling forward into a dream.

"Wanna say a prayer?" Gerbasi asked. "I'll give you a minute."

Shellane did not answer, fascinated by the particularity of his senses, the thousand details.

"You hear what I said, Roy? Want me to give you a minute?"

"Now would be good," said Shellane.

IN THE BEGINNING there was the memory of pain, a pain so vast and white it seemed less a condition of the mind and body than the country of his birth. But it was only a memory and did not afflict him long. As he moved through the dark, fogbound country of his death, he came to think that being shot had not left him much the worse for wear. He recalled what Grace had said about dying and realized that he, too, felt stronger, more settled in his head . . . and yet he also felt out of sorts, plagued by an ill-defined sense of wrongness and foreboding. He presumed this feeling would intensify once he reached the black house, and that it probably contributed to the low energy and aimlessness of its residents; but he told himself that none of them had been informed with such clear purpose, such determination, and he believed this would shield him from the effect. Even after he saw the gabled roof rising from fog and the black fist protruding from the wall, after he opened the door and was drawn inside, he remained hopeful, focused on his intention to find Grace and escape with her. Where they might escape to . . . well, that was not something he had given a great deal of thought. The potentials of the afterlife no doubt incorporated worse places than the house, and should they succeed in reaching a better one, what would they do then? There were many things he might have considered before acting. Matters of personal as well as metaphysical consequence. But they involved questions best answered by him and Grace together, and so would have to wait a judgment.

Upon opening the door, he was admitted to a corridor that appeared to be endless, an unrelieved perspective of black doors and black walls, black floors and ceiling, the surfaces of the boards shiny like newly exposed veins of coal. From each door he passed, he received an impression of menace and he wondered if his ability to smell such a psychic reek had been enhanced by his transition. The black perspective continued to recede. If there was an end to the corridor, he had made no appreciable progress toward it. He would have to pick a door and deal with whatever lay behind it. But before he could finalize this decision, Grace spoke from behind him, giving him a start, just as she had on their first morning on the beach.

"Hello, Roy," she said.

She was standing about fifteen feet away, two of the uglies crouched at her side, flanking her like faithful hounds. Her hair was loose about her shoulders and she wore a white, filmy gown, flimsy as a peignoir, its ultra-feminity at odds with her customary clothing. She betrayed no hint of anxiety, no uncertainty, and her smile was an act of disdainful aggression. She absently trailed the fingers of her left hand across the scalp of one of the uglies, and it trembled, rolling its sunken eyes toward her.

"Grace . . ." Stunned, unable to match her coolness, her poise, with anything he knew about her, Shellane was at a loss.

"Roy!" She made the name a husky mockery of passion and laughed. "Thanks for getting rid of Avery. That was so sweet! I knew you wouldn't let me down." Her tone grew chilly. "All that bullshit self-involvement you do! You're too much of a coward to admit you're a bully, so you invent these moral dilemmas to hide the truth from yourself. I knew you'd find a way to kill him. It's who you are." She gave her hair a toss. "Things couldn't have worked out better. You'll be much more fun than Avery. He wasn't a deep thinker, but you'll drive yourself crazy trying to understand what's going on. You'll be all understanding at first. You'll try to make me into something I'm not. An unhappy woman brutalized in life and empowered by death. It's only natural I act out my resentments, and you'll think if you give me time, I'll get over it. You'll drown yourself in that kind of crap. Take my advice, Roy. The only thing you need to understand is that I'm a lot smarter than you."

In her frilly glory, she reminded him of the figures on the cakes in an X-rated bakery near his apartment in Detroit. Shellane couldn't believe he had been so wrong about her.

"Come on!" she said. "Deep down you must have known the truth. Nobody could love something like you."

Stiffly, he said, "This is about revenge?"

"You say that like it's trivial! Haven't you ever been hurt?" She giggled. "Before now, I mean. Didn't you just want to fuck the bitch up? Tear her life apart . . . like what she did to you? Don't undervalue revenge. Thinking about it may be the only thing that's going to keep you sane."

Incredulous, he said, "Why . . . how did you bring me here? To the lake? I don't—"

"I didn't do anything. You found me. You found the house. Your whole life you've been looking for a place that fit you perfectly. That's how you see it, anyway. The truth is, you were looking for a suitable punishment." She tipped her head coquettishly and said, "And here you are!"

"But what did—"

"No more clues. Figure it out yourself . . . if you can. I'm not sure *I* understand it. But understanding's way overrated. Try and stay in the moment."

"I can still take us out of here, Grace," he said. "It—"

"Don't you get it? I don't want to leave! This is my little slice of heaven. I own this place. It's mine. I'm not about to give up what I've won."

The uglies strained forward, craning their necks, making whimpering sounds.

"When I came here," Grace went on, "when I saw all these fucked-up people, hurting themselves the same way in death as they did when they were alive, I swore I'd break the mold. I was fed up with taking a beating, and I worked hard to get where I am. But I don't think it's in you, Roy. What you did in life was run, and you're not going to change here." She patted the uglies' heads with rough affection. "The boys are dying for some exercise. So in a minute I'm going to let you do what you do best."

His mind burned with questions she would never answer . . . or that she never *could* answer. And that, he thought, was key. She didn't have all the answers. If she was the queen of the house, why hadn't the people he talked to known who she was? Maybe they were dissembling, afraid to speak, but it might be that Grace was not the only power here, and that there was still power to be had by someone resourceful enough to grasp it.

"I can hear the wheels spinning." Grace tapped her forehead. "You go, Roy! If anybody can beat the odds, it's a great big criminal type like you!"

The uglies surged forward, but she snapped at them and they heeled.

"I won't be able to hold them much longer," said Grace, "so if you want a head start . . ." She shrugged, smiled sweetly. "Your call, lover."

As he turned to the door behind him, he was astonished to find that he still loved her, that mixed in with the shocks bred by her duplicity were skeins of longing and the hope he could persuade her that their relationship had not merely been a device, part of her scheme to kill her husband. He refused to believe she was that accomplished an actress. The iron hand of the doorknob clasped his fingers snugly and the contact put a cold charge in his emotions. Love notwithstanding, if she wanted a game, he'd give her one; but then his anger was drowned beneath a tide of terrible recognitions. The hopelessness of his situation; the complexity of the problem he confronted; and most disabling of all, the appropriateness of the punishment he faced. To run ceaselessly, to hide, to exist—however fractionally—without the consolations that had made his old existence endurable. He understood why the lake had seemed such a good fit. It was to be his resting place, his final worldly destination. He'd spend eternity, if eternity there was, scurrying through the maze of that black, sedated house like a rat in a ruin and mooning about the lake where death and love had found him. He entered the room, passing through flickering white lights into the shadowy space beyond and thought once again of Grace, her clean beauty, all the simple qualities he had desired. Dressed in her frillies, voice dripping with sarcasm, she no longer seemed to embody those qualities, to be someone toward whom he had any relation, and it was not desire, not love, not guilt, not even regret or sorrow that ruled him now. Those emotions were going to shades, draining of color and force. It was hate, a freshly excavated core of it, that urged him on as he began to run.

AFTERWORD

My favorite ghost story is Henry James's *The Turn of the Screw.* As ghosts are by nature elusive and allusive; to my mind, the best ghost stories are studies in ambiguity, and—in addition to being masterfully written—James's story sets the standard in this regard.

KELLY LINK's stories have recently appeared in *Conjunctions* and *McSweeney's Mammoth Treasury of Thrilling Tales*. Her first collection, *Stranger Things Happen*, was published in 2001. She has won a World Fantasy Award, a Nebula Award, and the James Tiptree, Jr., Award. She works with her husband, Gavin J. Grant, on the zine *Lady Churchill's Rosebud Wristlet*, and is the editor of *Trampoline*, an anthology just out from Small Beer Press.

THE HORTLAK

KELLY LINK

ERIC WAS NIGHT, and Batu was day. The girl, Charley, was the moon. Every night, she drove past the All-Night in her long, noisy, green Chevy, a dog hanging out the passenger window. It wasn't ever the same dog, although they all had the same blissful expression. They were doomed, but they didn't know it.

Bız buradan çok hoş, landık.
We like it here very much.

The All-Night Convenience was a fully stocked, self-sufficient organism, like the *Starship Enterprise*, or the *Kon-Tiki*. Batu went on and on about this. They didn't work retail anymore. They were on a voyage of discovery, one in which they had no need to leave the All-Night, not even to do laundry. Batu washed his pajamas and the extra uniforms in the sink in the back. He even washed Eric's clothes. That was the kind of friend Batu was.

Burada tatil için mi bulunuyorsunuz?
Are you here on holiday?

All during his shift, Eric listened for Charley's car. First she went by on her way to the shelter and then, during her shift, she took the dogs out driving, past the store first in one direction and then back again, two or three times in one night, the lights of her headlights picking out the long, black gap of the Ausible Chasm, a bright slap across the windows of the All-Night. Eric's heart lifted whenever a car went past.

The zombies came in, and he was polite to them, and failed to understand what they wanted, and sometimes real people came in and bought candy or cigarettes or beer. The zombies were never around when the real people were around, and Charley never showed up when the zombies were there.

Charley looked like someone from a Greek play, Electra, or Cassandra. She looked like someone had just set her favorite city on fire. Eric had thought that, even before he knew about the dogs.

Sometimes, when she didn't have a dog in the Chevy, Charley came into the All-Night Convenience to buy a Mountain Dew, and then she and Batu would go outside to sit on the curb. Batu was teaching her Turkish. Sometimes Eric went outside as well, to smoke a cigarette. He didn't really smoke, but it meant he got to look at Charley, the way the moonlight sat on her like a hand. Sometimes she looked back. Wind would rise up, out of the Ausible Chasm, across Ausible Chasm Road, into the parking lot of the All-Night, tugging at Batu's pajama bottoms, pulling away the cigarette smoke that hung out of Eric's mouth. Charley's bangs would float up off her forehead, until she clamped them down with her fingers.

Batu said he was not flirting. He didn't have a thing for Charley. He was interested in her because Eric was interested. Batu wanted to know what Charley's story was: he said he needed to know if she was good enough for Eric, for the All-Night Convenience. There was a lot at stake.

WHAT ERIC WANTED to know was, why did Batu have so many pajamas? But Eric didn't want to seem nosy. There wasn't a lot of space in the All-Night. If Batu wanted Eric to know about the pajamas, then one day he'd tell him. It was as simple as that.

RECENTLY, BATU HAD evolved past the need for more than two or three hours sleep, which was good in some ways and bad in others. Eric had a suspicion he might figure out how to talk to Charley if Batu were tucked away, back in the storage closet, dreaming his own sweet dreams, and not scheming schemes, doing all the flirting on Eric's behalf, so that Eric never had to say a thing.

Eric had even rehearsed the start of a conversation. Charley would say, "Where's Batu?" and Eric would say, "Asleep." Or even, "Sleeping in the closet."

Erkek arkadaş var mi?
Do you have a boyfriend?

Charley's story: She worked night shifts at the animal shelter. Every night, when Charley got to work, she checked the list to see which dogs were on the schedule. She took the dogs—any that weren't too ill, or too mean—out for one last drive around town. Then she drove them back and she put them to sleep. She did this with an injection. She sat on the floor and petted them until they weren't breathing anymore.

When she was telling Batu this, Batu sitting far too close to her, Eric not close enough, Eric had this thought, which was what it would be like to lie down and put his head on Charley's leg. But the longest conversation that he'd ever managed with Charley was with Charley on one side of the counter, him on the other, when he'd explained that they weren't taking money anymore, at least not unless people wanted to give them money.

"I want a Mountain Dew," Charley had said, making sure Eric understood that part.

"I know," Eric said. He tried to show with his eyes how much he knew, and how much he didn't know, but wanted to know.

"But you don't want me to pay you for it."

"I'm supposed to give you what you want," Eric said, "and then you give me what you want to give me. It doesn't have to be about money. It doesn't even have to be something, you know, tangible. Sometimes people tell Batu their dreams if they don't have anything interesting in their wallets."

"All I want is a Mountain Dew," Charley said. But she must have seen the panic on Eric's face, and she dug in her pocket. Instead of change, she pulled out a set of dog tags and plunked it down on the counter.

"This dog is no longer alive," she said. "It wasn't a very big dog, and I think it was part Chihuahua and part Collie, and how pitiful is that. You should have seen it. Its owner brought it in because it would jump up on her bed in the morning, lick her face, and get so excited that it would pee. I don't know, maybe she thought someone else would want to adopt an ugly little bedwetting dog, but nobody did, and so now it's not alive anymore. I killed it."

"I'm sorry," Eric said. Charley leaned her elbows against the counter. She was so close he could smell her smell: chemical, burnt, doggy. There were dog hairs on her clothes.

"I killed it," Charley said. She sounded angry at him. "Not you."

When Eric looked at her, he saw that that city was still on fire. It was still burning down, and Charley was watching it burn. She was still holding the dog tags. She let go and they lay there on the counter until Eric picked them up and put them in the register.

"This is all Batu's idea," Charley said. "Right?" She went outside and sat on the curb, and in a while Batu came out of the storage closet and went outside as well. Batu's pajama bottoms were silk. There were smiling hydrocephalic cartoon cats on them, and the cats carried children in their mouths. Either the children were mouse-sized, or the cats were bear-sized.

The children were either screaming or laughing. Batu's pajama top was red flannel, faded, with guillotines, and heads in baskets.

Eric stayed inside. He leaned his face against the window every once in a while, as if he could hear what they were saying. But even if he could have heard them, he guessed he wouldn't have understood. The shapes their mouths made were shaped like Turkish words. Eric hoped they were talking about retail.

Kar yağacak.
It's going to snow.

The way the All-Night worked at the moment was Batu's idea. They sized up the customers before they got to the counter—that had always been part of retail. If the customer was the right sort, then Batu or Eric gave the customers what they said they needed, and the customers paid with money sometimes, and sometimes with other things: pot, books on tape, souvenir maple-syrup tins. They were near the border. They got a lot of Canadians. Eric suspected someone, maybe a traveling Canadian pajama salesman, was supplying Batu with novelty pajamas.

Siz de mi bekliyorsunuz?
Are you waiting, too?

What Batu thought Eric should say to Charley, if he really liked her: "Come live with me. Come live at the All-Night."

What Eric thought about saying to Charley: "If you're going away, take me with you. I'm about to be twenty years old, and I've never been to college. I sleep days in a storage closet, wearing someone else's pajamas. I've worked retail jobs since I was sixteen. I know people are hateful. If you need to bite someone, you can bite me."

Başka bir yere gidelim mi?
Shall we go somewhere else?

Charley drives by. There is a little black dog in the passenger window, leaning out to swallow the fast air. There is a yellow dog. An Irish setter. A Doberman. Akitas. Charley has rolled the window so far down that these dogs could jump out, if they wanted, when she stops the car at a light. But the dogs don't jump. So Charley drives them back again.

BATU SAID IT was clear Charley had a great capacity for hating, and also a great capacity for love. Charley's hatred was seasonal: in the months after

Christmas, Christmas puppies started growing up. People got tired of trying to housetrain them. All February, all March, Charley hated people. She hated people in December, too, just for practice.

Being in love, Batu said, like working retail, meant that you had to settle for being hated, at least part of the year. That was what the months after Christmas were all about. Neither system—not love, not retail—was perfect. When you looked at dogs, you saw this, that love didn't work.

Batu said it was likely that Charley, both her person and her Chevy, were infested with dog ghosts. These ghosts were different from the zombies. Non-human ghosts, he said, were the most difficult of all ghosts to dislodge, and dogs were worst of all. There is nothing as persistent, as loyal, as *clingy*, as a dog.

"So can you see these ghosts?" Eric said.

"Don't be ridiculous," Batu said. "You can't see that kind of ghost. You smell them."

"What do they smell like?" Eric said. "How do you get rid of them?"

"Either you smell it or you don't," Batu said. "It's not something I can describe. And it isn't a serious thing. More like dandruff, except they don't make a shampoo for it. Maybe that's what we should be selling: shampoo that gets rid of ghosts, the dog kind and the zombies, all that kind of thing. Our problem is that we're new-style retail, but everything we stock is the same old crap."

"People need Mountain Dew," Eric said. "And aspirin."

"I know," Batu said. "It just makes me crazy sometimes."

Civarda turistik yerler var mı, acaba?
Are there any tourist attractions around here, I wonder?

Eric woke up and found it was dark. It was always dark when he woke up, and this was always a surprise. There was a little window on the back wall of the storage closet, that framed the dark like a picture. You could feel the cold night air propping up the walls of the All-Night, thick and wet as glue.

Batu had let him sleep in. Batu was considerate of other people's sleep.

All day long, in Eric's dreams, store managers had arrived, one after another, announced themselves, expressed dismay at the way Batu had reinvented—*compromised*—convenience retail. In Eric's dream, Batu had put his large, handsome arm over the shoulder of the store managers, promised to explain everything in a satisfactory manner, if they would only come and see. The store managers had all gone, in a docile, trusting way, trotting after Batu, across the road, looking both ways, to the edge of the Ausible Chasm. They stood there, in Eric's dream, peering down into the Chasm, and then Batu had given them a little push, a small push, and that was the end of those store managers, and Batu walked back across the road to wait for the next store managers.

Eric bathed standing up at the sink and put on his uniform. He brushed his teeth. The closet smelled like sleep.

It was the middle of February, and there was snow in the All-Night parking lot. Batu was clearing the parking lot, carrying shovelfuls of snow across the road, dumping the snow into the Ausible Chasm. Eric went outside for a smoke and watched. He didn't offer to help. He was still upset about the way Batu had behaved in his dream.

There was no moon, but the snow was lit by its own whiteness. There was the shadowy figure of Batu, carrying in front of him the shadowy scoop of the shovel, full of snow, like an enormous spoon full of falling light, which was still falling all around them. The snow came down, and Eric's smoke went up and up.

He walked across the road to where Batu stood, peering down into the Ausible Chasm. Down in the Chasm, it was no darker than the kind of dark the rest of the world, including Eric, had had to get used to. Snow fell into the Chasm, the way snow fell on the rest of the world. And yet there was a wind coming out of the Chasm that worried Eric.

"What do you think is down there?" Batu said.

"Zombie Land," Eric said. He could almost taste it. "Zomburbia. They have everything down there. There's even supposed to be a drive-in movie theater down there, somewhere, that shows old black-and-white horror movies, all night long. Zombie churches with AA meetings for zombies, down in the basements, every Thursday night."

"Yeah?" Batu said. "Zombie bars, too? Where they serve zombies Zombies?"

Eric said, "My friend Dave went down once, when we were in high school, on a dare. He used to tell us all kinds of stories. Said he was going to apply to Zombie U. and get a full scholarship, on account of living people were a minority down there. But he went to Arizona instead."

"You ever go?" Batu said, pointing with his empty shovel at the narrow, crumbly path that went down into the Chasm.

"I never went to college. I've never even been to Canada," Eric said. "Not even when I was in high school, to buy beer."

ALL NIGHT THE zombies came out of the Chasm, holding handfuls of snow. They carried the snow across the road, and into the parking lot, and left it there. Batu was back in the office, sending off faxes, and Eric was glad about this, that Batu couldn't see what the zombies were up to.

Zombies came into the store, tracking in salt and melting snow. Eric hated mopping up after the zombies.

He sat on the counter, facing the road, hoping Charley would drive by soon. Two weeks ago, Charley had bitten a man who'd brought his dog to the animal shelter to be put down.

The man was bringing his dog because it had bit him, he said, but Charley said you knew when you saw this guy, and when you saw the dog, that the dog had had a very good reason.

This man had a tattoo of a mermaid coiled around his meaty forearm, and even this mermaid had an unpleasant look to her: scaly, corseted bottom; tiny black-dot eyes; a sour, fangy smile. Charley said it was as if even the mermaid was telling her to bite the arm, and so she did. When she did, the dog went nuts. The guy dropped its leash. He was trying to get Charley off his arm. The dog, misunderstanding the situation, or rather, understanding the situation but not the larger situation, had grabbed Charley by her leg, sticking its teeth into her calf.

Both Charley and the dog's owner had needed stitches. But it was the dog who was doomed. Nothing had changed that.

Charley's boss at the shelter was going to fire her, any time soon—in fact, he had fired her. But they hadn't found someone to take her shift yet, and so she was working there for a few more days, under a different name. Everyone at the shelter understood why she'd had to bite the man.

Charley said she was going to drive all the way across Canada. Maybe keep on going, up into Alaska. Go watch bears pick through garbage.

"Before a bear hibernates," she told Batu and Eric, "it eats this special diet. Nuts and these particular leaves. It sleeps all winter and never goes to the bathroom. So when she wakes up in spring, she's still constipated and the first thing she does is take this really painful shit. And then she goes and jumps in a river. She's really pissed off now, about everything. When she comes out of the river, she's covered in ice. She goes on a rampage, and she's insane with rage, and she's invulnerable, like she's wearing armor. Isn't that great? That bear can take a bite out of anything it wants."

Uykum geldi.
My sleep has come.

The snow kept falling. Sometimes it stopped. Charley came by. Eric had bad dreams. Batu did not go to bed. When the zombies came in, he followed them around the store, taking notes. The zombies didn't care at all. They were done with all that.

Batu was wearing Eric's favorite pajamas. These were blue, and had towering Hokusai-style white-blue waves, and up on the waves, there were boats with owls looking owlish. If you looked closely, you could see that the owls were gripping newspapers in their wings, and if you looked even closer, you could read the date and the headline:

"Tsunami Tsweeps Pussy Overboard, All is Lots."

Batu had spent a lot of time reorganizing the candy aisle according to chewiness and meltiness. The week before, he had arranged it so that if you took the first letter of every candy, reading across from left to right, and then down, it had spelled out the first sentence of *To Kill A Mockingbird*, and then also a line of Turkish poetry. Something about the moon.

The zombies came and went, and Batu put his notebook away. He said, "I'm going to go ahead and put jerky with Sugar Daddies. It's almost a candy. It's very chewy. About as chewy as you can get. Chewy Meat Gum."

"Frothy Meat Drink," Eric said automatically. They were always thinking of products that no one would ever want to buy, and that no one would ever try to sell.

"Squeezable Pork. *It's on your mind, it's in your mouth, it's pork.* Remember that ad campaign? She can come live with us," Batu said. It was the same old speech, only a little more urgent each time he gave it. "The All-Night needs women, especially women like Charley. She falls in love with you, I don't mind one bit."

"What about you?" Eric said.

"What about me?" Batu said. "Charley and I have the Turkish language. That's enough. Tell me something I need. I don't even need sleep!"

"What are you talking about?" Eric said. He hated when Batu talked about Charley, except that he loved hearing her name.

Batu said, "The All-Night is a great place to raise a family. Everything you need, right here. Diapers, Vienna Sausages, grape-scented Magic Markers, Moon Pies—kids like Moon Pies—and then one day, when they're tall enough, we teach them how to operate the register."

"There are laws against that," Eric said. "Mars needs women. Not the All-Night. And we're running out of Moon Pies." He turned his back on Batu.

SOME OF BATU'S pajamas worry Eric. He won't wear these, although Batu has told him that he may wear any pajamas he likes.

For example, ocean liners navigating icebergs on a pair of pajama bottoms. A man with an enormous pair of scissors, running after women whose long hair whips out behind them like red and yellow flags, they are moving so fast. Spiderwebs with houses stuck to them. An embroidered pajama top that records the marriage of the bearded woman and the tightrope walker, who perches above the aisle on a silken cord. The flower-girl is a dwarf. Someone has woven roses and lilies of the valley into the bride's beard. The minister has no arms. He stands at the altar like a stork, the sleeves of his vestments pinned up like flat black wings, holding the Bible with the toes of his left foot.

There is a pajama bottom embroidered with the wedding night.

Some of the pajamas are plain on the outside. Eric once put his foot down into a pair, once, before he saw what was on the insides.

A few nights ago, about two or three in the morning, a woman came into the store. Batu was over by the magazines, and the woman went and stood next to Batu.

Batu's eyes were closed, although that doesn't necessarily mean he was asleep. The woman stood and flicked through magazines, and then at some point she realized that the man standing there with his eyes closed was wearing pajamas. She stopped reading through *People* magazine, and started reading Batu's pajamas instead. Then she gasped, and poked Batu with a skinny finger.

"Where did you get those?" she said. "How on earth did you get those?"

Batu opened his eyes. "Excuse me," he said. "May I help you find something?"

"You're wearing my diary," the woman said. Her voice went up and up in a wail. "That's my handwriting! That's the diary that I kept when I was fourteen! But it had a lock on it, and I hid it under my mattress, and I never let anyone read it. Nobody ever read it!"

Batu held out his arm. "That's not true," he said. "I've read it. You have very nice handwriting. Very distinctive. My favorite part is when—"

The woman screamed. She put her hands over her ears and walked backward, down the aisle, and still screaming, turned around and ran out of the store.

"What was that about?" Eric said. "What was up with her?"

"I don't know," Batu said. "The thing is, I thought she looked familiar! And I was right. Hah! What are the odds, you think, the woman who kept that diary coming in the store like that?"

"Maybe you shouldn't wear those anymore," Eric said. "Just in case she comes back."

Gelebilir miyim?
Can I come?

Batu had originally worked Tuesday through Saturday, second shift. Now he was all day, every day. Eric worked all night, all nights. They didn't need anyone else, except maybe Charley.

What had happened was this. One of the managers had left, supposedly to have a baby, although she had not looked in the least bit pregnant, Batu said, and besides, it was clearly not Batu's kid, because of the vasectomy. Then, shortly after the incident with the man in the trenchcoat, the other manager had quit, claiming to be sick of that kind of shit. No one was sent to replace him, so Batu had stepped in.

The door rang and a customer came into the store. Canadian. Not a zombie. Eric turned around in time to see Batu duck down, slipping around the corner of the candy aisle and heading toward the storage closet.

The customer bought a Mountain Dew, Eric too disheartened to explain that cash was no longer necessary. He could feel Batu, fretting in the storage closet, listening to this old-style retail transaction. When the customer was gone, Batu came out again.

"Do you ever wonder," Eric said, "if the company will ever send another manager?" He saw again the dream-Batu, the dream-managers, the cartoonish, unbridgeable gap of the Ausible Chasm.

"They won't," Batu said.

"They might," Eric said.

"They won't," Batu said.

"How do you know for sure?" Eric said. "What if they do?"

"It was a bad idea in the first place," Batu said. He gestured toward the parking lot and the Ausible Chasm. "Not enough steady business."

"So why do we stay here?" Eric said. "How do we change the face of retail if nobody ever comes in here except joggers and truckers and zombies and Canadians? I mean, I tried to explain about how new-style retail worked the other night—to this woman—and she told me to fuck off. She acted like I was insane."

"You just have to ignore people like that. The customer isn't always right. Sometimes the customer is an asshole. That's the first rule of retail," Batu said. "But it's not like anywhere else is better. Before this, when I was working for the CIA, that was a shitty job. Believe me, this is better."

"The thing I hate is how they look at us," Eric said. "As if we don't really exist. As if we're ghosts. As if they're the real people and we're not."

"We used to go to this bar, sometimes, me and the people I worked with," Batu said. "Only we have to pretend that we don't know each other. No fraternizing. So we all sit there, along the bar, and don't say a word to each other. All these guys, all of us, we could speak maybe five hundred languages, dialects, whatever, between us. But we don't talk in this bar. Just sit and drink and sit and drink. All us Agency spooks, all in a row. Used to drive the bartender crazy. He knew what we were. We used to leave nice tips. Didn't matter to him."

"So did you ever kill people?" Eric said. He never knew whether or not Batu was joking about the CIA thing.

"Do I look like a killer?" Batu said, standing there in his pajamas, rumpled and red-eyed. When Eric burst out laughing, he smiled and yawned and scratched his head.

WHEN OTHER EMPLOYEES had quit the All-Night, for various reasons of their own, Batu had not replaced them.

Around this same time, Batu's girlfriend had kicked him out, and with Eric's permission, he had moved into the storage closet. That had been just *before* Christmas, and it was a few days *after* Christmas when Eric's mother lost her job as a security guard at the mall, and decided she was going to go find Eric's father. She'd gone hunting online, and made a list of names she thought he might be going under. She had addresses as well.

Eric wasn't sure what she was going to do if she found his father, and he didn't think she knew, either. She said she just wanted to talk, but Eric knew she kept a gun in the glove compartment of her car. Before she left, Eric had copied down her list of names and addresses, and sent out Christmas cards to all of them. It was the first time he'd ever had a reason to send out Christmas cards, and it had been difficult, finding the right things to say in them, especially since they probably weren't his father, no matter what his mother thought. Not all of them, anyway.

Before she left, Eric's mother had put most of the furniture in storage. She'd sold everything else, including Eric's guitar and his books, at a yard sale one Saturday morning while Eric was working an extra shift at the All-Night.

The rent was still paid through the end of January, but after his mother left, Eric had worked longer and longer hours at the store, and then, one morning, he didn't bother going home. What had he been thinking, anyway, living at home with his mother? He was a high-school graduate. He had his whole life in front of him. The All-Night, and Batu, they needed him. Batu said this attitude showed Eric was destined for great things at the All-Night.

Every night Batu sent off faxes to the *Weekly World News*, and to the *National Enquirer*, and to *The New York Times*. These faxes concerned the Ausible Chasm and the zombies. Someday someone would send reporters. It was all part of the plan, which was going to change the way retail worked. It was going to be a whole different world, and Eric and Batu were going to be right there at the beginning. They were going to be famous heroes. Revolutionaries. Heroes of the Revolution. Batu said that Eric didn't need to understand that part of the plan yet. It was essential to the plan that Eric didn't ask questions.

Ne zaman gelecksiniz?
When will you come back?

The zombies were like Canadians in that they looked enough like real people at first, to fool you. But when you looked closer, you saw they were from some other place, where things were different, where even the same things, the things that went on everywhere, were just a little bit different.

The zombies didn't talk at all, or they said things that didn't make sense.

"Wooden hat," one zombie said to Eric, "Glass leg. Drove around all day in my wife. Did you ever hear me on the radio?" They tried to pay Eric for things that the All-Night didn't sell.

Real people, the ones who weren't heading toward Canada or away from Canada, mostly had better things to do than drive out to the All-Night at 3:00 A.M. So real people, in a way, were even weirder, when they came in. Eric kept a close eye on the real people. Once a guy had pulled a gun on him—there was no way to understand that, but on the other hand, you knew exactly what was going on. With the zombies, who knew?

Not even Batu knew what the zombies were up to. Sometimes he said that they were just another thing you had to deal with in retail. They were the kind of customer that you couldn't ever satisfy, the kind of customer who wanted something you couldn't give them, who had no other currency, except currency that was sinister, unwholesome, confusing, and probably dangerous.

Meanwhile, the things that the zombies tried to purchase were plainly things that they had brought with them into the store—things that had fallen, or been thrown into the Ausible Chasm, like pieces of safety glass. Rocks from the bottom of Ausible Chasm. Beetles. The zombies liked shiny things, broken things, trash like empty soda bottles, handfuls of leaves, sticky dirt, dirty sticks.

Eric thought maybe Batu had it wrong. Maybe it wasn't supposed to be a transaction. Maybe the zombies just wanted to give Eric something. But what was he going to do with their leaves? Why him? What was he supposed to give them in return? "You keep it," he'd tell them. "Dead leaves are on special this week."

Eventually, when it was clear Eric didn't understand, the zombies drifted off, away from the counter and around the aisles again, or out the doors, making their way like raccoons, scuttling back across the road, still clutching their leaves. Batu would put away his notebook, go into the storage closet, and send off his faxes.

The zombie customers made Eric feel guilty. He hadn't been trying hard enough. The zombies were never rude, or impatient, or tried to shoplift things. He hoped that they found what they were looking for. After all, he would be dead someday, too, and on the other side of the counter.

Maybe his friend Dave had been telling the truth and there was a country down there that you could visit, just like Canada. Maybe when the zombies got all the way to the bottom, they got into zippy zombie cars and drove off to their zombie jobs, or back home again, to their sexy zombie wives, or maybe they went off to the zombie bank to make their deposits of stones, leaves, linty, birdsnesty tangles, all the other debris real people didn't know the value of.

IT WASN'T JUST the zombies. Weird stuff happened in the middle of the day, too. When there were still managers and other employers, once, on Batu's shift, a guy had come in wearing a trenchcoat and a hat. Outside, it must have been ninety degrees, and Batu admitted he had felt a little spooked about the trenchcoat thing, but there was another customer, a jogger, poking at the bottled waters to see which were coldest. Trenchcoat guy walked around the store, putting candy bars and safety razors in his pockets, like he was getting ready for Halloween. Batu had thought about punching the alarm. "Sir?" he said. "Excuse me, sir?"

The man walked up and stood in front of the counter. Batu couldn't take his eyes off the trenchcoat. It was like the guy was wearing an electric fan strapped to his chest, under the trenchcoat, and the fan was blowing things around underneath. You could hear the fan buzzing. It made sense, (Batu said) he'd thought: This guy had his own air-conditioning unit under there. Pretty neat, although you still wouldn't want to go trick-or-treating at this guy's house.

"Hot enough for you?" the man said, and Batu saw that this guy was sweating. He twitched, and a bee flew out of the gray trenchcoat sleeve. Batu and the man both watched it fly away. Then the man opened his trenchcoat, flapped his arms, gently, gently, and the bees inside his trenchcoat began to leave the man in long, clotted, furious trails, until the whole store was vibrating with clouds of bees. Batu ducked under the counter. Trenchcoat man, bee guy, reached over the counter, dinged the register in a calm and experienced way so that the drawer popped open, and scooped all the bills out of the till.

Then he walked back out again and left all his bees. He got in his car and drove away. That's the way that all All-Night stories end, with someone driving away.

But they had to get a beekeeper to come in, to smoke the bees out. Batu got stung three times, once on the lip, once on his stomach, and once when he put his hand into the register and found no money, only a bee. The jogger sued the All-Night parent company for a lot of money, and Batu and Eric didn't know what had happened with that.

Karanlik ne zman basar?
When does it get dark?

Eric has been having this dream recently. In the dream, he's up behind the counter in the All-Night, and then his father is walking down the aisle of the All-Night, past the racks of magazines and toward the counter, his father's hands full of black stones. Which is ridiculous: his father is alive, and not only that, but living in another state, maybe in a different time zone, probably under a different name.

When he told Batu about it, Batu said, "Oh, that dream. I've had it, too."

"About your father?" Eric said.

"About your father," Batu said. "Who do you think I meant, *my* father?"

"You haven't ever met my father," Eric said.

"I'm sorry if it upsets you, but it was definitely your father," Batu said. "You look just like him. If I dream about him again, what do you want me to do? Ignore him? Pretend he isn't there?"

Eric never knew when Batu was pulling his leg. Dreams could be a touchy subject with Batu. Eric thought maybe Batu was nostalgic about sleep, collecting pajamas the way people who were nostalgic about their childhood collected toys.

ANOTHER DREAM, ONE that Eric hasn't told Batu about. In this dream, Charley comes in. When she gets up to the counter, Eric realizes that he's got one of Batu's pajama tops on, one of the inside-out ones. Things are rubbing against his arms, his back, his stomach, transferring themselves, like tattoos, to his skin.

And he hasn't got any pants on.

Batık gemilerle ilgileniyorum.
I'm interested in sunken ships.

"You need to make your move," Batu said. He said it over and over, day after day, until Eric was sick of hearing it. "Any day now, the shelter is going to find someone to replace her, and Charley will split. Who knows where she'll end up? Tell you what you should do, you tell her you want to adopt a dog. Give it a home. We've got room here. Dogs are good practice for when you and Charley are parents."

"How do you know?" Eric said. He knew he sounded exasperated. He couldn't help it. "That makes no sense at all. If dogs are good practice, then what kind of mother is Charley going to be? What are you saying? So say Charley has a kid, you're saying she's going to put it down if it cries at night or wets the bed?"

"That's not what I'm saying at all," Batu said. "The only thing I'm worried about, Eric, really, is whether or not Charley may be too old. It takes longer to have kids when you're her age. Things can go wrong."

"What are you talking about?" Eric said. "Charley's not old."

"How old do you think she is?" Batu said. "So what do you think? Should the toothpaste and the condiments go next to the Elmer's glue and the hair gel and lubricants? Make a shelf of sticky things? Or should I put it with the chewing tobacco and the mouthwash, and make a little display of things that you spit?"

"Sure," Eric said. "Make a little display. I don't know how old Charley is, maybe she's my age? Nineteen? A little older?"

Batu laughed. "A little older? So how old do you think I am?"

"I don't know," Eric said. He squinted at Batu. "Thirty-five? Forty?"

Batu looked pleased. "You know, since I started sleeping less, I think I've stopped getting older. I may be getting younger. You keep on getting a good night's sleep, and we're going to be the same age pretty soon. Come take a look at this and tell me what you think."

"Not bad," Eric said. A car went past, swerved, and honked, and drove on. Not a Chevy. "Looks like we're running low on some stuff."

"It's not such a big deal," Batu said. He knelt down in the aisle, marking off inventory on his clipboard. "No big thing if Charley's older than you think. Nothing wrong with older women. And it's good you're not bothered about the ghost dogs, or the biting thing. Everyone's got problems. The only real concern I have is about her car."

"What about her car?" Eric said.

"Well," Batu said. "It isn't a problem if she's going to live here. She can park it here for as long as she wants. That's what the parking lot is for. But whatever you do, if she invites you to go for a ride, don't go for a ride."

"Why not?" Eric said. "What are you talking about?"

"Think about it," Batu said. "All those dog ghosts." He scooted down the aisle on his butt. Eric went after him. "Every time she drives by here with some poor dog, that dog is doomed. That car is bad luck. The passenger side especially. You want to stay out of that car. I'd rather climb down into the Ausible Chasm."

Something cleared its throat; a zombie had come into the store. It stood behind Batu, looking down at him. Batu looked up. Eric retreated down the aisle, toward the counter.

"Stay out of her car," Batu said, ignoring the zombie.

"And who will be fired out of the cannon?" the zombie said. It was wearing a suit and tie. "My brother will be fired out of the cannon."

"Why can't you talk like sensible people?" Batu said, turning around. Sitting on the floor, he sounded as if he were about to cry. He swatted at the zombie.

The zombie coughed again, yawning. It grimaced at them. Something was snagged on its gray lips now, and the zombie put up its hand. It tugged, dragging at the thing in its mouth, coughing out a black, glistening, wadded rope. The zombie's mouth stayed open, as if to show that there was nothing else in there, even as it held the wet black rope out to Batu. It hung down from its hands, and became pajamas. Batu looked back at Eric. "I don't want them," he said. He looked shy.

"What should I do?" Eric said. He hovered by the magazines. Charlize Theron was grinning at him, as if she knew something he didn't.

"You shouldn't be here." It wasn't clear whether Batu was speaking to Eric or to the zombie. "I have all the pajamas I need." Eric could hear the longing in his voice.

The zombie said nothing. It dropped the pajamas into Batu's lap.

"Stay out of Charley's car!" Batu said to Eric. He closed his eyes, and began to snore.

"Shit," Eric said to the zombie. "How did you do that?"

There was another zombie in the store now. The first zombie took Batu's arms and the second zombie took Batu's feet. They dragged him down the aisle and toward the storage closet. Eric came out from behind the counter.

"What are you doing?" he said. "You're not going to eat him, are you?"

But the zombies had Batu in the closet now. They put the black pajamas on him, yanking them over the other pair of pajamas. They lifted Batu up onto the mattress and pulled the blanket over him, up to his chin.

Eric followed the zombies out of the storage closet. He shut the door behind him. "So I guess he's going to sleep for a while," he said. "That's a good thing, right? He needed to get some sleep. So how did you do that with the pajamas? Are you the ones who are always giving him pajamas? Is there some kind of freaky pajama factory down there? Is he going to wake up?"

The zombies ignored Eric. They held hands and went down the aisles, stopping to consider candy bars and Tampax and toilet paper and all the things that you spit. They wouldn't buy anything. They never did.

Eric went back to the counter. He sat behind the register for a while. Then he went back to the storage closet and looked at Batu. Batu was snoring. His eyelids twitched, and there was a tiny, knowing smile on his face, as if he were dreaming, and everything was being explained to him, at last, in this dream. It was hard to feel worried about someone who looked like that. Eric would have been jealous, except he knew that no one ever managed to hold onto those explanations, once you woke up. Not even Batu.

Hangi yol daha kısa?
Which is the shorter route?
Hangi yol daha kolay?
Which is the easier route?

Charley came by at the beginning of her shift. She didn't come inside the All-Night. Instead, she stood out in the parking lot, beside her car, looking out across the road, at the Ausible Chasm. The car hung low to the ground, as if the trunk were full of things. When Eric went outside, he saw that there was a suitcase in the back seat. If there were ghost dogs, Eric couldn't see them, but there were doggy smudges on the windows.

"Where's Batu?" Charley said.

"Asleep," Eric said. He realized that he'd never figured out how the conversation would go after that.

He said, "Are you going someplace?"

"I'm going to work," Charley said. "Just like normal."

"Good," Eric said. "Normal is good." He stood and looked at his feet. A zombie wandered into the parking lot. It nodded at them, and went into the All-Night.

"Aren't you going to go back inside?" Charley said.

"In a bit," Eric said. "It's not like they ever find what they need in there." But he kept an eye on the All-Night, and on the zombie, in case it headed toward the storage closet.

"So how old are you?" Eric said. "I mean, can I ask you that? How old you are?"

"How old are you?" Charley said right back. She seemed amused.

"I'm almost twenty," Eric said. "I know I look older."

"No you don't," Charley said. "You look exactly like you're almost twenty."

"So how old are you?" Eric said again.

"How old do you think I am?" Charley said.

"About my age?" Eric said.

"That's sweet," Charley said. "Are you flirting with me? Yes? No? How about in dog years? How old would you say I am in dog years?"

The zombie had finished looking for whatever it was looking for inside the All-Night. It came outside and nodded to Charley and Eric. "Beautiful people," it said. "Why won't you ever visit my hand?"

"I'm sorry," Eric said.

The zombie turned its back on them. It tottered calmly across the road, looking neither to the left nor to the right, and went down the footpath into the Ausible Chasm.

"Have you?" Charley said. She pointed at the path.

"No," Eric said. "I mean, someday I will, I guess."

"Do you think they have pets down there? Dogs?" Charley said.

"I don't know," Eric said. "Regular dogs?"

"The thing I think about sometimes," Charley said, "is whether or not they have animal shelters, and if someone has to look after the dogs. If someone has to have a job where they put down dogs, down there. And if you do put dogs to sleep down there, then where do they wake up?"

"Batu says that if you need another job, you can come live with us at the All-Night," Eric said. He was shivering.

"Is *that* what Batu says?" Charley said. She started to laugh.

"I think he likes you," Eric said.

"I like him too," Charley said. "But not like that. And I don't want to live in a convenience store. No offense. I'm sure it's nice."

"It's okay," Eric said. "I don't know. I don't want to work retail my whole life."

"There are worse jobs," Charley said. She leaned against her car. "Maybe I'll stop by, later tonight. We could always go for a long ride, go somewhere else, and talk about retail."

"Like where? Where are you going?" Eric said. "Are you thinking about going to Turkey? Is that why Batu is teaching you Turkish?" He felt as if he were asleep and dreaming. He wanted to stand there and ask Charley questions all night long.

"I want to learn Turkish so that when I go somewhere else, I can pretend to be Turkish. I can pretend I *only* speak Turkish. That way no one will bother me," Charley said.

"Oh," Eric said. "I didn't know you let anyone else—you know, other people—ride in your car."

"It's not a big deal," Charley said. "We can do it some other time." Suddenly she looked much older.

"No, wait," Eric said. "I do want to go for a ride." *I want to come with you. Please take me with you.* "It's just that Batu's asleep. Someone has to look after him. Someone has to be awake to sell stuff."

"So are you going to work there your whole life?" Charley said. "Take care of Batu? Figure out how to rip off dead people?"

"What do you mean?" Eric said.

"Batu says the All-Night is thinking about opening up another store, down there," Charley said, waving across the road. "You and he are this big experiment in retail, according to him. Once the All-Night guys figure out what dead people want to buy, and whether or not they can pay for what they want, it's going to be huge. It's going to be like the discovery of America all over again."

"It's not like that," Eric said. He could feel his voice going up at the end, as if it was a question. He could almost smell what Batu meant about Charley's car. The ghosts, those dogs, were getting impatient. You could tell that. They were tired of the parking lot, they wanted to be going for a ride. "You don't understand. I don't think you understand?"

"Batu said that you have a real way with dead people," Charley said. "Most retail clerks flip out. Of course, you're from around here. Plus, you're young. You probably don't even understand about death yet. You're just like my dogs."

"I don't know what they want," Eric said. "The zombies."

"Nobody ever really knows what they want," Charley said. "Why should that change after you die?"

"Good point," Eric said. "So Batu's told you about our plan?"

"You shouldn't let Batu mess you around so much," Charley said. "I shouldn't be saying all this, I know, because Batu and I are friends. But we could be friends, too, you and me. You're sweet. It's okay that you don't talk much, although this is okay, too, us talking. Why don't you come for a drive with me?"

If there had been dogs inside her car, or the ghosts of dogs, then Eric would have heard them howling. Eric heard them howling. The dogs were telling him to beware. They were telling him to fuck off. Charley belonged to them. She was *their* murderer.

"I can't," Eric said, longing to hear Charley ask him again. "Not right now."

"Well, I'll stop by later, then," Charley said. She smiled at him and for a moment he was standing in that city where no one ever figured out how to put out that fire, and all the dead dogs howled again, and scratched at the smeary windows. "For a Mountain Dew. So you can think about it for a while."

She reached out and took Eric's hand in her hand. "Your hands are cold," she said. Her hands were hot. "You should go back inside."

Rengi beğenmiyorum.
I don't like the color.

It was already 4:00 A.M., and there still wasn't any sign of Charley when Batu came out of the back room, rubbing his eyes. The black pajamas were gone. Now he was wearing pajama bottoms with a field at night, and foxes running across it toward a tree with a circle of foxes sitting on their haunches around it. The outstretched tails of the running foxes were fat as zeppelins, with commas of flame hovering over them. Each little flame had a Hindenburg inside it, with a second littler flame above it, and so on. Some fires you just can't put out.

The pajama top was a color that Eric could not name. Dreary, creeping shapes lay upon it. Eric felt queasy when he looked at them.

"I just had the best dream," Batu said.

"You've been asleep for almost six hours," Eric said. When Charley came, he would go with her. He would stay with Batu. Batu needed him. He would go with Charley. He would go and come back. He wouldn't ever come back. He would send Batu postcards with bears on them. "So what was all that about, with the zombies?"

"I don't know what you're talking about," Batu said. He took an apple from the fruit display and polished it on his non-Euclidean pajama top. The apple took on a poisonous, whispery sheen. "Has Charley come by?"

"Yeah," Eric said. He and Charley would go to Las Vegas. They would buy Batu gold lamé pajamas. "I think you're right. I think she's about to leave town."

"Well, she can't!" Batu said. "That's not the plan. Here, I tell you what we'll do. You go outside and wait for her. Make sure she doesn't get away."

"She's not wanted by the police, Batu," Eric said. "She doesn't belong to us. She can leave town if she wants to."

"And you're okay with that?" Batu said. He yawned ferociously, and yawned again, and stretched, so that his eldritch pajama top heaved up and made Eric feel sick again.

"Not really," Eric said. He had already picked out a toothbrush, some toothpaste, and some novelty teeth, left over from Halloween, which he could give to Charley, maybe. "Are you okay? Are you going to fall asleep again? Can I ask you some questions?"

"What kind of questions?" Batu said, lowering his eyelids in a way that seemed both sleepy and cunning.

"Questions about our mission," Eric said. "About the All-Night and what we're doing here next to the Ausible Chasm. I need to understand what just happened with the zombies and the pajamas, and whether or not what happened is part of the plan, and whether or not the plan belongs to us, or whether the plan was planned by someone else, and we're just somebody else's big experiment in retail. Are we brand new, or are we just the same old thing?"

"This isn't a good time for questions," Batu said. He jerked his head toward the security cameras in a meaningful way. "In all the time that we've worked here, have I lied to you? Have I led you astray?"

"Well," Eric said. "That's what I need to know."

"Perhaps I haven't told you everything," Batu said. "But that's part of the plan. When I said that we were going to make everything new again, that we were going to reinvent retail, I was telling the truth. The plan is still the plan, and you are still part of that plan, and so is Charley."

"What about the pajamas?" Eric said. "What about the Canadians and the maple syrup and the people who come in to buy Mountain Dew?"

"You need to know this?" Batu said.

"Yes," Eric said. "Absolutely."

"Okay, then. My pajamas are *experimental CIA pajamas*," Batu said, out of the side of his mouth. "Like batteries. You've been charging them for me when you sleep. That's all I can say right now. Forget about the Canadians. They're just for practice. *That's* the least part of the plan, and anyway, the plan just changed. These pajamas the zombies just gave me—do you have any idea what this means?"

Eric shook his head no.

Batu said, "If they can give us pajamas, then they can give us other things. It's a matter of communication. If we can figure out what they need, then we can make them give us what we need."

"What do we need?" Eric said.

"We need you to go outside and wait for Charley," Batu said. "We don't have time for this. It's getting early. Charley gets off work any time now."

"Explain all of that again," Eric said. "What you just said. Explain the plan to me one more time."

"Look," Batu said. "Listen. Everybody is alive at first, right?"

"Right," Eric said.

"And everybody dies," Batu said. "Right?"

"Right," Eric said. A car drove by, but it still wasn't Charley.

"So everybody starts here," Batu said. "Not here, in the All-Night, but somewhere *here*, where we are. Where we live now. Where we live is here. The world. Right?"

"Right," Eric said. "Okay."

"And where we go is there," Batu said, flicking a finger toward the road. "Out there, down into the Ausible Chasm. Everybody goes there. And here we are, *here, the All-Night*, which is on the way to *there*."

"Right," Eric said.

"So it's like the Canadians," Batu said. "People are going someplace, and if they need something, they can stop here, to get it. But we need to know what they need. This is a whole new unexplored market demographic. The people we're working for stuck the All-Night right here, lit it up like a Christmas tree, and waited to see who stopped in and what they bought. I shouldn't be telling you this. This is all need-to-know information only."

"You mean the All-Night, or the CIA, or whoever, needs us to figure out how to sell things to zombies," Eric said.

"Forget about the CIA. Nobody has ever tried it before!" Batu said. "Can you believe that? Now will you go outside?"

"But is it our plan? Or are we just following someone else's plan?"

"Why does that matter to you?" Batu said. He put his hands on his head and tugged at his hair until it stood straight up.

"I thought we were on a mission," Eric said, "to help mankind. Womankind, too. Like the *Starship Enterprise*. But how are we helping anybody? What's new-style retail about this?"

"*Hello*," Batu said. "Did you see those pajamas? Look. On second thought, forget about the pajamas. You never saw them. Like I said, this is bigger than the All-Night. There are bigger fish that are fishing, if you know what I mean."

"No," Eric said. "I don't."

"Excellent," Batu said. His experimental CIA pajama top writhed and boiled. "Your job is to be helpful and polite. Be patient. Be *careful.* Wait for the zombies to make the next move. I send off some faxes. Meanwhile, we still need Charley. Charley is a natural-born saleswoman. She's been selling death for years. And she's got a real gift for languages—she'll be speaking zombie in no time. Think what kind of work she could do here! Go outside. When she drives by, you flag her down. Talk to her. Explain why she needs to come live here. But whatever you do, don't get in the car with her. That car is full of ghosts. The wrong kind of ghosts. The kind who are never going to understand the least little thing about meaningful transactions."

"I know," Eric said. "I could smell them."

"So are we clear on all this?" Batu said. "Or maybe you think I'm still lying to you. Or maybe you think I'm nuts?"

"I don't think you'd lie to me, exactly," Eric said. He put on his jacket.

"You better put on a hat, too," Batu said. "It's cold out there. You know, you're like a son to me, which is why I tell you to put on your hat. And if I lied to you, it would be for your own good, because I love you like a son. One day, Eric, all of this will be yours. Just trust me and do what I tell you. Trust the plan."

Eric said nothing. Batu patted him on the shoulder, pulled an All-Night shirt over his pajama top, and grabbed a banana and a Snapple. He settled in behind the counter. His hair was still a mess, but at 4:00 A.M., who was going to complain? Not Eric, not the zombies. Eric put on his hat, gave a little wave to Batu, which was either *glad we cleared all* that *up at last*, or else *so long!*, he wasn't sure which, and walked out of the All-Night. This is the last time, he thought, I will ever walk through this door. He didn't know how he felt about that.

ERIC STOOD OUTSIDE in the parking lot for a long time. Out in the bushes, on the other side of the road, he could hear the zombies, hunting for the things that were valuable to other zombies.

Some woman, a real person, but not Charley, drove into the parking lot. She went inside, and Eric thought he knew what Batu would say to her when she went to the counter. Batu would explain, when she tried to make her purchase, that he didn't want money. That wasn't what retail was really about. What Batu would want to know was what this woman really wanted. It was that simple, that complicated. Batu might try to recruit this woman, if she didn't seem litigious, and maybe that was a good thing. Maybe the All-Night really did need women.

Eric walked backward, away and then even farther away from the All-Night. The farther he got, the more beautiful he saw it was—it was all lit up like the moon. Was this what the zombies saw? What Charley saw when she drove by? He couldn't imagine how anyone could leave it behind and never come back.

He wondered if Batu had a pair of pajamas in his collection with All-Night Convenience Stores, light spilling out; the Ausible Chasm; a road, with zombies, and Charleys in Chevys, a different dog hanging out of every passenger window, driving down that road. Down on one leg of those pajamas, down the road a long ways, there would be bears dressed up in ice; Canadians; CIA operatives and tabloid reporters and All-Night executives; Las Vegas showgirls; G-men and bee men in trenchcoats; his mother's car, always getting farther and farther away. He wondered if zombies wore zombie pajamas, or if they'd just invented them for Batu. He tried to picture Charley wearing silk pajamas and a flannel bathrobe, but she didn't look comfortable in them. She still looked miserable and angry and hopeless, much older than Eric had ever realized.

He jumped up and down in the parking lot, trying to keep warm. The woman, when she came out of the store, gave him a funny look. He couldn't see Batu behind the counter. Maybe he'd fallen asleep again, or maybe he was sending off more faxes. But Eric didn't go back inside of the store. He was afraid of Batu's pajamas.

He was afraid of Batu.

He stayed outside, waiting for Charley.

But a few hours later, when Charley drove by—he was standing on the curb, keeping an eye out for her, she wasn't going to just slip away, he was determined to see her, to make sure that she saw him, to make her take him with her, wherever she was going—there was a Labrador in the passenger seat. The back seat of her car was full of dogs, real dogs and ghost dogs, and all of the dogs poking their doggy noses out of the windows at him. There wouldn't have been room for him, even if he'd been able to make her stop. But he ran out in the road anyway, like a damn dog, chasing after her car for as long as he could.

AFTERWORD

"Hortlak" means "ghost" in Turkish. There are several different kinds of ghosts in this story, but, more important, there are several different kinds of pajamas. As for Ausible Chasm, I've driven past the exit sign, but I've never stopped.

Two of my favorite ghost stories, "Lodgers" and "The Cold Flame," are by Joan Aiken. The third is H. R. Wakefield's "The Red Lodge." In both of the Joan Aiken stories, it's not the ghosts who are terrifying, it's the living people. "The Red Lodge," on the other hand, is crawling with ghosts and all of them are malignant. When I was a kid, I would lie in bed at night and read Helen Hoke's anthologies—it was in these anthologies that I (covers pulled up to my neck, not daring to sleep) first encountered these stories.

✠

GLEN HIRSHBERG grew up in Detroit and San Diego. He received his B.A. from Columbia University, and spent a sizable chunk of his college years watching Val Lewton movies at the Theatre 80 on St. Marks and bowling in the haunted alley under Barnard College. From there, it was off to Montana, where he received his M.F.A. and M.A., wrote incessantly, found his wife, and hung out at Freddy's Feed & Read (R.I.P.). He also has lived in Galway, Seattle, Charlotte, and now Los Angeles, writing and teaching all the while. His first novel, *The Snowman's Children*, was published in 2002. His ghost stories, most of which were created originally to tell his students on Halloween, have appeared in a number of anthologies, including *The Year's Best Fantasy and Horror, Best New Horror*, and *Dark Terrors 6. The Two Sams*, a collection of his supernatural fiction, has just been published.

DANCING MEN

GLEN HIRSHBERG

These are the last days of our lives so we give a signal maybe there still will be relatives or acquaintances of these persons. . . . They were tortured and burnt good-bye. . . .
—TESTIMONIAL FOUND AT CHELMNO

I

WE'D BEEN ALL afternoon in the Old Jewish Cemetery, where the green light filters through the trees and lies atop the tumbled tombstones like algae. Mostly, I think, the kids were tired. The two-week Legacy of the Holocaust tour I had organized had taken us to Zeppelin Field in Nuremberg, where downed electrical wires slither through the brittle grass, and Bebelplatz in East Berlin, where ghost-shadows of burned books flutter in their chamber in the ground like white wings. We'd spent our nights not sleeping on sleeper trains east to Auschwitz and Birkenau and our days on public transport, traipsing through the fields of dead and the monuments to them, and all seven high-school juniors in my care had had enough.

From my spot on a bench alongside the roped-off stone path that meandered through the grounds and back out to the streets of Josefov, I watched six of my seven charges giggling and chattering around the final resting place of Rabbi Loew. I'd told them the story of the Rabbi, and the clay man he'd supposedly created and then animated, and now they were running their hands over his tombstone, tracing Hebrew letters they couldn't read, chanting "*Amet,*" the word I'd taught them, in low voices and laughing. As of yet, nothing had risen from the dirt. The Tribe, they'd taken to calling themselves, after I told them that the Wandering Jews didn't really work, historically, since the essential characteristic of the Wanderer himself was his solitude.

There are teachers, I suppose, who would have been considered members of the Tribe by the Tribe, particularly on a summer trip, far from home and school and television and familiar language. But I had never quite been that sort of teacher.

Nor was I the only excluded member of our traveling party. Lurking not far from me, I spotted Penny Berry, the quietest member of our group and the only goy, staring over the graves into the trees with her expressionless eyes half-closed and her lipstickless lips curled into the barest hint of a smile. Her auburn hair sat cocked on the back of her head in a tight, precise ponytail, like arrows in a quiver. When she saw me watching, she wandered over, and I swallowed a sigh. It wasn't that I didn't like Penny, exactly. But she asked uncomfortable questions, and she knew how to wait for answers, and she made me nervous for no reason I could explain.

"Hey, Mr. Gadeuszki," she said, her enunciation studied, perfect. She'd made me teach her how to say it right, grind the s and z and k together into that single, Slavic snarl of sound. "What's with the stones?"

She gestured at the tiny gray pebbles placed across the tops of several nearby tombstones. The ones on the slab nearest us glinted in the warm, green light like little eyes. "In memory," I said. I thought about sliding over on the bench to make room for her, then thought that would only make both of us even more awkward.

"Why not flowers?" Penny said.

I sat still, listening to the clamor of new-millennium Prague just beyond the stone wall that enclosed the cemetery. "Jews bring stones."

A few minutes later, when she realized I wasn't going to say anything else, Penny moved off in the general direction of the Tribe. I watched her go, allowed myself a few more peaceful seconds. Probably, I thought, it was time to move us along. We had the Astronomical Clock left to see today, puppet theatre tickets for tonight, the plane home to Cleveland in the morning. And just because the kids were tired didn't mean they would tolerate loitering here much longer. For seven summers in a row, I had taken kids on some sort of exploring trip. "Because you've got nothing better to do," one member of the Tribe cheerfully informed me one night the preceding week. Then he'd said, "Oh my God, I was just kidding, Mr. G."

And I'd had to reassure him that I knew he was, I just always looked like that.

"That's true, you do," he'd said, and returned to his tripmates.

Now, I rubbed my hand over the stubble on my shaven scalp, stood, and blinked as my family name—in its original Polish spelling—flashed behind my eyelids again, looking just the way it had this morning amongst all the other names etched into the Pinkas Synagogue wall. The ground went slippery underneath me, the tombstones slid sideways in the grass, and I teetered and sat down hard.

When I lifted my head and opened my eyes, the Tribe had swarmed around me, a whirl of backwards baseball caps and tanned legs and Nike symbols. "I'm fine," I said quickly, stood up, and to my relief, I found I did feel fine, couldn't really imagine what had just happened. "Slipped."

"Kind of," said Penny Berry from the edge of the group, and I avoided looking her way.

"Time to go, kids. Lots more to see."

It has always surprised me when they do what I say, because mostly, they do. It's not me, really. The social contract between teachers and students may be the oldest mutually accepted enacted ritual on this earth, and its power is stronger than most people imagine.

We passed between the last of the graves, through a low stone opening. The dizziness, or whatever it had been, was gone, and I felt only a faint tingling in my fingertips as I drew my last breath of that too-heavy air, thick with loam and grass springing from bodies stacked a dozen deep in the ground.

The side street beside the Old-New Synagogue was crammed with tourists, their purses and backpacks open like the mouths of grotesquely overgrown chicks. Into those open mouths went wooden puppets and embroidered kepot and Chamsa hands from the rows of stalls that lined the sidewalk; the walls, I thought, of an all-new, much more ingenious sort of ghetto. In a way, this place had become exactly what Hitler had meant for it to be: a Museum of a Dead Race, only the paying customers were descendants of the Race, and they spent money in amounts he could never have dreamed. The ground had begun to roll under me again, and I closed my eyes. When I opened them, the tourists had cleared in front of me, and I saw the stall, a lopsided wooden hulk on bulky brass wheels. It tilted toward me, the puppets nailed to its side, leering and chattering while the Gypsy leaned out from between them, nose studded with a silver star, grinning.

He touched the toy nearest him, set it rocking on its terrible, thin wire. "*Loh-ootkawve divahd-law,*" he said, and then I was down, flat on my face in the street.

I don't know how I wound up on my back. Somehow, somebody had rolled me over. I couldn't breathe. My stomach felt squashed, as though there was something squatting on it, wooden and heavy, and I jerked, gagged, opened my eyes, and the light blinded me.

"I didn't," I said, blinking, brain flailing. I wasn't even sure I'd been all the way unconscious, couldn't have been out more than a few seconds. But the way the light affected my eyes, it was as though I'd been buried for a month.

"Dobry den, dobry den," said a voice over me, and I squinted, teared up, blinked into the Gypsy's face, the one from the stall, and almost screamed. Then he touched my forehead, and he was just a man, red Manchester United cap on his head, black eyes kind as they hovered around mine. The cool hand he laid against my brow had a wedding ring on it, and the silver star in his nose caught the afternoon light.

I meant to say I was okay, but what came out was "I didn't" again.

The Gypsy said something else to me. The language could have been Czech or Slovakian or neither. I didn't know enough to tell the difference, and my ears weren't working right. In them I could feel a painful, persistent pressure.

The Gypsy stood, and I saw my students clustered behind him like a knot I'd drawn taut. When they saw me looking, they burst out babbling, and I shook my head, tried to calm them, and then I felt their hands on mine, pulling me to a sitting position. The world didn't spin. The ground stayed still. The puppet stall I would not look at kept its distance.

"Mr. G., are you all right?" one of them asked, her voice shrill, slipping toward panic.

Then Penny Berry knelt beside me and looked straight into me, and I could see her formidable brain churning behind those placid gray-green eyes, the color of Lake Erie when it's frozen.

"Didn't what?" she asked.

And I answered, because I had no choice. "Kill my grandfather."

II

THEY PROPPED ME at my desk in our *pension* not far from the Charles Bridge and brought me a glass of "nice water," which was one of our traveling jokes. It was what the too-thin waitress at Terezin—the "town presented to the Jews by the Nazis," as the old propaganda film we saw at the museum proclaimed—thought we were saying when we asked for ice.

For a while, the Tribe sat on my bed and talked quietly to each other and refilled my glass for me. But after thirty minutes or so, when I hadn't keeled over again and wasn't babbling and seemed my usual sullen, solid, bald self, they started shuffling around, playing with my curtains, ignoring me. One of them threw a pencil at another. For a short while, I almost forgot about the nausea churning in my stomach, the trembling in my wrists, the puppets bobbing on their wires in my head.

"Hey," I said. I had to say it twice more to get their attention. I usually do.

Finally, Penny noticed and said, "Mr. Gadeuszki's trying to say something," and they slowly quieted down.

I put my quivering hands on my lap under the desk and left them there. "Why don't you kids get back on the Metro and go see the Clock?"

The Tribe members looked at each other uncertainly. "Really," I told them. "I'm fine. When's the next time you're going to be in Prague?"

They were good kids, these kids, and they looked unsure for a few seconds longer. In the end, though, they started trickling toward the door, and I thought I'd gotten them out until Penny Berry stepped in front of me.

"You killed your grandfather," she said.

"Didn't," I snarled, and Penny blinked, and everyone whirled to stare at me. I took a breath, almost got control of my voice. "I said I didn't kill him."

"Oh," Penny said. She was on this trip not because of any familial or cultural heritage but because this was the most interesting experience she could find to devour this month. She was pressing me now because she suspected that I had something more startling to share than Prague did, for the moment. And she was always hungry.

Or maybe she was just lonely, confused about the kid she had never quite been and the world she didn't quite feel part of. Which would make her more than a little like me. Which might explain why she had always annoyed me as much as she did.

"It's stupid," I said. "It's nothing."

Penny didn't move. In my memory, the little wooden man on his wire quivered, twitched, began to rock side to side.

"I need to write it down," I said, trying to sound gentle. Then I lied. "Maybe I'll show you when I'm done."

Five minutes later, I was alone in my room with a fresh glass of nice water and a stack of unlined, blank white paper I had scavenged from the computer printer downstairs. I picked up my black pen, and in an instant, there was sand on my tongue and desert sun on my neck and that horrid, gasping breathing like snake-rattle in my ears, and for the first time in many, many years, I was home.

III

IN JUNE OF 1978, on the day after school let out, I was sitting in my bedroom in Albuquerque, New Mexico, thinking about absolutely nothing when my dad came in and sat down on my bed and said, "I want you to do something for me."

In my nine years of life, my father had almost never asked me to do anything for him. As far as I could tell, he had very few things that he wanted. He worked at an insurance firm and came home at exactly 5:30 every night and played an hour of catch with me before dinner or, sometimes, walked me to the ice-cream shop. After dinner, he sat on the black couch in the den reading paperback mystery novels until 9:30. The paperbacks were all old, with bright yellow or red covers featuring men in trenchcoats and women with black dresses sliding down the curves in their bodies like tar.

It made me nervous, sometimes, just watching my father's hands on the covers. I asked him once why he liked those kinds of books, and he just shook his head. "All those people," he said, sounding, as usual, like he was speaking to me through a tin can from a great distance. "Doing all those things." At exactly 9:30, every single night I can remember, my father clicked off the lamp next to the couch and touched me on the head if I was up and went to bed.

"What do you want me to do?" I asked that June morning, though I didn't much care. This was the first weekend of summer vacation, and I had months of free time in front of me, and I never knew quite what to do with it, anyway.

"What I tell you, okay?" my father said.

Without even thinking, I said, "Sure."

And he said, "Good. I'll tell Grandpa you're coming." Then he left me gaping on the bed while he went into the kitchen to use the phone.

My grandfather lived seventeen miles from Albuquerque in a red adobe hut in the middle of the desert. The only sign of humanity anywhere around him was the ruins of a small pueblo maybe half a mile away. Even now, what I remember most about my grandfather's house is the desert rolling up to and through it in an endless, never-receding red tide. From the back steps, I could see the pueblo, honeycombed with caves like a giant beehive tipped on its side, empty of bees but buzzing as the wind whipped through it.

Four years before, my grandfather had told my parents to knock off the token visits. Then he'd had his phone shut off. As far as I knew, none of us had seen him since.

All my life, he'd been dying. He had emphysema and some kind of weird allergic condition that turned swatches of his skin pink. The last time I'd been with him, he'd just sat in a chair in a tank top, breathing through a tube. He'd looked like a piece of petrified wood.

The next morning, a Sunday, my father packed my green camp duffel bag with a box of new, unopened baseball cards and the transistor radio my mother had given me for my birthday the year before, then loaded it and me into the grimy green Datsun he always meant to wash and didn't. "Time to go," he told me in his mechanical voice, and I was still too startled by what was happening to protest as he led me outside. Moments before, a morning thunderstorm had rocked the whole house, but now the sun was up, searing the whole sky orange. Our street smelled like creosote and green chili and adobe mud and salamander skin.

"I don't want to go," I said to my father.

"I wouldn't either, if I were you," he told me, and started the car.

"You don't even like him," I said.

My father just looked at me, and for an astonishing second, I thought he was going to snatch out his arms and hug me. But he looked away instead, dropped the car into gear, and drove us out of town.

All the way to my grandfather's house, we followed the thunderstorm. It must have been traveling at exactly our speed, because we never got any closer, and it never got further away. It just retreated before us, a big black wall of nothing, like a shadow the whole world cast, and every now and then streaks of lightning flew up the clouds like signal flares, but illuminated only the sand and mountains and rain.

"Why are we doing this?" I asked when my dad started slowing, studying the sand on his side of the car for the dirt track that led to my grandfather's.

"Want to drive?" he answered, gesturing to me to slide across the seat into his lap.

Again, I was startled. My dad always seemed willing enough to play catch with me. But he rarely generated ideas for things we could do together on his own. And the thought of sitting in his lap with his arms around me was too alien to fathom. I waited too long, and the moment passed. My father didn't ask again. Through the windshield, I watched the thunderstorm retreating, the wet road already drying in patches in the sun. The whole day felt distant, like someone else's dream.

"You know he was in the war, right?" my father said, and despite our crawling speed, he had to jam on the brakes to avoid passing the turnoff. No one, it seemed to me, could possibly have intended this to be a road. It wasn't dug or flattened or marked. Just a rumple in the earth.

"Yeah," I said.

That he'd been in the war was pretty much the only thing I knew about my grandfather. Actually, he'd been in the camps. After the war, he'd been in other camps in Israel for almost five years while Red Cross workers searched for living relatives and found none and finally turned him loose to make his way as best he could.

As soon as we were off the highway, sand-ghosts rose around the car, ticking against the trunk and the hood as we passed. Thanks to the thunderstorm, they left a wet, red residue like bug-smear on the hood and windshield.

"You know, now that I think about it," my father said, his voice flat as ever but the words clearer, somehow, and I found myself leaning closer to him to make sure I heard him over the churning wheels, ". . . he was even less of a grandfather to you than a dad to me." He rubbed a hand over the bald spot just beginning to spread over the top of his head like an egg yolk being squashed. I'd never seen him do that before. It made him look old.

My grandfather's house appeared before us like a druid mound. There was no shape to it. It had exactly one window, and that couldn't be seen from the street. No mailbox. Never in my life, I realized abruptly, had I had to sleep in there.

"Dad, please don't make me stay," I said as he stopped the car fifteen feet or so from the front door.

He looked at me, and his mouth turned down a little, and his shoulders tensed. Then he sighed. "Three days," he said, and got out.

When I was standing beside him, looking past the house at the distant pueblo, he said, "Your grandfather didn't ask for me, he asked for you. He won't hurt you. And he doesn't ask for much from us, or from anyone."

"Neither do you," I said.

After a while, and very slowly, as though remembering how, my father smiled. "And neither do you, Seth."

Neither the smile nor the statement reassured me.

"Just remember this, son. Your grandfather has had a very hard life, and not just because of the camps. He worked two jobs for twenty-five years to provide for my mother and me. He never called in sick. He never took vacations. And he was ecstatic when you were born."

That surprised me. "Really? How do you know?"

For the first time I could remember, my father blushed, and I thought maybe I'd caught him lying, and then I wasn't sure. He kept looking at me. "Well, he came to town, for one thing. Twice."

For a little longer, we stood together while the wind rolled over the rocks and sand. I couldn't smell the rain anymore, but I thought I could taste it, a little. Tall, leaning cacti prowled the waste around us like stick figures who'd escaped from one of my doodles. I was always doodling, then. Trying to get the shapes of things.

Finally, the thin, wooden door to the adobe clicked open, and out stepped Lucy, and my father straightened and put his hand on his bald spot again and put it back down.

She didn't live there, as far as I knew. But I'd never been to my grandfather's house when she wasn't in it. I knew she worked for some foundation that provided care to Holocaust victims, though she was Navajo, not Jewish, and that she'd been coming out here all my life to make my grandfather's meals, bathe him, keep him company. I rarely saw them speak to each other. When I was little and my grandmother was still alive and we were still welcome, Lucy used to take me to the pueblo after she'd finished with my grandfather and watch me climb around on the stones and peer into the empty caves and listen to the wind chase thousand-year-old echoes out of the walls.

There were gray streaks now in the black hair that poured down Lucy's shoulders, and I could see semicircular lines like tree rings in her dark, weathered cheeks. But I was uncomfortably aware, this time, of the way her breasts pushed her plain, white-denim shirt out of the top of her jeans while her eyes settled on mine, black and still.

"Thank you for coming," she said, as if I'd had a choice. When I didn't answer, she looked at my father. "Thank you for bringing him. We're set up out back."

I threw one last questioning glance at my father as Lucy started away, but he just looked bewildered or bored or whatever he generally was. And that made me angry. " 'Bye," I told him, and moved toward the house.

"Good-bye," I heard him say, and something in his tone unsettled me; it was too sad. I shivered, turned around, and my father said, "He want to see me?"

He looked thin, I thought, just another spindly cactus, holding my duffel bag out from his side. If he'd been speaking to me, I might have run to him. I wanted to. But he was watching Lucy, who had stopped at the edge of the square of patio cement outside the front door.

"I don't think so," she said, and came over to me and took my hand.

Without another word, my father tossed my duffel bag onto the miniature patio and climbed back in his car. For a moment, his eyes caught mine through the windshield, and I said, "Wait," but my father didn't hear me. I said it louder, and Lucy put her hand on my shoulder.

"This has to be done, Seth," she said.

"What does?"

"This way." She gestured toward the other side of the house, and I followed her there and stopped when I saw the hogan.

It sat next to the squat gray cactus I'd always considered the edge of my grandfather's yard. It looked surprisingly solid, its mud walls dry and gray and hard, its pocked, stumpy wooden pillars firm in the ground, almost as if they were real trees that had somehow taken root there.

"You live here now?" I blurted, and Lucy stared at me.

"Oh, yes, Seth. Me sleep-um ground. How." She pulled aside the hide curtain at the front of the hogan and ducked inside, and I followed.

I thought it would be cooler in there, but it wasn't. The wood and mud trapped the heat but blocked the light. I didn't like it. It reminded me of an oven, of Hansel and Gretel. And it reeked of the desert: burnt sand, hot wind, nothingness.

"This is where you'll sleep," Lucy said. "It's also where we'll work." She knelt and lit a beeswax candle and placed it in the center of the dirt floor in a scratched glass drugstore candlestick. "We need to begin right now."

"Begin what?" I asked, fighting down another shudder as the candlelight played over the room. Against the far wall, tucked under a miniature canopy constructed of metal poles and a tarpaulin, were a sleeping bag and a pillow. My bed, I assumed. Beside it sat a low, rolling table, and on the table were another candlestick, a cracked ceramic bowl, some matches, and the Dancing Man.

In my room in this *pension* in the Czech Republic, five thousand miles and twenty years removed from that place, I put my pen down and swallowed the entire glass of lukewarm water my students had left me. Then I got up and went to the window, staring out at the trees and the street. I was hoping to see my kids returning like ducks to a familiar pond, flapping their arms and jostling each other and squawking and laughing. Instead, I saw my own face, faint and featureless, too white in the window glass. I went back to the desk and picked up the pen.

The Dancing Man's eyes were all pupil, carved in two perfect ovals in the knottiest wood I had ever seen. The nose was just a notch, but the mouth was enormous, a giant O, like the opening of a cave. I was terrified of the thing even before I noticed that it was moving.

Moving, I suppose, is too grand a description. It . . . leaned. First one way, then the other, on a wire that ran straight through its belly. In a fit of panic, after a nightmare, I described it to my college roommate, a physics major, and he shrugged and said something about perfect balance and pendulums and gravity and the rotation of the earth. Except that the Dancing Man didn't just move side to side. It also wiggled down its wire, very slowly, until it reached the end. And then the wire tilted up, and it began to wiggle back. Slowly. Until it reached the other end. Back and forth. Side to side. Forever.

"Take the drum," Lucy said behind me, and I ripped my eyes away from the Dancing Man.

"What?" I said.

She gestured at the table, and I realized she meant the ceramic bowl. I didn't understand, and I didn't want to go over there. But I didn't know what else to do, and I felt ridiculous under Lucy's stare.

The Dancing Man was at the far end of its wire, leaning, mouth open. Trying to be casual, I snatched the bowl from underneath it and retreated to where Lucy knelt. The water inside the bowl made a sloshing sound but didn't splash out, and I held it away from my chest in surprise and noticed the covering stitched over the top. It was hide of some kind, moist when I touched it.

"Like this," said Lucy, and she leaned close and tapped on the skin of the drum. The sound was deep and tuneful, like a voice. I sat down next to Lucy. She tapped again, in a slow, repeating pattern. I put my hands where hers had been, and when she nodded at me, I began to play.

"Okay?" I said.

"Harder," Lucy said, and she reached into her pocket and pulled out a long, wooden stick. The candlelight flickered across the stick, and I saw the carving. A pine tree, and underneath it, roots that bulged along the base of the stick like long, black veins.

"What is that?" I asked.

"A rattle stick. My grandmother made it. I'm going to rattle it while you play. So if you would. Like I showed you."

I beat on the drum, and the sound came out dead in that airless space.

"For God's sake," Lucy snapped. "Harder." She had never been exceptionally friendly to me. But she'd been friendlier than this.

I slammed my hands down harder, and after a few beats, Lucy leaned back and nodded and watched. Not long after, she lifted her hand, stared at me as though daring me to stop her, and shook the stick. The sound it made was less rattle than buzz, as though it had wasps inside it. Lucy shook it a few more times, always at the same half-pause in my rhythm. Then her eyes rolled back in her head, and her spine arched, and my hand froze over the drum and Lucy snarled, "Don't stop."

After that, she began to chant. There was no tune to it, but a pattern, the pitch sliding up a little, down some, up a little more. When Lucy reached the top note, the ground under my crossed legs seemed to tingle, as though there were scorpions sliding out of the sand, but I didn't look down. I thought of the wooden figure on its wire behind me, but I didn't turn around. I played the drum, and I watched Lucy, and I kept my mouth shut.

We went on for a long, long time. After that first flush of fear, I was too mesmerized to think. My bones were tingling, too, and the air in the hogan was heavy. I couldn't get enough of it in my lungs. Tiny tidepools of sweat had formed in the hollow of Lucy's neck and under her ears and at the throat of her shirt. Under my palms, the drum was sweating, too, and the skin got slippery and warm. Not until Lucy stopped singing did I realize that I was rocking side to side. Leaning.

"Want lunch?" Lucy said, standing and brushing the earth off her jeans.

I put my hands out perpendicular, felt the skin prickle and realized my wrists had gone to sleep even as they pounded out the rhythm Lucy had taught me. When I stood, the floor of the hogan seemed unstable, like the bottom of one of those balloon tents my classmates sometimes had at birthday parties. I didn't want to look behind me, and then I did. The Dancing Man rocked slowly in no wind.

I turned around again, but Lucy had left the hogan. I didn't want to be alone in there, so I leapt through the hide curtain and winced against the sudden blast of sunlight and saw my grandfather.

He was propped on his wheelchair, positioned dead center between the hogan and the back of his house. He must have been there the whole time, I thought, and somehow I'd managed not to notice him when I came in, because unless he'd gotten a whole lot better in the years since I'd seen him last, he couldn't have wheeled himself out. And he looked worse.

For one thing, his skin was falling off. At every exposed place on him, I saw flappy folds of yellow-pink. What was underneath was uglier still, not red or bleeding, just not skin. Too dry. Too colorless. He looked like a corn husk. An empty one.

Next to him, propped on a rusty blue dolly, was a cylindrical silver oxygen tank. A clear tube ran from the nozzle at the top of the tank to the blue mask over my grandfather's nose and mouth. Above the mask, my grandfather's heavy-lidded eyes watched me, though they didn't seem capable of movement either. Leave him out here, I thought, and those eyes would simply fill up with sand.

"Come in, Seth," Lucy told me, without any word to my grandfather or acknowledgment that he was there.

I had my hand on the screen door, was halfway into the house, when I realized I'd heard him speak. I stopped. It had to have been him, I thought, and couldn't have been. I turned around and saw the back of his head tilting toward the top of the chair. Retracing my steps—I'd given him a wide berth—I returned to face him. The eyes stayed still, and the oxygen tank was silent. But the mask fogged, and I heard the whisper again.

"*Ruach*," he said. It was what he always called me, when he called me anything.

In spite of the heat, I felt goose bumps spring from my skin, all along my legs and arms. I couldn't move. I couldn't answer. I should say hello, I thought. Say something.

I waited instead. A few seconds later, the oxygen mask fogged again. "*Trees*," said the whisper voice. "*Screaming. In the trees.*" One of my grandfather's hands raised an inch or so off the arm of the chair and fell back into place.

"Patience," Lucy said from the doorway. "Come on, Seth." This time, my grandfather said nothing as I slipped past him into the house.

Lucy slid a bologna sandwich and a bag of Fritos and a plastic glass of apple juice in front of me. I lifted the sandwich, found that I couldn't imagine putting it in my mouth, and dropped it on the plate.

"Better eat," Lucy said. "We have a long day yet."

I ate, a little. Eventually, Lucy sat down across from me, but she didn't say anything else. She just gnawed a celery stick and watched the sand outside change color as the sun crawled west. The house was silent, the countertops and walls bare.

"Can I ask you something?" I finally asked.

Lucy was washing my plate in the sink. She didn't turn around, but she didn't say no.

"What are we doing? Out there, I mean."

No answer. Through the kitchen doorway, I could see my grandfather's living room, the stained wood floor, and the single brown armchair lodged against a wall, across from the TV. My grandfather had spent every waking minute of his life in this place for fifteen years or more, and there was no trace of him in it.

"It's a Way, isn't it?" I said, and Lucy shut the water off.

When she turned, her expression was the same as it had been all day, a little mocking, a little angry. She took a step toward the table.

"We learned about them at school," I said.

"Did you," she said.

"We're studying lots of Indian things."

The smile that spread over Lucy's face was ugly, cruel. Or maybe just tired. "Good for you," she said. "Come on. We don't have much time."

"Is this to make my grandfather better?"

"Nothing's going to make your grandfather better." Without waiting for me, she pushed through the screen door into the heat.

This time, I made myself stop beside my grandfather's chair. I could just hear the hiss of the oxygen tank, like steam escaping from the boiling ground. When no fog appeared in the blue mask and no words emerged from the hiss, I followed Lucy into the hogan and let the hide curtain fall shut.

All afternoon and into the evening, I played the water-drum while Lucy sang. By the time the air began to cool outside, the whole hogan was vibrating, and the ground, too. Whatever we were doing, I could feel the power in it. I was the beating heart of a living thing, and Lucy was its voice. Once, I found myself wondering just what we were setting loose or summoning here, and I stopped, for a single beat. But the silence was worse. The silence was like being dead. And I thought I could hear the thing behind me, the Dancing Man. If I inclined my head, stopped playing for too long, I almost believed I'd hear him whispering.

When Lucy finally rocked to her feet and walked out without speaking to me, it was evening, and the desert was alive. I sat shaking as the rhythm spilled out of me and the sand soaked it up. Then I stood, and that unsteady feeling came over me again, stronger this time, as if the air was wobbling, too, threatening to slide right off the surface of the earth. When I emerged from the hogan, I saw black spiders on the wall of my grandfather's house, and I heard wind and rabbits, and the first coyotes yipping somewhere to the west. My grandfather sat slumped in the same position he had been in hours and hours ago, which meant he had been baking out here all afternoon. Lucy was on the patio, watching the sun melt into the horizon's open mouth. Her skin was slick, and her hair was wet where it touched her ear and neck.

"Your grandfather's going to tell you a story," she said, sounding exhausted. "And you're going to listen."

My grandfather's head rolled upright, and I wished we were back in the hogan, doing whatever it was we'd been doing. At least there, I was moving, pounding hard enough to drown sound out. Maybe. The screen door slapped shut, and my grandfather looked at me. His eyes were deep, deep brown, almost black, and horribly familiar. Did my eyes look like that?

"*Ruach,*" he whispered, and I wasn't sure, but his whisper seemed stronger than it had before. The oxygen mask fogged and stayed fogged. The whisper kept coming, as though Lucy had spun a spigot and left it open. "*You will know . . . Now . . . Then the world . . . won't be yours . . . anymore.*" My grandfather shifted like some sort of giant, bloated sand-spider in the center of its web, and I heard his ruined skin rustle. Overhead, the whole sky went red.

"*At war's end . . .*" my grandfather hissed. "*Do you . . . understand?*" I nodded, transfixed. I could hear his breathing now, the ribs rising, parting, collapsing. The tank machinery had gone strangely silent. Was he breathing on his own, I wondered? Could he, still?

"*A few days. Do you understand? Before the Red Army came . . .*" He coughed. Even his cough sounded stronger. "*The Nazis took . . . me. And the Gypsies. From . . . our camp. To Chelmno.*"

I'd never heard the word before. I've almost never heard it since. But as my grandfather said it, another cough roared out of his throat, and when it was gone, the tank was hissing again. Still, my grandfather continued to whisper.

"*To die. Do you understand?*" Gasp. Hiss. Silence. "*To die. But not yet. Not . . . right away.*" Gasp. "*We came . . . by train, but open train. Not cattle car. Wasteland. Farmland. Nothing. And then trees.*" Under the mask, the lips twitched, and above it, the eyes closed completely. "*That first time. Ruach. All those . . . giant . . . green . . . trees. Unimaginable. To think anything . . . on the earth we knew . . . could live that long.*"

His voice continued to fade, faster than the daylight. A few minutes more, I thought, and he'd be silent again, just machine and breath, and I could sit out here in the yard and let the evening wind roll over me.

"*When they took . . . us off the train,*" my grandfather said, "*for one moment . . . I swear I smelled . . . leaves. Fat, green leaves . . . the new green . . . in them. Then the old smell . . . the only smell. Blood in dirt. The stink . . . of us. Piss. Shit. Open . . . sores. Skin on fire. Hnnn.*"

His voice trailed away, hardly-there air over barely moving mouth, and still he kept talking. "*Prayed for . . . some people . . . to die. They smelled . . . better. Dead. That was one prayer . . . always answered.*

"*They took us . . . into the woods. Not to barracks. So few of them. Ten. Maybe twenty. Faces like . . . possums. Stupid. Blank. No thoughts. We came to . . . ditches. Deep. Like wells. Half-full, already. They told us, 'Stand still . . . 'Breathe in.'* "

At first, I thought the ensuing silence was for effect. He was letting me smell it. And I did smell it, the earth and the dead people, and there were German soliders all around us, floating up out of the sand with black uniforms and white, blank faces. Then my grandfather crumpled forward, and I screamed for Lucy.

She came fast but not running and put a hand on my grandfather's back and another on his neck. After a few seconds, she straightened. "He's asleep," she told me. "Stay here." She wheeled my grandfather into the house, and she was gone a long time.

Sliding to a sitting position, I closed my eyes and tried not to hear my grandfather's voice. After a while, I thought I could hear bugs and snakes and something larger padding out beyond the cacti. I could feel the moonlight, too, white and cool on my skin. The screen door banged, and I opened my eyes to find Lucy moving toward me, past me, carrying a picnic basket into the hogan.

"I want to eat out here," I said quickly, and Lucy turned with the hide curtain in her hand.

"Why don't we go in?" she said, and the note of coaxing in her voice made me nervous. So did the way she glanced over her shoulder into the hogan, as though something in there had spoken.

I stayed where I was, and eventually, Lucy shrugged and let the curtain fall and dropped the basket at my feet. From the way she was acting, I thought she might leave me alone out there, but she sat down instead and looked at the sand and the cacti and the stars.

Inside the basket I found warmed canned chili in a plastic Tupperware container and fry bread with cinnamon-sugar and two cellophane-wrapped broccoli stalks that reminded me of uprooted miniature trees. In my ears, my grandfather's voice murmured, and to drown out the sound, I began to eat.

As soon as I was finished, Lucy began to stack the containers inside the basket, but she stopped when I spoke. "Please. Just talk to me a little."

She looked at me. The same look. As though we'd never even met. "Get some sleep. Tomorrow . . . well, let's just say tomorrow's a big day."

"For who?"

Lucy pursed her lips, and all at once, inexplicably, she seemed on the verge of tears. "Go to sleep."

"I'm not sleeping in the hogan," I told her.

"Suit yourself."

She was standing, and her back was to me now. I said, "Just tell me what kind of Way we're doing."

"An Enemy Way."

"What does it do?"

"It's nothing, Seth. Jesus Christ. It's silly. Your grandfather thinks it will help him talk. He thinks it will sustain him while he tells you what he needs to tell you. Don't worry about the goddamn Way. Worry about your grandfather, for once."

My mouth flew open, and my skin stung as though she'd slapped me. I started to protest, then found I couldn't, and didn't want to. All my life, I'd built my grandfather into a figure of fear, a gasping, grotesque monster in a wheelchair. And my father had let me. I started to cry.

"I'm sorry," I said.

"Don't apologize to me." Lucy walked to the screen door.

"Isn't it a little late?" I called after her, furious at myself, at my father, at Lucy. Sad for my grandfather. Scared and sad.

One more time, Lucy turned around, and the moonlight poured down the white streaks in her hair like wax through a mold. Soon, I thought, she'd be made of it.

"I mean, for my grandfather's enemies," I said. "The Way can't really do anything to them. Right?"

"His enemies are inside him," Lucy said, and left me.

For hours, it seemed, I sat in the sand, watching constellations explode out of the blackness, one after another, like firecrackers. In the ground, I heard night-things stirring. I thought about the tube in my grandfather's mouth, and the unspeakable hurt in his eyes—because that's what it was, I thought now, not boredom, not hatred—and the enemies inside him. And then, slowly, exhaustion overtook me. The taste of fry bread lingered in my mouth, and the starlight got brighter still. I leaned back on my elbows. And finally, at God knows what hour, I crawled into the hogan, under the tarpaulin canopy Lucy had made me, and fell asleep.

When I awoke, the Dancing Man was sliding down its wire toward me, and I knew, all at once, where I'd seen eyes like my grandfather's, and the old fear exploded through me all over again. How had he done it, I wondered? The carving on the wooden man's face was basic, the features crude. But the eyes were his. They had the same singular, almost oval shape, with identical little notches right near the tear ducts. The same too-heavy lids. Same expression, or lack of any.

I was transfixed, and I stopped breathing. All I could see were those eyes dancing toward me. Halfway down the wire, they seemed to stop momentarily, as though studying me, and I remembered something my dad had told me about wolves. "They're not trial-and-error animals," he'd said. "They wait and watch, wait and watch, until they're sure they know how the thing is done. And then they do it."

The Dancing Man began to weave again. First to one side, then the other, then back. If it reached the bottom of the wire, I thought—I *knew*—I would die. Or I would change. That was why Lucy was ignoring me. She had lied to me about what we were doing here. That was the reason they hadn't let my father stay. Leaping to my feet, I grabbed the Dancing Man around its clunky wooden base, and it came off the table with the faintest little suck, as though I'd yanked a weed out of the ground. I wanted to throw it, but I didn't dare. Instead, bent double, not looking at my clenched fist, I crab-walked to the entrance of the hogan, brushed back the hide curtain, slammed the Dancing Man down in the sand outside, and flung the curtain closed again. Then I squatted in the shadows, panting. Listening.

I crouched there a long time, watching the bottom of the curtain, expecting to see the Dancing Man slithering beneath it. But the hide stayed motionless, the hogan shadowy but still. I let myself sit back, and eventually, I slid into my sleeping bag again. I didn't expect to sleep anymore, but I did.

The smell of fresh fry bread woke me, and when I opened my eyes, Lucy was laying a tray of breads and sausage and juice on a red, woven blanket on the floor of the hogan. My lips tasted sandy, and I could feel grit in my clothes and between my teeth and under my eyelids, as though I'd been buried overnight and dug up again.

"Hurry," Lucy told me, in the same chilly voice as yesterday.

I threw back the sleeping bag and started to sit up and saw the Dancing Man gliding back along its wire, watching me. My whole body clenched, and I glared at Lucy and shouted, "How did that get back here?" Even as I said it, I realized that wasn't what I wanted to ask. More than how, I needed to know *when*. Exactly how long had it been hovering there without my knowing?

Without raising an eyebrow or even looking at me, Lucy shrugged and sat back. "Your grandfather wants you to have it," she said.

"I don't want it."

"Grow up."

Edging as far from the nightstand as possible, I shed the sleeping bag and sat down on the blanket and ate. Everything tasted sweet and sandy. My skin prickled with the intensifying heat. I still had a piece of fry bread and half a sausage left when I put my plastic fork down and looked at Lucy, who was arranging a new candle, settling the water-drum near me, tying her hair back with a red rubber band.

"Where did it come from?" I asked.

For the first time that day, Lucy looked at me, and this time, there really were tears in her eyes. "I don't understand your family," she said.

I shook my head. "Neither do I."

"Your grandfather's been saving that for you, Seth."

"Since when?"

"Since before you were born. Before your father was born. Before he ever imagined there could be a you."

This time, when the guilt came for me, it mixed with my fear rather than chasing it away, and I broke out sweating, and I thought I might be sick.

"You have to eat. Damn you," said Lucy.

I picked up my fork and squashed a piece of sausage into the fry bread and put it in my mouth. My stomach convulsed, but it accepted what I gave it.

I managed a few more bites. As soon as I pushed the plate back, Lucy shoved the drum onto my lap. I played while she chanted, and the sides of the hogan seemed to breathe in and out, very slowly. I felt drugged. Then I wondered if I had been. Had they sprinkled something over the bread? Was that the next step? And toward what? Erasing me, I thought, almost chanted. Erasing me, and my hands flew off the drum and Lucy stopped.

"All right," she said. "That's probably enough." Then, to my surprise, she actually reached out and tucked some of my hair behind my ear, then touched my face for a second as she took the drum from me. "It's time for your journey," she said.

I stared at her. The walls, I noticed, had stilled. I didn't feel any less strange, but a little more awake, at least. "Journey where?"

"You'll need water. And I've packed you a lunch." She slipped through the hide curtain, and I followed, dazed, and almost walked into my grandfather, parked right outside the hogan with a black towel on his head, so that his eyes and splitting skin were in shadow. On his peeling hands, he wore black-leather gloves. His hands, I thought, must be on fire.

Right at the moment I noticed that Lucy was no longer with us, the hiss from the oxygen tank sharpened, and my grandfather's lips moved beneath the mask. "*Ruach.*" This morning, the nickname sounded almost affectionate.

I waited, unable to look away. But the oxygen hiss settled again, like leaves after a gust of wind, and my grandfather said nothing more. A few seconds later, Lucy came back carrying a red backpack, which she handed to me.

"Follow the signs," she said, and turned me around until I was facing straight out from the road into the empty desert.

Struggling to life, I shook her hand off my shoulder. "Signs of what? What am I supposed to be doing?"

"Finding. Bringing back."

"I won't go," I said.

"You'll go," said Lucy coldly. "The signs will be easily recognizable, and easy to locate. I have been assured of that. All you have to do is pay attention."

"Assured by who?"

"The first sign, I am told, will be left by the tall, flowering cactus."

She pointed, which was unnecessary. A hundred yards or so from my grandfather's house, a spiky green cactus poked out of the rock and sand, supported on either side by two miniature versions of itself. A little cactus family, staggering in out of the waste.

I glanced at my grandfather under his mock cowl, Lucy with her ferocious black eyes trained on me. Tomorrow, I thought, my father would come for me, and with any luck, I would never have to come out here again.

Then, suddenly, I felt ridiculous, and sad, and guilty once more. Without even realizing what I was doing, I stuck my hand out and touched my grandfather's arm. The skin under his thin, cotton shirt depressed beneath my fingers like the squishy center of a misshapen pillow. It wasn't hot. It didn't feel alive at all. I yanked my hand back, and Lucy glared at me. Tears sprang to my eyes.

"Get out of here," she said, and I stumbled away into the sand.

I don't really think the heat intensified as soon as I stepped away from my grandfather's house. But it seemed to. Along my bare arms and legs, I could feel the little hairs curling as though singed. The sun had scorched the sky white, and the only place to look that didn't hurt my eyes was down. Usually, when I walked in the desert, I was terrified of scorpions, but not that day. It was impossible to imagine anything scuttling or stinging or even breathing out there. Except me.

I don't know what I expected to find. Footprints maybe, or animal scat, or something dead. Instead, stuck to the stem by a cactus needle, I found a yellow stick-em note. It said, "Pueblo."

Gently, avoiding the rest of the spiny needles, I removed the note. The writing was black and blocky. I glanced toward my grandfather's house, but he and Lucy were gone. The ceremonial hogan looked silly from this distance, like a little kid's pup tent.

Unlike the pueblo, I thought. I didn't even want to look that way, let alone go there. Already I could hear it, calling for me in a whisper that sounded far too much like my grandfather's. I could head for the road, I thought. Start toward town instead of the pueblo, and wait for a passing truck to carry me home. There would have to be a truck, sooner or later.

I did go to the road. But when I got there, I turned in the direction of the pueblo. I don't know why. I didn't feel as if I had a choice.

The walk, if anything, was too short. No cars passed. No road signs sprang from the dirt to point the way back to the world I knew. I watched the asphalt rise out of itself and roll in the heat, and I thought of my grandfather in the woods of Chelmno, digging graves in long, green shadows. Lucy had put ice in the thermos she gave me, and the cubes clicked against my teeth when I drank.

I walked, and I watched the desert, trying to spot a bird or a lizard. Even a scorpion would have been welcome. What I saw was sand, distant, colorless mountains, white sky, a world as empty of life and its echoes as the surface of Mars, and just as red.

Even the lone road sign pointing to the pueblo was rusted through, crusted with sand, the letters so scratched away that the name of the place was no longer legible. I'd never seen a tourist trailer here, or another living soul. Even calling it a pueblo seemed grandiose.

It was two sets of caves dug into the side of a cliff face, the top one longer than the bottom, so that together they formed a sort of gigantic, cracked harmonica for the desert wind to play. The roof and walls of the top set of caves had fallen in. The whole structure seemed more monument than ruin, a marker of a people who no longer existed rather than a place they had lived.

The bottom stretch of caves was largely intact, and as I stumbled toward them along the cracking macadam, I could feel their pull in my ankles. They seemed to be sucking the desert inside them, bit by bit. I stopped in front and listened.

I couldn't hear anything. I looked at the cracked, nearly square window openings, the doorless entryways leading into what had once been living spaces, the low, shadowed caves of dirt and rock. The whole pueblo just squatted there, inhaling sand through its dozens of dead mouths in a mockery of breath. I waited a while longer, but the open air didn't feel any safer, just hotter. If my grandfather's enemies were inside him, I suddenly wondered, and if we were calling them out, then where were they going? Finally, I ducked through the nearest entryway and stood in the gloom.

After a few seconds, my eyes adjusted. But there was nothing to see. Along the window openings, blown sand lay in waves and mounds, like miniature relief maps of the desert outside. At my feet lay tiny stones, too small to hide scorpions, and a few animal bones, none of them larger than my pinky, distinguishable primarily by the curve of them, their stubborn whiteness.

Then, as though my entry had triggered some sort of mechanical magic show, sound coursed into my ears. In the walls, tiny feet and bellies slithered and scuttled. Nothing rattled a warning. Nothing hissed. And the footsteps, when they came, came so softly that at first I mistook them for sand shifting along the sills and the cool, clay floor.

I didn't scream, but I staggered backward, lost my footing, slipped down, and I had the thermos raised and ready to swing when my father stepped out of the shadows and sat down cross-legged across the room from me.

"What . . ." I said, tears flying down my face, heart thudding.

My father said nothing. From the pocket of his plain, yellow, button-up shirt, he pulled a packet of cigarette paper and a pouch of tobacco, then rolled a cigarette in a series of quick, expert motions.

"You don't smoke," I said, and my father lit the cigarette and dragged air down his lungs with a rasp.

"Far as you know," he answered. The red-orange light looked like an open sore on his lips. Around us, the pueblo lifted, settled.

"Why does Grandpa call me 'Ruach'?" I snapped. And still, my father only sat and smoked. The smell tickled unpleasantly in my nostrils. "God, Dad. What's going on? What are you doing here, and—"

"Do you know what 'ruach' means?" he said.

I shook my head.

"It's a Hebrew word. It means ghost."

Hearing that was like being slammed to the ground. I couldn't get my lungs to work.

My father went on. "Sometimes, that's what it means. It depends what you use it with, you see? Sometimes, it means spirit, as in the spirit of God. Spirit of life. What God gave to his creations." He stubbed his cigarette in the sand, and the orange light winked out like an eye blinking shut. "And sometimes, it just means wind."

By my sides, I could feel my hands clutch sand as breath returned to my body. The sand felt cool, soft. "You don't know Hebrew either," I said.

"I made a point of knowing that."

"Why?"

"Because that's what he called me, too," my father said, and rolled a second cigarette but didn't light it. For a while, we sat. Then my father said, "Lucy called me two weeks ago. She told me it was time, and she said she needed a partner for your . . . ceremony. Someone to hide this, then help you find it. She said it was essential to the ritual." Reaching behind him, he produced a brown-paper grocery bag with the top rolled down and tossed it to me. "I didn't kill it," he said.

I stared at him, and more tears stung my eyes. Sand licked along the skin of my legs and arms and crawled up my shorts and sleeves, as though seeking pores, points of entry. Nothing about my father's presence here was reassuring. Nothing about him had ever been reassuring, or anything else, I thought furiously, and the fury felt good. It helped me move. I yanked the bag to me.

The first thing I saw when I ripped it open was an eye. It was yellow-going-gray, almost dry. Not quite, though. Then I saw the folded, black, ridged wings. A furry, broken body, twisted into a J. Except for the smell and the eye, it could have been a Halloween decoration.

"Is that a bat?" I whispered. Then I shoved the bag away and gagged.

My father glanced around at the walls, back at me. He made no move toward me. He was part of it, I thought wildly, he knew what they were doing, and then I pushed the thought away. It couldn't be true. "Dad, I don't understand," I pleaded.

"I know you're young," my father said. "He didn't do this to me until I left for college. But there's no more time, is there? You've seen him."

"Why do I have to do this at all?"

At that, my father's gaze swung down on me. He cocked his head, pursed his lips, as though I'd asked something completely incomprehensible. "It's your birthright," he said, and stood up.

We drove back to my grandfather's adobe in silence. The trip lasted less than five minutes. I couldn't even figure out what else to ask, let alone what I might do. I glanced at my father, wanted to scream at him, pound on him until he told me why he was acting this way.

Except that I wasn't sure he was acting anything but normal, for him. He didn't speak when he walked me to the ice-cream shop either. When we arrived at the adobe, he leaned across me to push my door open, and I grabbed his hand.

"Dad. At least tell me what the bat is for."

My father sat up, moved the air-conditioning lever right, then hard back to the left, as though he could surprise it into working. He always did this. It never worked. My father and his routines. "Nothing," he said. "It's a symbol."

"For what?"

"Lucy will tell you."

"But you know." I was almost snarling at him now.

"It stands for the skin at the tip of the tongue. It's the Talking God. Or part of it. I think. I'm sorry."

Gently, hand on my shoulder, he eased me out of the car before it occurred to me to wonder what he was apologizing for. But he surprised me by calling after me. "I promise you this, Seth," he said. "This is the last time in your life that you'll have to come here. Shut the door."

Too stunned and confused and scared to do anything else, I shut it, then watched as my father's car disintegrated into the first, far-off shadows of twilight. Already, too soon, I felt the change in the air, the night chill seeping through the gauze-dry day like blood through a bandage.

My grandfather and Lucy were waiting on the patio. She had her hand on his shoulder, her long hair gathered on her head, and without its dark frame, her face looked much older. And his—fully exposed now, without its protective shawl—looked like a rubber mask on a hook, with no bones inside to support it.

Slowly, my grandfather's wheelchair squeaked over the patio onto the hard sand as Lucy propelled it. I could do nothing but watch. The wheelchair stopped, and my grandfather studied me.

"*Ruach*," he said. There was still no tone in his voice. But there were no holes in it either, no gaps where last night his breath had failed him. "*Bring it to me.*"

It was my imagination, surely, or the first hint of breeze, that made the bag seem to squirm in my hands. This would be the last time, my father had said. I stumbled forward and dropped the paper bag in my grandfather's lap.

Faster than I'd ever seen him move, but still not fast, my grandfather crushed the bag against his chest. His head tilted forward, and I had the insane idea that he was about to sing to it, like a baby. But all he did was close his eyes and hold it.

"All right, that's enough," Lucy said, and took the bag from him. She touched him gently on the back but didn't look at me.

"What did he just do?" I asked, challenging her. "What did the bat do?"

Once more, Lucy smiled her slow, nasty smile. "Wait and see."

Then she was gone, and my grandfather and I were alone in the yard. The dark came drifting down the distant mountainsides like a fog bank, but faster. When it reached us, I closed my eyes and felt nothing except an instantaneous chill. When I opened my eyes, my grandfather was still watching me, head cocked a little on his neck. A wolf indeed.

"*Digging,*" he said. "*All we did, at first. Making pits deeper. The dirt so black. So soft. Like sticking your hands . . . inside an animal. All those trees leaning over us. Pines. Great white birches. Bark as smooth as baby skin. The Nazis gave us nothing to drink. Nothing to eat. But they paid us no attention either. I sat next to the Gypsy I had slept beside all through the war. On a single slab of rotted wood. We had shared body heat. Blood from each other's cuts and wounds. Infections. Lice.*

"*I never . . . even knew his name. Four years, six inches from each other . . . never knew it. Couldn't understand each other. Never really tried. He'd saved—*" a cough rattled my grandfather's entire body, and his eyes got wilder, began to bulge, and I thought he wasn't breathing and almost yelled for Lucy again, but he gathered himself and went on. "*Buttons,*" he said. "*You understand? From somewhere. Rubbed their edges on rocks. Posts. Anything handy. Until they were . . . sharp. Not to kill. Not as a weapon.*" More coughing. "*As a tool. To whittle.*"

"Whittle," I said automatically, as though talking in my sleep.

"*When he was starving. When he woke up screaming. When we had to watch children's . . . bodies dangle from gallows . . . until the first crows came for their eyes. When it was snowing, and . . . we had to march . . . barefoot . . . or stand outside all night. The Gypsy whittled.*"

Again, my grandfather's eyes ballooned in their sockets as though they would burst. Again came the cough, shaking him so hard that he almost fell from the chair. And again, he fought his body to stillness.

"*Wait,*" he gasped. "*You will wait. You must.*"

I waited. What else could I do?

A long while later, he said, "*Two little girls.*"

I stared at him. His words wrapped me like strands of a cocoon. "What?"

"*Listen. Two girls. The same ones, over and over. That's what . . . the Gypsy . . . whittled.*"

Dimly, in the part of my brain that still felt alert, I wondered how anyone could tell if two figures carved in God knows what with the sharpened edge of a button were the same girls.

But my grandfather just nodded. "*Even at the end. Even at Chelmno. In the woods. In the rare moments . . . when we weren't digging, and the rest of us . . . sat. He went straight for the trees. Put his hands on them like they were warm. Wept. First time, all war. Despite everything we saw, everything we knew . . . no tears from him, until then. When he came back, he had . . . strips of pine bark in his hands. And while everyone else slept . . . or froze . . . or died . . . he worked. All night. Under the trees.*

"*Every few hours . . . shipments came. Of people, you understand? Jews. We heard trains. Then, later, we saw creatures . . . between tree trunks. Thin. Awful. Like dead saplings walking. When the Nazis . . . began shooting . . . they fell with no sound. Poppoppop from the guns. Then silence. Things lying in leaves. In the wet.*

"*The killing wasn't . . . enough fun . . . for the Nazis, of course. They made us roll bodies . . . into the pits, with our hands. Then bury them. With our hands. Or our mouths. Sometimes our mouths. Dirt and blood. Bits of person in your teeth. A few of us laid down. Died on the ground. The Nazis didn't have . . . to tell us. We just . . . pushed anything dead . . . into the nearest pit. No prayers. No last look to see who it was. It was no one. Do you see? No one. Burying. Or buried. No difference.*

"*And still, all night, the Gypsy whittled.*

"*For the dawn . . . shipment . . . the Nazis tried . . . something new. Stripped the newcomers . . . then lined them up . . . on the lip of a pit . . . twenty, thirty at a time. Then they played . . . perforation games. Shoot up the body . . . down it . . . see if you could get it . . . to flap apart . . . before it fell. Open up, like a flower.*

"*All through the next day. And all the next night. Digging. Waiting. Whittling. Killing. Burying. Over and over. Sometime . . . late second day, maybe . . . I got angry. Not at the Nazis. For what? Being angry at human beings . . . for killing . . . for cruelty . . . like being mad at ice for freezing. It's just . . . what to expect. So I got angry . . . at the trees. For standing there. For being green, and alive. For not falling when bullets hit them.*

"*I started . . . screaming. Trying to. In Hebrew. In Polish. The Nazis looked up, and I thought they would shoot me. They laughed instead. One began to clap. A rhythm. See?*"

Somehow, my grandfather lifted his limp hands from the arms of the wheelchair and brought them together. They met with a sort of crackle, like dry twigs crumbling.

"*The Gypsy . . . just watched. Still weeping. But also . . . after a while . . . nodding.*"

All this time, my grandfather's eyes had seemed to swell, as though there was too much air being pumped into his body. But now, the air went out of him in a rush, and the eyes went dark, and the lids came down. I thought maybe he'd fallen asleep again, the way he had last night. But I still couldn't move. Dimly, I realized that the sweat from my long day's walking had cooled on my skin, and that I was freezing.

My grandfather's lids opened, just a little. He seemed to be peering at me from inside a trunk, or a coffin.

"I don't know how the Gypsy knew . . . that it was ending. That it was time. Maybe just because . . . it had been hours . . . half a day . . . between shipments. The world had gone . . . quiet. Us. Nazis. Trees. Corpses. There had been worse places . . . I thought . . . to stop living. Despite the smell.

"Probably, I was sleeping. I must have been, because the Gypsy shook me . . . by the shoulder. Then held out . . . what he'd made. He had it . . . balanced . . . on a stick he'd bent. So the carving moved. Back and forth. Up and down."

My mouth opened and then hung there. I was rock, sand, and the air moved through me and left me nothing.

" 'Life,' the Gypsy said to me, in Polish. Only Polish I ever heard him speak. 'Life. You see?'

"I shook . . . my head. He said it again. 'Life.' And then . . . I don't know how . . . but I did . . . see.

"I asked him . . . 'Why not you?' He took . . . from his pocket . . . one of his old carvings. The two girls. Holding hands. I hadn't noticed . . . the hands before. And I understood.

" 'My girls,' he said. 'Smoke. No more. Five years ago.' I understood that, too.

"I took the carving from him. We waited. We slept, side by side. One last time. Then the Nazis came.

"They made us stand. Hardly any of them now. The rest gone. Fifteen of us. Maybe less. They said something. German. None of us knew German. But to me . . . at least . . . the word meant . . . run.

"The Gypsy . . . just stood there. Died where he was. Under the trees. The rest . . . I don't know. The Nazi who caught me . . . laughing . . . a boy. Not much . . . older than you. Laughing. Awkward with his gun. Too big for him. I looked at my hand. Holding . . . the carving. The wooden man. 'Life,' I found myself chanting . . . instead of Shma. 'Life.' Then the Nazi shot me in the head. Bang."

And with that single word, my grandfather clicked off, as though a switch had been thrown. He slumped in his chair. My paralysis lasted a few more seconds, and then I started waving my hands in front of me, as if I could ward off what he'd told me, and I was so busy doing that that I didn't notice, at first, the way my grandfather's torso heaved and rattled. Whimpering, I lowered my hands, but by then, my grandfather wasn't heaving anymore, and he'd slumped forward further, and nothing on him was moving.

"LUCY!" I screamed, but she was already out of the house, wrestling my grandfather out of his chair to the ground. Her head dove down on my grandfather's as she shoved the mask up his face, but before their mouths even met, my grandfather coughed, and Lucy fell back, sobbing, tugging the mask back into place.

My grandfather lay where he'd been thrown, a scatter of bones in the dirt. He didn't open his eyes. The oxygen tank hissed, and the blue tube stretching to his mask filled with wet mist.

"How?" I whispered

Lucy swept tears from her eyes. "What?"

"He said he got shot in the head." And even as I said that, I felt it for the first time, that cold slithering up my intestines into my stomach, then my throat.

"Stop it," I said. But Lucy slid forward so that her knees were under my grandfather's head and ignored me. Overhead, I saw the moon half-embedded in the ridged black of the sky like the lidded eye of a gila monster. I stumbled around the side of the house, and without thinking about it, slipped into the hogan.

Once inside, I jerked the curtain down to block out the sight of Lucy and my grandfather and that moon, then drew my knees tight against my chest to pin that freezing feeling where it was. I stayed that way a long while, but whenever I closed my eyes, I saw people splitting open like peeled bananas, limbs strewn across bare, black ground like tree branches after a lightning storm, pits full of naked dead people.

I'd wished him dead, I realized. At the moment he tumbled forward in his chair, I'd hoped he was dead. And for what, exactly? For being in the camps? For telling me about it? For getting sick, and making me confront it?

But with astonishing, disturbing speed, the guilt over those thoughts passed. And when it was gone, I realized that the cold had seeped down my legs and up to my neck. It clogged my ears, coated my tongue like a paste, sealing the world out. All I could hear was my grandfather's voice, like blown sand against the inside of my skull. *Life.* He was inside me, I thought. He had erased me, taken my place. He was becoming me.

I threw my hands over my ears, which had no effect. My thoughts flashed through the last two days, the drumming and chanting, the dead bat in the paper bag, my father's good-bye, while that voice beat in my ears, attaching itself to my pulse. *Life.* And finally, I realized that I'd trapped myself. I was alone in the hogan in the dark. When I turned around, I would see the Dancing Man. It would be wiggling toward me with its mouth wide open. And it would be over, too late. It might already be.

Flinging my hands behind me, I grabbed the Dancing Man around its thin, black neck. I could feel it bob on its wire, and I half-expected it to squirm as I fought to my feet. It didn't, but its wooden skin gave where I pressed it, like real skin. Inside my head, the new voice kept beating.

At my feet on the floor lay the matches Lucy had used to light her ceremonial candles. I snatched up the matchbook, then threw the carved thing to the ground, where it smacked on its base and tipped over, face up, staring at me. I broke a match against the matchbox, then another. The third match lit.

For one moment, I held the flame over the Dancing Man. The heat felt wonderful crawling toward my fingers, a blazing, living thing, chasing back the cold inside me. I dropped the match, and the Dancing Man disintegrated in a spasm of white-orange flame.

And then, abruptly, there was nothing to be done. The hogan was a dirt-and-wood shelter; the night outside, the plain old desert night; the Dancing Man a puddle of red and black ash I scattered with my foot. Still cold, but mostly tired, I staggered back outside and sat down hard against the side of the hogan and closed my eyes.

Footsteps woke me, and I sat up and found, to my amazement, that it was daylight. I waited, tense, afraid to look up, and then I did.

My father was kneeling beside me on the ground.

"You're here already?" I asked.

"Your grandpa died, Seth," he said. In his zombie-Dad voice, though he touched my hand the way a real father would. "I've come to take you home."

IV

THE FAMILIAR COMMOTION in the hallway of the *pension* alerted me that my students had returned. One of them, but only one, stopped outside my door. I waited, holding my breath, wishing I'd snapped out the light. But Penny didn't knock, and after a few seconds, I heard her careful, precise footfall continuing toward her room. And so I was alone with my puppets and my memories and my horrible suspicions, the way I have always been.

I remember rousing myself out of the malaise I couldn't quite seem to shake—have never, for one instant, shaken since—during that last ride home from my grandfather's. "I killed him," I told my father, and when he glanced at me, expressionless, I told him all of it, the Dancing Man and the ceremony and the thoughts I'd had.

My father didn't laugh. He also didn't touch me. All he said was, "That's silly, Seth." And for a while, I thought it was.

But that day, in Prague, I was thinking of Rabbi Loew and his golem, the creature he infected with a sort of life. A creature that walked, talked, thought, saw, but couldn't taste. Couldn't feel.

I was thinking of my father, the way he always was. I am thinking of him now, as I look over these notes in my posterless, plain suburban Ohio apartment, with its cableless television and nearly bare cupboards and single shelf stacked with textbooks. If I'm right, then of course it was done to my father, too. I'm thinking of the way I only seem all the way real, even to me, when I see myself in the vividly reflective faces of my students.

It's possible, I realize, that nothing happened to me those last few days. It could have happened years before I was born. The Gypsy had offered what he offered, and my grandfather had accepted, and as a result become what he was. Might have been. If that's true, then my father and I are unexceptional in a way. Natural progeny. We simply inherited our natures and our limitations, the way all earthly creatures do.

But tonight I am thinking about the graves I saw on this summer's trip, and the millions of people in them, and the millions more without graves. The ones who are smoke. And I find that I can feel it, at last. Or that I've always felt it, without knowing what it was: the Holocaust, roaring down the generations like a wave of radiation, eradicating in everyone it touches the ability to trust people, experience joy, fall in love, believe in love when you see it in others. And I wonder what difference it makes, in the end, whether it really was my grandfather, or the approximation of him that the Gypsy made, who finally crawled out of the woods of Chelmno.

AFTERWORD

It's never been the ghosts, for me, as much as the places ghosts linger and the ways they affect the living. I love the bells, the empty streets, and the smell of the sea in Robert Aickman's "Ringing the Changes," so it always made perfect sense to me that the bride goes outside to dance with the dead. I love the wretched town; the shadows in the mirror, and those gaping fireplaces in Ramsey Campbell's "The Chimney," which is still this good Jewish boy's favorite Christmas story. I love the graveyard and the snow at the end of Joyce's "The Dead," the scariest love story I know. And if I could, I'm pretty sure I'd live in Shirley Jackson's Hill House (in *The Haunting of*. . .). I've been living there anyway, in one way or another, ever since the first time I read that perfect opening paragraph and started chanting myself to sleep with it when I was twelve years old.

ABOUT THE EDITOR

ELLEN DATLOW is editor of SCI FICTION, the fiction area of SCIFI.COM, the Sci Fi Channel's Web site. She was fiction editor of *Omni* for more than seventeen years, and also edited the webzine *Event Horizon*.

She has edited a number of anthologies, including *Little Deaths*, *Alien Sex*, *Lethal Kisses*, *Vanishing Acts* (a science fiction anthology on the theme of endangered species), and with Terri Windling, she edits the annual *Year's Best Fantasy and Horror*. In addition, she and Windling have coedited *A Wolf at the Door* and *Swan Sister* (for middle grades), *The Green Man: Tales from the Mythic Forest*, and the six-volume adult fairy tales anthology series beginning with *Snow White, Blood Red*. She has won the World Fantasy Award six times, the Bram Stoker Award once, and the Hugo Award once. She lives in Manhattan. Her Web site is www.datlow.com.